DECEPTION POINT

www.**books**at**transworld**.co.uk

Also by Dan Brown

Digital Fortress
Angels and Demons
The Da Vinci Code

For more information on Dan Brown and his books, see his website
at www.danbrown.com

DECEPTION POINT

DAN BROWN

BANTAM PRESS

LONDON · TORONTO · SYDNEY · AUCKLAND · JOHANNESBURG

TRANSWORLD PUBLISHERS
61–63 Uxbridge Road, London W5 5SA
a division of The Random House Group Ltd

RANDOM HOUSE AUSTRALIA (PTY) LTD
20 Alfred Street, Milsons Point, Sydney,
New South Wales 2061, Australia

RANDOM HOUSE NEW ZEALAND LTD
18 Poland Road, Glenfield, Auckland 10, New Zealand

RANDOM HOUSE SOUTH AFRICA (PTY) LTD
Isle of Houghton, Corner of Boundary Road & Carse O'Gowrie,
Houghton 2198, South Africa

First published in Great Britain in 2002 by Corgi Books
a division of Transworld Publishers.

The hardcover edition published 2005 by Bantam Press,
a division of Transworld Publishers.

A catalogue record for this book is available from the British Library.
ISBN 0593057430

Typeset in Berling Roman by
Kestrel Data, Exeter, Devon.

Printed and bound in Great Britain by
Clays Ltd, Bungay, Suffolk.

Papers used by Transworld Publishers are natural, recyclable products
made from wood grown in sustainable forests. The manufacturing processes
conform to the environmental regulations of the country of origin.

Acknowledgements

With warm thanks to Jason Kaufman for his superb guidance and insightful editorial skills; Blythe Brown for her tireless research and creative input; Bill Scott-Kerr for his enthusiasm for my work and for navigating it so expertly across the Atlantic; my good friend Jake Elwell at Wieser & Wieser; the National Security Archive; the NASA Public Affairs Office; Stan Planton, who continues to be a source for information on all things; the National Security Agency; glaciologist Martin O. Jeffries; and the superb minds of Brett Trotter, Thomas D. Nadeau, and Jim Barrington. Thanks also to Connie and Dick Brown, the U.S. Intelligence Policy Documentation Project, Suzanne O'Neill, Margie Wachtel, Morey Stettner, Owen King, Alison McKinnell, Mary and Stephen Gorman, Dr Karl Singer, Dr Michael I. Latz of Scripps Institute of Oceanography, April at Micron Electronics, Esther Sung, the National Air and Space Museum, Dr Gene Allmendinger, the incomparable Heide Lange at Sanford J. Greenburger Associates, and John Pike at the Federation of American Scientists.

The Delta Force, the National Reconnaissance Office, and the Space Frontier Foundation are real organizations. All technologies described in this novel exist.

If this discovery is confirmed, it will surely be one of the most stunning insights into our universe that science has ever uncovered. Its implications are as far-reaching and awe-inspiring as can be imagined. Even as it promises answers to some of our oldest questions, it poses still others even more fundamental.

President Bill Clinton, in a press conference
following a discovery known as ALH84001
on August 7, 1996

Death, in this forsaken place, could come in countless forms. Geologist Charles Brophy had endured the savage splendor of this terrain for years, and yet nothing could prepare him for a fate as barbarous and unnatural as the one about to befall him.

As Brophy's four huskies pulled his sled of geologic sensing equipment across the tundra, the dogs suddenly slowed, looking skyward.

'What is it, girls?' Brophy asked, stepping off the sled.

Beyond the gathering storm clouds, a twin-rotor transport helicopter arched in low, hugging the glacial peaks with military dexterity.

That's odd, he thought. He never saw helicopters this far north. The aircraft landed fifty yards away, kicking up a stinging spray of granulated snow. His dogs whined, looking wary.

When the chopper doors slid open, two men descended. They were dressed in full-weather whites, armed with rifles, and moved toward Brophy with urgent intent.

'Dr Brophy?' one called.

The geologist was baffled. 'How did you know my name? Who are you?'

'Take out your radio, please.'

'I'm sorry?'

'Just do it.'

Bewildered, Brophy pulled his radio from his parka.

'We need you to transmit an emergency communiqué. Decrease your radio frequency to one hundred kilohertz.'

One hundred kilohertz? Brophy felt utterly lost. *Nobody can receive anything that low.* 'Has there been an accident?'

The second man raised his rifle and pointed it at Brophy's head. 'There's no time to explain. Just do it.'

Trembling, Brophy adjusted his transmission frequency.

The first man now handed him a note card with a few lines typed on it. 'Transmit this message. Now.'

Brophy looked at the card. 'I don't understand. This information is incorrect. I didn't—'

The man pressed his rifle hard against the geologist's temple.

Brophy's voice was shaking as he transmitted the bizarre message.

'Good,' the first man said. 'Now get yourself and your dogs into the chopper.'

At gunpoint, Brophy maneuvered his reluctant dogs and sled up a skid ramp into the cargo bay. As soon as they were settled, the chopper lifted off, turning westward.

'Who the hell are you?' Brophy demanded, breaking a sweat inside his parka. *And what was the meaning of that message?*

The men said nothing.

As the chopper gained altitude, the wind tore through the open door. Brophy's four huskies, still rigged to the loaded sled, were whimpering now.

'At least close the door,' Brophy demanded. 'Can't you see my dogs are frightened!'

The men did not respond.

As the chopper rose to 4,000 feet, it banked steeply out over a series of ice chasms and crevasses. Suddenly, the men stood. Without a word, they gripped the heavily laden sled and pushed it out the open door. Brophy watched in horror as his dogs scrambled in vain against the enormous weight. In an instant the animals disappeared, dragged howling out of the chopper.

Brophy was already on his feet screaming when the men grabbed him. They hauled him to the door. Numb with fear, Brophy swung his fists, trying to fend off the powerful hands pushing him outward.

It was no use. Moments later he was tumbling toward the chasms below.

CHAPTER 1

Toulos Restaurant, adjacent to Capitol Hill, boasts a politically incorrect menu of baby veal and horse carpaccio, making it an ironic hotspot for the quintessential Washingtonian power breakfast. This morning Toulos was busy – a cacophony of clanking silverware, espresso machines, and cellphone conversations.

The maitre d' was sneaking a sip of his morning Bloody Mary when the woman entered. He turned with a practiced smile.

'Good morning,' he said. 'May I help you?'

The woman was attractive, in her mid-thirties, wearing gray, pleated flannel pants, conservative flats, and an ivory Laura Ashley blouse. Her posture was straight – chin raised ever so slightly – not arrogant, just strong. The woman's hair was light brown and fashioned in Washington's most popular style – the 'anchorwoman' – a lush feathering, curled under at the shoulders . . . long enough to be sexy, but short enough to remind you she was probably smarter than you.

'I'm a little late,' the woman said, her voice unassuming. 'I have a breakfast meeting with Senator Sexton.'

The maitre d' felt an unexpected tingle of nerves. *Senator Sedgewick Sexton.* The senator was a regular here and currently one of the country's most famous men. Last week, having swept all twelve Republican primaries on Super Tuesday, the senator was virtually guaranteed his party's nomination for President of the United States. Many believed the senator had a superb chance of stealing the White House from the embattled President next fall. Lately Sexton's face seemed to be on every national magazine, his campaign slogan plastered all across America: 'Stop spending. Start mending.'

'Senator Sexton is in his booth,' the maitre d' said. 'And you are?'

'Rachel Sexton. His daughter.'

How foolish of me, he thought. The resemblance was quite apparent. The woman had the senator's penetrating eyes and refined carriage –

that polished air of resilient nobility. Clearly the senator's classic good looks had not skipped generations, although Rachel Sexton seemed to carry her blessings with a grace and humility her father could learn from.

'A pleasure to have you, Ms Sexton.'

As the maitre d' led the senator's daughter across the dining area, he was embarrassed by the gauntlet of male eyes following her . . . some discreet, others less so. Few women dined at Toulos and even fewer who looked like Rachel Sexton.

'Nice body,' one diner whispered. 'Sexton already find himself a new wife?'

'That's his daughter, you idiot,' another replied.

The man chuckled. 'Knowing Sexton, he'd probably screw her anyway.'

When Rachel arrived at her father's table, the senator was on his cellphone talking loudly about one of his recent successes. He glanced up at Rachel only long enough to tap his Cartier and remind her she was late.

I missed you, too, Rachel thought.

Her father's first name was Thomas, although he'd adopted his middle name long ago. Rachel suspected it was because he liked the alliteration. Senator Sedgewick Sexton. The man was a silver-haired, silver-tongued political animal who had been anointed with the slick look of a soap opera doctor, which seemed appropriate considering his talents of impersonation.

'Rachel!' Her father clicked off his phone and stood to kiss her cheek.

'Hi, Dad.' She did not kiss him back.

'You look exhausted.'

And so it begins, she thought. 'I got your message. What's up?'

'I can't ask my daughter out for breakfast?'

Rachel had learned long ago her father seldom requested her company unless he had some ulterior motive.

Sexton took a sip of coffee. 'So, how are things with you?'

'Busy. I see your campaign's going well.'

'Oh, let's not talk business.' Sexton leaned across the table, lowering his voice. 'How's that guy at the State Department I set you up with?'

Rachel exhaled, already fighting the urge to check her watch. 'Dad, I really haven't had time to call him. And I wish you'd stop trying to—'

'You've got to make time for the important things, Rachel. Without love, everything else is meaningless.'

A number of comebacks came to mind, but Rachel chose silence. Being the bigger person was not difficult when it came to her father. 'Dad, you wanted to see me? You said this was important.'

'It is.' Her father's eyes studied her closely.

Rachel felt part of her defenses melt away under his gaze, and she cursed the man's power. The senator's eyes were his gift – a gift Rachel suspected would probably carry him to the White House. On cue, his eyes would well with tears, and then, an instant later, they would clear, opening a window to an impassioned soul, extending a bond of trust to all. *It's all about trust*, her father always said. The senator had lost Rachel's years ago, but he was quickly gaining the country's.

'I have a proposition for you,' Senator Sexton said.

'Let me guess,' Rachel replied, attempting to refortify her position. 'Some prominent divorcé looking for a young wife?'

'Don't kid yourself, honey. You're not that young anymore.'

Rachel felt the familiar shrinking sensation that so often accompanied meetings with her father.

'I want to throw you a life raft,' he said.

'I wasn't aware I was drowning.'

'You're not. The President is. You should jump ship before it's too late.'

'Haven't we had this conversation?'

'Think about your future, Rachel. You can come work for me.'

'I hope that's not why you asked me to breakfast.'

The senator's veneer of calm broke ever so slightly. 'Rachel, can't you see that your working for him reflects badly on me? And on my campaign.'

Rachel sighed. She and her father had been through this. 'Dad, I don't work for the President. I haven't even *met* the President. I work in Fairfax, for God's sake!'

'Politics is perception, Rachel. It *appears* you work for the President.'

Rachel exhaled, trying to keep her cool. 'I worked too hard to get this job, Dad. I'm not quitting.'

The senator's eyes narrowed. 'You know, sometimes your selfish attitude really—'

'Senator Sexton?' A reporter materialized beside the table.

Sexton's demeanor thawed instantly. Rachel groaned and took a croissant from the basket on the table.

'Ralph Sneeden,' the reporter said. '*Washington Post.* May I ask you a few questions?'

The senator smiled, dabbing his mouth with a napkin. 'My pleasure, Ralph. Just make it quick. I don't want my coffee getting cold.'

The reporter laughed on cue. 'Of course, sir.' He pulled out a minirecorder and turned it on. 'Senator, your television ads call for legislation ensuring equal salaries for women in the workplace . . . as well as for tax cuts for new families. Can you comment on your rationale?'

'Sure. I'm simply a huge fan of strong women and strong families.'

Rachel practically choked on her croissant.

'And on the subject of families,' the reporter followed up, 'you talk a lot about education. You've proposed some highly controversial budget cuts in an effort to allocate more funds to our nation's schools.'

'I believe the children are our future.'

Rachel could not believe her father had sunk to quoting pop songs.

'Finally, sir,' the reporter said, 'you've taken an enormous jump in the polls these past few weeks. The President has got to be worried. Any thoughts on your recent success?'

'I think it has to do with trust. Americans are starting to see that the President cannot be trusted to make the tough decisions facing this nation. Runaway government spending is putting this country deeper in debt every day, and Americans are starting to realize that it's time to stop spending and start mending.'

Like a stay of execution from her father's rhetoric, the pager in Rachel's handbag went off. Normally the harsh electronic beeping was an unwelcome interruption, but at the moment, it sounded almost melodious.

The senator glared indignantly at having been interrupted.

Rachel fished the pager from her handbag and pressed a preset sequence of five buttons, confirming that she was indeed the person holding the pager. The beeping stopped, and the LCD began blinking. In fifteen seconds she would receive a secure text message.

Sneeden grinned at the senator. 'Your daughter is obviously a busy woman. It's refreshing to see you two still find time in your schedules to dine together.'

'As I said, family comes first.'

Sneeden nodded, and then his gaze hardened. 'Might I ask, sir, how you and your daughter manage your conflicts of interest?'

'Conflicts?' Senator Sexton cocked his head with an innocent look of confusion. 'What conflicts do you mean?'

Rachel glanced up, grimacing at her father's act. She knew exactly where this was headed. *Damn reporters*, she thought. Half of them were on political payrolls. The reporter's question was what journalists called a *grapefruit* – a question that was supposed to look like a tough inquiry but was in fact a scripted favor to the senator – a slow lob pitch that her father could line up and smash out of the park, clearing the air about a few things.

'Well, sir . . .' The reporter coughed, feigning uneasiness over the question. 'The conflict is that your daughter works for your opponent.'

Senator Sexton exploded in laughter, defusing the question instantly. 'Ralph, first of all, the President and I are not *opponents*. We are simply two patriots who have different ideas about how to run the country we love.'

The reporter beamed. He had his sound bite. 'And second?'

'Second, my daughter is not employed by the President; she is employed by the intelligence community. She compiles intel reports and sends them to the White House. It's a fairly low-level position.' He paused and looked at Rachel. 'In fact, dear, I'm not sure you've even *met* the President, have you?'

Rachel stared, her eyes smoldering.

The beeper chirped, drawing Rachel's gaze to the incoming message on the LCD screen.

– RPRT DIRNRO STAT –

She deciphered the shorthand instantly and frowned. The message was unexpected, and most certainly bad news. At least she had her exit cue.

'Gentlemen,' she said. 'It breaks my heart, but I have to go. I'm late for work.'

'Ms Sexton,' the reporter said quickly, 'before you go, I was wondering if you could comment on the rumors that you called this breakfast meeting to discuss the possibility of leaving your current post to work for your father's campaign?'

Rachel felt like someone had thrown hot coffee in her face. The question took her totally off guard. She looked at her father and sensed in his smirk that the question had been prepped. She wanted to climb across the table and stab him with a fork.

The reporter shoved the recorder into her face. 'Miss Sexton?'

Rachel locked eyes with the reporter. 'Ralph, or whoever the hell you are, get this straight: I have no intention of abandoning my job to work for Senator Sexton, and if you print anything to the contrary, you'll need a shoehorn to get that recorder out of your ass.'

The reporter's eyes widened. He clicked off his recorder, hiding a grin. 'Thank you both.' He disappeared.

Rachel immediately regretted the outburst. She had inherited her father's temper, and she hated him for it. *Smooth, Rachel. Very smooth.*

Her father glared disapprovingly. 'You'd do well to learn some poise.'

Rachel began collecting her things. 'This meeting is over.'

The senator was apparently done with her anyway. He pulled out his cellphone to make a call. ''Bye, sweetie. Stop by the office one of these days and say hello. And get married, for God's sake. You're thirty-three years old.'

'Thirty-*four*,' she snapped. 'Your secretary sent a card.'

He clucked ruefully. 'Thirty-four. Almost an old maid. You know by the time I was thirty-four, I'd already—'

'Married Mom and screwed the neighbor?' The words came out louder than Rachel had intended, her voice hanging naked in an ill-timed lull. Diners nearby glanced over.

Senator Sexton's eyes flash-froze, two ice-crystals boring into her. 'You watch yourself, young lady.'

Rachel headed for the door. *No, you watch yourself, Senator.*

CHAPTER **2**

The three men sat in silence inside their ThermaTech storm tent. Outside, an icy wind buffeted the shelter, threatening to tear it from its moorings. None of the men took notice; each had seen situations far more threatening than this one.

Their tent was stark white, pitched in a shallow depression, out of sight. Their communication devices, transport, and weapons were all state-of-the-art. The group leader was code-named Delta-One. He was muscular and lithe with eyes as desolate as the topography on which he was stationed.

The military chronograph on Delta-One's wrist emitted a sharp beep. The sound coincided in perfect unison with beeps emitted from the chronographs worn by the other two men.

Another thirty minutes had passed.

It was time. Again.

Reflexively, Delta-One left his two partners and stepped outside into the darkness and pounding wind. He scanned the moonlit horizon with infrared binoculars. As always, he focused on the structure. It was 1,000 meters away – an enormous and unlikely edifice rising from the barren terrain. He and his team had been watching it for ten days now, since its construction. Delta-One had no doubt that the information inside would change the world. Lives already had been lost to protect it.

At the moment, everything looked quiet outside the structure.

The true test, however, was what was happening *inside*.

Delta-One reentered the tent and addressed his two fellow soldiers. 'Time for a flyby.'

Both men nodded. The taller of them, Delta-Two, opened a laptop computer and turned it on. Positioning himself in front of the screen, Delta-Two placed his hand on a mechanical joystick and gave it a short jerk. A thousand meters away, hidden deep within the building, a surveillance robot the size of a mosquito received his transmission and sprang to life.

CHAPTER **3**

Rachel Sexton was still steaming as she drove her white Integra up Leesburg Highway. The bare maples of the Falls Church foothills rose stark against a crisp March sky, but the peaceful setting did little to calm her anger. Her father's recent surge in the polls should have endowed him with a modicum of confident grace, and yet it seemed only to fuel his self-importance.

The man's deceit was doubly painful because he was the only immediate family Rachel had left. Rachel's mother had died three years ago, a devastating loss whose emotional scars still raked at Rachel's heart. Rachel's only solace was knowing that the death, with ironic compassion, had liberated her mother from a deep despair over a miserable marriage to the senator.

Rachel's pager beeped again, pulling her thoughts back to the road in front of her. The incoming message was the same.

– RPRT DIRNRO STAT –

Report to the director of NRO stat. She sighed. *I'm coming, for God's sake!*

With rising uncertainty, Rachel drove to her usual exit, turned onto the private access road, and rolled to a stop at the heavily armed sentry booth. This was 14225 Leesburg Highway, one of the most secretive addresses in the country.

While the guard scanned her car for bugs, Rachel gazed out at the mammoth structure in the distance. The 1,000,000-square-foot complex sat majestically on 68 forested acres just outside D.C. in Fairfax, Virginia. The building's facade was a bastion of one-way glass that reflected the army of satellite dishes, antennas, and rayodomes on the surrounding grounds, doubling their already awe-inspiring numbers.

Two minutes later, Rachel had parked and crossed the manicured grounds to the main entrance, where a carved granite sign announced

NATIONAL RECONNAISSANCE OFFICE (NRO)

The two armed Marines flanking the bulletproof revolving door stared straight ahead as Rachel passed between them. She felt the same sensation she always felt as she pushed through these doors . . . that she was entering the belly of a sleeping giant.

Inside the vaulted lobby, Rachel sensed the faint echoes of hushed conversations all around her, as if the words were sifting down from the offices above. An enormous tiled mosaic proclaimed the NRO directive:

ENABLING U.S. GLOBAL INFORMATION SUPERIORITY,
DURING PEACE AND THROUGH WAR.

The walls here were lined with massive photographs – rocket launches, submarine christenings, intercept installations – towering achievements that could be celebrated only within these walls.

Now, as always, Rachel felt the problems of the outside world fading behind her. She was entering the shadow world. A world where the problems thundered in like freight trains, and the solutions were meted out with barely a whisper.

As Rachel approached the final checkpoint, she wondered what kind of problem had caused her pager to ring twice in the last thirty minutes.

'Good morning, Ms Sexton.' The guard smiled as she approached the steel doorway.

Rachel returned the smile as the guard held out a tiny swab for Rachel to take.

'You know the drill,' he said.

Rachel took the hermetically sealed cotton swab and removed the plastic covering. Then she placed it in her mouth like a thermometer.

She held it under her tongue for two seconds. Then, leaning forward, she allowed the guard to remove it. The guard inserted the moistened swab into a slit in a machine behind him. The machine took four seconds to confirm the DNA sequences in Rachel's saliva. Then a monitor flickered on, displaying Rachel's photo and security clearance.

The guard winked. 'Looks like you're still you.' He pulled the used swab from the machine and dropped it through an opening, where it was instantly incinerated. 'Have a good one.' He pressed a button and the huge steel doors swung open.

As Rachel made her way into the maze of bustling corridors beyond, she was amazed that even after six years here she was still daunted by the colossal scope of this operation. The agency encompassed six other U.S. installations, employed over ten thousand agents, and had operating costs of over $10 billion per year.

In total secrecy, the NRO built and maintained an astonishing arsenal of cutting-edge spy technologies: worldwide electronic intercepts; spy satellites; silent, embedded relay chips in telecomm products; even a global naval-recon network known as Classic Wizard, a secret web of 1,456 hydrophones mounted on seafloors around the world, capable of monitoring ship movements anywhere on the globe.

NRO technologies not only helped the United States win military conflicts, but they provided an endless stream of peacetime data to agencies such as the CIA, NSA, and Department of Defense, helping them thwart terrorism, locate crimes against the environment, and give policymakers the data needed to make informed decisions on an enormous array of topics.

Rachel worked here as a 'gister.' Gisting, or data reduction, required analyzing complex reports and distilling their essence or 'gist' into concise, single-page briefs. Rachel had proven herself a natural. *All those years of cutting through my father's bullshit*, she thought.

Rachel now held the NRO's premiere gisting post – intelligence liaison to the White House. She was responsible for sifting through the NRO's daily intelligence reports, deciding which stories were relevant to the President, distilling those reports into single-page briefs, and then forwarding the synopsized material to the President's

National Security Adviser. In NRO-speak, Rachel Sexton 'manufactured finished product and serviced *the* customer.'

Although the job was difficult and required long hours, the position
was a badge of honor for her, a way to assert her independence from
her father. Senator Sexton had offered countless times to support
Rachel if she would quit the post, but Rachel had no intention of
becoming financially beholden to a man like Sedgewick Sexton. Her
mother was testimony to what could happen when a man like that
held too many cards.

The sound of Rachel's pager echoed in the marble hall.

Again? She didn't even bother to check the message.

Wondering what the hell was going on, she boarded the elevator,
skipped her own floor, and went straight to the top.

CHAPTER 4

To call the NRO director a plain man was in itself an over-
statement. NRO Director William Pickering was diminutive, with
pale skin, a forgettable face, a bald head, and hazel eyes, which
despite having gazed upon the country's deepest secrets, appeared as
two shallow pools. Nonetheless, to those who worked under him,
Pickering towered. His subdued personality and unadorned
philosophies were legendary at the NRO. The man's quiet diligence,
combined with his wardrobe of plain black suits, had earned him
the nickname the 'Quaker.' A brilliant strategist and the model of
efficiency, the Quaker ran his world with an unrivaled clarity. His
mantra: 'Find the truth. Act on it.'

When Rachel arrived in the director's office, he was on the phone.
Rachel was always surprised by the sight of him: William Pickering
looked nothing like a man who wielded enough power to wake the
President at any hour.

Pickering hung up and waved her in. 'Agent Sexton, have a seat.'
His voice had a lucid rawness to it.

'Thank you, sir.' Rachel sat.

Despite most people's discomfort around William Pickering's blunt demeanor, Rachel had always liked the man. He was the exact antithesis of her father . . . physically unimposing, anything but charismatic, and he did his duty with a selfless patriotism, shunning the spotlight her father loved so much.

Pickering removed his glasses and gazed at her. 'Agent Sexton, the President called me about a half hour ago. In direct reference to you.'

Rachel shifted in her seat. Pickering was known for getting to the point. *One hell of an opening*, she thought. 'Not a problem with one of my gists, I hope.'

'On the contrary. He says the White House is impressed with your work.'

Rachel exhaled silently. 'So what did he want?'

'A meeting with you. In person. Immediately.'

Rachel's unease sharpened. 'A personal meeting? About *what*?'

'Damn good question. He wouldn't tell me.'

Now Rachel was lost. Keeping information from the director of the NRO was like keeping Vatican secrets from the Pope. The standing joke in the intelligence community was that if William Pickering didn't know about it, it hadn't happened.

Pickering stood, pacing now in front of his window. 'He asked that I contact you immediately and send you to meet with him.'

'Right now?'

'He sent transportation. It's waiting outside.'

Rachel frowned. The President's request was unnerving on its own account, but it was the look of concern on Pickering's face that really worried her. 'You obviously have reservations.'

'I sure as hell do!' Pickering showed a rare flash of emotion. 'The President's timing seems almost callow in its transparency. You are the daughter of the man who is currently challenging him in the polls, and he demands a private meeting with you? I find this highly inappropriate. Your father no doubt would agree.'

Rachel knew Pickering was right – not that she gave a damn what her father thought. 'Do you not trust the President's motives?'

'My oath is to provide intel support to the current White House administration, not pass judgment on their politics.'

Typical Pickering response, Rachel realized. William Pickering made no bones about his view of politicians as transitory figureheads who passed fleetingly across a chessboard whose real players were men like Pickering himself – seasoned 'lifers' who had been around long enough to understand the game with some perspective. Two full terms in the White House, Pickering often said, was not nearly enough to comprehend the true complexities of the global political landscape.

'Maybe it's an innocent request,' Rachel offered, hoping the President was above trying some sort of cheap campaign stunt. 'Maybe he needs a reduction of some sensitive data.'

'Not to sound belittling, Agent Sexton, but the White House has access to plenty of qualified gisting personnel if they need it. If it's an internal White House job, the President should know better than to contact you. And if not, then he sure as hell should know better than to request an NRO asset and then refuse to tell me what he wants it for.'

Pickering always referred to his employees as assets, a manner of speech many found disconcertingly cold.

'Your father is gaining political momentum,' Pickering said. 'A *lot* of it. The White House has got to be getting nervous.' He sighed. 'Politics is a desperate business. When the President calls a secret meeting with his challenger's daughter, I'd guess there's more on his mind than intelligence gists.'

Rachel felt a distant chill. Pickering's hunches had an uncanny tendency to be dead on. 'And you're afraid the White House feels desperate enough to introduce *me* into the political mix?'

Pickering paused a moment. 'You are not exactly silent about your feelings for your father, and I have little doubt the President's campaign staff is aware of the rift. It occurs to me that they may want to use you against him somehow.'

'Where do I sign up?' Rachel said, only half joking.

Pickering looked unimpressed. He gave her a stern stare. 'A word of warning, Agent Sexton. If you feel that your personal issues with your father are going to cloud your judgment in dealing with the President, I strongly advise that you decline the President's request for a meeting.'

'Decline?' Rachel gave a nervous chuckle. 'I obviously can't refuse the President.'

'No,' the director said, 'but I can.'

His words rumbled a bit, reminding Rachel of the other reason Pickering was called the 'Quaker.' Despite being a small man, William Pickering could cause political earthquakes if he were crossed.

'My concerns here are simple,' Pickering said. 'I have a responsibility to protect the people who work for me, and I don't appreciate even the vague implication that one of them might be used as a pawn in a political game.'

'What do you recommend I do?'

Pickering sighed. 'My suggestion is that you meet with him. Commit to nothing. Once the President tells you what the hell is on his mind, call me. If I think he's playing political hardball with you, trust me, I'll pull you out so fast the man won't know what hit him.'

'Thank you, sir.' Rachel sensed a protective aura from the director that she often longed for in her own father. 'And you said the President already sent a car?'

'Not exactly.' Pickering frowned and pointed out the window.

Uncertain, Rachel went over and gazed out in the direction of Pickering's outstretched finger.

A snub-nosed MH-60G PaveHawk helicopter sat idling on the lawn. One of the fastest choppers ever made, this PaveHawk was emblazoned with the White House insignia. The pilot stood nearby, checking his watch.

Rachel turned to Pickering in disbelief. 'The White House sent a *PaveHawk* to take me fifteen miles into D.C.?'

'Apparently the President hopes you are either impressed or intimidated.' Pickering eyed her. 'I suggest you are neither.'

Rachel nodded. She was both.

Four minutes later, Rachel Sexton exited the NRO and climbed into the waiting helicopter. Before she had even buckled herself in, the craft was airborne, banking hard across the Virginia woods. Rachel gazed out at the blur of trees beneath her and felt her pulse rising. It would have risen faster had she known this chopper would never reach the White House.

CHAPTER **5**

The frigid wind battered the fabric of the ThermaTech tent, but Delta-One hardly noticed. He and Delta-Three were focused on their comrade, who was manipulating the joystick in his hand with surgical dexterity. The screen before them displayed a live video transmission from a pinpoint camera mounted aboard the microrobot.

The ultimate surveillance tool, Delta-One thought, still amazed every time they powered it up. Lately, in the world of micromechanics, fact seemed to be outpacing fiction.

Micro Electro Mechanical Systems (MEMS) – microbots – were the newest tool in high-tech surveillance – 'fly on the wall technology,' they called it.

Literally.

Although microscopic, remote-controlled robots sounded like science fiction, in fact they had been around since the 1990s. *Discovery* magazine had run a cover story in May 1997 on microbots, featuring both 'flying' and 'swimming' models. The swimmers – nanosubs the size of salt grains – could be injected into the human bloodstream *à la* the movie *Fantastic Voyage*. They were now being used by advanced medical facilities to help doctors navigate arteries by remote control, observe live intravenous video transmissions, and locate arterial blockages without ever lifting a scalpel.

Contrary to intuition, building a *flying* microbot was an even simpler business. The aerodynamics technology for getting a machine to fly had been around since Kittyhawk, and all that remained had been the issue of miniaturization. The first flying microbots, designed by NASA as unmanned exploration tools for future Mars missions, had been several inches long. Now, however, advances in nanotechnology, lightweight energy-absorbent materials, and micromechanics had made the flying microbots a reality.

The true breakthrough had come from the new field biomimics –

copying Mother Nature. Miniature dragonflies, as it turned out, were the ideal prototype for these agile and efficient flying microbots. The PH2 model Delta-Two was currently flying was only one centimeter long – the size of a *mosquito* – and employed a dual pair of transparent, hinged, silicon-leaf wings, giving it unparalleled mobility and efficiency in the air.

The microbot's refueling mechanism had been another breakthrough. The first microbot prototypes could only recharge their energy cells by hovering directly beneath a bright light source, not ideal for stealth or use in dark locales. The newer prototypes, however, could recharge simply by parking within a few inches of a magnetic field. Conveniently, in modern society, magnetic fields were ubiquitous and discreetly placed – power outlets, computer monitors, electric motors, audio speakers, cellphones – it seemed there was never any shortage of obscure recharging stations. Once a microbot had been introduced successfully into a locale, it could transmit audio and video almost indefinitely. The Delta Force's PH2 had been transmitting for over a week now with no trouble whatsoever.

Now, like an insect hovering inside a cavernous barn, the airborne microbot hung silently in the still air of the structure's massive central room. With a bird's-eye view of the space below, the microbot circled silently above unsuspecting occupants – technicians, scientists, specialists in countless fields of study. As the PH2 circled, Delta-One spotted two familiar faces engaged in conversation. They would be a telling mark. He told Delta-Two to drop down and have a listen.

Manipulating the controls, Delta-Two switched on the robot's sound sensors, oriented the microbot's parabolic amplifier, and decreased the robot's elevation until it was ten feet over the scientists' heads. The transmission was faint, but discernible.

'I still can't believe it,' one scientist was saying. The excitement in his voice had not diminished since his arrival here forty-eight hours ago.

The man with whom he was talking obviously shared the enthusiasm. 'In your lifetime . . . did you ever think you would witness anything like this?'

'Never,' the scientist replied, beaming. 'It's all a magnificent dream.'

Delta-One had heard enough. Clearly everything inside was proceeding as expected. Delta-Two maneuvered the microbot away from the conversation and flew it back to its hiding place. He parked the tiny device undetected near the cylinder of an electric generator. The PH2's power cells immediately began recharging for the next mission.

CHAPTER 6

Rachel Sexton's thoughts were lost in the morning's bizarre developments as her PaveHawk transport tore across the morning sky, and it was not until the helicopter rocketed out across Chesapeake Bay that she realized they were heading in entirely the wrong direction. The initial flash of confusion instantly gave way to trepidation.

'Hey!' she yelled to the pilot. 'What are you doing?' Her voice was barely audible over the rotors. 'You're supposed to be taking me to the White House!'

The pilot shook his head. 'Sorry, ma'am. The President is not at the White House this morning.'

Rachel tried to remember if Pickering had specifically mentioned the White House or whether she had simply assumed. 'So where is the President?'

'Your meeting with him is elsewhere.'

No shit. 'Where elsewhere?'

'Not far now.'

'That's not what I asked.'

'Sixteen more miles.'

Rachel scowled at him. *This guy should be a politician.* 'Do you dodge bullets as well as you dodge questions?'

The pilot did not answer.

*   *   *

It took less than seven minutes for the chopper to cross the Chesapeake. When land was in sight again, the pilot banked north and skirted a narrow peninsula, where Rachel saw a series of runways and military-looking buildings. The pilot dropped down toward them, and Rachel then realized what this place was. The six launch-pads and charred rocket towers were a good clue, but if that was not enough, the roof of one of the buildings had been painted with two enormous words: WALLOPS ISLAND.

Wallops Island was one of NASA's oldest launch sites. Still used today for satellite launches and testing of experimental aircraft, Wallops was NASA's base away from the spotlight.

The President is at Wallops Island? It made no sense.

The chopper pilot aligned his trajectory with a series of three runways that ran the length of the narrow peninsula. They seemed to be heading for the far end of the center runway.

The pilot began to slow. 'You will be meeting the President in his office.'

Rachel turned, wondering if the guy was joking. 'The President of the United States has an office on Wallops Island?'

The pilot looked dead serious. 'The President of the United States has an office wherever he likes, ma'am.'

He pointed toward the end of the runway. Rachel saw the mammoth shape glistening in the distance, and her heart almost stopped. Even at 300 yards, she recognized the light blue hull of the modified 747.

'I'm meeting him aboard the . . .'

'Yes, ma'am. His home away from home.'

Rachel stared out at the massive aircraft. The military's cryptic designation for this prestigious plane was VC-25-A, although the rest of the world knew it by another name: Air Force One.

'Looks like you're in the *new* one this morning,' the pilot said, motioning to the numbers on the plane's tail fin.

Rachel nodded blankly. Few Americans knew that there were actually two Air Force Ones in service – a pair of identical, specially configured 747-200-Bs, one with the tail number 28000 and the other 29000. Both planes had cruising speeds of 600 mph and had been modified for in-flight refueling, giving them virtually unlimited range.

As the PaveHawk settled onto the runway beside the President's plane, Rachel now understood the references to Air Force One being the commander-in-chief's 'portable home court advantage.' The machine was an intimidating sight.

When the President flew to other countries to meet heads of state, he often requested – for security purposes – that the meeting take place on the runway aboard his jet. Although some of the motives were security, certainly another incentive was to gain a negotiating edge through raw intimidation. A visit to Air Force One was far more intimidating than any trip to the White House. The six-foot-high letters along the fuselage trumpeted 'UNITED STATES OF AMERICA.' A female English cabinet member had once accused President Nixon of 'waving his manhood in her face' when he asked her to join him aboard Air Force One. Later the crew jokingly nicknamed the plane 'Big Dick.'

'Ms Sexton?' A blazer-clad Secret Serviceman materialized outside the chopper and opened the door for her. 'The President is waiting for you.'

Rachel got out of the chopper and gazed up the steep gangway at the bulging hull. *Into the flying phallus.* She had once heard the flying 'Oval Office' had over four thousand square feet of interior floor space, including four separate private sleeping quarters, berths for a twenty-six-member flight crew, and two galleys capable of providing food for fifty people.

Climbing the stairway, Rachel felt the Secret Serviceman on her heels, urging her upward. High above, the cabin door stood open like a tiny puncture wound on the side of a gargantuan silver whale. She moved toward the darkened entryway and felt her confidence starting to ebb.

Easy, Rachel. It's just a plane.

On the landing, the Secret Serviceman politely took her arm and guided her into a surprisingly narrow corridor. They turned right, walked a short distance, and emerged into a luxurious and spacious cabin. Rachel immediately recognized it from photographs.

'Wait here,' the serviceman said, and he disappeared.

Rachel stood alone in Air Force One's famous wood-paneled fore cabin. This was the room used for meetings, entertaining dignitaries, and, apparently, for scaring the hell out of first-time passengers. The room spanned the entire width of the plane, as did its thick tan carpeting. The furnishings were impeccable – cordovan leather arm-chairs around a bird's-eye maple meeting table, burnished brass floor lamps beside a continental sofa, and hand-etched crystal glassware on a mahogany wet bar.

Supposedly, Boeing designers had carefully laid out this fore cabin to provide passengers with 'a sense of order mixed with tranquility.' Tranquility, however, was the last thing Rachel Sexton was feeling at the moment. The only thing she could think of was the number of world leaders who had sat in this very room and made decisions that shaped the world.

Everything about this room said power, from the faint aroma of fine pipe tobacco to the ubiquitous presidential seal. The eagle clasping the arrows and olive branches was embroidered on throw pillows, carved into the ice bucket, and even printed on the cork coasters on the bar. Rachel picked up a coaster and examined it.

'Stealing souvenirs already?' a deep voice asked behind her.

Startled, Rachel wheeled, dropping the coaster on the floor. She knelt awkwardly to retrieve it. As she grasped the coaster, she turned to see the President of the United States gazing down at her with an amused grin.

'I'm not royalty, Ms Sexton. There's really no need to kneel.'

CHAPTER 7

Senator Sedgewick Sexton savored the privacy of his Lincoln stretch limousine as it snaked through Washington's morning traffic toward his office. Across from him, Gabrielle Ashe, his twenty-four-year-old personal assistant, read him his daily schedule. Sexton was barely listening.

I love Washington, he thought, admiring the assistant's perfect shape beneath her cashmere sweater. *Power is the greatest aphrodisiac of all . . . and it brings women like this to D.C. in droves.*

Gabrielle was a New York Ivy Leaguer with dreams of being a senator herself one day. *She'll make it too*, Sexton thought. She was incredible-looking and sharp as a whip. Above all, she understood the rules of the game.

Gabrielle Ashe was black, but her tawny coloring was more of a deep cinnamon or mahogany, the kind of comfortable in-between that Sexton knew bleeding heart 'whites' could endorse without feeling like they were giving away the farm. Sexton described Gabrielle to his cronies as Halle Berry's looks with Hillary Clinton's brains and ambition, although sometimes he thought even that was an understatement.

Gabrielle had been a tremendous asset to his campaign since he'd promoted her to his personal campaign assistant three months ago. And to top it all off, she was working for free. Her compensation for a sixteen-hour workday was learning the ropes in the trenches with a seasoned politician.

Of course, Sexton gloated, *I've persuaded her to do a bit more than just work.* After promoting Gabrielle, Sexton had invited her to a late night 'orientation session' in his private office. As expected, his young assistant arrived starstruck and eager to please. With a slow-moving patience mastered over decades, Sexton worked his magic . . . building up Gabrielle's trust, carefully stripping away her inhibitions, exhibiting tantalizing control, and finally seducing her right there in his office.

Sexton had little doubt the encounter had been one of the most sexually gratifying experiences of the young woman's life, and yet, in the light of the day, Gabrielle clearly regretted the indiscretion. Embarrassed, she offered to resign. Sexton refused. Gabrielle stayed on, but she made her intentions very clear. The relationship had been strictly business ever since.

Gabrielle's pouty lips were still moving. '. . . don't want you to be lackadaisical going into this CNN debate this afternoon. We still don't know who the White House is sending as opposition. You'll want to peruse these notes I typed.' She handed him a folder.

Sexton took the folder, savoring the scent of her perfume mixed with the plush leather seats.

'You aren't listening,' she said.

'Certainly am.' He grinned. 'Forget about this CNN debate. Worse case scenario, the White House snubs me by sending some low-level campaign intern. Best case scenario, they send a bigwig, and I eat him for lunch.'

Gabrielle frowned. 'Fine. I've included a list of the most probable hostile topics in your notes.'

'The usual suspects no doubt.'

'With one new entry. I think you might face some hostile backlash from the gay community for your comments last night on *Larry King*.'

Sexton shrugged, barely listening. 'Right. The same-sex marriage thing.'

Gabrielle gave him a disapproving look. 'You *did* come out against it pretty strongly.'

Same-sex marriages, Sexton thought in disgust. *If it were up to me, the faggots wouldn't even have the right to vote*. 'Okay, I'll turn it down a notch.'

'Good. You've been pushing the envelope a bit on some of these hot topics lately. Don't get cocky. The public can turn in an instant. You're gaining now, and you have momentum. Just ride it out. There's no need to hit the ball out of the park today. Just keep it in play.'

'Any news from the White House?'

Gabrielle looked pleasantly baffled. 'Continued silence. It's official; your opponent has become the "Invisible Man." '

Sexton could barely believe his good fortune lately. For months, the President had been working hard on the campaign trail. Then suddenly, a week ago, he had locked himself in the Oval Office, and nobody had seen or heard from him since. It was as if the President simply could not face Sexton's groundswell of voter support.

Gabrielle ran a hand through her straightened black hair. 'I hear the White House campaign staff is as confused as we are. The President is offering no explanation for his vanishing act, and everyone over there is furious.'

'Any theories?' Sexton asked.

Gabrielle gazed at him over her scholarly glasses. 'As it turns out, I got some interesting data this morning from a contact of mine in the White House.'

Sexton recognized the look in her eyes. Gabrielle Ashe had scored some insider information again. Sexton wondered if she were giving some presidential aide backseat blow jobs in exchange for campaign secrets. Sexton didn't care . . . so long as the information kept coming.

'Rumor has it,' his assistant said, lowering her voice, 'the President's strange behavior all started last week after an emergency private briefing with the administrator of NASA. Apparently the President emerged from the meeting looking dazed. He immediately cleared his schedule, and he's been in close contact with NASA ever since.'

Sexton certainly liked the sound of that. 'You think maybe NASA delivered some more bad news?'

'Seems a logical explanation,' she said hopefully. 'Although it would have to be pretty critical to make the President drop everything.'

Sexton considered it. Obviously, whatever was going on with NASA had to be bad news. *Otherwise the President would throw it in my face.* Sexton had been pounding the President pretty hard on NASA funding lately. The space agency's recent string of failed missions and gargantuan budget overruns had earned NASA the dubious honor of becoming Sexton's unofficial poster child against big government overspending and inefficiency. Admittedly, attacking NASA – one of the most prominent symbols of American pride – was not the way most politicians would think of winning votes, but Sexton had a weapon few other politicians had – Gabrielle Ashe. And her impeccable instincts.

The savvy young woman had come to Sexton's attention several months ago when she was working as a coordinator in Sexton's Washington campaign office. With Sexton trailing badly in the primary polls and his message of government overspending falling on deaf ears, Gabrielle Ashe wrote him a note suggesting a radical new campaign angle. She told the senator he should attack NASA's huge budget overruns and continued White House bailouts as the quintessential example of President Herney's careless overspending.

'NASA is costing Americans a fortune,' Gabrielle wrote, including a list of financial figures, failures, and bailouts. 'Voters have no idea. They would be horrified. I think you should make NASA a political issue.'

Sexton groaned at her naïveté. 'Yeah, and while I'm at it, I'll rail against singing the national anthem at baseball games.'

In the weeks that followed, Gabrielle continued to send information about NASA across the senator's desk. The more Sexton read, the more he realized this young Gabrielle Ashe had a point. Even by government agency standards, NASA was an astounding money pit – expensive, inefficient, and in recent years, grossly incompetent.

One afternoon Sexton was doing an on-air interview about education. The host was pressing Sexton about where he would find funding for his promised overhaul of public schools. In response, Sexton decided to test Gabrielle's NASA theory with a half-joking response. 'Money for education?' he said. 'Well, maybe I'll cut the space program in half. I figure if NASA can spend fifteen billion a year in space, I should be able to spend seven and a half billion on the kids here on earth.'

In the transmission booth, Sexton's campaign managers gasped in horror at the careless remark. After all, entire campaigns had been sunk by far less than taking a potshot at NASA. Instantly, the phone lines at the radio station lit up. Sexton's campaign managers cringed; the space patriots were circling for the kill.

Then something unexpected happened.

'Fifteen billion a year?' the first caller said, sounding shocked. 'With a *B?* Are you telling me that my son's math class is overcrowded because schools can't afford enough teachers, and NASA is spending fifteen billion dollars a year taking pictures of space dust?'

'Um . . . that's right,' Sexton said warily.

'Absurd! Does the President have the power to do something about that?'

'Absolutely,' Sexton replied, gaining confidence. 'A President can veto the budget request of any agency he or she deems overfunded.'

'Then you have my vote, Senator Sexton. Fifteen billion for space research, and our kids don't have teachers. It's outrageous! Good luck, sir. I hope you go all the way.'

The next caller came on the line. 'Senator, I just read that NASA's

International Space Station is way overbudget and the President is thinking of giving NASA emergency funding to keep the project going. Is that true?'

Sexton jumped at this one. 'True!' He explained that the space station was originally proposed as a joint venture, with twelve countries sharing the costs. But after construction began, the station's budget spiraled wildly out of control, and many countries dropped out in disgust. Rather than scrapping the project, the President decided to cover everyone's expenses. 'Our cost for the ISS project,' Sexton announced, 'has risen from the proposed eight billion to a staggering *one hundred* billion dollars!'

The caller sounded furious. 'Why the hell doesn't the President pull the plug?'

Sexton could have kissed the guy. 'Damn good question. Unfortunately, one third of the building supplies are already in orbit, and the President spent *your* tax dollars putting them there, so pulling the plug would be admitting he made a multibillion-dollar blunder with *your* money.'

The calls kept coming. For the first time, it seemed Americans were waking up to the idea that NASA was an option – not a national fixture.

When the show was over, with the exception of a few NASA diehards calling in with poignant overtures about man's eternal quest for knowledge, the consensus was in: Sexton's campaign had stumbled onto the holy grail of campaigning – a new 'hot button' – a yet untapped controversial issue that struck a nerve with voters.

In the weeks that followed, Sexton trounced his opponents in five crucial primaries. He announced Gabrielle Ashe as his new personal campaign assistant, praising her for her work in bringing the NASA issue to the voters. With the wave of a hand, Sexton had made a young African-American woman a rising political star, and the issue of his racist and sexist voting record disappeared overnight.

Now, as they sat together in the limousine, Sexton knew Gabrielle had yet again proven her worth. Her new information about last week's secret meeting between the NASA administrator and the President certainly suggested more NASA troubles were brewing – perhaps another country pulling funding from the space station.

As the limousine passed the Washington Monument, Senator Sexton could not help but feel he had been anointed by destiny.

CHAPTER 8

Despite having ascended to the most powerful political office in the world, President Zachary Herney was average in height, with a slender build and narrow shoulders. He had a freckled face, bifocals, and thinning black hair. His unimposing physique, however, stood in stark contrast to the almost princely love the man commanded from those who knew him. It was said that if you met Zach Herney once, you would walk to the ends of the earth for him.

'So glad you could make it,' President Herney said, reaching out to shake Rachel's hand. His grasp was warm and sincere.

Rachel fought the frog in her throat. 'Of . . . course, Mr President. An honor to meet you.'

The President gave her a comforting grin, and Rachel sensed firsthand the legendary Herney affability. The man possessed an easygoing countenance political cartoonists loved because no matter how skewed a rendition they drew, no one ever mistook the man's effortless warmth and amiable smile. His eyes mirrored sincerity and dignity at all times.

'If you follow me,' he said in a cheery voice, 'I've got a cup of coffee with your name on it.'

'Thank you, sir.'

The President pressed the intercom and called for some coffee in his office.

As Rachel followed the President through the plane, she could not help but notice that he looked extremely happy and well rested for a man who was down in the polls. He was also very casually dressed – blue jeans, a polo shirt, and L.L. Bean hiking boots.

Rachel tried to make conversation. 'Doing . . . some hiking, Mr President?'

'Not at all. My campaign advisers have decided this should be my new look. What do you think?'

Rachel hoped for his sake that he wasn't serious. 'It's very . . . um . . . *manly*, sir.'

Herney was deadpan. 'Good. We're thinking it will help me win back some of the women's vote from your father.' After a beat, the President broke into a broad smile. 'Ms Sexton, that was a *joke*. I think we both know I'll need more than a polo shirt and blue jeans to win this election.'

The President's openness and good humor were quickly evaporating any tension Rachel felt about being there. What this President lacked in physical brawn, he more than made up for in diplomatic rapport. Diplomacy was about people skills, and Zach Herney had the gift.

Rachel followed the President toward the back of the plane. The deeper they went, the less the interior resembled a plane – curved hallways, wallpapered walls, even an exercise room complete with StairMaster and rowing machine. Oddly, the plane seemed almost entirely deserted.

'Traveling alone, Mr President?'

He shook his head. 'Just landed, actually.'

Rachel was surprised. *Landed from where?* Her intel briefs this week had included nothing about presidential travel plans. Apparently he was using Wallops Island to travel quietly.

'My staff deplaned right before you arrived,' the President said. 'I'm headed back to the White House shortly to meet them, but I wanted to meet you here instead of my office.'

'Trying to intimidate me?'

'On the contrary. Trying to respect you, Ms Sexton. The White House is anything but private, and news of a meeting between the two of us would put you in an awkward position with your father.'

'I appreciate that, sir.'

'It seems you're managing a delicate balancing act quite gracefully, and I see no reason to disrupt that.'

Rachel flashed on her breakfast meeting with her father and doubted that it qualified as 'graceful.' Nonetheless, Zach Herney was going out of his way to be decent, and he certainly didn't have to.

'May I call you Rachel?' Herney asked.

'Of course.' *May I call you Zach?*

'My office,' the President said, ushering her through a carved maple door.

The office aboard Air Force One certainly was cozier than its White House counterpart, but its furnishings still carried an air of austerity. The desk was mounded with papers, and behind it hung an imposing oil painting of a classic, three-masted schooner under full sail trying to outrun a raging storm. It seemed a perfect metaphor for Zach Herney's presidency at the moment.

The President offered Rachel one of the three executive chairs facing his desk. She sat. Rachel expected him to sit behind his desk, but instead he pulled one of the chairs up and sat next to her.

Equal footing, she realized. *The master of rapport.*

'Well, Rachel,' Herney said, sighing tiredly as he settled into his chair. 'I imagine you've got to be pretty damned confused to be sitting here right now, am I right?'

Whatever was left of Rachel's guard crumbled away with the candor in the man's voice. 'Actually, sir, I'm baffled.'

Herney laughed out loud. 'Terrific. It's not every day I can baffle someone from the NRO.'

'It's not every day someone from the NRO is invited aboard Air Force One by a President in hiking boots.'

The President laughed again.

A quiet rap on the office door announced the arrival of coffee. One of the flight crew entered with a steaming pewter pot and two pewter mugs on a tray. At the President's bidding, she laid the tray on the desk and disappeared.

'Cream and sugar?' the President asked, standing up to pour.

'Cream, please.' Rachel savored the rich aroma. *The President of the United States is personally serving me coffee?*

Zach Herney handed her a heavy pewter mug. 'Authentic Paul Revere,' he said. 'One of the little luxuries.'

Rachel sipped the coffee. It was the best she had ever tasted.

'Anyhow,' the President said, pouring himself a cup and sitting back down, 'I've got limited time here, so let's get to business.' The President plopped a sugar cube in his coffee and gazed up at her. 'I imagine Bill Pickering warned you that the only reason I would want to see you would be to use you to my political advantage?'

'Actually, sir, that's *exactly* what he said.'

The President chuckled. 'Always the cynic.'

'So he's wrong?'

'Are you kidding?' the President laughed. 'Bill Pickering is never wrong. He's dead-on as usual.'

CHAPTER 9

Gabrielle Ashe gazed absently out the window of Senator Sexton's limousine as it moved through the morning traffic toward Sexton's office building. She wondered how the hell she had arrived at this point in her life. Personal assistant to Senator Sedgewick Sexton. This was exactly what she had wanted, wasn't it?

I'm sitting in a limousine with the next President of the United States.

Gabrielle stared across the car's plush interior at the senator, who seemed to be far away in his own thoughts. She admired his handsome features and perfect attire. He looked presidential.

Gabrielle had first seen Sexton speak when she was a poli-sci major at Cornell University three years ago. She would never forget how his eyes probed the audience, as if sending a message directly to her – *trust me.* After Sexton's speech, Gabrielle waited in line to meet him.

'Gabrielle Ashe,' the senator said, reading her name tag. 'A lovely name for a lovely young woman.' His eyes were reassuring.

'Thank you, sir,' Gabrielle replied, feeling the man's strength as she shook his hand. 'I was really impressed by your message.'

'Glad to hear it!' Sexton thrust a business card into her hand. 'I'm always looking for bright young minds who share my vision. When you get out of school, track me down. My people may have a job for you.'

Gabrielle opened her mouth to thank him, but the senator was already on to the next person in line. Nonetheless, in the months that followed, Gabrielle found herself following Sexton's career on television. She watched with admiration as he spoke out against big government spending – spearheading budget cuts, streamlining the IRS to work more effectively, trimming fat at the DEA, and even abolishing redundant civil service programs. Then, when the senator's wife died suddenly in a car crash, Gabrielle watched in awe as Sexton somehow turned the negative into a positive. Sexton rose above his personal pain and declared to the world that he would be running for the presidency and dedicating the remainder of his public service to his wife's memory. Gabrielle decided right then and there that she wanted to work closely with Senator Sexton's presidential campaign.

Now she had gotten as close as anyone could get.

Gabrielle recalled the night she had spent with Sexton in his plush office, and she cringed, trying to block out the embarrassing images in her mind. *What was I thinking?* She knew she should have resisted, but somehow she'd found herself unable. Sedgewick Sexton had been an idol of hers for so long . . . and to think he wanted *her*.

The limousine hit a bump, jarring her thoughts back to the present.

'You okay?' Sexton was watching her now.

Gabrielle flashed a hurried smile. 'Fine.'

'You aren't still thinking about that drudge, are you?'

She shrugged. 'I'm still a little worried, yeah.'

'Forget it. The drudge was the best thing that ever happened to my campaign.'

A drudge, Gabrielle had learned the hard way, was the political equivalent of leaking information that your rival used a penis enlarger or subscribed to *Stud Muffin* magazine. Drudging wasn't a glamorous tactic, but when it paid off, it paid off big.

Of course, when it backfired . . .

And backfire it had. For the White House. About a month ago, the President's campaign staff, unsettled by the slipping polls, had decided to get aggressive and leak a story they suspected to be true – that Senator Sexton had engaged in an affair with his personal assistant, Gabrielle Ashe. Unfortunately for the White House, there was no hard evidence. Senator Sexton, a firm believer in the best defense is a strong offense, seized the moment for attack. He called a national press conference to proclaim his innocence and outrage. *I cannot believe*, he said, gazing into the cameras with pain in his eyes, *that the President would dishonor my wife's memory with these malicious lies.*

Senator Sexton's performance on TV was so convincing that Gabrielle herself practically believed they had not slept together. Seeing how effortlessly he lied, Gabrielle realized that Senator Sexton was indeed a dangerous man.

Lately, although Gabrielle was certain she was backing the *strongest* horse in this presidential race, she had begun to question whether she was backing the *best* horse. Working closely with Sexton had been an eye-opening experience – akin to a behind-the-scenes tour of Universal Studios, where one's childlike awe over the movies is sullied by the realization that Hollywood isn't magic after all.

Although Gabrielle's faith in Sexton's message remained intact, she was beginning to question the messenger.

CHAPTER 10

'What I am about to tell you, Rachel,' the President said, 'is classified "UMBRA." Well beyond your current security clearance.'

Rachel felt the walls of Air Force One closing in around her. The President had flown her to Wallops Island, invited her onboard his plane, poured her coffee, told her flat out that he intended to use her to political advantage against her own father, and now he was announcing he intended to give her classified information illegally. However affable Zach Herney appeared on the surface, Rachel Sexton had just learned something important about him. This man took control in a hurry.

'Two weeks ago,' the President said, locking eyes with her, 'NASA made a discovery.'

The words hung a moment in the air before Rachel could process them. *A NASA discovery?* Recent intelligence updates had suggested nothing out of the ordinary going on with the space agency. Of course, these days a 'NASA discovery' usually meant realizing they'd grossly underbudgeted some new project.

'Before we talk further,' the President said, 'I'd like to know if you share your father's cynicism over space exploration.'

Rachel resented the comment. 'I certainly hope you didn't call me here to ask me to control my father's rants against NASA.'

He laughed. 'Hell, no. I've been around the Senate long enough to know that *nobody* controls Sedgewick Sexton.'

'My father is an opportunist, sir. Most successful politicians are. And unfortunately NASA has made itself an opportunity.' The recent string of NASA errors had been so unbearable that one either had to laugh or cry – satellites that disintegrated in orbit, space probes that never called home, the International Space Station budget rising tenfold and member countries bailing out like rats from a sinking ship. Billions were being lost, and Senator Sexton was riding it like a wave – a wave that seemed destined to carry him to the shores of 1600 Pennsylvania Avenue.

'I will admit,' the President continued, 'NASA has been a walking disaster area lately. Every time I turn around, they give me yet another reason to slash their funding.'

Rachel saw her opening for a foothold and took it. 'And yet, sir, didn't I just read that you bailed them out last week with another three million in emergency funding to keep them solvent?'

The President chuckled. 'Your father was pleased with that one, wasn't he?'

'Nothing like sending ammunition to your executioner.'

'Did you hear him on *Nightline*? "Zach Herney is a space addict, and the taxpayers are funding his habit." '

'But you keep proving him right, sir.'

Herney nodded. 'I make it no secret that I'm an enormous fan of NASA. I always have been. I was a child of the space race – Sputnik, John Glenn, Apollo 11 – and I have never hesitated to express my feelings of admiration and national pride for our space program. In my mind, the men and women of NASA are history's modern pioneers. They attempt the impossible, accept failure, and then go back to the drawing board while the rest of us stand back and criticize.'

Rachel remained silent, sensing that just below the President's calm exterior was an indignant rage over her father's endless anti-NASA rhetoric. Rachel found herself wondering what the hell NASA had found. The President was certainly taking his time coming to the point.

'Today,' Herney said, his voice intensifying, 'I intend to change your entire opinion of NASA.'

Rachel eyed him with uncertainty. 'You have my vote already, sir. You may want to concentrate on the rest of the country.'

'I intend to.' He took a sip of coffee and smiled. 'And I'm going to ask you to help me.' Pausing, he leaned toward her. 'In a most unusual way.'

Rachel could now feel Zach Herney scrutinizing her every move, like a hunter trying to gauge if his prey intended to run or fight. Unfortunately, Rachel saw nowhere to run.

'I assume,' the President said, pouring them both more coffee, 'that you're aware of a NASA project called EOS?'

Rachel nodded. 'Earth Observation System. I believe my father has mentioned EOS once or twice.'

The weak attempt at sarcasm drew a frown from the President. The truth was that Rachel's father mentioned the Earth Observation System every chance he got. It was one of NASA's most controversial big-ticket ventures – a constellation of five satellites designed to look down from space and analyze the planet's environment: ozone depletion, polar ice melt, global warming, rainforest defoliation. The intent was to provide environmentalists with never before seen macroscopic data so that they could plan better for earth's future.

Unfortunately, the EOS project had been wrought with failure. Like so many NASA projects of late, it had been plagued with costly overruns right from the start. And Zach Herney was the one taking the heat. He had used the support of the environmental lobby to push the $1.4 billion EOS project through Congress. But rather than delivering the promised contributions to global earth science, EOS had spiraled quickly into a costly nightmare of failed launches, computer malfunctions, and somber NASA press conferences. The only smiling face lately was that of Senator Sexton, who was smugly

reminding voters just how much of *their* money the President had
spent on EOS and just how lukewarm the returns had been.

The President dropped a sugar cube into his mug. 'As surprising as
this may sound, the NASA discovery I'm referring to was *made* by
EOS.'

Now Rachel felt lost. If EOS had enjoyed a recent success, NASA
certainly would have announced it, wouldn't they? Her father had
been crucifying EOS in the media, and the space agency could use any
good news they could find.

'I've heard nothing,' Rachel said, 'about any EOS discovery.'

'I know. NASA prefers to keep the good news to themselves for a
while.'

Rachel doubted it. 'In my experience, sir, when it comes to NASA,
no news is generally bad news.' Restraint was not a forte of the
NASA public relations department. The standing joke at the NRO
was that NASA held a press conference every time one of their
scientists so much as farted.

The President frowned. 'Ah, yes. I forget I'm talking to one of
Pickering's NRO security disciples. Is he still moaning and groaning
about NASA's loose lips?'

'Security is his business, sir. He takes it very seriously.'

'He damn well better. I just find it hard to believe that two agencies
with so much in common constantly find something to fight about.'

Rachel had learned early in her tenure under William Pickering that
although both NASA and the NRO were space-related agencies, they
had philosophies that were polar opposites. The NRO was a defense
agency and kept all of its space activities classified, while NASA was
academic and excitedly publicized all of its breakthroughs around the
globe – often, William Pickering argued, at the risk of national
security. Some of NASA's finest technologies – high-resolution lenses
for satellite telescopes, long-range communications systems, and radio
imaging devices – had a nasty habit of appearing in the intelligence
arsenal of hostile countries and being used to spy against us. Bill
Pickering often grumbled that NASA scientists had big brains . . . and
even bigger mouths.

A more pointed issue between the agencies, however, was the fact
that because NASA handled the NRO's satellite launches, many of

NASA's recent failures directly affected the NRO. No failure had been more dramatic than that of 12 August 1998, when a NASA/ Air Force Titan 4 rocket blew up forty seconds into launch and obliterated its payload – a *$1.2 billion* NRO satellite code-named Vortex 2. Pickering seemed particularly unwilling to forget that one.

'So why hasn't NASA gone public about this recent success?' Rachel challenged. 'They certainly could use some good news right now.'

'NASA is being silent,' the President declared, 'because I *ordered* them to be.'

Rachel wondered if she had heard him correctly. If so, the President was committing some kind of political hara-kiri that she did not understand.

'This discovery,' the President said, 'is . . . shall we say . . . nothing short of astounding in its ramifications.'

Rachel felt an uneasy chill. In the world of intelligence, 'astounding ramifications' seldom meant good news. She now wondered if all the EOS secrecy was on account of the satellite system having spotted some impending environmental disaster. 'Is there a problem?'

'No problem at all. What EOS discovered is quite wonderful.'

Rachel fell silent.

'Suppose, Rachel, that I told you NASA has just made a discovery of such scientific importance . . . such earth-shattering significance . . . that it validated every dollar Americans have ever spent in space?'

Rachel could not imagine.

The President stood up. 'Let's take a walk, shall we?'

CHAPTER 11

Rachel followed President Herney out onto the glistening gangway of Air Force One. As they descended the stairs, Rachel felt the bleak March air clearing her mind. Unfortunately, clarity only made the President's claims seem more outlandish than before.

NASA made a discovery of such scientific importance that it validates every dollar Americans have ever spent in space?

Rachel could only imagine that a discovery of that magnitude would only center on one thing – the holy grail of NASA – contact with extraterrestrial life. Unfortunately, Rachel knew enough about *that* particular holy grail to know it was utterly implausible.

As an intelligence analyst, Rachel constantly fielded questions from friends who wanted to know about the alleged government cover-ups of alien contact. She was consistently appalled by the theories her 'educated' friends bought into – crashed alien saucers hidden in secret government bunkers, extraterrestrial corpses kept on ice, even unsuspecting civilians being abducted and surgically probed.

It was all absurd, of course. There were no aliens. No cover-ups.

Everyone in the intelligence community understood that the vast majority of sightings and alien abductions were simply the product of active imaginations or moneymaking hoaxes. When authentic photographic UFO evidence *did* exist, it had a strange habit of occurring near U.S. military airbases that were testing advanced classified aircraft. When Lockheed began air-testing a radical new jet called the Stealth Bomber, UFO sightings around Edwards Air Force Base increased fifteenfold.

'You have a skeptical look on your face,' the President said, eyeing her askance.

The sound of his voice startled Rachel. She glanced over, unsure how to respond. 'Well . . .' She hesitated. 'May I assume, sir, that we are not talking about alien spacecrafts or little green men?'

The President looked quietly amused. 'Rachel, I think you'll find this discovery far more intriguing than science fiction.'

Rachel was relieved to hear NASA had not been so desperate as to try selling the President on an alien story. Nonetheless, his comment served only to deepen the mystery. 'Well,' she said, 'whatever NASA found, I must say the timing is exceptionally convenient.'

Herney paused on the gangway. 'Convenient? How so?'

How so? Rachel stopped and stared. 'Mr President, NASA is currently in a life or death battle to justify its very existence, and you are under attack for continuing to fund it. A major NASA breakthrough right now would be a panacea for both NASA and your campaign. Your critics will obviously find the timing highly suspect.'

'So . . . are you calling me a liar or a fool?'

Rachel felt a knot rise in her throat. 'I meant no disrespect, sir. I simply—'

'Relax.' A faint grin grew on Herney's lips, and he started to descend again. 'When the NASA administrator first told me about this discovery, I flat out rejected it as absurd. I accused him of masterminding the most transparent political sham in history.'

Rachel felt the knot in her throat dissolve somewhat.

At the bottom of the ramp, Herney stopped and looked at her. 'One reason I've asked NASA to keep their discovery under wraps is to protect them. The magnitude of this find is well beyond anything NASA has ever announced. It will make landing men on the moon seem insignificant. Because everyone, myself included, has so much to gain – and lose – I thought it prudent for someone to double-check the NASA data before we step into the world spotlight with a formal announcement.'

Rachel was startled. 'Certainly you can't mean *me*, sir?'

The President laughed. 'No, this is not your area of expertise. Besides, I've already achieved verification through extragovernmental channels.'

Rachel's relief gave way to a new mystification. 'Extragovernmental, sir? You mean you used the *private* sector? On something this classified?'

The President nodded with conviction. 'I put together an external confirmation team – four civilian scientists – non-NASA personnel with big names and serious reputations to protect. They used their own equipment to make observations and come to their own conclusions. Over the past forty-eight hours, these civilian scientists have confirmed the NASA discovery beyond the shadow of a doubt.'

Now Rachel was impressed. The President had protected himself with typical Herney aplomb. By hiring the ultimate team of skeptics – outsiders who had nothing to gain by confirming the NASA discovery – Herney had immunized himself against suspicions that this might be a desperate NASA ploy to justify its budget, reelect their NASA-friendly President, and ward off Senator Sexton's attacks.

'Tonight at eight P.M.,' Herney said, 'I will be calling a press conference at the White House to announce this discovery to the world.'

Rachel felt frustrated. Herney had essentially told her nothing. 'And this discovery is *what*, precisely?'

The President smiled. 'You will find patience a virtue today. This discovery is something you need to see for yourself. I need you to understand this situation fully before we proceed. The administrator of NASA is waiting to brief you. He will tell you everything you need to know. Afterward, you and I will further discuss your role.'

Rachel sensed an impending drama in the President's eyes and recalled Pickering's hunch that the White House had something up its sleeve. Pickering, it appeared, was right, as usual.

Herney motioned to a nearby airplane hangar. 'Follow me,' he said, walking toward it.

Rachel followed, confused. The building before them had no windows, and its towering bay doors were sealed. The only access seemed to be a small entryway on the side. The door was ajar. The President guided Rachel to within a few feet of the door and stopped.

'End of the line for me,' he said, motioning to the door. 'You go through there.'

Rachel hesitated. 'You're not coming?'

'I need to return to the White House. I'll speak to you shortly. Do you have a cellphone?'

'Of course, sir.'

'Give it to me.'

Rachel produced her phone and handed it to him, assuming he intended to program a private contact number into it. Instead, he slipped her phone into his pocket.

'You're now off-the-grid,' the President said. 'All your responsibilities at work have been covered. You will not speak to anyone else today without express permission from myself or the NASA administrator. Do you understand?'

Rachel stared. *Did the President just steal my cellphone?*

'After the administrator briefs you on the discovery, he will put you in contact with me via secure channels. I'll talk to you soon. Good luck.'

Rachel looked at the hangar door and felt a growing uneasiness.

President Herney put a reassuring hand on her shoulder and nodded toward the door. 'I assure you, Rachel, you will not regret assisting me in this matter.'

Without another word, the President strode toward the PaveHawk that had brought Rachel in. He climbed aboard, and took off. He never once looked back.

CHAPTER 12

Rachel Sexton stood alone on the threshold of the isolated Wallops hangar and peered into the blackness beyond. She felt like she was on the cusp of another world. A cool and musty breeze flowed outward from the cavernous interior, as if the building were breathing.

'Hello?' she called out, her voice wavering slightly.

Silence.

With rising trepidation, she stepped over the threshold. Her vision went blank for an instant as her eyes became accustomed to the dimness.

'Ms Sexton, I presume?' a man's voice said, only yards away.

Rachel jumped, wheeling toward the sound. 'Yes, sir.'

The hazy shape of a man approached.

As Rachel's vision cleared, she found herself standing face to face with a young, stone-jawed buck in a NASA flight suit. His body was fit and muscle-bound, his chest bedecked with countless patches.

'Commander Wayne Loosigian,' the man said. 'Sorry if I startled you, ma'am. It's pretty dark in here. I haven't had a chance to open the bay doors yet.' Before Rachel could respond, the man added, 'It will be my honor to be your pilot this morning.'

'Pilot?' Rachel stared at the man. *I just had a pilot.* 'I'm here to see the administrator.'

'Yes, ma'am. My orders are to transport you to him immediately.'

It took a moment for the statement to sink in. When it hit her, she felt a stab of deceit. Apparently, her travels were not over. 'Where *is* the administrator?' Rachel demanded, wary now.

'I do not have that information,' the pilot replied. 'I will receive his coordinates after we are airborne.'

Rachel sensed that the man was telling the truth. Apparently she and Director Pickering were not the only two people being kept in the dark this morning. The President was taking the issue of security very seriously, and Rachel felt embarrassed by how quickly and effortlessly the President had taken her 'off-the-grid.' *Half an hour in the field, and I'm already stripped of all communication, and my director has no idea where I am.*

Standing now before her stiff-backed NASA pilot, Rachel had little doubt her morning plans were cast in stone. This carnival ride was leaving with Rachel onboard whether she liked it or not. The only question was where it was headed.

The pilot strode over to the wall and pressed a button. The far side of the hangar began sliding loudly to one side. Light poured in from the outside, silhouetting a large object in the center of the hangar.

Rachel's mouth fell open. *God help me.*

There in the middle of the hangar stood a ferocious-looking black fighter jet. It was the most streamlined aircraft Rachel had ever seen.

'You *are* joking,' she said.

'Common first reaction, ma'am, but the F-14 Tomcat Split-tail is a highly proven craft.'

It's a missile with wings.

The pilot led Rachel toward his craft. He motioned to the dual cockpit. 'You'll be riding in back.'

'Really?' She gave him a tight smile. 'And here I thought you wanted me to drive.'

After donning a thermal flight suit over her clothes, Rachel found herself climbing into the cockpit. Awkwardly, she wedged her hips into the narrow seat.

'NASA obviously has no fat-assed pilots,' she said.

The pilot gave a grin as he helped Rachel buckle herself in. Then he slid a helmet over her head.

'We'll be flying pretty high,' he said. 'You'll want oxygen.' He pulled an oxygen mask from the side dash and began snapping it onto her helmet.

'I can manage,' Rachel said, reaching up and taking over.

'Of course, ma'am.'

Rachel fumbled with the molded mouthpiece and then finally snapped it onto her helmet. The mask's fit was surprisingly awkward and uncomfortable.

The commander stared at her for a long moment, looking vaguely amused.

'Is something wrong?' she demanded.

'Not at all, ma'am.' He seemed to be hiding a smirk. 'Hack sacks are under your seat. Most people get sick their first time in a split-tail.'

'I should be fine,' Rachel assured him, her voice muffled by the smothering fit of the mask. 'I'm not prone to motion sickness.'

The pilot shrugged. 'A lot of Navy Seals say the same thing, and I've cleaned plenty of Seal puke out of my cockpit.'

She nodded weakly. *Lovely.*

'Any questions before we go?'

Rachel hesitated a moment and then tapped on the mouthpiece cutting into her chin. 'It's cutting off my circulation. How do you wear these things on long flights?'

The pilot smiled patiently. 'Well, ma'am, we don't usually wear them upside down.'

Poised at the end of the runway, engines throbbing beneath her, Rachel felt like a bullet in a gun waiting for someone to pull the trigger. When the pilot pushed the throttle forward, the Tomcat's twin Lockheed 345 engines roared to life, and the entire world shook. The brakes released, and Rachel slammed backward in her seat. The jet tore down the runway and lifted off within a matter of seconds. Outside, the earth dropped away at a dizzying rate.

Rachel closed her eyes as the plane rocketed skyward. She wondered where she had gone wrong this morning. She was supposed to be at a desk writing gists. Now she was straddling a testosterone-fueled torpedo and breathing through an oxygen mask.

By the time the Tomcat leveled out at 45,000 feet, Rachel was feeling queasy. She willed herself to focus her thoughts elsewhere. Gazing down at the ocean nine miles below, Rachel felt suddenly far from home.

Up front, the pilot was talking to someone on the radio. When the conversation ended, the pilot hung up the radio, and immediately banked the Tomcat sharply left. The plane tipped almost to the vertical, and Rachel felt her stomach do a somersault. Finally, the plane leveled out again.

Rachel groaned. 'Thanks for the warning, hotshot.'

'I'm sorry, ma'am, but I've just been given the classified coordinates of your meeting with the administrator.'

'Let me guess,' Rachel said. 'Due north?'

The pilot seemed confused. 'How did you know that?'

Rachel sighed. *You gotta love these computer-trained pilots.* 'It's nine A.M., sport, and the sun is on our right. We're flying north.'

There was a moment of silence from the cockpit. 'Yes, ma'am, we'll be traveling north this morning.'

'And how *far* north are we going?'

The pilot checked the coordinates. 'Approximately three thousand miles.'

Rachel sat bolt upright. 'What?' She tried to picture a map, unable even to imagine what was *that* far north. 'That's a four-hour flight!'

'At our current speed, yes,' the pilot said. 'Hold on, please.'

Before Rachel could respond, the man retracted the F-14's wings into low-drag position. An instant later, Rachel felt herself slammed into her seat yet again as the plane shot forward as though it had been standing still. Within a minute they were cruising at almost 1,500 miles per hour.

Rachel was feeling dizzy now. As the sky tore by with blinding speed, she felt an uncontrollable wave of nausea hit her. The President's voice echoed faintly. *I assure you, Rachel, you will not regret assisting me in this matter.*

Groaning, Rachel reached for her hack sack. *Never trust a politician.*

CHAPTER **13**

Although he disliked the menial filth of public taxis, Senator Sedgewick Sexton had learned to endure the occasional demeaning moment along his road to glory. The grungy Mayflower cab that had just deposited him in the lower parking garage of the Purdue Hotel afforded Sexton something his stretch limousine could not – anonymity.

He was pleased to find this lower level deserted, only a few dusty cars dotting a forest of cement pillars. As he made his way diagonally across the garage on foot, Sexton glanced at his watch.

11:15 A.M. Perfect.

The man with whom Sexton was meeting was always touchy about punctuality. Then again, Sexton reminded himself, considering who the man represented, he could be touchy about any damned thing he wanted.

Sexton saw the white Ford Windstar minivan parked in exactly the same spot as it had been for every one of their meetings – in the eastern corner of the garage, behind a row of trash bins. Sexton would have preferred to meet this man in a suite upstairs, but he certainly understood the precautions. This man's friends had not gotten to where they were by being careless.

As Sexton moved toward the van, he felt the familiar edginess that he always experienced before these encounters. Forcing himself to relax his shoulders, he climbed into the passenger's seat with a cheery wave. The dark-haired gentleman in the driver's seat did not smile. The man was almost seventy years old, but his leathery complexion exuded a toughness appropriate to his post as figurehead of an army of brazen visionaries and ruthless entrepreneurs.

'Close the door,' the man said, his voice callous.

Sexton obeyed, tolerating the man's gruffness graciously. After all, this man represented men who controlled enormous sums of money, much of which had been pooled recently to poise Sedgewick Sexton on the threshold of the most powerful office in the world. These meetings, Sexton had come to understand, were less strategy sessions than they were monthly reminders of just how beholden the senator had become to his benefactors. These men were expecting a serious return on their investment. The 'return,' Sexton had to admit, was a shockingly bold demand; and yet, almost more incredibly, it was something that would be within Sexton's sphere of influence once he took the Oval Office.

'I assume,' Sexton said, having learned how this man liked to get down to business, 'that another installment has been made?'

'It has. And as usual, you are to use these funds solely for your campaign. We have been pleased to see the polls shifting consistently in your favor, and it appears your campaign managers have been spending our money effectively.'

'We're gaining fast.'

'As I mentioned to you on the phone,' the old man said, 'I have persuaded six more to meet with you tonight.'

'Excellent.' Sexton had blocked off the time already.

The old man handed Sexton a folder. 'Here is their information. Study it. They want to know you understand their concerns specifically. They want to know you are sympathetic. I suggest you meet them at your residence.'

'My home? But I usually meet—'

'Senator, these six men run companies that possess resources well in excess of the others you have met. These men are the big fish, and they are wary. They have more to gain and therefore more to lose. I've worked hard to persuade them to meet with you. They will require special handling. A personal touch.'

Sexton gave a quick nod. 'Absolutely. I can arrange a meeting at my home.'

'Of course, they will want total privacy.'

'As will I.'

'Good luck,' the old man said. 'If tonight goes well, it could be your last meeting. These men alone can provide what is needed to push the Sexton campaign over the top.'

Sexton liked the sound of that. He gave the old man a confident smile. 'With luck, my friend, come election time, we will all claim victory.'

'Victory?' The old man scowled, leaning toward Sexton with ominous eyes. 'Putting you in the White House is only the *first step* toward victory, Senator. I assume you have not forgotten that.'

CHAPTER 14

The White House is one of the smallest presidential mansions in the world, measuring only 170 feet in length, 85 feet in depth, and sitting on a mere 18 acres of landscaped grounds. Architect James Hoban's plan for a boxlike stone structure with a hipped roof, balustrade, and columnar entrance, though clearly unoriginal, was selected from the open design contest by judges who praised it as 'attractive, dignified, and flexible.'

President Zach Herney, even after three and a half years in the White House, seldom felt at home here among the maze of chandeliers, antiques, and armed Marines. At the moment, however, as he strode toward the West Wing, he felt invigorated and oddly at ease, his feet almost weightless on the plush carpeting.

Several members of the White House staff looked up as the President approached. Herney waved and greeted each by name. Their responses, though polite, were subdued and accompanied by forced smiles.

'Good morning, Mr President.'

'Nice to see you, Mr President.'

'Good day, sir.'

As the President made his way toward his office, he sensed whisperings in his wake. There was an insurrection afoot inside the White House. For the past couple of weeks, the disillusionment at 1600 Pennsylvania Avenue had been growing to a point where Herney was starting to feel like Captain Bligh – commanding a struggling ship whose crew was preparing for mutiny.

The President didn't blame them. His staff had worked grueling hours to support him in the upcoming election, and now, all of a sudden, it seemed the President was fumbling the ball.

Soon they will understand, Herney told himself. *Soon I'll be the hero again.*

He regretted having to keep his staff in the dark for so long, but secrecy was absolutely critical. And when it came to keeping secrets, the White House was known as the leakiest ship in Washington.

Herney arrived in the waiting room outside the Oval Office and gave his secretary a cheery wave. 'You look nice this morning, Dolores.'

'You too, sir,' she said, eyeing his casual attire with unveiled disapproval.

Herney lowered his voice. 'I'd like you to organize a meeting for me.'

'With whom, sir?'

'The entire White House staff.'

His secretary glanced up. 'Your *entire* staff, sir? All one hundred and forty-five of them?'

'Exactly.'

She looked uneasy. 'Okay. Shall I set it up in . . . the Briefing Room?'

Herney shook his head. 'No. Let's set it up in my office.'

Now she stared. 'You want to see your *entire* staff inside the Oval Office?'

'Exactly.'

'All at once, sir?'

'Why not? Set it up for four P.M.'

The secretary nodded as though humoring a mental patient. 'Very well, sir. And the meeting is regarding . . . ?'

'I have an important announcement to make to the American people tonight. I want my staff to hear it first.'

A sudden dejected look swept across his secretary's face, almost as if she had secretly been dreading this moment. She lowered her voice. 'Sir, are you pulling out of the race?'

Herney burst out laughing. 'Hell no, Dolores! I'm gearing up to fight!'

She looked doubtful. The media reports had all been saying President Herney was throwing the election.

He gave her a reassuring wink. 'Dolores, you've done a terrific job for me these past few years, and you'll do a terrific job for me for another four. We're *keeping* the White House. I swear it.'

His secretary looked like she wanted to believe it. 'Very well, sir. I'll alert the staff. Four P.M.'

As Zach Herney entered the Oval Office, he couldn't help but smile at the image of his entire staff crammed into the deceptively small chamber.

Although this great office had enjoyed many nicknames over the years – the Loo, Dick's Den, the Clinton Bedroom – Herney's favorite was 'the Lobster Trap.' It seemed most fitting. Each time a newcomer entered the Oval Office, disorientation set in immediately. The symmetry of the room, the gently curving walls, the discreetly disguised doorways in and out, all gave visitors the dizzying sense they'd been blindfolded and spun around. Often, after a meeting in the Oval Office, a visiting dignitary would stand up, shake hands with the President, and march straight into a storage closet. Depending on how the meeting had gone, Herney would either stop the guest in time or watch in amusement as the visitor embarrassed himself.

Herney had always believed the most dominating aspect of the Oval Office was the colorful American eagle emblazoned on the room's oval carpet. The eagle's left talon clutched an olive branch and his right a bundle of arrows. Few outsiders knew that during times of peace, the eagle faced left – toward the olive branch. But in times of war, the eagle mysteriously faced right – toward the arrows. The mechanism behind this little parlor trick was the source of quiet speculation among White House staff because it was traditionally known only by the President and the head of housekeeping. The truth behind the enigmatic eagle, Herney had found to be disappointingly mundane. A storage room in the basement contained the second oval carpet, and housekeeping simply swapped the carpets in the dead of night.

Now, as Herney gazed down at the peaceful, left-gazing eagle,

he smiled to think that perhaps he should swap carpets in honor of
the little war he was about to launch against Senator Sedgewick
Sexton.

CHAPTER **15**

The U.S. Delta Force is the sole fighting squad whose actions are
granted complete presidential immunity from the law.

Presidential Decision Directive 25 (PDD 25) grants Delta Force
soldiers 'freedom from all legal accountability,' including exception
from the 1876 Posse Comitatus Act, a statute imposing criminal
penalties for anyone using the military for personal gain, domestic
law enforcement, or unsanctioned covert operations. Delta Force
members are handpicked from the Combat Applications Group
(CAG), a classified organization within the Special Operations
Command in Fort Bragg, North Carolina. Delta Force soldiers are
trained killers – experts in SWAT operations, rescuing hostages,
surprise raids, and elimination of covert enemy forces.

Because Delta Force missions usually involve high levels of secrecy,
the traditional multitiered chain of command is often circumvented in
favor of 'monocaput' management – a single controller who holds
authority to control the unit as he or she sees fit. The controller tends
to be a military government powerbroker with sufficient rank or
influence to run the mission. Regardless of the identity of their
controller, Delta Force missions are classified at the highest level, and
once a mission is completed, Delta Force soldiers never speak of it
again – not to one another, and not to their commanding officers
within Special Ops.

Fly. Fight. Forget.

The Delta team currently stationed above the 82nd Parallel was
doing no flying or fighting. They were simply watching.

Delta-One had to admit that this had been a most unusual mission
so far, but he had learned long ago never to be surprised by what he

was asked to do. In the past five years he had been involved in Middle East hostage rescues, tracking and exterminating terrorist cells working inside the United States, and even the discreet elimination of several dangerous men and women around the globe.

Just last month his Delta team had used a flying microbot to induce a lethal heart attack in a particularly malicious South American drug lord. Using a microbot equipped with a hairline titanium needle containing a potent vasoconstrictor, Delta-Two had flown the device into the man's house through an open second-story window, found the man's bedroom, and then pricked him on the shoulder while he was sleeping. The microbot was back out the window and 'feet dry' before the man woke up with chest pain. The Delta team was already flying home by the time his victim's wife was calling the paramedics.

No breaking and entering.

Death by natural causes.

It had been a thing of beauty.

More recently, another microbot stationed inside a prominent senator's office to monitor his personal meetings had captured images of a lurid sexual encounter. The Delta team jokingly referred to that mission as 'insertion behind enemy lines.'

Now, after being trapped on surveillance duty inside this tent for the last ten days, Delta-One was ready for this mission to be over.

Remain in hiding.

Monitor the structure – inside and out.

Report to your controller any unexpected developments.

Delta-One had been trained never to feel any emotion regarding his assignments. This mission, however, had certainly raised his heart rate when he and his team were first briefed. The briefing had been 'faceless' – every phase explained via secure electronic channels. Delta-One had never met the controller responsible for this mission.

Delta-One was preparing a dehydrated protein meal when his watch beeped in unison with the others. Within seconds the CrypTalk communications device beside him blinked on alert. He stopped what he was doing and picked up the handheld communicator. The other two men watched in silence.

'Delta-One,' he said, speaking into the transmitter.

The two words were instantly identified by the voice recognition software inside the device. Each word was then assigned a reference number, which was encrypted and sent via satellite to the caller. On the caller's end, at a similar device, the numbers were decrypted, translated back into words using a predetermined, self-randomizing dictionary. Then the words were spoken aloud by a synthetic voice. Total delay, eighty milliseconds.

'Controller here,' said the person overseeing the operation. The robotic tone of the CrypTalk was eerie – inorganic and androgynous. 'What is your op status?'

'Everything proceeding as planned,' Delta-One replied.

'Excellent. I have an update on the time frame. The information goes public tonight at eight P.M. Eastern.'

Delta-One checked his chronograph. *Only eight more hours.* His job here would be finished soon. That was encouraging.

'There is another development,' the controller said. 'A new player has entered the arena.'

'What new player?'

Delta-One listened. *An interesting gamble.* Someone out there was playing for keeps. 'Do you think she can be trusted?'

'She needs to be watched very closely.'

'And if there is trouble?'

There was no hesitation on the line. 'Your orders stand.'

CHAPTER **16**

Rachel Sexton had been flying due north for over an hour. Other than a fleeting glimpse of Newfoundland, she had seen nothing but water beneath the F-14 for the entire journey.

Why did it have to be water? she thought, grimacing. Rachel had plunged through the ice on a frozen pond while ice-skating when she was seven. Trapped beneath the surface, she was certain she would die. It had been her mother's powerful grasp that finally yanked Rachel's waterlogged body to safety. Ever since that harrowing ordeal,

Rachel had battled a persistent case of hydrophobia – a distinct wariness of open water, especially cold water. Today, with nothing but the North Atlantic as far as Rachel could see, her old fears had come creeping back.

Not until the pilot checked his bearings with Thule airbase in northern Greenland did Rachel realize how far they had traveled. *I'm above the Arctic Circle?* The revelation intensified her uneasiness. *Where are they taking me? What has NASA found?* Soon the blue-gray expanse below her became speckled with thousands of stark white dots.

Icebergs.

Rachel had seen icebergs only once before in her life, six years ago when her mother persuaded Rachel to join her on an Alaskan mother-daughter cruise. Rachel had suggested countless alternative *land*-based vacations, but her mother was insistent. 'Rachel, honey,' her mother had said, 'two thirds of this planet is covered with water, and sooner or later, you've got to learn to deal with it.' Mrs Sexton was a resilient New Englander intent on raising a strong daughter.

The cruise had been the last trip Rachel and her mother ever took. *Katherine Wentworth Sexton.* Rachel felt a distant pang of loneliness. Like the howling wind outside the plane, the memories came tearing back, pulling at her the way they always did. Their final conversation had been by phone. Thanksgiving morning.

'I'm so sorry, Mom,' Rachel said, phoning home from a snowbound O'Hare Airport. 'I know our family has never spent Thanksgiving Day apart. It looks like today will be our first.'

Rachel's mom sounded crushed. 'I was so looking forward to seeing you.'

'Me too, Mom. Think of me eating airport food while you and Dad feast on turkey.'

There was a pause on the line. 'Rachel, I wasn't going to tell you until you got here, but your father says he has too much work to make it home this year. He'll be staying at his D.C. suite for the long weekend.'

'What?' Rachel's surprise gave way immediately to anger. 'But, it's Thanksgiving. The Senate isn't in session! He's less than two hours away. He should be with you!'

'I know. He says he's exhausted – far too tired to drive. He's decided he needs to spend this weekend curled up with his backlog of work.'

Work? Rachel was skeptical. A more likely guess was that Senator Sexton would be curled up with another woman. His infidelities, though discreet, had been going on for years. Mrs Sexton was no fool, but her husband's affairs were always accompanied by persuasive alibis and pained indignity at the mere suggestion he could be unfaithful. Finally, Mrs Sexton saw no alternative but to bury her pain by turning a blind eye. Although Rachel had urged her mother to consider divorce, Katherine Wentworth Sexton was a woman of her word. *Till death do us part,* she told Rachel. *Your father blessed me with you – a beautiful daughter – and for that I thank him. He will have to answer for his actions to a higher power someday.*

Now, standing in the airport, Rachel's anger was simmering. 'But, this means you'll be alone for Thanksgiving!' She felt sick to her stomach. The senator deserting his family on Thanksgiving Day was a new low, even for him.

'Well . . .' Mrs Sexton said, her voice disappointed but decisive. 'I obviously can't let all this food go to waste. I'll drive it up to Aunt Ann's. She's always invited us up for Thanksgiving. I'll give her a call right now.'

Rachel felt only marginally less guilty. 'Okay. I'll be home as soon as I can. I love you, Mom.'

'Safe flight, sweetheart.'

It was 10:30 that night when Rachel's taxi finally pulled up the winding driveway of the Sextons' luxurious estate. Rachel immediately knew something was wrong. Three police cars sat in the driveway. Several news vans too. All the house lights were on. Rachel dashed in, her heart racing.

A Virginia State policeman met her at the doorway. His face was grim. He didn't have to say a word. Rachel knew. There had been an accident.

'Route Twenty-five was slick with freezing rain,' the officer said. 'Your mother went off the road into a wooded ravine. I'm sorry. She died on impact.'

Rachel's body went numb. Her father, having returned immediately when he got the news, was now in the living room holding a small press conference, stoically announcing to the world that his wife had passed away in a crash on her way back from Thanksgiving dinner with family.

Rachel stood in the wings, sobbing through the entire event.

'I only wish,' her father told the media, his eyes tearful, 'that I had been home for her this weekend. This never would have happened.'

You should have thought of that years ago, Rachel cried, her loathing for her father deepening with every passing instant.

From that moment on, Rachel divorced herself from her father in the way Mrs Sexton never had. The senator barely seemed to notice. He suddenly had gotten very busy using his late wife's fortunes to begin courting his party's nomination for president. The sympathy vote didn't hurt either.

Cruelly now, three years later, even at a distance the senator was making Rachel's life lonely. Her father's run for the White House had put Rachel's dreams of meeting a man and starting a family on indefinite hold. For Rachel it had become far easier to take herself completely out of the social game than to deal with the endless stream of power-hungry Washingtonian suitors hoping to snag a grieving, potential 'first daughter' while she was still in their league.

Outside the F-14, the daylight had started to fade. It was late winter in the Arctic – a time of perpetual darkness. Rachel realized she was flying into a land of permanent night.

As the minutes passed, the sun faded entirely, dropping below the horizon. They continued north, and a brilliant three-quarter moon appeared, hanging white in the crystalline glacial air. Far below, the ocean waves shimmered, the icebergs looking like diamonds sewn into a dark sequin mesh.

Finally, Rachel spotted the hazy outline of land. But it was not what she had expected. Looming out of the ocean before the plane was an enormous snowcapped mountain range.

'Mountains?' Rachel asked, confused. 'There are mountains *north* of Greenland?'

'Apparently,' the pilot said, sounding equally surprised.

As the nose of the F-14 tipped downward, Rachel felt an eerie weightlessness. Through the ringing in her ears she could hear a repeated electronic ping in the cockpit. The pilot had apparently locked on to some kind of directional beacon and was following it in.

As they passed below 3,000 feet, Rachel stared out at the dramatic moonlit terrain beneath them. At the base of the mountains, an expansive, snowy plain swept wide. The plateau spread gracefully seaward about ten miles until it ended abruptly at a sheer cliff of solid ice that dropped vertically into the ocean.

It was then that Rachel saw it. A sight like nothing she had ever seen anywhere on earth. At first she thought the moonlight must be playing tricks on her. She squinted down at the snowfields, unable to comprehend what she was looking at. The lower the plane descended, the clearer the image became.

What in the name of God?

The plateau beneath them was striped . . . as if someone had painted the snow with three huge striations of silver paint. The glistening strips ran parallel to the coastal cliff. Not until the plane dropped past 500 feet did the optical illusion reveal itself. The three silver stripes were deep troughs, each one over thirty yards wide. The troughs had filled with water and frozen into broad, silvery channels that stretched in parallel across the plateau. The white berms between them were mounded dikes of snow.

As they dropped toward the plateau, the plane started bucking and bouncing in heavy turbulence. Rachel heard the landing gear engage with a heavy clunk, but she still saw no landing strip. As the pilot struggled to keep the plane under control, Rachel peered out and spotted two lines of blinking strobes straddling the outermost ice trough. She realized to her horror what the pilot was about to do.

'We're landing on *ice?*' she demanded.

The pilot did not respond. He was concentrating on the buffeting wind. Rachel felt a drag in her gut as the craft decelerated and dropped toward the ice channel. High snow berms rose on either side of the aircraft, and Rachel held her breath, knowing the slightest miscalculation in the narrow channel would mean certain death. The wavering plane dropped lower between the berms, and the turbulence suddenly disappeared. Sheltered there from the wind, the plane touched down perfectly on the ice.

The Tomcat's rear thrusters roared, slowing the plane. Rachel exhaled. The jet taxied about a hundred yards farther and rolled to a stop at a red line spray-painted boldly across the ice.

The view to the right was nothing but a wall of snow in the moonlight – the side of an ice berm. The view on the left was identical. Only through the windshield ahead of them did Rachel have any visibility . . . an endless expanse of ice. She felt like she had landed on a dead planet. Aside from the line on the ice, there were no signs of life.

Then Rachel heard it. In the distance, another engine was approaching. Higher pitched. The sound grew louder until a machine came into view. It was a large, multitreaded snow tractor churning toward them up the ice trough. Tall and spindly, it looked like a towering futuristic insect grinding toward them on voracious spinning feet. Mounted high on the chassis was an enclosed Plexiglas cabin with a rack of floodlights illuminating its way.

The machine shuddered to a halt directly beside the F-14. The door on the Plexiglas cabin opened, and a figure climbed down a ladder onto the ice. He was bundled from head to foot in a puffy white jumpsuit that gave the impression he had been inflated.

Mad Max meets the Pillsbury Dough Boy, Rachel thought, relieved at least to see this strange planet was inhabited.

The man signaled for the F-14 pilot to pop the hatch.

The pilot obeyed.

When the cockpit opened, the gust of air that tore through Rachel's body chilled her instantly to the core.

Close the damn lid!

'Ms Sexton?' the figure called up to her. His accent was American. 'On behalf of NASA, I welcome you.'

Rachel was shivering. *Thanks a million.*

'Please unhook your flight harness, leave your helmet in the craft, and deplane by using the fuselage toeholds. Do you have any questions?'

'Yes,' Rachel shouted back. 'Where the hell am I?'

CHAPTER 17

Marjorie Tench – senior adviser to the President – was a loping skeleton of a creature. Her gaunt six-foot frame resembled an Erector Set construction of joints and limbs. Overhanging her precarious body was a jaundiced face whose skin resembled a sheet of parchment paper punctured by two emotionless eyes. At fifty-one, she looked seventy.

Tench was revered in Washington as a goddess in the political arena. She was said to possess analytical skills that bordered on the clairvoyant. Her decade running the State Department's Bureau of Intelligence and Research had helped hone a lethally sharp, critical mind. Unfortunately, accompanying Tench's political savvy came an icy temperament that few could endure for more than a few minutes. Marjorie Tench had been blessed with all the brains of a super-computer – and the warmth of one, too. Nonetheless, President Zach Herney had little trouble tolerating the woman's idiosyncrasies; her intellect and hard work were almost single-handedly responsible for putting Herney in office in the first place.

'Marjorie,' the President said, standing to welcome her into the Oval Office. 'What can I do for you?' He did not offer her a seat. The typical social graces did not apply to women like Marjorie Tench. If Tench wanted a seat, she would damn well take one.

'I see you set the staff briefing for four o'clock this afternoon.' Her voice was raspy from cigarettes. 'Excellent.'

Tench paced a moment, and Herney sensed the intricate cogs of her mind turning over and over. He was grateful. Marjorie Tench was one of the select few on the President's staff who was fully aware of the NASA discovery, and her political savvy was helping the President plan his strategy.

'This CNN debate today at one o'clock,' Tench said, coughing. 'Who are we sending to spar with Sexton?'

Herney smiled. 'A junior campaign spokesperson.' The political tactic of frustrating the 'hunter' by never sending him any big game was as old as debates themselves.

'I have a better idea,' Tench said, her barren eyes finding his. 'Let me take the spot myself.'

Zach Herney's head shot up. 'You?' *What the hell is she thinking?* 'Marjorie, you don't do media spots. Besides, it's a midday cable show. If I send my senior adviser, what kind of message does that send? It makes us look like we're panicking.'

'Exactly.'

Herney studied her. Whatever convoluted scheme Tench was hatching, there was no way in hell Herney would permit her to appear on CNN. Anyone who had ever laid eyes on Marjorie Tench knew there was a reason she worked *behind* the scenes. Tench was a frightful-looking woman – not the kind of face a President wanted delivering the White House message.

'I am taking this CNN debate,' she repeated. This time she was not asking.

'Marjorie,' the President maneuvered, feeling uneasy now, 'Sexton's campaign will obviously claim your presence on CNN is proof the White House is running scared. Sending out our big guns early makes us look desperate.'

The woman gave a quiet nod and lit a cigarette. 'The more desperate we look, the better.'

For the next sixty seconds, Marjorie Tench outlined why the President would be sending her to the CNN debate instead of some lowly campaign staffer. When Tench was finished, the President could only stare in amazement.

Once again, Marjorie Tench had proven herself a political genius.

CHAPTER 18

The Milne Ice Shelf is the largest solid ice floe in the Northern Hemisphere. Located above the 82nd Parallel on the northernmost coast of Ellesmere Island in the high Arctic, the Milne Ice Shelf is 4 miles wide and reaches thicknesses of over three hundred feet.

Now, as Rachel climbed into the Plexiglas enclosure atop the ice tractor, she was grateful for the extra parka and gloves waiting for her on her seat, as well as the heat pouring out of the tractor's vents. Outside, on the ice runway, the F-14's engines roared, and the plane began taxiing away.

Rachel looked up in alarm. 'He's leaving?'

Her new host climbed into the tractor, nodding. 'Only science personnel and immediate NASA support team members are allowed on-site.'

As the F-14 tore off into the sunless sky, Rachel felt suddenly marooned.

'We'll be taking the IceRover from here,' the man said. 'The administrator is waiting.'

Rachel gazed out at the silvery path of ice before them and tried to imagine what the hell the administrator of NASA was doing up here.

'Hold on,' the NASA man shouted, working some levers. With a grinding growl, the machine rotated ninety degrees in place like a treaded army tank. It was now facing the high wall of a snow berm.

Rachel looked at the steep incline and felt a ripple of fear. *Surely he doesn't intend to—*

'Rock and roll!' The driver popped the clutch, and the craft accelerated directly toward the slope. Rachel let out a muffled cry and held on. As they hit the incline, the spiked treads tore into the snow, and the contraption began to climb. Rachel was certain they would tip over backward, but the cabin remained surprisingly horizontal as the treads clawed up the slope. When the huge machine heaved up onto the crest of the berm, the driver brought it to a stop and beamed at his white-knuckled passenger. 'Try *that* in an SUV! We took the shock-system design from the Mars Pathfinder and popped it on this baby! Worked like a charm.'

Rachel gave a wan nod. 'Neat.'

Sitting now atop the snow berm, Rachel looked out at the inconceivable view. One more large berm stood before them, and then the undulations stopped abruptly. Beyond, the ice smoothed into a glistening expanse that was inclined ever so slightly. The moonlit sheet of ice stretched out into the distance, where it eventually narrowed and snaked up into the mountains.

'That's the Milne Glacier,' the driver said, pointing up into the mountains. 'Starts up there and flows down into this wide delta that we're sitting on now.'

The driver gunned the engine again, and Rachel held on as the craft accelerated down the steep face. At the bottom, they clawed across another ice river and rocketed up the next berm. Mounting the crest and quickly skimming down the far side, they slid out onto a smooth sheet of ice and started crunching across the glacier.

'How far?' Rachel saw nothing but ice in front of them.

'About two miles ahead.'

Rachel thought it seemed far. The wind outside pounded the IceRover in relentless gusts, rattling the Plexiglas as if trying to hurl them back toward the sea.

'That's the katabatic wind,' the driver yelled. 'Get used to it!' He explained that this area had a permanent offshore gale called the katabatic – Greek for flowing downhill. The relentless wind was apparently the product of heavy, cold air 'flowing' down the glacial face like a raging river downhill. 'This is the only place on earth,' the driver added, laughing, 'where hell actually freezes over!'

Several minutes later, Rachel began to see a hazy shape in the distance in front of them – the silhouette of an enormous white dome emerging from the ice. Rachel rubbed her eyes. *What in the world . . . ?*

'*Big* Eskimos up here, eh?' the man joked.

Rachel tried to make sense of the structure. It looked like a scaled-down Houston Astrodome.

'NASA put it up a week and a half ago,' he said. 'Multistage inflatable plexipolysorbate. Inflate the pieces, affix them to one another, connect the whole thing to the ice with pitons and wires. Looks like an enclosed big top tent, but it's actually the NASA prototype for the portable habitat we hope to use on Mars someday. We call it a "habisphere." '

'Habisphere?'

'Yeah, get it? Because it's not a *whole* sphere, it's only *habi-sphere*.'

Rachel smiled and stared out at the bizarre building now looming closer on the glacial plain. 'And because NASA hasn't gone to Mars yet, you guys decided to have a big sleepover out here instead?'

The man laughed. 'Actually, I would have preferred Tahiti, but fate pretty much decided the location.'

Rachel gazed uncertainly up at the edifice. The off-white shell was a ghostly contour against a dark sky. As the IceRover neared the structure, it ground to a stop at a small door on the side of the dome, which was now opening. Light from inside spilled out onto the snow. A figure stepped out. He was a bulky giant wearing a black fleece pullover that amplified his size and made him look like a bear. He moved toward the IceRover.

Rachel had no doubt who the huge man was: Lawrence Ekstrom, administrator of NASA.

The driver gave a solacing grin. 'Don't let his size fool you. The guy's a pussycat.'

More like a tiger, Rachel thought, well acquainted with Ekstrom's reputation for biting the heads off those who stood in the way of his dreams.

When Rachel climbed down from the IceRover, the wind almost blew her over. She wrapped the coat around herself and moved toward the dome.

The NASA administrator met her halfway, extending a huge gloved paw. 'Ms Sexton. Thank you for coming.'

Rachel nodded uncertainly and shouted over the howling wind, 'Frankly, sir, I'm not sure I had much choice.'

*   *   *

A thousand meters farther up the glacier, Delta-One gazed through infrared binoculars and watched as the administrator of NASA ushered Rachel Sexton into the dome.

CHAPTER **19**

NASA administrator Lawrence Ekstrom was a giant of a man, ruddy and gruff, like an angry Norse god. His prickly blond hair was cropped military short above a furrowed brow, and his bulbous nose was spidered with veins. At the moment, his stony eyes drooped with the weight of countless sleepless nights. An influential aerospace strategist and operations adviser at the Pentagon before his appointment to NASA, Ekstrom had a reputation for surliness matched only by his incontestable dedication to whatever mission was at hand.

As Rachel Sexton followed Lawrence Ekstrom into the habisphere, she found herself walking through an eerie, translucent maze of hallways. The labyrinthine network appeared to have been fashioned by hanging sheets of opaque plastic across tautly strung wires. The floor of the maze was nonexistent – a sheet of solid ice, carpeted with strips of rubber matting for traction. They passed a rudimentary living area lined with cots and chemical toilets.

Thankfully, the air in the habisphere was warm, albeit heavy with the mingled potpourri of indistinguishable smells that accompany humans in tight quarters. Somewhere a generator droned, apparently the source of the electricity that powered the bare bulbs hanging from draped extension cords in the hallway.

'Ms Sexton,' Ekstrom grunted, guiding her briskly toward some unknown destination. 'Let me be candid with you right from the start.' His tone conveyed anything but pleasure to have Rachel as his guest. 'You are here because the *President* wants you here. Zach Herney is a personal friend of mine and a faithful NASA supporter. I respect him. I owe him. And I trust him. I do not question his direct orders, even when I resent them. Just so there is no confusion, be aware that I do not share the President's enthusiasm for involving you in this matter.'

Rachel could only stare. *I traveled 3,000 miles for this kind of hospitality?* This guy was no Martha Stewart. 'With all due respect,' she fired back, 'I am *also* under presidential orders. I have not been told my purpose here. I made this trip on good faith.'

'Fine,' Ekstrom said. 'Then I will speak bluntly.'

'You've made a damn good start.'

Rachel's tough response seemed to jolt the administrator. His stride slowed a moment, his eyes clearing as he studied her. Then, like a snake uncoiling, he heaved a long sigh and picked up the pace.

'Understand,' Ekstrom began, 'that you are here on a classified NASA project against my better judgment. Not only are you a representative of the NRO, whose director enjoys dishonoring NASA personnel as loose-lipped children, but you are the daughter of the man who has made it his personal mission to destroy my agency. This should be NASA's hour in the sun; my men and women have endured a lot of criticism lately and deserve this moment of glory. However, due to a torrent of skepticism spearheaded by *your* father, NASA finds itself in a political situation where my hardworking personnel are forced to share the spotlight with a handful of random civilian scientists and the daughter of the man who is trying to destroy us.'

I am not my father, Rachel wanted to shout, but this was hardly the moment to debate politics with the head of NASA. 'I did not come here for the spotlight, sir.'

Ekstrom glared. 'You may find you have no alternative.'

The comment took her by surprise. Although President Herney had said nothing specific about her assisting him in any sort of 'public' way, William Pickering had certainly aired his suspicions that Rachel might become a political pawn. 'I'd like to know what I'm doing here,' Rachel demanded.

'You and me both. I do not have that information.'

'I'm sorry?'

'The President asked me to brief you fully on our discovery the moment you arrived. Whatever role he wants you to play in this circus is between you and him.'

'He told me your Earth Observation System had made a discovery.'

Ekstrom glanced sidelong at her. 'How familiar are you with the EOS project?'

'EOS is a constellation of five NASA satellites which scrutinize the earth in different ways – ocean mapping, geologic fault analyses, polar ice-melt observation, location of fossil fuel reserves—'

'Fine,' Ekstrom said, sounding unimpressed. 'So you're aware of the newest addition to the EOS constellation? It's called PODS.'

Rachel nodded. The Polar Orbiting Density Scanner (PODS) was designed to help measure the effects of global warming. 'As I understand it, PODS measures the thickness and hardness of the polar ice cap?'

'In effect, yes. It uses spectral band technology to take composite density scans of large regions and find softness anomalies in the ice – slush spots, internal melting, large fissures – indicators of global warming.'

Rachel was familiar with composite density scanning. It was like a subterranean ultrasound. NRO satellites had used similar technology to search for subsurface density variants in Eastern Europe and locate mass burial sites, which confirmed for the President that ethnic cleansing was indeed going on.

'Two weeks ago,' Ekstrom said, 'PODS passed over this ice shelf and spotted a density anomaly that looked nothing like anything we'd expected to see. Two hundred feet beneath the surface, perfectly embedded in a matrix of solid ice, PODS saw what looked like an amorphous globule about ten feet in diameter.'

'A water pocket?' Rachel asked.

'No. Not liquid. Strangely, this anomaly was *harder* than the ice surrounding it.'

Rachel paused. 'So . . . it's a boulder or something?'

Ekstrom nodded. 'Essentially.'

Rachel waited for the punch line. It never came. *I'm here because NASA found a big rock in the ice?*

'Not until PODS calculated the density of this rock did we get excited. We immediately flew a team up here to analyze it. As it turns out, the rock in the ice beneath us is significantly *more* dense than any type of rock found here on Ellesmere Island. More dense, in fact, than any type of rock found within a four-hundred-mile radius.'

Rachel gazed down at the ice beneath her feet, picturing the huge rock down there somewhere. 'You're saying someone *moved* it here?'

Ekstrom looked vaguely amused. 'The stone weighs more than eight tons. It is embedded under two *hundred* feet of solid ice, meaning it has been there untouched for over three hundred years.'

Rachel felt tired as she followed the administrator into the mouth of a long, narrow corridor, passing between two armed NASA workers who stood guard. Rachel glanced at Ekstrom. 'I assume there's a logical explanation for the stone's presence here . . . and for all this secrecy?'

'There most certainly is,' Ekstrom said, deadpan. 'The rock PODS found is a meteorite.'

Rachel stopped dead in the passageway and stared at the administrator. 'A *meteorite?*' A surge of disappointment washed over her. A meteorite seemed utterly anticlimactic after the President's big buildup. *This discovery will single-handedly justify all of NASA's past expenditures and blunders?* What was Herney thinking? Meteorites were admittedly one of the rarest rocks on earth, but NASA discovered meteorites all the time.

'This meteorite is one of the largest ever found,' Ekstrom said, standing rigid before her. 'We believe it is a fragment of a larger meteorite documented to have hit the Arctic Ocean in the seventeen hundreds. Most likely, this rock was thrown as ejecta from that ocean impact, landed on the Milne Glacier, and was slowly buried by snow over the past three hundred years.'

Rachel scowled. This discovery changed nothing. She felt a growing suspicion that she was witnessing an overblown publicity stunt by a desperate NASA and White House – two struggling entities attempting to elevate a propitious find to the level of earth-shattering NASA victory.

'You don't look too impressed,' Ekstrom said.

'I guess I was just expecting something . . . else.'

Ekstrom's eyes narrowed. 'A meteorite of this size is a very rare find, Ms Sexton. There are only a few larger in the world.'

'I realize—'

'But the *size* of the meteorite is not what excites us.'

Rachel glanced up.

'If you would permit me to finish,' Ekstrom said, 'you will learn that *this* meteorite displays some rather astonishing characteristics never before seen in any meteorite. Large or small.' He motioned down the passageway. 'Now, if you would follow me, I'll introduce you to someone more qualified than I am to discuss this find.'

Rachel was confused. 'Someone more qualified than the administrator of NASA?'

Ekstrom's Nordic eyes locked in on hers. 'More qualified, Ms Sexton, insofar as he is a civilian. I had assumed because you are a professional data analyst that you would prefer to get your data from an *unbiased* source.'

Touché. Rachel backed off.

She followed the administrator down the narrow corridor, where they dead-ended at a heavy, black drapery. Beyond the drape, Rachel could hear the reverberant murmur of countless voices rumbling on the other side, echoing as if in a giant open space.

Without a word, the administrator reached up and pulled aside the curtain. Rachel was blinded by a dazzling brightness. Hesitant, she stepped forward, squinting into the glistening space. As her eyes adjusted, she gazed out at the massive room before her and drew an awestruck breath.

'My God,' she whispered. *What is this place?*

CHAPTER **20**

The CNN production facility outside of Washington, D.C., is one of 212 studios worldwide that link via satellite to the global headquarters of Turner Broadcasting System in Atlanta.

It was 1:45 P.M. when Senator Sedgewick Sexton's limousine pulled into the parking lot. Sexton was feeling smug as he got out and strode toward the entrance. He and Gabrielle were greeted inside by a pot-bellied CNN producer who wore an effusive smile.

'Senator Sexton,' the producer said. 'Welcome. Great news. We

just found out who the White House sent as a sparring partner for
you.' The producer gave a foreboding grin. 'I hope you brought your
game face.' He motioned through the production glass out into the
studio.

Sexton looked through the glass and almost fell over. Staring back
at him, through the smoky haze of her cigarette, was the ugliest face
in politics.

'Marjorie Tench?' Gabrielle blurted. 'What the hell is *she* doing
here?'

Sexton had no idea, but whatever the reason, her presence here was
fantastic news – a clear sign that the President was in desperation
mode. Why else would he send his senior adviser to the front lines?
President Zach Herney was rolling out the big guns, and Sexton
welcomed the opportunity.

The bigger the foe, the harder they fall.

The senator had no doubt that Tench would be a sly opponent, but
gazing now at the woman, Sexton could not help but think that the
President had made a serious error in judgment. Marjorie Tench was
hideous-looking. At the moment, she sat slouched in her chair,
smoking a cigarette, her right arm moving in languid rhythm back and
forth to her thin lips like a giant praying mantis feeding.

Jesus, Sexton thought, *if there was ever a face that should stick to
radio.*

The few times Sedgewick Sexton had seen the White House senior
adviser's jaundiced mug in a magazine, he could not believe he was
looking at one of the most powerful faces in Washington.

'I don't like this,' Gabrielle whispered.

Sexton barely heard her. The more he considered the opportunity,
the more he liked it. Even more fortuitous than Tench's media-
unfriendly face was Tench's reputation on one key issue: Marjorie
Tench was extremely vocal that America's leadership role in the
future could only be secured through technological superiority. She
was an avid supporter of high-tech government R&D programs, and,
most important – NASA. Many believed it was Tench's behind-the-
scenes pressure that kept the President positioned so staunchly behind
the failing space agency.

Sexton wondered if perhaps the President was now punishing

Tench for all the bad advice about supporting NASA. *Is he throwing his senior adviser to the wolves?*

Gabrielle Ashe gazed through the glass at Marjorie Tench and felt a growing uneasiness. This woman was smart as hell *and* she was an unexpected twist. Those two facts had her instincts tingling. Considering the woman's stance on NASA, the President sending her to face-off against Senator Sexton seemed ill-advised. But the President was certainly no fool. Something told Gabrielle this interview was bad news.

Gabrielle already sensed the senator salivating over his odds, which did little to curb her concern. Sexton had a habit of going overboard when he got cocky. The NASA issue had been a welcome boost in the polls, but Sexton had been pushing very hard lately, she thought. Plenty of campaigns had been lost by candidates who went for the knockout when all they needed was to finish the round.

The producer looked eager for the impending blood match. 'Let's get you set up, Senator.'

As Sexton headed for the studio, Gabrielle caught his sleeve. 'I know what you're thinking,' she whispered. 'But just be smart. Don't go overboard.'

'Overboard? Me?' Sexton grinned.

'Remember this woman is very good at what she does.'

Sexton gave her a suggestive smirk. 'So am I.'

CHAPTER **21**

The cavernous main chamber of NASA's habisphere would have been a strange sight anywhere on earth, but the fact that it existed on an Arctic ice shelf made it that much more difficult for Rachel Sexton to assimilate.

Staring upward into a futuristic dome crafted of white interlocking triangular pads, Rachel felt like she had entered a colossal sanatorium.

The walls sloped downward to a floor of solid ice, where an army of halogen lamps stood like sentinels around the perimeter, casting stark light skyward and giving the whole chamber an ephemeral luminosity.

Snaking across the ice floor, black foam carpet-runners wound like boardwalks through a maze of portable scientific work stations. Amid the electronics, thirty or forty white-clad NASA personnel were hard at work, conferring happily and talking in excited tones. Rachel immediately recognized the electricity in the room.

It was the thrill of new discovery.

As Rachel and the administrator circled the outer edge of the dome, she noted the surprised looks of displeasure from those who recognized her. Their whispers carried clearly in the reverberant space.

Isn't that Senator Sexton's daughter?

What the hell is SHE doing here?

I can't believe the administrator is even speaking to her!

Rachel half expected to see voodoo dolls of her father dangling everywhere. The animosity around her, though, was not the only emotion in the air; Rachel also sensed a distinct smugness – as if NASA clearly knew who would be having the last laugh.

The administrator led Rachel toward a series of tables where a lone man sat at a computer work station. He was dressed in a black turtleneck, wide-whale corduroys, and heavy boat shoes, rather than the matching NASA weather gear everyone else seemed to be wearing. He had his back to them.

The administrator asked Rachel to wait as he went over and spoke to the stranger. After a moment, the man in the turtleneck gave him a congenial nod and started shutting down his computer. The administrator returned.

'Mr Tolland will take it from here,' he said. 'He's another one of the President's recruits, so you two should get along fine. I'll join you later.'

'Thank you.'

'I assume you've heard of Michael Tolland?'

Rachel shrugged, her brain still taking in the incredible surround-ings. 'Name doesn't ring a bell.'

The man in the turtleneck arrived, grinning. 'Doesn't ring a bell?'

His voice was resonant and friendly. 'Best news I've heard all day. Seems I never get a chance to make a first impression anymore.'

When Rachel glanced up at the newcomer, her feet froze in place. She knew the man's handsome face in an instant. Everyone in America did.

'Oh,' she said, blushing as the man shook her hand. 'You're *that* Michael Tolland.'

When the President had told Rachel he had recruited top-notch civilian scientists to authenticate NASA's discovery, Rachel had imagined a group of wizened nerds with monogrammed calculators. Michael Tolland was the antithesis. One of the best known 'science celebrities' in America today, Tolland hosted a weekly documentary called *Amazing Seas*, during which he brought viewers face-to-face with spellbinding oceanic phenomena – underwater volcanoes, ten-foot sea worms, killer tidal waves. The media hailed Tolland as a cross between Jacques Cousteau and Carl Sagan, crediting his knowledge, unpretentious enthusiasm, and lust for adventure as the formula that had rocketed *Amazing Seas* to the top of the ratings. Of course, most critics admitted, Tolland's rugged good looks and self-effacing charisma probably didn't hurt his popularity with the female audience.

'Mr Tolland . . .' Rachel said, fumbling the words a bit. 'I'm Rachel Sexton.'

Tolland smiled a pleasant, crooked smile. 'Hi, Rachel. Call me Mike.'

Rachel found herself uncharacteristically tongue-tied. Sensory overload was setting in . . . the habisphere, the meteorite, the secrets, finding herself unexpectedly face-to-face with a television star. 'I'm surprised to see you here,' she said, attempting to recover. 'When the President told me he'd recruited civilian scientists for authentication of a NASA find, I guess I expected . . .' She hesitated.

'*Real* scientists?' Tolland grinned.

Rachel flushed, mortified. 'That's not what I meant.'

'Don't worry about it,' Tolland said. 'That's all I've heard since I got here.'

The administrator excused himself, promising to catch up with them later. Tolland turned now to Rachel with a curious look. 'The administrator tells me your father is Senator Sexton?'

Rachel nodded. *Unfortunately*.

'A Sexton spy behind enemy lines?'

'Battle lines are not always drawn where you might think.'

An awkward silence.

'So tell me,' Rachel said quickly, 'what's a world-famous ocean-ographer doing on a glacier with a bunch of NASA rocket scientists?'

Tolland chuckled. 'Actually, some guy who looked a lot like the President asked me to do him a favor. I opened my mouth to say "Go to hell," but somehow I blurted, "Yes, sir." '

Rachel laughed for the first time all morning. 'Join the club.'

Although most celebrities seemed smaller in person, Rachel thought Michael Tolland appeared taller. His brown eyes were just as vigilant and passionate as they were on television, and his voice carried the same modest warmth and enthusiasm. Looking to be a weathered and athletic forty-five, Michael Tolland had coarse black hair that fell in a permanent windswept tuft across his forehead. He had a strong chin and a carefree mannerism that exuded confidence. When he'd shaken Rachel's hand, the callused roughness of his palms reminded her he was not a typical 'soft' television personality but rather an accomplished seaman and hands-on researcher.

'To be honest,' Tolland admitted, sounding sheepish, 'I think I was recruited more for my PR value than for my scientific knowledge. The President asked me to come up and make a documentary for him.'

'A documentary? About a *meteorite*? But you're an oceanographer.'

'That's exactly what I told him! But he said he didn't know of any meteorite documentarians. He told me my involvement would help bring mainstream credibility to this find. Apparently he plans to broadcast my documentary as part of tonight's big press conference when he announces the discovery.'

A celebrity spokesman. Rachel sensed the savvy political maneuverings of Zach Herney at work. NASA was often accused of talking over the public's head. Not this time. They'd pulled in the master scientific communicator, a face Americans already knew and trusted when it came to science.

Tolland pointed kitty-corner across the dome to a far wall where a press area was being set up. There was a blue carpet on the ice, television cameras, media lights, a long table with several microphones. Someone was hanging a backdrop of a huge American flag.

'That's for tonight,' he explained. 'The NASA administrator and some of his top scientists will be connected live via satellite to the White House so they can participate in the President's eight o'clock broadcast.'

Appropriate, Rachel thought, pleased to know Zach Herney didn't plan to cut NASA out of the announcement entirely.

'So,' Rachel said with a sigh, 'is someone finally going to tell me what's so special about this meteorite?'

Tolland arched his eyebrows and gave her a mysterious grin. 'Actually, what's so special about this meteorite is best *seen*, not explained.' He motioned for Rachel to follow him toward the neighboring work area. 'The guy stationed over here has plenty of samples he can show you.'

'Samples? You actually have *samples* of the meteorite?'

'Absolutely. We've drilled quite a few. In fact, it was the initial core samples that alerted NASA to the importance of the find.'

Unsure of what to expect, Rachel followed Tolland into the work area. It appeared deserted. A cup of coffee sat on a desk scattered with rock samples, calipers, and other diagnostic gear. The coffee was steaming.

'Marlinson!' Tolland yelled, looking around. No answer. He gave a frustrated sigh and turned to Rachel. 'He probably got lost trying to find cream for his coffee. I'm telling you, I went to Princeton postgrad with this guy, and he used to get lost in his own dorm. Now he's a National Medal of Science recipient in astrophysics. Go figure.'

Rachel did a double take. 'Marlinson? You don't by any chance mean the famous Corky Marlinson, do you?'

Tolland laughed. 'One and the same.'

Rachel was stunned. 'Corky Marlinson is *here*?' Marlinson's ideas on gravitational fields were legendary among NRO satellite engineers. 'Marlinson is one of the President's civilian recruits?'

'Yeah, one of the *real* scientists.'

Real is right, Rachel thought. Corky Marlinson was as brilliant and respected as they came.

'The incredible paradox about Corky,' Tolland said, 'is that he can quote you the distance to Alpha Centauri in millimeters, but he can't tie his own necktie.'

'I wear clip-ons!' a nasal, good-natured voice barked nearby. 'Efficiency over style, Mike. You Hollywood types don't understand that!'

Rachel and Tolland turned to the man now emerging from behind a large stack of electronic gear. He was squat and rotund, resembling a pug dog with bubble eyes and a thinning, comb-over haircut. When the man saw Tolland standing with Rachel, he stopped in his tracks.

'Jesus Christ, Mike! We're at the friggin' North Pole and you still manage to meet gorgeous women. I knew I should have gone into television!'

Michael Tolland was visibly embarrassed. 'Ms Sexton, please excuse Mr Marlinson. What he lacks in tact, he more than makes up for in random bits of totally useless knowledge about our universe.'

Corky approached. 'A true pleasure, ma'am. I didn't catch your name.'

'Rachel,' she said. 'Rachel Sexton.'

'Sexton?' Corky let out a playful gasp. 'No relation to that short-sighted, depraved senator, I hope!'

Tolland winced. 'Actually, Corky, Senator Sexton is Rachel's father.'

Corky stopped laughing and slumped. 'You know, Mike, it's really no wonder I've never had any luck with the ladies.'

CHAPTER 22

Prize-winning astrophysicist Corky Marlinson ushered Rachel and Tolland into his work area and began sifting through his tools and rock samples. The man moved like a tightly wound spring about to explode.

'All right,' he said, quivering excitedly, 'Ms Sexton, you're about to get the Corky Marlinson thirty-second meteorite primer.'

Tolland gave Rachel a be-patient wink. 'Bear with him. The man really wanted to be an actor.'

'Yeah, and Mike wanted to be a respected scientist.' Corky rooted around in a shoebox and produced three small rock samples and aligned them on his desk. 'These are the three main classes of meteorites in the world.'

Rachel looked at the three samples. All appeared as awkward spheroids about the size of golf balls. Each had been sliced in half to reveal its cross section.

'All meteorites,' Corky said, 'consist of varying amounts of nickel-iron alloys, silicates, and sulfides. We classify them on the basis of their metal-to-silicate ratios.'

Rachel already had the feeling Corky Marlinson's meteorite 'primer' was going to be more than thirty seconds.

'This first sample here,' Corky said, pointing to a shiny, jet-black stone, 'is an iron-core meteorite. Very heavy. This little guy landed in Antarctica a few years back.'

Rachel studied the meteorite. It most certainly looked otherworldly – a blob of heavy grayish iron whose outer crust was burned and blackened.

'That charred outer layer is called a fusion crust,' Corky said. 'It's the result of extreme heating as the meteor falls through our atmosphere. All meteorites exhibit that charring.' Corky moved quickly to the next sample. 'This next one is what we call a stony-iron meteorite.'

Rachel studied the sample, noting that it too was charred on the outside. This sample, however, had a light-greenish tint, and the cross section looked like a collage of colorful angular fragments resembling a kaleidoscopic puzzle.

'Pretty,' Rachel said.

'Are you kidding, it's *gorgeous*!' Corky talked for a minute about the high olivine content causing the green luster, and then he reached dramatically for the third and final sample, handing it to Rachel.

Rachel held the final meteorite in her palm. This one was grayish brown in color, resembling granite. It felt heavier than a terrestrial stone, but not substantially. The only indication suggesting it was anything other than a normal rock was its fusion crust – the scorched outer surface.

'This,' Corky said with finality, 'is called a stony meteorite. It's the most common class of meteorite. More than ninety percent of meteorites found on earth are of this category.'

Rachel was surprised. She had always pictured meteorites more like the first sample – metallic, alien-looking blobs. The meteorite in her hand looked anything but extraterrestrial. Aside from the charred exterior, it looked like something she might step over on the beach.

Corky's eyes were bulging now with excitement. 'The meteorite buried in the ice here at Milne is a stony meteorite – a lot like the one in your hand. Stony meteorites appear almost identical to our terrestrial igneous rocks, which makes them tough to spot. Usually a blend of lightweight silicates – feldspar, olivine, pyroxene. Nothing too exciting.'

I'll say, Rachel thought, handing the sample back to him. 'This one looks like a rock someone left in a fireplace and burned.'

Corky burst out laughing. 'One *hell* of a fireplace! The meanest blast furnace ever built doesn't come close to reproducing the heat a meteoroid feels when it hits our atmosphere. They get ravaged!'

Tolland gave Rachel an empathetic smile. 'This is the good part.'

'Picture this,' Corky said, taking the meteorite sample from Rachel. 'Let's imagine this little fella is the size of a house.' He held the sample high over his head. 'Okay . . . it's in space . . . floating across our solar system . . . cold-soaked from the temperature of space to minus one hundred degrees Celsius.'

Tolland was chuckling to himself, apparently already having seen Corky's reenactment of the meteorite's arrival on Ellesmere Island.

Corky began lowering the sample. 'Our meteorite is moving toward earth . . . and as it's getting very close, our gravity locks on . . . accelerating . . . accelerating . . .'

Rachel watched as Corky sped up the sample's trajectory, mimicking the acceleration of gravity.

'Now it's moving fast,' Corky exclaimed. 'Over ten miles per second – thirty-six thousand miles per hour! At one hundred and thirty-five kilometers above the earth's surface, the meteorite begins to encounter friction with the atmosphere.' Corky shook the sample violently as he lowered it toward the ice. 'Falling below one hundred kilometers, it's starting to glow! Now the atmospheric density is increasing, and the friction is incredible! The air around the meteoroid is becoming incandescent as the surface material melts from the heat.' Corky started making burning and sizzling sound effects. 'Now it's falling past the eighty-kilometer mark, and the exterior becomes heated to over eighteen hundred degrees Celsius!'

Rachel watched in disbelief as the presidential award-winning astrophysicist shook the meteorite more fiercely, sputtering out juvenile sound effects.

'Sixty kilometers!' Corky was shouting now. 'Our meteoroid encounters the atmospheric wall. The air is too dense! It violently decelerates at more than three hundred times the force of gravity!' Corky made a screeching braking sound and slowed his descent dramatically. 'Instantly, the meteorite cools and stops glowing. We've hit dark flight! The meteoroid's surface hardens from its molten stage to a charred fusion crust.'

Rachel heard Tolland groan as Corky knelt on the ice to perform the coup de grâce – earth impact.

'Now,' Corky said, 'our huge meteorite is skipping across our lower atmosphere . . .' On his knees, he arched the meteorite toward the ground on a shallow slant. 'It's headed toward the Arctic Ocean . . . on an oblique angle . . . falling . . . looking almost like it will skip off the ocean . . . falling . . . and . . .' He touched the sample to the ice. 'BAM!'

Rachel jumped.

'The impact is cataclysmic! The meteorite explodes. Fragments fly off, skipping and spinning across the ocean.' Corky went into slow motion now, rolling and tumbling the sample across the invisible ocean toward Rachel's feet. 'One piece keeps skimming, tumbling toward Ellesmere Island . . .' He brought it right up to her toe. 'It skips off the ocean, bouncing up onto land . . .' He moved it up and over the tongue of her shoe and rolled it to a stop on top of her foot near her ankle. 'And finally comes to rest high on the Milne Glacier, where snow and ice quickly cover it, protecting it from atmospheric erosion.' Corky stood up with a smile.

Rachel's mouth fell slack. She gave an impressed laugh. 'Well, Dr Marlinson, that explanation was exceptionally . . .'

'Lucid?' Corky offered.

Rachel smiled. 'In a word.'

Corky handed the sample back to her. 'Look at the cross section.'

Rachel studied the rock's interior a moment, seeing nothing.

'Tilt it into the light,' Tolland prompted, his voice warm and kind. 'And look closely.'

Rachel brought the rock close to her eyes and tilted it against the dazzling halogens reflecting overhead. Now she saw it – tiny metallic globules glistening in the stone. Dozens of them were peppered throughout the cross section like minuscule droplets of mercury, each only about a millimeter across.

'Those little bubbles are called "chondrules," ' Corky said. 'And they occur *only* in meteorites.'

Rachel squinted at the droplets. 'Granted, I've never seen anything like this in an earth rock.'

'Nor will you!' Corky declared. 'Chondrules are one geologic structure we simply do not have on earth. Some chondrules are exceptionally old – perhaps made up of the earliest materials in the universe. Other chondrules are much younger, like the ones in your hand. The chondrules in that meteorite date only about one hundred and ninety million years old.'

'One hundred ninety million years is *young?*'

'Heck, yes! In cosmological terms, that's yesterday. The point here, though, is that this sample contains *chondrules* – conclusive meteoric evidence.'

'Okay,' Rachel said. 'Chondrules are conclusive. Got it.'

'And finally,' Corky said, heaving a sigh, 'if the fusion crust and chondrules don't convince you, we astronomers have a foolproof method to confirm meteoric origin.'

'Being?'

Corky gave a casual shrug. 'We simply use a petrographic polarizing microscope, an X-ray fluorescence spectrometer, a neutron activation analyzer, or an induction-coupled plasma spectrometer to measure ferromagnetic ratios.'

Tolland groaned. 'Now he's showing off. What Corky means is that we can prove a rock is a meteorite simply by measuring its chemical content.'

'Hey, ocean boy!' Corky chided. 'Let's leave the science to the scientists, shall we?' He immediately turned back to Rachel. 'In earth rocks, the mineral nickel occurs in either extremely high percentages or extremely low; nothing in the middle. In meteorites, though, the nickel content falls within a midrange set of values. Therefore, if we analyze a sample and find the nickel content reflects a midrange value, we can guarantee beyond the shadow of a doubt that the sample is a meteorite.'

Rachel felt exasperated. 'Okay, gentlemen, fusion crusts, chondrules, midrange nickel contents, all of which prove it's from space. I get the picture.' She laid the sample back on Corky's table. 'But why am I here?'

Corky heaved a portentous sigh. 'You want to see a sample of the meteorite NASA found in the ice underneath us?'

Before I die here, please.

This time Corky reached in his breast pocket and produced a small, disk-shaped piece of stone. The slice of rock was shaped like an audio CD, about half an inch thick, and appeared to be similar in composition to the stony meteorite she had just seen.

'This is a slice of a core sample that we drilled yesterday.' Corky handed the disk to Rachel.

The appearance certainly was not earth-shattering. Like the sample she had seen earlier, it was an orangish-white, heavy rock. Part of the rim was charred and black, apparently a segment of the meteorite's outer skin. 'I see the fusion crust,' she said.

Corky nodded. 'Yeah, this sample was taken from near the outside of the meteorite, so it still has some crust on it.'

Rachel tilted the disk in the light and spotted the tiny metallic globules. 'And I see the chondrules.'

'Good,' Corky said, his voice tense with excitement. 'And I can tell you from having run this thing through a petrographic polarizing microscope that its nickel content is midrange – nothing like a terrestrial rock. Congratulations, you've now successfully confirmed the rock in your hand came from space.'

Rachel looked up, confused. 'Dr Marlinson, it's a meteorite. It's *supposed* to come from space. Am I missing something here?'

Corky and Tolland exchanged knowing looks. Tolland put a hand on Rachel's shoulder and whispered, 'Flip it over.'

Rachel turned the disk over so she could see the other side. It took only an instant for her brain to process what she was looking at.

Then the truth hit her like a truck.

Impossible! she gasped, and yet as she stared at the rock she realized her definition of 'impossible' had just changed forever. Embedded in the stone was a form that in an earth specimen might be considered commonplace, and yet in a meteorite was utterly inconceivable.

'It's . . .' Rachel stammered, almost unable to speak the word. 'It's . . . a *bug*! This meteorite contains the fossil of a bug!'

Both Tolland and Corky were beaming. 'Welcome aboard,' Corky said.

The torrent of emotions that gripped Rachel left her momentarily mute, and yet even in her bewilderment, she could clearly see that this fossil, beyond question, had once been a living biological organism. The petrified impression was about three inches long and looked to be the underside of some kind of huge beetle or crawling insect. Seven pairs of hinged legs were clustered beneath a protective outer shell, which seemed to be segmented in plates like that of an armadillo.

Rachel felt dizzy. 'An insect from space . . .'

'It's an isopod,' Corky said. 'Insects have three pairs of legs, not seven.'

Rachel did not even hear him. Her head was spinning as she studied the fossil before her.

'You can clearly see,' Corky said, 'that the dorsal shell is segmented in plates like a terrestrial pill bug, and yet the two prominent tail-like appendages differentiate it as something closer to a louse.'

Rachel's mind had already tuned Corky out. The classification of the species was totally irrelevant. The puzzle pieces now came crashing into place – the President's secrecy, the NASA excitement . . .

There is a fossil in this meteorite! Not just a speck of bacteria or microbes, but an advanced life-form! Proof of life elsewhere in the universe!

CHAPTER **23**

Ten minutes into the CNN debate, Senator Sexton wondered how he could have been worried at all. Marjorie Tench was grossly overestimated as an opponent. Despite the senior adviser's reputation for ruthless sagacity, she was turning out to be more of a sacrificial lamb than a worthy opponent.

Granted, early in the conversation Tench had grabbed the upper hand by hammering the senator's prolife platform as biased against women, but then, just as it seemed Tench was tightening her grip, she'd made a careless mistake. While questioning how the senator expected to fund educational improvements without raising taxes, Tench made a snide allusion to Sexton's constant scapegoating of NASA.

Although NASA was a topic Sexton definitely intended to address toward the end of the discussion, Marjorie Tench had opened the door early. *Idiot!*

'Speaking of NASA,' Sexton segued casually, 'can you comment on the rumors I keep hearing that NASA has suffered another recent failure?'

Marjorie Tench did not flinch. 'I'm afraid I have not heard that rumor.' Her cigarette voice was like sandpaper.

'So, no comment?'

'I'm afraid not.'

Sexton gloated. In the world of media sound bites, 'no comment' translated loosely to 'guilty as charged.'

'I see,' Sexton said. 'And how about the rumors of a secret, emergency meeting between the President and the administrator of NASA?'

This time Tench looked surprised. 'I'm not sure what meeting you're referring to. The President takes many meetings.'

'Of course, he does.' Sexton decided to go straight at her. 'Ms Tench, you are a great supporter of the space agency, is that right?'

Tench sighed, sounding tired of Sexton's pet issue. 'I believe in the importance of preserving America's technological edge – be that military, industry, intelligence, telecommunications. NASA is certainly part of that vision. Yes.'

In the production booth, Sexton could see Gabrielle's eyes telling him to back off, but Sexton could taste blood. 'I'm curious, ma'am, is it *your* influence behind the President's continued support of this obviously ailing agency?'

Tench shook her head. 'No. The President is also a staunch believer in NASA. He makes his own decisions.'

Sexton could not believe his ears. He had just given Marjorie Tench a chance to partially exonerate the President by personally accepting some of the blame for NASA funding. Instead, Tench had thrown it right back at the President. *The President makes his own decisions.* It seemed Tench was already trying to distance herself from a campaign in trouble. No big surprise. After all, when the dust settled, Marjorie Tench would be looking for a job.

Over the next few minutes, Sexton and Tench parried. Tench made some weak attempts to change the subject, while Sexton kept pressing her on the NASA budget.

'Senator,' Tench argued, 'you want to cut NASA's budget, but do you have any idea how many high-tech jobs will be lost?'

Sexton almost laughed in the woman's face. *This gal is considered the smartest mind in Washington?* Tench obviously had something to learn about the demographics of this country. High-tech jobs were inconsequential in comparison to the huge numbers of hardworking blue-collar Americans.

Sexton pounced. 'We're talking about *billions* in savings here, Marjorie, and if the result is that a bunch of NASA scientists have to get in their BMWs and take their marketable skills elsewhere, then so be it. I'm committed to being tough on spending.'

Marjorie Tench fell silent, as if reeling from that last punch.

The CNN host prompted, 'Ms Tench? A reaction?'

The woman finally cleared her throat and spoke. 'I guess I'm just surprised to hear that Mr Sexton is willing to establish himself as so staunchly anti-NASA.'

Sexton's eyes narrowed. *Nice try, lady.* 'I am not anti-NASA, and I resent the accusation. I am simply saying that NASA's budget is indicative of the kind of runaway spending that your President endorses. NASA said they could build the shuttle for five billion; it cost twelve billion. They said they could build the space station for eight billion; now it's one hundred billion.'

'Americans are leaders,' Tench countered, 'because we set lofty goals and stick to them through the tough times.'

'That national pride speech doesn't work on me, Marge. NASA has overspent its allowance three times in the past two years and crawled back to the President with its tail between its legs and asked for more money to fix its mistakes. Is that national pride? If you want to talk about national pride, talk about strong schools. Talk about universal health care. Talk about smart kids growing up in a country of opportunity. *That's* national pride!'

Tench glared. 'May I ask you a direct question, Senator?'

Sexton did not respond. He simply waited.

The woman's words came out deliberately, with a sudden infusion of grit. 'Senator, if I told you that we could not explore space for less than NASA is currently spending, would you act to abolish the space agency altogether?'

The question felt like a boulder landing in Sexton's lap. Maybe Tench wasn't so stupid after all. She had just blindsided Sexton with a 'fence-buster' – a carefully crafted yes/no question designed to force a fence-straddling opponent to choose clear sides and clarify his position once and for all.

Instinctively Sexton tried sidestepping. 'I have no doubt that with proper management NASA can explore space for a lot less than we are currently—'

'Senator Sexton, answer the question. Exploring space is a danger-ous and costly business. It's much like building a passenger jet. We should either do it *right* – or not at all. The risks are too great. My question remains: If you become president, and you are faced with the decision to continue NASA funding at its current level or entirely scrap the U.S. space program, which would you choose?'

Shit. Sexton glanced up at Gabrielle through the glass. Her expression echoed what Sexton already knew. *You're committed. Be direct. No waffling.* Sexton held his chin high. 'Yes. I would transfer

NASA's current budget directly into our school systems if faced with that decision. I would vote for our children over space.'

The look on Marjorie Tench's face was one of absolute shock. 'I'm stunned. Did I hear you correctly? As president, you would act to *abolish* this nation's space program?'

Sexton felt an anger simmering. Now Tench was putting words in his mouth. He tried to counter, but Tench was already talking.

'So you're saying, Senator, for the record, that you would do away with the agency that put men on the moon?'

'I am saying that the space race is over! Times have changed. NASA no longer plays a critical role in the lives of everyday Americans and yet we continue to fund them as though they do.'

'So you don't think space is the future?'

'Obviously space is the future, but NASA is a dinosaur! Let the private sector explore space. American taxpayers shouldn't have to open their wallets every time some Washington engineer wants to take a billion-dollar photograph of Jupiter. Americans are tired of selling out their children's future to fund an outdated agency that provides so little in return for its gargantuan costs!'

Tench sighed dramatically. 'So little in return? With the exception perhaps of the SETI program, NASA has had enormous returns.'

Sexton was shocked that the mention of SETI had even escaped Tench's lips. Major blunder. *Thanks for reminding me.* The Search for Extraterrestrial Intelligence was NASA's most abysmal money pit ever. Although NASA had tried to give the project a facelift by renaming it 'Origins' and shuffling some of its objectives, it was still the same losing gamble.

'Marjorie,' Sexton said, taking his opening, 'I'll address SETI only because you mention it.'

Oddly, Tench looked almost eager to hear this.

Sexton cleared his throat. 'Most people are not aware that NASA has been looking for ET for thirty-five years now. And it's a pricey treasure hunt – satellite dish arrays, huge transceivers, millions in salaries to scientists who sit in the dark and listen to blank tape. It's an embarrassing waste of resources.'

'You're saying there's nothing up there?'

'I'm saying that if any other government agency had spent forty-five million over thirty-five years and had not produced *one* single result, they would have been axed a long time ago.' Sexton paused to let the gravity of the statement settle in. 'After thirty-five years, I think it's pretty obvious we're not going to find extraterrestrial life.'

'And if you're wrong?'

Sexton rolled his eyes. 'Oh, for heaven's sake, Ms Tench, if I'm wrong I'll eat my hat.'

Marjorie Tench locked her jaundiced eyes on Senator Sexton. 'I'll remember you said that, Senator.' She smiled for the first time. 'I think we *all* will.'

Six miles away, inside the Oval Office, President Zach Herney turned off the television and poured himself a drink. As Marjorie Tench had promised, Senator Sexton had taken the bait – hook, line, and sinker.

CHAPTER 24

Michael Tolland felt himself beaming empathetically as Rachel Sexton gaped in silence at the fossilized meteorite in her hand. The refined beauty of the woman's face now seemed to dissolve into the expression of innocent wonder – a young girl who had just seen Santa Claus for the first time.

I know just how you feel, he thought.

Tolland had been struck the same way only forty-eight hours ago. He too had been stunned into silence. Even now, the scientific and philosophical implications of the meteorite astounded him, forcing him to rethink everything he had ever believed about nature.

Tolland's oceanographic discoveries included several previously unknown deepwater species, and yet this 'space bug' was another level of breakthrough altogether. Despite Hollywood's propensity for casting extraterrestrials as little green men, astrobiologists and science buffs all agreed that given the sheer numbers and adaptability of

earth's insects, extraterrestrial life would in all probability be buglike
if it were ever discovered.

Insects were members of the phylum Arthropoda – creatures having
hard outer skeletons and jointed legs. With over 1.25 million known
species and an estimated five hundred thousand still to be classified,
earth's 'bugs' outnumbered all of the other animals combined. They
made up 95 percent of all the planet's species and an astounding
40 percent of the planet's biomass.

It was not so much the bugs' abundance that impressed as it was
their resilience. From the Antarctic ice beetle to Death Valley's
sun scorpion, bugs happily inhabited deadly ranges in temperature,
dryness, and even pressure. They also had mastered exposure to the
most deadly force known in the universe – radiation. Following a
nuclear test in 1945, air force officers had donned radiation suits and
examined ground zero, only to discover cockroaches and ants happily
carrying on as if nothing had happened. Astronomers realized that
an arthropod's protective exoskeleton made it a perfectly viable
candidate to inhabit the countless radiation-saturated planets where
nothing else could live.

It appeared the astrobiologists had been right, Tolland thought. *ET is
a bug.*

Rachel's legs felt weak beneath her. 'I can't . . . believe it,' she said,
turning the fossil in her hands. 'I never thought . . .'

'Give it some time to sink in,' Tolland said, grinning. 'Took me
twenty-four hours to get my feet back under me.'

'I see we have a newcomer,' said an uncharacteristically tall Asian
man, walking over to join them.

Corky and Tolland seemed to deflate instantly with the man's
arrival. Apparently the moment of magic had been shattered.

'Dr Wailee Ming,' the man said, introducing himself. 'Chairman of
paleontology at UCLA.'

The man carried himself with the pompous rigidity of renaissance
aristocracy, continuously stroking the out-of-place bow tie that he
wore beneath his knee-length camel-hair coat. Wailee Ming was
apparently not one to let a remote setting come in the way of his prim
appearance.

'I'm Rachel Sexton.' Her hand was still trembling as she shook Ming's smooth palm. Ming was obviously another of the President's civilian recruits.

'It would be my pleasure, Ms Sexton,' the paleontologist said, 'to tell you anything you want to know about these fossils.'

'And plenty you *don't* want to know,' Corky grumbled.

Ming fingered his bow tie. 'My paleontologic specialty is extinct Arthropoda and Mygalomorphae. Obviously the most impressive characteristic of this organism is—'

'—is that it's from another friggin' planet!' Corky interjected.

Ming scowled and cleared his throat. 'The most impressive characteristic of this organism is that it fits *perfectly* into our Darwinian system of terrestrial taxonomy and classification.'

Rachel glanced up. *They can classify this thing?* 'You mean kingdom, phylum, species, that sort of thing?'

'Exactly,' Ming said. 'This species, if found on earth, would be classified as the order Isopoda and would fall into a class with about two thousand species of lice.'

'*Lice?*' she said. 'But it's huge.'

'Taxonomy is not size specific. House cats and tigers are related. Classification is about physiology. This species is clearly a louse: it has a flattened body, seven pairs of legs, and a reproductive pouch identical in structure to wood lice, pill bugs, beach hoppers, sow bugs, and gribbles. The other fossils clearly reveal more specialized—'

'Other fossils?'

Ming glanced at Corky and Tolland. 'She doesn't know?'

Tolland shook his head.

Ming's face brightened instantly. 'Ms Sexton, you haven't heard the good part yet.'

'There are more fossils,' Corky interjected, clearly trying to steal Ming's thunder. '*Lots* more.' Corky scurried over to a large manila envelope and retrieved a folded sheet of oversized paper. He spread it out on the desk in front of Rachel. 'After we drilled some cores, we dropped an X-ray camera down. This is a graphic rendering of the cross section.'

Rachel looked at the X-ray printout on the table, and immediately had to sit down. The three-dimensional cross section of the meteorite was packed with dozens of these bugs.

'Paleolithic records,' Ming said, 'are usually found in heavy concentrations. Often times, mud slides trap organisms en masse, covering nests or entire communities.'

Corky grinned. 'We think the collection in the meteorite represents a nest.' He pointed to one of the bugs on the printout. 'And there's mommy.'

Rachel looked at the specimen in question, and her jaw dropped. The bug looked to be about two feet long.

'Big-ass louse, eh?' Corky said.

Rachel nodded, dumbstruck, as she pictured lice the size of bread loaves wandering around on some distant planet.

'On earth,' Ming said, 'our bugs stay relatively small because gravity keeps them in check. They can't grow larger than their exoskeletons can support. However, on a planet with diminished gravity, insects could evolve to much greater dimensions.'

'Imagine swatting mosquitoes the size of condors,' Corky joked, taking the core sample from Rachel and slipping it into his pocket.

Ming scowled. 'You had better not be stealing that!'

'Relax,' Corky said. 'We've got eight tons more where this came from.'

Rachel's analytical mind churned through the data before her. 'But how can life from space be so similar to life on earth? I mean, you're saying this bug *fits* in our Darwinian classification?'

'Perfectly,' Corky said. 'And believe it or not, a lot of astronomers have predicted that extraterrestrial life would be very similar to life on earth.'

'But why?' she demanded. 'This species came from an entirely different environment.'

'Panspermia.' Corky smiled broadly.

'I beg your pardon?'

'Panspermia is the theory that life was *seeded* here from another planet.'

Rachel stood up. 'You're losing me.'

Corky turned to Tolland. 'Mike, you're the primordial seas guy.'

Tolland looked happy to take over. 'Earth was once a lifeless planet,

Rachel. Then suddenly, as if overnight, life exploded. Many biologists think the explosion of life was the magical result of an ideal mixture of elements in the primordial seas. But we've never been able to reproduce that in a lab, so religious scholars have seized that failure as proof of God, meaning life could not exist unless God touched the primordial seas and infused them with life.'

'But we astronomers,' Corky declared, 'came up with another explanation for the overnight explosion of life on earth.'

'Panspermia,' Rachel said, now understanding what they were talking about. She had heard the panspermia theory before but didn't know its name. 'The theory that a meteorite splashed into the primordial soup, bringing the first seeds of microbial life to earth.'

'Bingo,' Corky said. 'Where they percolated and sprang to life.'

'And if *that's* true,' Rachel said, 'then the underlying ancestry of earth's life-forms and extraterrestrial life-forms would be identical.'

'Double bingo.'

Panspermia, Rachel thought, still barely able to grasp the implications. 'So, not only does this fossil confirm that life exists elsewhere in the universe, but it practically *proves* panspermia . . . that life on earth was seeded from elsewhere in the universe.'

'Triple bingo.' Corky flashed her an enthusiastic nod. 'Technically, we may *all* be extraterrestrials.' He put his fingers over his head like two antennas, crossed his eyes, and wagged his tongue like some kind of insect.

Tolland looked at Rachel with a pathetic grin. 'And this guy's the pinnacle of our evolution.'

CHAPTER 25

Rachel Sexton felt a dreamlike mist swirling around her as she walked across the habisphere, flanked by Michael Tolland. Corky and Ming followed close behind.

'You okay?' Tolland asked, watching her.

Rachel glanced over, giving a weak smile. 'Thanks. It's just . . . so much.'

Her mind reeled back to the infamous 1997 NASA discovery – ALH84001 – a Mars meteorite that NASA claimed contained fossil traces of bacterial life. Sadly, only weeks after NASA's triumphant press conference, several civilian scientists stepped forward with proof that the rock's 'signs of life' were really nothing more than kerogen produced by terrestrial contamination. NASA's credibility had taken a huge hit over that gaffe. The *New York Times* took the opportunity to sarcastically redefine the agency's acronym: NASA – NOT ALWAYS SCIENTIFICALLY ACCURATE.

In that same edition, paleobiologist Stephen Jay Gould summed up the problems with ALH84001 by pointing out that the evidence in it was chemical and inferential, rather than 'solid,' like an unambiguous bone or shell.

Now, however, Rachel realized NASA had found irrefutable proof. No skeptical scientist could possibly step forward and question *these* fossils. NASA was no longer touting blurry, enlarged photos of alleged microscopic bacteria – they were offering up real meteorite samples where bio-organisms visible to the naked eye had been embedded in the stone. *Foot-long lice!*

Rachel had to laugh when she realized she'd been a childhood fan of a song by David Bowie that referred to 'spiders from Mars.' Few would have guessed how close the androgynous British pop star would come to foreseeing astrobiology's greatest moment.

As the distant strains of the song ran through Rachel's mind, Corky hurried up behind her. 'Has Mike bragged about his documentary yet?'

Rachel replied, 'No, but I'd love to hear about it.'

Corky slapped Tolland on the back. 'Go for it, big boy. Tell her why the President decided that the most important moment in science history should be handed over to a snorkeling TV star.'

Tolland groaned. 'Corky, if you don't mind?'

'Fine, I'll explain,' Corky said, prying his way in between them. 'As you probably know, Ms Sexton, the President will be giving a press conference tonight to tell the world about the meteorite. Because the vast majority of the world is made up of half-wits, the President asked Mike to come onboard and dumb everything down for them.'

'Thanks, Corky,' Tolland said. 'Very nice.' He looked at Rachel. 'What Corky's trying to say is that because there's so much scientific data to convey, the President thought a short visual documentary about the meteorite might help make the information more accessible to mainstream America, many of whom, oddly, don't have advanced degrees in astrophysics.'

'Did you know,' Corky said to Rachel, 'that I've just learned our nation's President is a closet fan of *Amazing Seas*?' He shook his head in mock disgust. 'Zach Herney – the ruler of the free world – has his secretary tape Mike's program so he can decompress after a long day.'

Tolland shrugged. 'The man's got taste, what can I say?'

Rachel was now starting to realize just how masterful the President's plan was. Politics was a media game, and Rachel could already imagine the enthusiasm and scientific credibility the face of Michael Tolland on-screen would bring to the press conference. Zach Herney had recruited the ideal man to endorse his little NASA coup. Skeptics would be hard-pressed to challenge the President's data if it came from the nation's top television science personality as well as several respected civilian scientists.

Corky said, 'Mike's already taken video depositions from all of us civilians for his documentary, as well as from most of the top NASA specialists. And I'll bet my National Medal that *you're* next on his list.'

Rachel turned and eyed him. 'Me? What are you talking about? I have no credentials. I'm an intelligence liaison.'

'Then why did the President send you up here?'

'He hasn't told me yet.'

An amused grin crossed Corky's lips. 'You're a White House intelligence liaison who deals in clarification and authentication of data, right?'

'Yes, but nothing scientific.'

'*And* you're the daughter of the man who built a campaign around criticizing the money NASA has wasted in space?'

Rachel could hear it coming.

'You have to admit, Ms Sexton,' Ming chimed in, 'a deposition from you would give this documentary a whole new dimension of credibility. If the President sent you up here, he must want you to participate somehow.'

Rachel again flashed on William Pickering's concern that she was being used.

Tolland checked his watch. 'We should probably head over,' he said, motioning toward the center of the habisphere. 'They should be getting close.'

'Close to what?' Rachel asked.

'Extraction time. NASA is bringing the meteorite to the surface. It should be up any time now.'

Rachel was stunned. 'You guys are actually *removing* an eight-ton rock from under two hundred feet of solid ice?'

Corky looked gleeful. 'You didn't think NASA was going to leave a discovery like this buried in the ice, did you?'

'No, but . . .' Rachel had seen no signs of large-scale excavation equipment anywhere inside the habisphere. 'How the heck is NASA planning on getting the meteorite out?'

Corky puffed up. 'No problem. You're in a room full of rocket scientists!'

'Blather,' Ming scoffed, looking at Rachel. 'Dr Marlinson enjoys flexing other people's muscles. The truth is that everyone here was stumped about how to get the meteorite out. It was *Dr Mangor* who proposed a viable solution.'

'I haven't met Dr Mangor.'

'Glaciologist from the University of New Hampshire,' Tolland said. 'The fourth and final civilian scientist recruited by the President. And Ming here is correct, it was Mangor who figured it out.'

'Okay,' Rachel said. 'So what did this guy propose?'

'Gal,' Ming corrected, sounding smitten. 'Dr Mangor is a *woman*.'

'Debatable,' Corky grumbled. He looked over at Rachel. 'And by the way, Dr Mangor is going to hate *you*.'

Tolland shot Corky an angry look.

'Well, she will!' Corky defended. 'She'll hate the competition.'

Rachel felt lost. 'I'm sorry? Competition?'

'Ignore him,' Tolland said. 'Unfortunately, the fact that Corky is a total moron somehow escaped the National Science Committee. You and Dr Mangor will get along fine. She is a professional. She's considered one of the world's top glaciologists. She actually moved to Antarctica for a few years to study glacial movement.'

'Odd,' Corky said, 'I heard UNH took up a donation and sent her there so they could get some peace and quiet on campus.'

'Are you aware,' Ming snapped, seeming to have taken the comment personally, 'that Dr Mangor almost died down there! She got lost in a storm and lived on seal blubber for five weeks before anyone found her.'

Corky whispered to Rachel, 'I heard no one was looking.'

CHAPTER **26**

The limousine ride back from the CNN studio to Sexton's office felt long for Gabrielle Ashe. The senator sat across from her, gazing out the window, obviously gloating over the debate.

'They sent Tench to an afternoon cable show,' he said, turning with a handsome smile. 'The White House is getting frantic.'

Gabrielle nodded, noncommittal. She'd sensed a look of smug satisfaction on Marjorie Tench's face as the woman drove off. It made her nervous.

Sexton's personal cellphone rang, and he fished in his pocket to grab it. The senator, like most politicians, had a hierarchy of phone numbers at which his contacts could reach him, depending on how important they were. Whoever was calling him now was at the top of the list; the call was coming in on Sexton's private line, a number even Gabrielle was discouraged to call.

'Senator Sedgewick Sexton,' he chimed, accentuating the musical quality of his name.

Gabrielle couldn't hear the caller over the sound of the limo, but Sexton listened intently, replying with enthusiasm. 'Fantastic. I'm so pleased you called. I'm thinking six o'clock? Super. I have an apartment here in D.C. Private. Comfortable. You have the address, right? Okay. Looking forward to meeting you. See you tonight then.'

Sexton hung up, looking pleased with himself.

'New Sexton fan?' Gabrielle asked.

'They're multiplying,' he said. 'This guy's a heavy hitter.'

'Must be. Meeting him in your apartment?' Sexton usually defended the sanctified privacy of his apartment like a lion protecting its only remaining hiding place.

Sexton shrugged. 'Yeah. Thought I'd give him the personal touch. This guy might have some pull in the home stretch. Got to keep making those personal connections, you know. It's all about trust.'

Gabrielle nodded, pulling out Sexton's daily planner. 'You want me to put him in your calendar?'

'No need. I'd planned to take a night at home anyway.'

Gabrielle found tonight's page and noticed it was already shaded out in Sexton's handwriting with the bold letters 'P.E.' – Sexton shorthand for either personal event, private evening, or piss-off everyone; nobody was quite sure which. From time to time, the senator scheduled himself a 'P.E.' night so he could hole up in his apartment, take his phones off the hook, and do what he enjoyed most – sip brandy with old cronies and pretend he'd forgotten about politics for the evening.

Gabrielle gave him a surprised look. 'So you're actually letting business intrude on prescheduled P.E. time? I'm impressed.'

'This guy happened to catch me on a night when I've got some time. I'll talk to him for a little while. See what he has to say.'

Gabrielle wanted to ask who this mystery caller was, but Sexton clearly was being intentionally vague. Gabrielle had learned when not to pry.

As they turned off the beltway and headed back toward Sexton's office building, Gabrielle glanced down again at the P.E. time blocked out in Sexton's planner and had the strange sensation Sexton knew this call was coming.

CHAPTER **27**

The ice at the center of the NASA habisphere was dominated by an eighteen-foot tripod structure of composite scaffolding, which looked like a cross between an oil rig and an awkward model of the Eiffel Tower. Rachel studied the device, unable to fathom how it could be used to extract the enormous meteorite.

Beneath the tower, several winches had been screwed into steel plates affixed to the ice with heavy bolts. Threaded through the winches, iron cables banked upward over a series of pulleys atop the tower. From there, the cables plunged vertically downward into narrow bore holes drilled in the ice. Several large NASA men took turns tightening the winches. With each new tightening, the cables slithered a few inches upward through the bore holes, as if the men were raising an anchor.

I'm clearly missing something, Rachel thought, as she and the others moved closer to the extraction site. The men seemed to be hoisting the meteorite directly *through* the ice.

'EVEN TENSION! DAMN IT!' a woman's voice screamed nearby, with all the grace of a chain saw.

Rachel looked over to see a small woman in a bright yellow snowsuit smeared with grease. She had her back to Rachel, but even so, Rachel had no trouble guessing that she was in charge of this operation. Making notations on a clipboard, the woman stalked back and forth like a disgusted drillmaster.

'*Don't tell me you ladies are tired!*'

Corky called out, 'Hey, Norah, quit bossing those poor NASA boys and come flirt with me.'

The woman did not even turn around. 'Is that you, Marlinson? I'd know that weenie little voice anywhere. Come back when you reach puberty.'

Corky turned to Rachel. 'Norah keeps us warm with her charm.'

'I heard that, space boy,' Dr Mangor fired back, still making notes. 'And if you're checking out my ass, these snow pants add thirty pounds.'

'No worries,' Corky called. 'It's not your woolly-mammoth butt that drives me wild, it's your winning personality.'

'Bite me.'

Corky laughed again. 'I have great news, Norah. Looks like you're not the only woman the President recruited.'

'No shit. He recruited *you*.'

Tolland took over. 'Norah? Have you got a minute to meet someone?'

At the sound of Tolland's voice, Norah immediately stopped what she was doing and turned around. Her hardened demeanor dissolved instantly. 'Mike!' She rushed over, beaming. 'Haven't seen you in a few hours.'

'I've been editing the documentary.'

'How's my segment?'

'You look brilliant and lovely.'

'He used special effects,' Corky said.

Norah ignored the remark, glancing now at Rachel with a polite but standoffish smile. She looked back at Tolland. 'I hope you're not cheating on me, Mike.'

Tolland's rugged face flushed slightly as he made introductions. 'Norah, I'd like you to meet Rachel Sexton. Ms Sexton works in the intelligence community and is here at the request of the President. Her father is Senator Sedgewick Sexton.'

The introduction brought a confused look to Norah's face. 'I won't even pretend to understand that one.' Norah did not remove her gloves as she gave Rachel's hand a half-hearted shake. 'Welcome to the top of the world.'

Rachel smiled. 'Thanks.' She was surprised to see that Norah Mangor, despite the toughness of her voice, had a pleasant and impish countenance. Her pixie haircut was brown with streaks of gray, and her eyes were keen and sharp – two ice crystals. There was a steely confidence about her that Rachel liked.

'Norah,' Tolland said. 'Have you got a minute to share what you're doing with Rachel?'

Norah arched her eyebrows. 'You two on a first-name basis already? My, my.'

Corky groaned. 'I told you, Mike.'

Norah Mangor showed Rachel around the base of the tower while Tolland and the others trailed behind, talking among themselves.

'See those bore holes in the ice under the tripod?' Norah asked, pointing, her initial put-out tone softening now to one of rapt fervor for her work.

Rachel nodded, gazing down at the holes in the ice. Each was about a foot in diameter and had a steel cable inserted into it.

'Those holes are left over from when we drilled core samples and took X-rays of the meteorite. Now we're using them as entry points to lower heavy-duty screw eyes down the empty shafts and screw them into the meteorite. After that, we dropped a couple hundred feet of braided cable down each hole, snagged the screw eyes with industrial hooks, and now we're simply winching it up. It's taking these ladies several hours to get it to the surface, but it's coming.'

'I'm not sure I follow,' Rachel said. 'The meteorite is under thousands of tons of ice. How are you lifting it?'

Norah pointed to the top of the scaffolding where a narrow beam of pristine red light shone vertically downward toward the ice beneath the tripod. Rachel had seen it earlier and assumed it was simply some sort of visual indicator – a pointer demarking the spot where the object was buried.

'That's a gallium arsennide semiconductor laser,' Norah said.

Rachel looked more closely at the beam of light and now saw that it had actually melted a tiny hole in the ice and shone down into the depths.

'Very hot beam,' Norah said. 'We're heating the meteorite as we lift.'

When Rachel grasped the simple brilliance of the woman's plan, she was impressed. Norah had simply aimed the laser beam downward, melting through the ice until the beam hit the meteorite. The stone, being too dense to be melted by a laser, began absorbing the laser's heat, eventually getting warm enough to melt the ice around it. As the NASA men hoisted the hot meteorite, the heated rock, combined with the upward pressure, melted the surrounding ice, clearing a pathway to raise it to the surface. The melt water accumulating over the meteorite simply seeped back down around the edges of the stone to refill the shaft.

Like a hot knife through a frozen stick of butter.

Norah motioned to the NASA men on the winches. 'The generators can't handle this kind of strain, so I'm using manpower to lift.'

'That's crap!' one of the workers interjected. 'She's using manpower because she likes to see us sweat!'

'Relax,' Norah fired back. 'You girls have been bitching for two days that you're cold. I cured that. Now keep pulling.'

The workers laughed.

'What are the pylons for?' Rachel asked, pointing to several orange highway cones positioned around the tower at what appeared to be random locations. Rachel had seen similar cones dispersed around the dome.

'Critical glaciology tool,' Norah said. 'We call them SHABAs. That's short for "step here and break ankle." ' She picked up one of the pylons to reveal a circular bore hole that plunged like a bottomless well into the depths of the glacier. 'Bad place to step.' She replaced the pylon. 'We drilled holes all over the glacier for a structural continuity check. As in normal archeology, the number of years an object has been buried is indicated by how *deep* beneath the surface it's found. The farther down one finds it, the longer it's been there. So when an object is discovered under the ice, we can date that object's arrival by how much ice has accumulated on top of it. To make sure our core dating measurements are accurate, we check multiple areas of the ice sheet to confirm that the area is one solid slab and hasn't been disrupted by earthquake, fissuring, avalanche, what have you.'

'So how does this glacier look?'

'Flawless,' Norah said. 'A perfect, solid slab. No fault lines or glacial turnover. This meteorite is what we call a "static fall." It's been in the ice untouched and unaffected since it landed in 1716.'

Rachel did a double take. 'You know the exact *year* it fell?'

Norah looked surprised by the question. 'Hell, yes. That's why they called me in. I read ice.' She motioned to a nearby pile of cylindrical tubes of ice. Each looked like a translucent telephone pole and was marked with a bright orange tag. 'Those ice cores are a frozen geologic record.' She led Rachel over to the tubes. 'If you look closely you can see individual layers in the ice.'

Rachel crouched down and could indeed see that the tube was made up of what appeared to be countless strata of ice with subtle differences in luminosity and clarity. The layers varied between paper thin to about a quarter of an inch thick.

'Each winter brings a heavy snowfall to the ice shelf,' Norah said, 'and each spring brings a partial thaw. So we see a new compression layer every season. We simply start at the top – the most recent winter – and count backward.'

'Like counting rings on a tree.'

'It's not quite that simple, Ms Sexton. Remember, we're measuring *hundreds* of feet of layerings. We need to read climatological markers to benchmark our work – precipitation records, airborne pollutants, that sort of thing.'

Tolland and the others joined them now. Tolland smiled at Rachel. 'She knows a lot about ice, doesn't she?'

Rachel felt oddly happy to see him. 'Yeah, she's amazing.'

'And for the record,' Tolland nodded, 'Dr Mangor's 1716 date is right on. NASA came up with the exact same year of impact well before we even got here. Dr Mangor drilled her own cores, ran her own tests, and confirmed NASA's work.'

Rachel was impressed.

'And coincidentally,' Norah said, '1716 is the exact year early explorers claimed to have seen a bright fireball in the sky over northern Canada. The meteor became known as the Jungersol Fall, after the name of the exploration's leader.'

'So,' Corky added, 'the fact that the core dates *and* the historic record match is virtual proof that we're looking at a fragment of the same meteorite that Jungersol recorded seeing in 1716.'

'Dr Mangor!' one of the NASA workers called out. 'Leader hasps are starting to show!'

'Tour's over, folks,' Norah said. 'Moment of truth.' She grabbed a folding chair, climbed up onto it, and shouted out at the top of her lungs. '*Surfacing in five minutes, everyone!*'

All around the dome, like Pavlovian dogs responding to a dinner bell, the scientists dropped what they were doing and hurried toward the extraction zone.

Norah Mangor put her hands on her hips and surveyed her domain. 'Okay, let's raise the *Titanic*.'

CHAPTER **28**

'**Step aside!**' Norah hollered, moving through the growing crowd. The workers scattered. Norah took control, making a show of checking the cable tensions and alignments.

'Heave!' one of the NASA men yelled. The men tightened their winches, and the cables ascended another six inches out of the hole.

As the cables continued to move upward, Rachel felt the crowd inching forward in anticipation. Corky and Tolland were nearby, looking like kids at Christmas. On the far side of the hole, the hulking frame of NASA administrator Lawrence Ekstrom arrived, taking a position to watch the extraction.

'Hasps!' one of the NASA men yelled. 'Leaders are showing!'

The steel cables rising through the boreholes changed from silver braid to yellow leader chains.

'Six more feet! Keep it steady!'

The group around the scaffolding fell into a rapt silence, like onlookers at a séance awaiting the appearance of some divine specter – everyone straining for the first glimpse.

Then Rachel saw it.

Emerging from the thinning layer of ice, the hazy form of the meteorite began to show itself. The shadow was oblong and dark, blurry at first, but getting clearer every moment as it melted its way upward.

'Tighter!' a technician yelled. The men tightened the winches, and the scaffolding creaked.

'Five more feet! Keep the tension even!'

Rachel could now see the ice above the stone beginning to bulge upward like a pregnant beast about to give birth. Atop the hump, surrounding the laser's point of entry, a small circle of surface ice began to give way, melting, dissolving into a widening hole.

'Cervix is dilated!' someone shouted. 'Nine hundred centimeters!'

A tense laughter broke the silence.

'Okay, kill the laser!'

Someone threw a switch, and the beam disappeared.

And then it happened.

Like the fiery arrival of some paleolithic god, the huge rock broke the surface with a hiss of steam. Through the swirling fog, the hulking shape rose out of the ice. The men manning the winches strained harder until finally the entire stone broke free of the frozen restraints and swung, hot and dripping, over an open shaft of simmering water.

Rachel felt mesmerized.

Dangling there on its cables, dripping wet, the meteorite's rugged surface glistened in the fluorescent lights, charred and rippled with the appearance of an enormous petrified prune. The rock was smooth and rounded on one end, this section apparently blasted away by friction as it streaked through the atmosphere.

Looking at the charred fusion crust, Rachel could almost see the meteor rocketing earthward in a furious ball of flames. Incredibly, that was centuries ago. Now, the captured beast hung there on its cables, water dripping from its body.

The hunt was over.

Not until this moment had the drama of this event truly struck Rachel. The object hanging before her was from another world, millions of miles away. And trapped within it was evidence – no, *proof* – that man was not alone in the universe.

The euphoria of the moment seemed to grip everyone at the same instant, and the crowd broke into spontaneous hoots and applause. Even the administrator seemed caught up in it. He clapped his men and women on the back, congratulating them. Looking on, Rachel felt a sudden joy for NASA. They'd had some tough luck in the past. Finally things were changing. They deserved this moment.

The gaping hole in the ice now looked like a small swimming pool in the middle of the habisphere. The surface of the 200-foot-deep pool of melted water sloshed for a while against the icy walls of the shaft and then finally grew calm. The waterline in the shaft was a good four feet beneath the glacier's surface, the discrepancy caused by both the removal of the meteorite's mass and ice's property of shrinking as it melts.

Norah Mangor immediately set up SHABA pylons all around the hole. Although the hole was clearly visible, any curious soul who ventured too close and accidentally slipped in would be in dire jeopardy. The walls of the shaft were solid ice, with no footholds, and climbing out unassisted would be impossible.

Lawrence Ekstrom came padding across the ice toward them. He moved directly to Norah Mangor and shook her hand firmly. 'Well done, Dr Mangor.'

'I'll expect lots of praise in print,' Norah replied.

'You'll get it.' The administrator turned now to Rachel. He looked happier, relieved. 'So, Ms Sexton, is the professional skeptic convinced?'

Rachel couldn't help but smile. 'Stunned is more like it.'

'Good. Then follow me.'

Rachel followed the administrator across the habisphere to a large metal box that resembled an industrial shipping container. The box was painted with military camouflage patterns and stenciled letters: P-S-C.

'You'll call the President from in here,' Ekstrom said.

Portable Secure Comm, Rachel thought. These mobile communications booths were standard battlefield installations, although Rachel had never expected to see one used as part of a peacetime NASA mission. Then again, Administrator Ekstrom's background was the Pentagon, so he certainly had access to toys like this. From the stern faces on the two armed guards watching over the PSC, Rachel got the distinct impression that contact with the outside world was made only with express consent from Administrator Ekstrom.

Looks like I'm not the only one who is off-the-grid.

Ekstrom spoke briefly with one of the guards outside the trailer and then returned to Rachel. 'Good luck,' he said. Then he left.

A guard rapped on the trailer door, and it opened from within. A technician emerged and motioned for Rachel to enter. She followed him in.

The inside of the PSC was dark and stuffy. In the bluish glow of the lone computer monitor, Rachel could make out racks of telephone gear, radios, and satellite telecommunications devices. She already felt claustrophobic. The air inside was bitter, like a basement in winter.

'Sit here, please, Ms Sexton.' The technician produced a rolling stool and positioned Rachel in front of a flat-screen monitor. He arranged a microphone in front of her and placed a bulky pair of AKG headphones on her head. Checking a logbook of encryption passwords, the technician typed a long series of keys on a nearby device. A timer materialized on the screen in front of Rachel.

00:60 SECONDS

The technician gave a satisfied nod as the timer began to count down. 'One minute until connection.' He turned and left, slamming the door behind him. Rachel could hear the bolt lock outside.

Great.

As she waited in the dark, watching the sixty-second clock slowly count down, she realized that this was the first moment of privacy she'd had since early that morning. She'd woken up today without the slightest inkling of what lay ahead. *Extraterrestrial life*. As of today, the most popular modern myth of all time was no longer a myth.

Rachel was just now starting to sense how truly devastating this meteorite would be to her father's campaign. Although NASA funding had no business being on a political par with abortion rights, welfare, and health care, her father had *made* it an issue. Now it was going to blow up in his face.

Within hours, Americans would feel the thrill of a NASA triumph all over again. There would be teary-eyed dreamers. Slack-jawed scientists. Children's imaginations running free. Issues of dollars and cents would fade away as petty, overshadowed by this monumental moment. The President would emerge like a phoenix, transforming himself into a hero, while in the midst of the celebration, the businesslike senator would suddenly appear small-minded, a penny-pinching scrooge with no American sense of adventure.

The computer beeped, and Rachel glanced up.

00:05 SECONDS

The screen in front of her flickered suddenly, and a blurry image of the White House seal materialized on-screen. After a moment, the image dissolved into the face of President Herney.

'Hello, Rachel,' he said, a mischievous glint in his eye. 'I trust you've had an interesting afternoon?'

CHAPTER **29**

The office of Senator Sedgewick Sexton was located in the Philip A. Hart Senate Office Building on C Street to the northeast of the Capitol. The building was a neomodern grid of white rectangles that critics claimed looked more like a prison than an office building. Many who worked there felt the same.

On the third floor, Gabrielle Ashe's long legs paced briskly back and forth in front of her computer terminal. On the screen was a new e-mail message. She was not sure what to make of it.

The first two lines read:

> SEDGEWICK WAS IMPRESSIVE ON CNN.
> I HAVE MORE INFORMATION FOR YOU.

Gabrielle had been receiving messages like this for the last couple of weeks. The return address was bogus, although she'd been able to track it to a 'whitehouse.gov' domain. It seemed her mysterious informant was a White House insider, and whoever it was had become Gabrielle's source for all kinds of valuable political information recently, including the news of a covert meeting between the NASA administrator and the President.

Gabrielle had been leery of the e-mails at first, but when she checked out the tips, she was amazed to find the information consistently accurate and helpful – classified information on NASA overexpenditures, costly upcoming missions, data showing that NASA's search for extraterrestrial life was grossly overfunded and pathetically unproductive, even internal opinion polls warning that NASA was the issue turning voters away from the President.

To enhance her perceived value to the senator, Gabrielle had not informed him she was receiving unsolicited e-mail help from inside the White House. Instead, she simply passed the information to him as coming from 'one of her sources.' Sexton was always appreciative and seemed to know better than to ask *who* her source was. She could tell he suspected Gabrielle was doing sexual favors. Troublingly, it didn't seem to bother him in the least.

Gabrielle stopped pacing and looked again at the newly arrived message. The connotations of all the e-mails were clear: someone inside the White House wanted Senator Sexton to win this election and was helping him do it by aiding his attack against NASA.

But who? And why?

A rat from a sinking ship, Gabrielle decided. In Washington it was not at all uncommon for a White House employee, fearing his President was about to be ousted from office, to offer quiet favors to the apparent successor in hopes of securing power or another position after the changeover. It seemed someone smelled Sexton victory and was buying stock early.

The message currently on Gabrielle's screen made her nervous. It was like none other she had ever received. The first two lines didn't bother her so much. It was the last two:

EAST APPOINTMENT GATE, 4:30 P.M.

COME ALONE.

Her informant had never before asked to meet in person. Even so, Gabrielle would have expected a more subtle location for a face-to-face meeting. *East Appointment Gate?* Only one East Appointment Gate existed in Washington, as far as she knew. *Outside the White House? Is this some kind of joke?*

Gabrielle knew she could not respond via e-mail; her messages were always bounced back as undeliverable. Her correspondent's account was anonymous. Not surprising.

Should I consult Sexton? She quickly decided against it. He was in a meeting. Besides, if she told him about this e-mail, she'd have to tell

him about the others. She decided her informant's offer to meet in
public in broad daylight must be to make Gabrielle feel safe. After all,
this person had done nothing but help her for the last two weeks. He
or she was obviously a friend.

Reading the e-mail one last time, Gabrielle checked the clock. She
had an hour.

CHAPTER 30

The NASA administrator was feeling less edgy now that the
meteorite was successfully out of the ice. *Everything is falling into
place,* he told himself as he headed across the dome to the work area
of Michael Tolland. *Nothing can stop us now.*

'How's it coming?' Ekstrom asked, striding up behind the television
scientist.

Tolland glanced up from his computer, looking tired but enthusiastic. 'Editing is almost done. I'm just overlaying some of the extraction
footage your people shot. Should be done momentarily.'

'Good.' The President had asked Ekstrom to upload Tolland's
documentary to the White House as soon as possible.

Although Ekstrom had been cynical about the President's desire
to use Michael Tolland on this project, seeing the rough cuts of
Tolland's documentary had changed Ekstrom's mind. The television
star's spirited narrative, combined with his interviews of the civilian
scientists, had been brilliantly fused into a thrilling and compre-
hensible fifteen minutes of scientific programming. Tolland had
achieved effortlessly what NASA so often failed to do – describe a
scientific discovery at the level of the average American intellect
without being patronizing.

'When you're done editing,' Ekstrom said, 'bring the finished
product over to the press area. I'll have someone upload a digital copy
to the White House.'

'Yes, sir.' Tolland went back to work.

Ekstrom moved on. When he arrived at the north wall, he was encouraged to find the habisphere's 'press area' had come together nicely. A large blue carpet had been rolled out on the ice. Centered on the rug sat a long symposium table with several microphones, a NASA drape, and an enormous American flag as a backdrop. To complete the visual drama, the meteorite had been transported on a pallet sled to its position of honor, directly in front of the symposium table.

Ekstrom was pleased to see the mood in the press area was one of celebration. Much of his staff was now crowded around the meteorite, holding their hands out over its still-warm mass like campers around a campfire.

Ekstrom decided that this was the moment. He walked over to several cardboard boxes sitting on the ice behind the press area. He'd had the boxes flown in from Greenland this morning.

'Drinks are on me!' he yelled, handing out cans of beer to his cavorting staff.

'Hey, boss!' someone yelled. 'Thanks! It's even cold!'

Ekstrom gave a rare smile. 'I've been keeping it on ice.'

Everyone laughed.

'Wait a minute!' someone else yelled, scowling good-naturedly at his can. 'This stuff's Canadian! Where's your patriotism?'

'We're on a budget, here, folks. Cheapest stuff I could find.'

More laughter.

'*Attention shoppers,*' one of the NASA television crew yelled into a megaphone. '*We're about to switch to media lighting. You may experience temporary blindness.*'

'And no kissing in the dark,' someone yelled. 'This is a family program!'

Ekstrom chuckled, enjoying the raillery as his crew made final adjustments to the spotlights and accent lighting.

'Switching to media lighting in five, four, three, two . . .'

The dome's interior dimmed rapidly as the halogen lamps shut down. Within seconds, all the lights were off. An impenetrable darkness engulfed the dome.

Someone let out a mock scream.

'Who pinched my ass?' someone yelled, laughing.

The blackness lasted only a moment before it was pierced by the intense glare of media spotlights. Everyone squinted. The transformation was now complete; the north quadrant of the NASA habisphere had become a television studio. The remainder of the dome now looked like a gaping barn at night. The only light in the other sections was the muted reflection of the media lights reflecting off the arched ceiling and throwing long shadows across the now deserted work stations.

Ekstrom stepped back into the shadows, gratified to see his team carousing around the illuminated meteorite. He felt like a father at Christmas, watching his kids enjoy themselves around the tree.

God knows they deserve it, Ekstrom thought, never suspecting what calamity lay ahead.

CHAPTER 31

The weather was changing.

Like a mournful harbinger of impending conflict, the katabatic wind let out a plaintive howl and gusted hard against the Delta Force's shelter. Delta-One finished battening down the storm coverings and went back inside to his two partners. They'd been through this before. It would soon pass.

Delta-Two was staring at the live video feed from the microbot. 'You better look at this,' he said.

Delta-One came over. The inside of the habisphere was in total darkness except for the bright lighting on the north side of the dome near the stage. The remainder of the habisphere appeared only as a dim outline. 'It's nothing,' he said. 'They're just testing their television lighting for tonight.'

'The lighting's not the problem.' Delta-Two pointed to the dark blob in the middle of the ice – the water-filled hole from which the meteorite had been extracted. '*That's* the problem.'

Delta-One looked at the hole. It was still surrounded by pylons, and the surface of the water appeared calm. 'I don't see anything.'

'Look again.' He maneuvered the joystick, spiraling the microbot down toward the surface of the hole.

As Delta-One studied the darkened pool of melted water more closely, he saw something that caused him to recoil in shock. 'What the . . . ?'

Delta-Three came over and looked. He too looked stunned. 'My God. Is that the extraction pit? Is the water supposed to be doing that?'

'No,' Delta-One said. 'It sure as hell isn't.'

CHAPTER **32**

Although Rachel Sexton was currently sitting inside a large metal box situated 3,000 miles from Washington, D.C., she felt the same pressure as if she'd been summoned to the White House. The videophone monitor before her displayed a crystal clear image of President Zach Herney seated in the White House communications room before the presidential seal. The digital audio connection was flawless, and with the exception of an almost imperceptible delay, the man could have been in the next room.

Their conversation was upbeat and direct. The President seemed pleased, though not at all surprised, by Rachel's favorable assessment of NASA's find and of his choice to use Michael Tolland's captivating persona as a spokesman. The President's mood was good-natured and jocular.

'As I'm sure you will agree,' Herney said, his voice growing more serious now, 'in a perfect world, the ramifications of this discovery would be purely scientific in nature.' He paused, leaning forward, his face filling the screen. 'Unfortunately, we don't live in a perfect world, and this NASA triumph is going to be a political football the moment I announce it.'

'Considering the conclusive proof and who you've recruited for endorsements, I can't imagine how the public or any of your opposition will be able to do anything other than accept this discovery as confirmed fact.'

Herney gave an almost sad chuckle. 'My political opponents will *believe* what they see, Rachel. My concerns are that they won't *like* what they see.'

Rachel noted how careful the President was being not to mention her father. He spoke only in terms of 'the opposition' or 'political opponents.' 'And you think your opposition will cry conspiracy simply for political reasons?' she asked.

'That is the nature of the game. All anyone needs to do is cast a faint doubt, saying that this discovery is some kind of political fraud concocted by NASA and the White House, and all of a sudden, I'm facing an inquiry. The newspapers forget NASA has found proof of extraterrestrial life, and the media starts focusing on uncovering evidence of a conspiracy. Sadly, any innuendo of conspiracy with respect to this discovery will be bad for science, bad for the White House, bad for NASA, and, quite frankly, bad for the country.'

'Which is why you postponed announcing until you had full confirmation and some reputable civilian endorsements.'

'My goal is to present this data in so incontrovertible a way that any cynicism is nipped in the bud. I want this discovery celebrated with the untainted dignity it deserves. NASA merits no less.'

Rachel's intuition was tingling now. *What does he want from me?*

'Obviously,' he continued, 'you're in a unique position to help me. Your experience as an analyst as well as your obvious ties to my opponent give you enormous credibility with respect to this discovery.'

Rachel felt a growing disillusionment. *He wants to use me . . . just like Pickering said he would!*

'That said,' Herney continued, 'I would like to ask that you endorse this discovery *personally*, for the record, as my White House intelligence liaison . . . and as the daughter of my opponent.'

There it was. On the table.

Herney wants me to endorse.

Rachel really had thought Zach Herney was above this kind

of spiteful politics. A public endorsement from Rachel would immediately make the meteorite a *personal* issue for her father, leaving the senator unable to attack the discovery's credibility without attacking the credibility of his own daughter – a death sentence for a 'families first' candidate.

'Frankly, sir,' Rachel said, looking into the monitor, 'I'm stunned you would ask me to do that.'

The President looked taken aback. 'I thought you would be excited to help out.'

'Excited? Sir, my differences with my father aside, this request puts me in an impossible position. I have enough problems with my father without going head-to-head with him in some kind of public death match. Despite my admitted dislike of the man, he *is* my father, and pitting me against him in a public forum frankly seems beneath you.'

'Hold on!' Herney waved his hands in surrender. 'Who said anything about a public forum?'

Rachel paused. 'I assume you'd like me to join the administrator of NASA on the podium for the eight o'clock press conference.'

Herney's guffaw boomed in the audio speakers. 'Rachel, what kind of man do you think I am? Do you really imagine I'd ask someone to stab her father in the back on national television?'

'But, you said—'

'And do you think I would make the NASA administrator share the limelight with the daughter of his arch enemy? Not to burst your bubble, Rachel, but this press conference is a *scientific* presentation. I'm not sure your knowledge of meteorites, fossils, or ice structures would lend the event much credibility.'

Rachel felt herself flush. 'But then . . . what endorsement did you have in mind?'

'One more appropriate to your position.'

'Sir?'

'You are my White House intelligence liaison. You brief my staff on issues of national importance.'

'You want me to endorse this for your *staff*?'

Herney still looked amused by the misunderstanding. 'Yes, I do. The skepticism I'll face *outside* the White House is nothing compared to what I'm facing from my staff right now. We're in the midst of a full-scale mutiny here. My credibility in-house is shot. My staff has begged me to cut back NASA funding. I've ignored them, and it's been political suicide.'

'Until now.'

'Exactly. As we discussed this morning, this discovery's timing will seem suspect to political cynics, and nobody's as cynical as my staff is at the moment. Therefore, when they hear this information for the first time, I want it to come from—'

'You haven't told your *staff* about the meteorite?'

'Only a few top advisers. Keeping this discovery a secret has been a top priority.'

Rachel was stunned. *No wonder he's facing a mutiny.* 'But this is not my usual area. A meteorite could hardly be considered an *intelligence-related gist.*'

'Not in the traditional sense, but it certainly has all the elements of your usual work – complex data that needs to be distilled, substantial political ramifications—'

'I am not a meteorite specialist, sir. Shouldn't your staff be briefed by the administrator of NASA?'

'Are you kidding? Everyone here hates him. As far as my staff is concerned, Ekstrom is the snake-oil salesman who has lured me into bad deal after bad deal.'

Rachel could see the point. 'How about Corky Marlinson? The National Medal in Astrophysics? He's got far more credibility than I do.'

'My staff is made up of politicians, Rachel, not scientists. You've met Dr Marlinson. I think he's terrific, but if I let an astrophysicist loose on my team of left-brain, think-inside-the-box intellectuals, I'll end up with a herd of deer in the headlights. I need someone accessible. You're the one, Rachel. My staff knows your work, and considering your family name, you're about as unbiased a spokesperson as my staff could hope to hear from.'

Rachel felt herself being pulled in by the President's affable style. 'At least you admit my being the daughter of your opponent has something to do with your request.'

The President gave a sheepish chuckle. 'Of course it does. But, as you can imagine, my staff will be briefed one way or another, no matter what you decide. You are not the cake, Rachel, you are simply the icing. You are the individual most qualified to do this briefing, and you also happen to be a close relative of the man who wants to kick my staff out of the White House next term. You've got credibility on two accounts.'

'You should be in sales.'

'As a matter of fact, I am. As is your father. And to be honest, I'd like to close a deal for a change.' The President removed his glasses and looked into Rachel's eyes. She felt a touch of her father's power in him. 'I am asking you as a favor, Rachel, and also because I believe it is part of your job. So which is it? Yes or no? Will you brief my staff on this matter?'

Rachel felt trapped inside the tiny PSC trailer. *Nothing like the hard sell.* Even from 3,000 miles away, Rachel could feel the strength of his will pressing through the video screen. She also knew this was a perfectly reasonable request, whether she liked it or not.

'I'd have conditions,' Rachel said.

Herney arched his eyebrows. 'Being?'

'I meet your staff in private. No reporters. This is a private briefing, not a public endorsement.'

'You have my word. Your meeting is already slated for a very private location.'

Rachel sighed. 'All right then.'

The President beamed. 'Excellent.'

Rachel checked her watch, surprised to see it was already a little past four o'clock. 'Hold on,' she said, puzzled, 'if you're going live at eight P.M., we don't have time. Even in that vile contraption you sent me up here in, I couldn't get back to the White House for another couple of hours at the very fastest. I'd have to prepare my remarks and—'

The President shook his head. 'I'm afraid I didn't make myself clear. You'll be doing the briefing from where you are via video conference.'

'Oh.' Rachel hesitated. 'What time did you have in mind?'

'Actually,' Herney said, grinning. 'How about right now? Everyone is already assembled, and they're staring at a big blank television set. They're waiting for you.'

Rachel's body tensed. 'Sir, I'm totally unprepared. I can't possibly—'

'Just tell them the truth. How hard is that?'

'But—'

'Rachel,' the President said, leaning toward the screen. 'Remember, you compile and relay data for a living. It's what you do. Just talk about what's going on up there.' He reached up to flick a switch on his video transmission gear, but paused. 'And I think you'll be pleased to find I've set you up in a position of power.'

Rachel didn't understand what he meant, but it was too late to ask. The President threw the switch.

The screen in front of Rachel went blank for a moment. When it refreshed, Rachel was staring at one of the most unnerving images she had ever seen. Directly in front of her was the White House Oval Office. It was packed. Standing room only. The entire White House staff appeared to be there. And every one of them was staring at her. Rachel now realized her view was from atop the President's desk.

Speaking from a position of power. Rachel was sweating already.

From the looks on the faces of the White House staffers, they were as surprised to see Rachel as she was to see them.

'Ms Sexton?' a raspy voice called out.

Rachel searched the sea of faces and found who had spoken. It was a lanky woman just now taking a seat in the front row. Marjorie Tench. The woman's distinctive appearance was unmistakable, even in a crowd.

'Thank you for joining us, Ms Sexton,' Marjorie Tench said, sounding smug. 'The President tells us you have some news?'

CHAPTER **33**

Enjoying the darkness, paleontologist Wailee Ming sat alone in quiet reflection at his private work area. His senses were alive with anticipation for tonight's event. *Soon I will be the most famous paleontologist in the world.* He hoped Michael Tolland had been generous and featured Ming's comments in the documentary.

As Ming savored his impending fame, a faint vibration shuddered through the ice beneath his feet, causing him to jump up. His earthquake instinct from living in Los Angeles made him hyper-sensitive to even the faintest palpitations of the ground. At the moment, though, Ming felt foolish to realize the vibration was perfectly normal. *It's just ice calving,* he reminded himself, exhaling. He still hadn't gotten used to it. Every few hours, a distant explosion rumbled through the night as somewhere along the glacial frontier a huge block of ice cracked off and fell into the sea. Norah Mangor had a nice way of putting it. *New icebergs being born . . .*

On his feet now, Ming stretched his arms. He looked across the habisphere, and off in the distance beneath the blaze of television spotlights, he could see a celebration was getting underway. Ming was not much for parties and headed in the opposite direction across the habisphere.

The labyrinth of deserted work areas now felt like a ghost town, the entire dome taking on an almost sepulchral feel. A chill seemed to have settled inside, and Ming buttoned up his long, camel-hair coat.

Up ahead he saw the extraction shaft – the point from which the most magnificent fossils in all of human history had been taken. The giant metal tripod had now been stowed and the pool sat alone, surrounded by pylons like some kind of shunned pothole on a vast parking lot of ice. Ming wandered over to the pit, standing a safe distance back, peering into the 200-foot-deep pool of frigid water. Soon it would refreeze, erasing all traces that anyone had ever been here.

The pool of water was a beautiful sight, Ming thought. Even in the dark.

Especially in the dark.

Ming hesitated at the thought. Then it registered.

There's something wrong.

As Ming focused more closely on the water, he felt his previous contentedness give way to a sudden whirlwind of confusion. He blinked his eyes, stared again, and then quickly turned his gaze across the dome . . . fifty yards away toward the mass of people celebrating in the press area. He knew they could not see him way over here in the dark.

I should tell someone about this, shouldn't I?

Ming looked again at the water, wondering what he would tell them. Was he seeing an optical illusion? Some kind of strange reflection?

Uncertain, Ming stepped beyond the pylons and squatted down at the edge of the pit. The water level was four feet below the ice level, and he leaned down to get a better look. Yes, something was definitely strange. It was impossible to miss, and yet it had not become visible until the lights in the dome had gone out.

Ming stood up. Somebody definitely needed to hear about this. He started off at a hurried pace toward the press area. Completing only a few steps, Ming slammed on the brakes. *Good God!* He spun back toward the hole, his eyes going wide with realization. It had just dawned on him.

'Impossible!' he blurted aloud.

And yet Ming knew that was the only explanation. *Think carefully*, he cautioned. *There must be a more reasonable rationale.* But the harder Ming thought, the more convinced he was of what he was seeing. *There is no other explanation!* He could not believe that NASA and Corky Marlinson had somehow missed something this incredible, but Ming wasn't complaining.

This is Wailee Ming's discovery now!

Trembling with excitement, Ming ran to a nearby work area and found a beaker. All he needed was a little water sample. Nobody was going to believe this!

CHAPTER 34

'As intelligence liaison to the White House,' Rachel Sexton was saying, trying to keep her voice from shaking as she addressed the crowd on the screen before her, 'my duties include traveling to political hot spots around the globe, analyzing volatile situations, and reporting to the President and White House staff.'

A bead of sweat formed just below her hairline and Rachel dabbed it away, silently cursing the President for dropping this briefing into her lap with zero warning.

'Never before have my travels taken me to quite this exotic a spot.' Rachel motioned stiffly to the cramped trailer around her. 'Believe it or not, I am addressing you right now from above the Arctic Circle on a sheet of ice that is over three hundred feet thick.'

Rachel sensed a bewildered anticipation in the faces on the screen before her. They obviously knew they had been packed into the Oval Office for a reason, but certainly none of them imagined it would have anything to do with a development above the Arctic Circle.

The sweat was beading again. *Get it together, Rachel. This is what you do.* 'I sit before you tonight with great honor, pride, and . . . above all, excitement.'

Blank looks.

Screw it, she thought, angrily wiping the sweat away. *I didn't sign up for this.* Rachel knew what her mother would say if she were here now: *When in doubt, just spit it out!* The old Yankee proverb embodied one of her mom's basic beliefs – that all challenges can be overcome by speaking the truth, no matter how it comes out.

Taking a deep breath, Rachel sat up tall and looked straight into the camera. 'Sorry, folks, if you're wondering how I could be sweating my butt off above the Arctic Circle . . . I'm a little nervous.'

The faces before her seemed to jolt back a moment. Some uneasy laughter.

'In addition,' Rachel said, 'your boss gave me about ten seconds' warning before telling me I would be facing his entire staff. This baptism by fire is not exactly what I had in mind for my first visit to the Oval Office.'

More laughter this time.

'And,' she said, glancing down at the bottom of the screen, 'I had certainly not imagined I would be sitting at the President's desk . . . much less *on* it!'

This brought a hearty laugh and some broad smiles. Rachel felt her muscles starting to relax. *Just give it to them straight.*

'Here's the situation.' Rachel's voice now sounded like her own. Easy and clear. 'President Herney has been absent from the media spotlight this past week not because of his lack of interest in his campaign, but rather because he has been engrossed in another matter. One he felt was far more important.'

Rachel paused, her eyes making contact now with her audience.

'There has been a scientific discovery made in a location called the Milne Ice Shelf in the high Arctic. The President will be informing the world about it in a press conference tonight at eight o'clock. The find was made by a group of hardworking Americans who have endured a string of tough luck lately and deserve a break. I'm talking about NASA. You can be proud to know that your President, with apparent clairvoyant confidence, has made a point of standing beside NASA lately through thick and thin. Now, it appears his loyalty is going to be rewarded.'

It was not until that very instant that Rachel realized how historically momentous this was. A tightness rose in her throat, and she fought it off, plowing onward.

'As an intelligence officer who specializes in the analysis and verification of data, I am one of several people the President has called upon to examine the NASA data. I have examined it personally as well as conferring with several specialists – both government and civilian – men and women whose credentials are beyond reproach and whose stature is beyond political influence. It is my professional opinion that the data I am about to present to you is factual in its origins and unbiased in its presentation. Moreover, it is my personal opinion that the President, in good faith to his office and the American people, has shown admirable care and restraint in delaying an announcement I know he would have loved to have made last week.'

Rachel watched the crowd before her exchanging puzzled looks. They all returned their gaze to her, and she knew she had their undivided attention.

'Ladies and gentlemen, you are about to hear what I'm sure you will agree is one of the most exciting pieces of information ever revealed in this office.'

CHAPTER **35**

The aerial view currently being transmitted to the Delta Force by the microbot circling inside the habisphere looked like something that would win an avant-garde film contest – the dim lighting, the glistening extraction hole, and the well-dressed Asian lying on the ice, his camel-hair coat splayed around him like enormous wings. He was obviously trying to extract a water sample.

'We've got to stop him,' said Delta-Three.

Delta-One agreed. The Milne Ice Shelf held secrets his team was authorized to protect with force.

'How do we stop him?' Delta-Two challenged, still gripping the joystick. 'These microbots are not equipped.'

Delta-One scowled. The microbot currently hovering inside the habisphere was a recon model, stripped down for longer flight. It was about as lethal as a housefly.

'We should call the controller,' Delta-Three stated.

Delta-One stared intently at the image of the solitary Wailee Ming, perched precariously on the rim of the extraction pit. Nobody was anywhere near him – and ice cold water had a way of muffling one's ability to scream. 'Give me the controls.'

'What are you doing?' the soldier on the joystick demanded.

'What we were *trained* to do,' Delta-One snapped, taking over. 'Improvise.'

CHAPTER **36**

Wailee Ming lay on his stomach beside the extraction hole, his right arm extended over the rim trying to extract a water sample. His eyes were definitely not playing tricks on him; his face, now only a yard or so from the water, could see everything perfectly.

This is incredible!

Straining harder, Ming maneuvered the beaker in his fingers, trying to reach down to the surface of the water. All he needed was another few inches.

Unable to extend his arm any farther, Ming repositioned himself closer to the hole. He pressed the toes of his boots against the ice and firmly replanted his left hand on the rim. Again, he extended his right arm as far as he could. *Almost.* He shifted a little closer. *Yes!* The edge of the beaker broke the surface of the water. As the liquid flowed into the container, Ming stared in disbelief.

Then, without warning, something utterly inexplicable occurred. Out of the darkness, like a bullet from a gun, flew a tiny speck of metal. Ming only saw it for a fraction of a second before it smashed into his right eye.

The human instinct to protect one's eyes was so innately ingrained, that despite Ming's brain telling him that any sudden movements risked his balance, he recoiled. It was a jolting reaction more out of surprise than pain. Ming's left hand, closest to his face, shot up reflexively to protect the assaulted eyeball. Even as his hand was in motion, Ming knew he had made a mistake. With all of his weight leaning forward, and his only means of support suddenly gone, Wailee Ming teetered. He recovered too late. Dropping the beaker and trying to grab on to the slick ice to stop his fall, he slipped – plummeting forward into the darkened hole.

The fall was only four feet, and yet as Ming hit the icy water head first he felt like his face had hit pavement at fifty miles an hour. The liquid that engulfed his face was so cold it felt like burning acid. It brought an instantaneous spike of panic.

Upside down and in the darkness, Ming was momentarily disoriented, not knowing which way to turn toward the surface. His heavy camel-hair coat kept the icy blast from his body – but only for a second or two. Finally righting himself, Ming came sputtering up for air, just as the water found its way to his back and chest, engulfing his body in a lung-crushing vise of cold.

'Hee . . . lp,' he gasped, but Ming could barely pull in enough air to let out a whimper. He felt like the wind had been knocked out of him.

'Heee . . . lp!' His cries were inaudible even to himself. Ming clambered toward the side of the extraction pit and tried to pull himself out. The wall before him was vertical ice. Nothing to grab. Underwater, his boots kicked the side of the wall, searching for a foothold. Nothing. He strained upward, reaching for the rim. It was only a foot out of reach.

Ming's muscles were already having trouble responding. He kicked his legs harder, trying to propel himself high enough up the wall to grab the rim. His body felt like lead, and his lungs seemed to have shrunk to nothing, as if they were being crushed by a python. His water-laden coat was getting heavier by the second, pulling him downward. Ming tried to pull it off his body, but the heavy fabric stuck.

'Help . . . me!'

The fear came on in torrents now.

Drowning, Ming had once read, was the most horrific death imaginable. He had never dreamed he would find himself on the verge of experiencing it. His muscles refused to cooperate with his mind, and already he was fighting just to keep his head above water. His soggy clothing pulled him downward as his numb fingers scratched the sides of the pit.

His screams were only in his mind now.

And then it happened.

Ming went under. The sheer terror of being conscious of his own impending death was something he never imagined he would experience. And yet here he was . . . sinking slowly down the sheer ice wall of a 200-foot-deep hole in the ice. Multitudes of thoughts flashed before his eyes. Moments from his childhood. His career. He wondered if anyone would find him down here. Or would he simply sink to the bottom and freeze there . . . entombed in the glacier for all time.

Ming's lungs were screaming for oxygen. He held his breath, still trying to kick toward the surface. *Breathe!* He fought the reflex, clamping his insensate lips together. *Breathe!* He tried in vain to swim upward. *Breathe!* At that instant, in a deadly battle of human reflex against reason, Ming's breathing instinct overcame his ability to keep his mouth closed.

Wailee Ming inhaled.

The water crashing into his lungs felt like scalding oil on his sensitive pulmonary tissue. He felt like he was burning from the inside out. Cruelly, water does not kill immediately. Ming spent seven horrifying seconds inhaling in the icy water, each breath more painful than the last, each inhalation offering none of what his body so desperately craved.

Finally, as Ming slid downward into the icy darkness, he felt himself going unconscious. He welcomed the escape. All around him in the water Ming saw tiny glowing specks of light. It was the most beautiful thing he had ever seen.

CHAPTER 37

The East Appointment Gate of the White House is located on East Executive Avenue between the Treasury Department and the East Lawn. The reinforced perimeter fence and cement bollards installed after the attack on the Marine barracks in Beirut give this entry an air that is anything but welcoming.

Outside the gate, Gabrielle Ashe checked her watch, feeling a growing nervousness. It was 4:45 P.M., and still nobody had made contact.

EAST APPOINTMENT GATE, 4:30 P.M. COME ALONE.

Here I am, she thought. *Where are you?*

Gabrielle scanned the faces of the tourists milling about, waiting for someone to catch her eye. A few men looked her over and moved on. Gabrielle was beginning to wonder if this had been such a good idea. She sensed the Secret Serviceman in the sentry shack had his eye on her now. Gabrielle decided her informant had gotten cold feet. Gazing one last time through the heavy fence toward the White House, Gabrielle sighed and turned to go.

'Gabrielle Ashe?' the Secret Serviceman called out behind her.

Gabrielle wheeled, her heart catching in her throat. *Yes?*

The man in the guard shack waved her over. He was lean with a humorless face. 'Your party is ready to see you now.' He unlocked the main gate and motioned for her to enter.

Gabrielle's feet refused to move. 'I'm coming inside?'

The guard nodded. 'I was asked to apologize for keeping you waiting.'

Gabrielle looked at the open doorway and still could not move. *What's going on?* This was not at all what she had expected.

'You are Gabrielle Ashe, are you not?' the guard demanded, looking impatient now.

'Yes, sir, but—'

'Then I strongly suggest you follow me.'

Gabrielle's feet jolted into motion. As she stepped tentatively over the threshold, the gate slammed shut behind her.

CHAPTER 38

Two days without sunlight had rearranged Michael Tolland's biological clock. Although his watch said it was late afternoon, Tolland's body insisted it was the middle of the night. Now, having put the finishing touches on his documentary, Michael Tolland had downloaded the entire video file onto a digital video disk and was making his way across the darkened dome. Arriving at the illuminated press area, he delivered the disk to the NASA media technician in charge of overseeing the presentation.

'Thanks, Mike,' the technician said, winking as he held up the video disk. 'Kind of redefines "must-see TV," eh?'

Tolland gave a tired chuckle. 'I hope the President likes it.'

'No doubt. Anyhow, your work is done. Sit back and enjoy the show.'

'Thanks.' Tolland stood in the brightly lit press area and surveyed the convivial NASA personnel toasting the meteorite with cans of Canadian beer. Even though Tolland wanted to celebrate, he felt exhausted, emotionally drained. He glanced around for Rachel Sexton, but apparently she was still talking to the President.

He wants to put her on-air, Tolland thought. Not that he blamed him; Rachel would be a perfect addition to the cast of meteorite spokespeople. In addition to her good looks, Rachel exuded an accessible poise and self-confidence that Tolland seldom saw in the women he met. Then again, most of the women Tolland met were in television – either ruthless power women or gorgeous on-air 'personalities' who lacked exactly that.

Now, slipping quietly away from the crowd of bustling NASA employees, Tolland navigated the web of pathways across the dome, wondering where the other civilian scientists had disappeared to. If they felt half as drained as he did, they should be in the bunking area grabbing a catnap before the big moment. Ahead of him in the distance, Tolland could see the circle of SHABA pylons around the deserted extraction pit. The empty dome overhead seemed to echo with the hollow voices of distant memories. Tolland tried to block them out.

Forget the ghosts, he willed himself. They often haunted him at times like these, when he was tired or alone – times of personal triumph or celebration. *She should be with you right now*, the voice whispered. Alone in the darkness, he felt himself reeling backward into oblivion.

Celia Birch had been his sweetheart in graduate school. One Valentine's Day, Tolland took her to her favorite restaurant. When the waiter brought Celia's dessert, it was a single rose and a diamond ring. Celia understood immediately. With tears in her eyes, she spoke a single word that made Michael Tolland as happy as he'd ever been.

'Yes.'

Filled with anticipation, they bought a small house near Pasadena, where Celia got a job as a science teacher. Although the pay was modest, it was a start, and it was also close to Scripps Institute of Oceanography in San Diego, where Tolland had landed his dream job aboard a geologic research ship. Tolland's work meant he was away for three or four days at a time, but his reunions with Celia were always passionate and exciting.

While at sea, Tolland began videotaping some of his adventures for Celia, making minidocumentaries of his work onboard the ship. After one trip, he returned with a grainy home video that he'd shot out of the window of a deepwater submersible – the first footage ever shot of a bizarre chemotropic cuttlefish that nobody even knew existed. On camera, as he narrated the video, Tolland was practically bursting out of the submarine with enthusiasm.

Literally thousands of undiscovered species, he gushed, *live in these depths! We've barely scratched the surface! There are mysteries down here that none of us can imagine!*

Celia was enthralled with her husband's ebullience and concise scientific explanation. On a whim, she showed the tape to her science class, and it became an instant hit. Other teachers wanted to borrow it. Parents wanted to make copies. It seemed everyone was eagerly awaiting Michael's next installment. Celia suddenly had an idea. She called a college friend of hers who worked for NBC and sent her a videotape.

Two months later, Michael Tolland came to Celia and asked her to take a walk with him on Kingman Beach. It was their special place, where they always went to share their hopes and dreams.

'I have something I want to tell you,' Tolland said.

Celia stopped, taking her husband's hands as the water lapped around their feet. 'What is it?'

Tolland was bursting. 'Last week, I got a call from NBC television. They think I should host an oceanic documentary series. It's perfect. They want to make a pilot next year! Can you believe it?'

Celia kissed him, beaming. 'I believe it. You'll be great.'

Six months later, Celia and Tolland were sailing near Catalina when Celia began complaining of pain in her side. They ignored it for a few weeks, but finally it got too much. Celia went in to have it checked out.

In an instant, Tolland's dream life shattered into a hellish nightmare. Celia was ill. Very ill.

'Advanced stages of lymphoma,' the doctors explained. 'Rare in people her age, but certainly not unheard of.'

Celia and Tolland visited countless clinics and hospitals, consulting with specialists. The answer was always the same. Incurable.

I will not accept that! Tolland immediately quit his job at Scripps Institute, forgot all about the NBC documentary, and focused all of his energy and love on helping Celia get well. She fought hard too, bearing the pain with a grace that only made him love her more. He took her for long walks on Kingman Beach, made her healthy meals, and told her stories of the things they would do when she got better.

But it was not to be.

Only seven months had passed when Michael Tolland found himself sitting beside his dying wife in a stark hospital ward. He no longer recognized her face. The savageness of the cancer was rivaled only by the brutality of the chemotherapy. She was left a ravaged skeleton. The final hours were the hardest.

'Michael,' she said, her voice raspy. 'It's time to let go.'

'I can't.' Tolland's eyes welled.

'You're a survivor,' Celia said. 'You have to be. Promise me you'll find another love.'

'I'll never want another.' Tolland meant it.

'You'll have to learn.'

Celia died on a crystal clear Sunday morning in June. Michael Tolland felt like a ship torn from its moorings and thrown adrift in a raging sea, his compass smashed. For weeks he spun out of control. Friends tried to help, but his pride could not bear their pity.

You have a choice to make, he finally realized. *Work or die*.

Hardening his resolve, Tolland threw himself back into *Amazing Seas*. The program quite literally saved his life. In the four years that followed, Tolland's show took off. Despite the matchmaking efforts of his friends, Tolland endured only a handful of dates. All were fiascos or mutual disappointments, so Tolland finally gave up and blamed his busy travel schedule for his lack of social life. His best friends knew better, though; Michael Tolland simply was not ready.

The meteorite extraction pit loomed before Tolland now, pulling him from his painful reverie. He shook off the chill of his memories and approached the opening. In the darkened dome, the melt water in the hole had taken on an almost surreal and magical beauty. The surface of the pool was shimmering like a moonlit pond. Tolland's eyes were drawn to specks of light on the top layer of the water, as if someone had sprinkled blue-green sparkles onto the surface. He stared a long moment at the shimmering.

Something about it seemed peculiar.

At first glance, he thought the gleaming water was simply reflecting the glow of the spotlights from across the dome. Now he saw this was not the case at all. The shimmers possessed a greenish tint and seemed to pulse in a rhythm, as if the surface of the water were alive, illuminating itself from within.

Unsettled, Tolland stepped beyond the pylons for a closer look.

Across the habisphere, Rachel Sexton exited the PSC trailer into darkness. She paused a moment, disoriented by the shadowy vault around her. The habisphere was now a gaping cavern, lit only by incidental effulgence radiating out from the stark media lights against the north wall. Unnerved by the darkness around her, she headed instinctively for the illuminated press area.

Rachel felt pleased with the outcome of her briefing of the White House staff. Once she'd recovered from the President's little stunt, she'd smoothly conveyed everything she knew about the meteorite. As she spoke, she watched the expressions on the faces of the President's staff go from incredulous shock, to hopeful belief, and finally to awestruck acceptance.

'Extraterrestrial life?' she had heard one of them exclaim. 'Do you know what that means?'

'Yes,' another replied. 'It means we're going to win this election.'

As Rachel approached the dramatic press area, she imagined the impending announcement and couldn't help but wonder if her father really deserved the presidential steamroller that was about to blindside him, crushing his campaign in a single blow.

The answer, of course, was yes.

Whenever Rachel Sexton felt any soft spot for her father, all she had to do was remember her mother. Katherine Sexton. The pain and shame Sedgewick Sexton had brought on her was reprehensible . . . coming home late every night, looking smug and smelling of perfume. The feigned religious zeal her father hid behind – all the while lying and cheating, knowing Katherine would never leave him.

Yes, she decided, *Senator Sexton was about to get exactly what he deserved*.

The crowd in the press area was jovial. Everyone held beers. Rachel moved through the crowd feeling like a coed at a frat party. She wondered where Michael Tolland had gone.

Corky Marlinson materialized beside her. 'Looking for Mike?'

Rachel started. 'Well . . . no . . . sort of.'

Corky shook his head in disgust. 'I knew it. Mike just left. I think he was headed back to go grab a few winks.' Corky squinted across the dusky dome. 'Although it looks like you can still catch him.' He gave her a puggish smile and pointed. 'Mike becomes mesmerized every time he sees water.'

Rachel followed Corky's outstretched finger toward the center of the dome, where the silhouette of Michael Tolland stood, gazing down into the water in the extraction pit.

'What's he doing?' she asked. 'That's kind of dangerous over there.'

Corky grinned. 'Probably taking a leak. Let's go push him.'

Rachel and Corky crossed the darkened dome toward the extraction pit. As they drew close to Michael Tolland, Corky called out.

'Hey, aqua man! Forget your swimsuit?'

Tolland turned. Even in the dimness, Rachel could see his expression was uncharacteristically grave. His face looked oddly illuminated, as if he were being lit from below.

'Everything okay, Mike?' she asked.

'Not exactly.' Tolland pointed into the water.

Corky stepped over the pylons and joined Tolland at the edge of the shaft. Corky's mood seemed to cool instantly when he looked in the water. Rachel joined them, stepping past the pylons to the edge of the pit. When she peered into the hole, she was surprised to see specks of blue-green light shimmering on the surface. Like neon dust particles floating in the water. They seemed to be pulsating green. The effect was beautiful.

Tolland picked up a shard of ice off the glacial floor and tossed it into the water. The water phosphoresced at the point of impact, glowing with a sudden green splash.

'Mike,' Corky said, looking uneasy, 'please tell me you know what that is.'

Tolland frowned. 'I know exactly what this is. My question is, what the hell is it doing *here*?'

CHAPTER 39

'We've got flagellates,' Tolland said, staring into the luminescent water.

'Flatulence?' Corky scowled. 'Speak for yourself.'

Rachel sensed Michael Tolland was in no joking mood.

'I don't know how it could have happened,' Tolland said, 'but somehow this water contains bioluminescent dinoflagellates.'

'Bioluminescent what?' Rachel said. *Speak English.*

'Monocelled plankton capable of oxidizing a luminescent catalyst called luceferin.'

That was English?

Tolland exhaled and turned to his friend. 'Corky, there any chance the meteorite we pulled out of that hole had living organisms on it?'

Corky burst out laughing. 'Mike, be serious!'

'I am serious.'

'No chance, Mike! Believe me, if NASA had any inkling whatsoever that there were extraterrestrial organisms living on that rock, you can be damn sure they never would have extracted it into the open air.'

Tolland looked only partially comforted, his relief apparently clouded by a deeper mystery. 'I can't be for sure without a microscope,' Tolland said, 'but it looks to me like this is a bioluminescent plankton from the phylum Pyrrophyta. Its name means fire plant. The Arctic Ocean is filled with it.'

Corky shrugged. 'So why'd you ask if they were from space?'

'Because,' Tolland said, 'the meteorite was buried in glacial ice – *fresh*water from snowfalls. The water in that hole is glacial melt and has been frozen for three centuries. How could ocean creatures get in there?'

Tolland's point brought a long silence.

Rachel stood at the edge of the pool and tried to get her mind around what she was looking at. *Bioluminescent plankton in the extraction shaft. What does it mean?*

'There's got to be a crack somewhere down there,' Tolland said. 'It's the only explanation. The plankton must have entered the shaft through a fissure in the ice that allowed ocean water to seep in.'

Rachel didn't understand. 'Seep in? From where?' She recalled her long IceRover ride in from the ocean. 'The coast is a good two miles from here.'

Both Corky and Tolland gave Rachel an odd look. 'Actually,' Corky said, 'the ocean is directly *underneath* us. This slab of ice is floating.'

Rachel stared at the two men, feeling utterly perplexed. 'Floating? But . . . we're on a glacier.'

'Yes, we're on a glacier,' Tolland said, 'but we're not over land. Glaciers sometimes flow off a landmass and fan out over water. Because ice is lighter than water, the glacier simply continues to flow, floating out over the ocean like an enormous ice raft. That's the definition of an ice *shelf* . . . the floating section of a glacier.' He paused. 'We're actually almost a mile out to sea at the moment.'

Shocked, Rachel instantly became wary. As she adjusted her mental picture of her surroundings, the thought of standing over the Arctic Ocean brought with it a sense of fear.

Tolland seemed to sense her uneasiness. He stamped his foot reassuringly on the ice. 'Don't worry. This ice is three hundred feet thick, with two hundred of those feet floating below the water like an ice cube in a glass. Makes the shelf very stable. You could build a skyscraper on this thing.'

Rachel gave a wan nod, not entirely convinced. The misgivings aside, she now understood Tolland's theory about the origins of the plankton. *He thinks there's a crack that goes all the way down to the ocean, allowing plankton to come up through it into the hole.* It was feasible, Rachel decided, and yet it involved a paradox that bothered her. Norah Mangor had been very clear about the integrity of the glacier, having drilled countless test cores to confirm its solidity.

Rachel looked at Tolland. 'I thought the glacier's perfection was the cornerstone of all the strata-dating records. Didn't Dr Mangor say the glacier had *no* cracks or fissures?'

Corky frowned. 'Looks like the ice queen muffed it.'

Don't say that too loudly, Rachel thought, *or you'll get an ice pick in the back.*

Tolland stroked his chin as he watched the phosphorescing creatures. 'There's literally no other explanation. There *must* be a crack. The weight of the ice shelf on top of the ocean must be pushing plankton-rich seawater up into the hole.'

One hell of a crack, Rachel thought. If the ice here was 300 feet thick and the hole was 200 feet deep, then this hypothetical crack had to pass through 100 feet of solid ice. *Norah Mangor's test cores showed no cracks.*

'Do me a favor,' Tolland said to Corky. 'Go find Norah. Let's hope to God she knows something about this glacier that she's not telling us. And find Ming, too, maybe he can tell us what these little glow-beasties are.'

Corky headed off.

'Better hurry,' Tolland called after him, glancing back into the hole. 'I could swear this bioluminescence is fading.'

Rachel looked at the hole. Sure enough, the green was not so brilliant now.

Tolland removed his parka and lay down on the ice next to the hole.

Rachel watched, confused. 'Mike?'

'I want to find out if there's any saltwater flowing in.'

'By lying on the ice without a coat?'

'Yup.' Tolland crawled on his belly to the edge of the hole. Holding one sleeve of the coat over the edge, he let the other sleeve dangle down the shaft until the cuff skimmed the water. 'This is a highly

accurate salinity test used by world-class oceanographers. It's called
''licking a wet jacket.'' '

Out on the ice shelf, Delta-One struggled with the controls, trying to
keep the damaged microbot in flight over the group now assembled
around the excavation pit. From the sounds of the conversation
beneath, he knew things were unraveling fast.

'Call the controller,' he said. 'We've got a serious problem.'

CHAPTER 40

Gabrielle Ashe had taken the White House public tour
countless times in her youth, secretly dreaming of someday working
inside the presidential mansion, and becoming part of the elite team
that charted the country's future. At the moment, however, she
would have preferred to be anywhere else in the world.

As the Secret Serviceman from the East Gate led Gabrielle into
an ornate foyer, she wondered what in the world her anonymous
informant was trying to prove. Inviting Gabrielle into the White
House was insane. *What if I'm seen?* Gabrielle had become quite
visible lately in the media as Senator Sexton's right-hand aide.
Certainly someone would recognize her.

'Ms Ashe?'

Gabrielle looked up. A kind-faced sentry in the foyer gave her
a welcoming smile. 'Look over there, please.' He pointed.

Gabrielle looked where he was pointing and was blinded by a
flashbulb.

'Thank you, ma'am.' The sentry led her to a desk and handed her
a pen. 'Please sign the entry log.' He pushed a heavy leather binder in
front of her.

Gabrielle looked at the log. The page before her was blank. She
recalled hearing once that all White House visitors sign on their own
blank page to preserve the privacy of their visit. She signed her name.

So much for a secret meeting.

Gabrielle walked through a metal detector, and was then given a cursory pat down.

The sentry smiled. 'Enjoy your visit, Ms Ashe.'

Gabrielle followed the Secret Serviceman fifty feet down a tiled hallway to a second security desk. Here, another sentry was assembling a guest pass that was just rolling out of a lamination machine. He punched a hole in it, affixed a neck cord, and slipped it over Gabrielle's head. The plastic was still warm. The photo on the ID was the snapshot they had taken fifteen seconds earlier down the hall.

Gabrielle was impressed. *Who says government is inefficient?*

They continued, the Secret Serviceman leading her deeper into the White House complex. Gabrielle was feeling more uneasy with every step. Whoever had extended the mysterious invitation certainly was not concerned about keeping the meeting private. Gabrielle had been issued an official pass, signed the guest log, and was now being marched in plain view through the first floor of the White House where public tours were gathered.

'And this is the China Room,' a tour guide was saying to a group of tourists, 'home of Nancy Reagan's $952 per setting red-rimmed china that sparked a debate over conspicuous consumption back in 1981.'

The Secret Serviceman led Gabrielle past the tour toward a huge marble staircase, where another tour was ascending. 'You are about to enter the thirty-two-hundred-square-foot East Room,' the guide was narrating, 'where Abigail Adams once hung John Adams's laundry. Then we will pass to the Red Room, where Dolley Madison liquored up visiting heads of state before James Madison negotiated with them.'

The tourists laughed.

Gabrielle followed past the stairway through a series of ropes and barricades into a more private section of the building. Here they entered a room Gabrielle had only seen in books and on television. Her breath grew short.

My God, this is the Map Room!

No tour ever came in here. The room's paneled walls could swing outward to reveal layer upon layer of world maps. This was the place where Roosevelt had charted the course of World War II.

Unsettlingly, it was also the room from which Clinton had admitted his affair with Monica Lewinsky. Gabrielle pushed that particular thought from her mind. Most important, the Map Room was a passageway into the West Wing – the area inside the White House where the true powerbrokers worked. This was the last place Gabrielle Ashe had expected to be going. She had imagined her e-mail was coming from some enterprising young intern or secretary working in one of the complex's more mundane offices. Apparently not.

I'm going into the West Wing . . .

The Secret Serviceman marched her to the very end of a carpeted hallway and stopped at an unmarked door. He knocked. Gabrielle's heart was pounding.

'It's open,' someone called from inside.

The man opened the door and motioned for Gabrielle to enter.

Gabrielle stepped in. The shades were down, and the room was dim. She could see the faint outline of a person sitting at a desk in the darkness.

'Ms Ashe?' The voice came from behind a cloud of cigarette smoke. 'Welcome.'

As Gabrielle's eyes accustomed to the dark, she began to make out an unsettlingly familiar face, and her muscles went taut with surprise. *THIS is who has been sending me e-mail?*

'Thank you for coming,' Marjorie Tench said, her voice cold.

'Ms . . . Tench?' Gabrielle stammered, suddenly unable to breathe.

'Call me Marjorie.' The hideous woman stood up, blowing smoke out of her nose like a dragon. 'You and I are about to become best friends.'

CHAPTER 41

Norah Mangor stood at the extraction shaft beside Tolland, Rachel, and Corky and stared into the pitch-black meteorite hole.

'Mike,' she said, 'you're cute, but you're insane. There's no bioluminescence here.'

Tolland now wished he'd thought to take some video; while Corky had gone to find Norah and Ming, the bioluminescence had begun fading rapidly. Within a couple of minutes, all the twinkling had simply stopped.

Tolland threw another piece of ice into the water, but nothing happened. No green splash.

'Where did they go?' Corky asked.

Tolland had a fairly good idea. Bioluminescence – one of nature's most ingenious defense mechanisms – was a natural response for plankton in distress. A plankton sensing it was about to be consumed by larger organisms would begin flashing in hopes of attracting much larger predators that would scare off the original attackers. In this case, the plankton, having entered the shaft through a crack, suddenly found themselves in a primarily freshwater environment and bioluminesced in panic as the freshwater slowly killed them. 'I think they died.'

'They were murdered,' Norah scoffed. 'The Easter Bunny swam in and ate them.'

Corky glared at her. 'I saw the luminescence too, Norah.'

'Was it before or after you took LSD?'

'Why would we lie about this?' Corky demanded.

'Men lie.'

'Yeah, about sleeping with other women, but never about bioluminescent plankton.'

Tolland sighed. 'Norah, certainly you're aware that plankton *do* live in the oceans beneath the ice.'

'Mike,' she replied with a glare, 'please don't tell me my business. For the record, there are over two hundred species of diatoms that thrive under Arctic ice shelves. Fourteen species of autotrophic nannoflagellates, twenty heterotrophic flagellates, forty heterotrophic dinoflagellates, and several metazoans, including polychaetes, amphipods, copepods, euphausids, and fish. Any questions?'

Tolland frowned. 'Clearly you know more about Arctic fauna than I do, and you agree there's plenty of life underneath us. So why are you so skeptical that we saw bioluminescent plankton?'

'Because, Mike, this shaft is *sealed*. It's a closed, freshwater environment. No ocean plankton could possibly get in here!'

'I tasted salt in the water,' Tolland insisted. 'Very faint, but present. Saltwater is getting in here somehow.'

'Right,' Norah said skeptically. 'You tasted salt. You licked the sleeve of an old sweaty parka, and now you've decided that the PODS density scans and fifteen separate core samples are inaccurate.'

Tolland held out the wet sleeve of his parka as proof.

'Mike, I'm not licking your damn jacket.' She looked into the hole. 'Might I ask why droves of alleged plankton decided to swim into this alleged crack?'

'Heat?' Tolland ventured. 'A lot of sea creatures are attracted by heat. When we extracted the meteorite, we heated it. The plankton may have been drawn instinctively toward the temporarily warmer environment in the shaft.'

Corky nodded. 'Sounds logical.'

'Logical?' Norah rolled her eyes. 'You know, for a prize-winning physicist and a world-famous oceanographer, you're a couple of pretty dense specimens. Has it occurred to you that even if there is a crack – which I can assure you there is not – it is physically impossible for any seawater to be flowing *into* this shaft.' She stared at both of them with pathetic disdain.

'But, Norah . . .' Corky began.

'Gentlemen! We're standing *above* sea level here.' She stamped her foot on the ice. 'Hello? This ice sheet rises a hundred feet above the sea. You might recall the big cliff at the end of this shelf? We're higher than the ocean. If there were a fissure into this shaft, the water would be flowing *out* of this shaft, not into it. It's called gravity.'

Tolland and Corky looked at each other.

'Shit,' Corky said. 'I didn't think of that.'

Norah pointed into the water-filled shaft. 'You may also have noticed that the water level isn't changing?'

Tolland felt like an idiot. Norah was absolutely right. If there had been a crack, the water would be flowing *out*, not in. Tolland stood in silence a long moment, wondering what to do next.

'Okay,' Tolland sighed. 'Apparently, the fissure theory makes no sense. But we saw bioluminescence in the water. The only conclusion is that this is not a closed environment after all. I realize much of your ice-dating data is built on the premise that the glacier is a solid block, but—'

'Premise?' Norah was obviously getting agitated. 'Remember, this was not just *my* data, Mike. NASA made the same findings. We *all* confirmed this glacier is solid. No cracks.'

Tolland glanced across the dome toward the crowd gathered around the press conference area. 'Whatever is going on, I think, in good faith, we need to inform the administrator and—'

'This is bullshit!' Norah hissed. 'I'm telling you this glacial matrix is pristine. I'm not about to have my core data questioned by a salt lick and some absurd hallucinations.' She stormed over to a nearby supply area and began collecting some tools. 'I'll take a proper water sample, and show you this water contains no saltwater plankton – living or dead!'

Rachel and the others looked on as Norah used a sterile pipette on a string to harvest a water sample from the melt pool. Norah placed several drops in a tiny device that resembled a miniature telescope. Then she peered through the oculus, pointing the device toward the light emanating from the other side of the dome. Within seconds she was cursing.

'Jesus Christ!' Norah shook the device and looked again. 'Damn it! Something's got to be wrong with this refractometer!'

'Saltwater?' Corky gloated.

Norah frowned. 'Partial. It's registering three percent brine – which is totally impossible. This glacier is a snow pack. Pure freshwater. There should be no salt.' Norah carried the sample to a nearby microscope and examined it. She groaned.

'Plankton?' Tolland asked.

'*G. polyhedra*,' she replied, her voice now sedate. 'It's one of the planktons we glaciologists commonly see in the oceans under ice shelves.' She glanced over at Tolland. 'They're dead now. Obviously they didn't survive long in a three percent saltwater environment.'

The four of them stood in silence a moment beside the deep shaft.

Rachel wondered what the ramifications of this paradox were for the overall discovery. The dilemma appeared minor when compared to the overall scope of the meteorite, and yet, as an intel analyst, Rachel had witnessed the collapse of entire theories based on smaller snags than this.

'What's going on over here?' The voice was a low rumble.

Everyone looked up. The bearish frame of the NASA administrator emerged from the dark.

'Minor quandary with the water in the shaft,' Tolland said. 'We're trying to sort it out.'

Corky sounded almost gleeful. 'Norah's ice data is screwed.'

'Bite me twice,' Norah whispered.

The administrator approached, his furry eyebrows lowering. 'What's wrong with the ice data?'

Tolland heaved an uncertain sigh. 'We're showing a three percent saltwater mix in the meteorite shaft, which contradicts the glaciology report that the meteorite was encased in a pristine freshwater glacier.' He paused. 'There's also plankton present.'

Ekstrom looked almost angry. 'Obviously that's impossible. There are no fissures in this glacier. The PODS scans confirmed that. This meteorite was sealed in a solid matrix of ice.'

Rachel knew Ekstrom was correct. According to NASA's density scans, the ice sheet was rock solid. Hundreds of feet of frozen glacier on all sides of the meteorite. No cracks. And yet as Rachel imagined how density scans were taken, a strange thought occurred to her . . .

'In addition,' Ekstrom was saying, 'Dr Mangor's core samples confirmed the solidity of the glacier.'

'Exactly!' Norah said, tossing the refractometer on a desk. 'Double corroboration. No fault lines in the ice. Which leaves us no explanation whatsoever for the salt and plankton.'

'Actually,' Rachel said, the boldness of her voice surprising even herself. 'There *is* another possibility.' The brainstorm had hit her from the most unlikely of memories.

Everyone was looking at her now, their skepticism obvious.

Rachel smiled. 'There's a perfectly sound rationale for the presence of salt and plankton.' She gave Tolland a wry look. 'And frankly, Mike, I'm surprised it didn't occur to you.'

CHAPTER 42

'Plankton *frozen* in the glacier?' Corky Marlinson sounded not at all sold on Rachel's explanation. 'Not to rain on your parade, but usually when things freeze they die. These little buggers were flashing us, remember?'

'Actually,' Tolland said, giving Rachel an impressed look, 'she may have a point. There are a number of species that enter suspended animation when their environment requires it. I did an episode on that phenomenon once.'

Rachel nodded. 'You showed northern pike that got frozen in lakes and had to wait until the thaw to swim away. You also talked about microorganisms called "waterbears" that became totally dehydrated in the desert, remained that way for decades, and then reinflated when rains returned.'

Tolland chuckled. 'So you really *do* watch my show?'

Rachel gave a slightly embarrassed shrug.

'What's your point, Ms Sexton?' Norah demanded.

'Her point,' Tolland said, 'which should have dawned on me earlier, is that one of the species I mentioned on that program was a kind of plankton that gets frozen in the polar ice cap every winter, hibernates inside the ice, and then swims away every summer when the ice cap thins.' Tolland paused. 'Granted the species I featured on the show was not the bioluminescent species we saw here, but maybe the same thing happened.'

'Frozen plankton,' Rachel continued, excited to have Michael Tolland so enthusiastic about her idea, 'could explain everything we're seeing here. At some point in the past, fissures could have opened in this glacier, filled with plankton-rich saltwater, and then refroze. What if there were *frozen* pockets of saltwater in this glacier? Frozen saltwater containing frozen plankton? Imagine if while you were raising the heated meteorite through the ice, it passed through a frozen saltwater pocket. The saltwater ice would have melted, releasing the plankton from hibernation, and giving us a small percentage of salt mixed in the freshwater.'

'Oh, for the love of God!' Norah exclaimed with a hostile groan. 'Suddenly *everyone's* a glaciologist!'

Corky also looked skeptical. 'But wouldn't PODS have spotted any brine ice pockets when it did its density scans? After all, brine ice and freshwater ice have different densities.'

'*Barely* different,' Rachel said.

'Three percent is a substantial difference,' Norah challenged.

'Yes, in a *lab*,' Rachel replied. 'But PODS takes its measurements from 120 miles up in space. Its computers were designed to differentiate between the obvious – ice and slush, granite and limestone.' She turned to the administrator. 'Am I right to assume that when PODS measures densities from space, it probably lacks the resolution to distinguish brine ice from fresh ice?'

The administrator nodded. 'Correct. A three percent differential is below PODS's tolerance threshold. The satellite would see brine ice and fresh ice as identical.'

Tolland now looked intrigued. 'This would also explain the static water level in the shaft.' He looked at Norah. 'You said the plankton species you saw in the extraction shaft was called—'

'*G. polyhedra*,' Norah declared. 'And now you're wondering if *G. polyhedra* is capable of hibernating inside the ice? You'll be pleased to know the answer is *yes*. Absolutely. *G. polyhedra* is found in droves around ice shelves, it bioluminesces, and it can hibernate inside the ice. Any other questions?'

Everyone exchanged looks. From Norah's tone, there was obviously some sort of 'but' – and yet it seemed she had just confirmed Rachel's theory.

'So,' Tolland ventured, 'you're saying it's possible, right? This theory makes sense?'

'Sure,' Norah said, 'if you're totally retarded.'

Rachel glared. 'I *beg* your pardon?'

Norah Mangor locked stares with Rachel. 'I imagine in your business, a little bit of knowledge is a dangerous thing? Well, trust me when I tell you that the same holds true for glaciology.' Norah's eyes shifted now, looking at each of the four people around her. 'Let me clarify this for everyone once and for all. The frozen brine pockets that Ms Sexton has proposed do occur. They are what glaciologists call interstices. Interstices, however, form not as pockets of saltwater but rather as highly branched networks of brine ice whose tendrils are as wide as a human hair. That meteorite would have had to pass through one hell of a dense series of interstices to release enough saltwater to create a three percent mixture in a pool that deep.'

Ekstrom scowled. 'So is it possible or not?'

'Not on your life,' Norah said flatly. 'Totally impossible. I would have hit pockets of brine ice in my core samples.'

'Core samples are drilled essentially in random spots, right?' Rachel asked. 'Is there any chance the cores' placements, simply by bad luck, could have missed a pocket of sea ice?'

'I drilled directly down *over* the meteorite. Then I drilled multiple cores only a few yards on either side. You can't get any closer.'

'Just asking.'

'The point is moot,' Norah said. 'Brine interstices occur only in *seasonal* ice – ice that forms and melts every season. The Milne Ice Shelf is *fast* ice – ice that forms in the mountains and holds fast until it migrates to the calving zone and falls into the sea. As convenient as frozen plankton would be for explaining this mysterious little phenomenon, I can guarantee there are no hidden networks of frozen plankton in this glacier.'

The group fell silent again.

Despite the stark rebuttal of the frozen plankton theory, Rachel's systematic analysis of the data refused to accept the rejection. Instinctively, Rachel knew that the presence of frozen plankton in the glacier beneath them was the simplest solution to the riddle. *The Law of Parsimony*, she thought. Her NRO instructors had driven it into her subconscious. *When multiple explanations exist, the simplest is usually correct.*

Norah Mangor obviously had a lot to lose if her ice-core data was wrong, and Rachel wondered if maybe Norah had seen the plankton, realized she'd made a mistake in claiming the glacier was solid, and was now simply trying to cover her tracks.

'All I know,' Rachel said, 'is that I just briefed the entire White

House staff and told them this meteorite was discovered in a pristine matrix of ice and had been sealed there, untouched by outside influence since 1716, when it broke off of a famous meteorite called the Jungersol. This fact now appears to be in some question.'

The NASA administrator was silent, his expression grave.

Tolland cleared his throat. 'I have to agree with Rachel. There was saltwater and plankton in the pool. No matter what the explanation is, that shaft is obviously not a closed environment. We can't say it is.'

Corky was looking uncomfortable. 'Um, folks, not to sound like the astrophysicist here, but in my field when we make mistakes, we're usually off by *billions* of years. Is this little plankton/saltwater mix-up really all that important? I mean, the perfection of the ice surrounding the meteorite in no way affects the meteorite itself, right? We still have the fossils. Nobody is questioning *their* authenticity. If it turns out we've made a mistake with the ice-core data, nobody will really care. All they'll care about is that we found proof of life on another planet.'

'I'm sorry, Dr Marlinson,' Rachel said, 'as someone who analyzes data for a living, I have to disagree. Any tiny flaw in the data NASA presents tonight has the potential to cast doubt over the credibility of the entire discovery. Including the authenticity of the fossils.'

Corky's jaw fell open. 'What are you talking about? Those fossils are irrefutable!'

'I know that. You know that. But if the public catches wind that NASA knowingly presented ice-core data that was in question, trust me, they will immediately start wondering what else NASA lied about.'

Norah stepped forward, eyes flashing. 'My ice-core data is *not* in question.' She turned to the administrator. 'I can *prove* to you, categorically, that there is no brine ice trapped anywhere in this ice shelf!'

The administrator eyed her a long moment. 'How?'

Norah outlined her plan. When she was done, Rachel had to admit, the idea sounded like a reasonable one.

The administrator did not look so sure. 'And the results will be definitive?'

'One hundred percent confirmation,' Norah assured him. 'If there's one goddamn ounce of frozen saltwater anywhere near that meteorite shaft, you will see it. Even a few droplets will light up on my gear like Times Square.'

The administrator's brow furrowed beneath his military buzz cut. 'There's not much time. The press conference is in a couple of hours.'

'I can be back in twenty minutes.'

'How far out on the glacier did you say you have to go?'

'Not far. Two hundred yards should do it.'

Ekstrom nodded. 'Are you certain it's safe?'

'I'll take flares,' Norah replied. 'And Mike will go with me.'

Tolland's head shot up. 'I will?'

'You sure as hell will, Mike! We'll be tethered. I'd appreciate a strong set of arms out there if the wind whips up.'

'But—'

'She's right,' the administrator said, turning to Tolland. 'If she goes, she can't go alone. I'd send some of my men with her, but frankly, I'd rather keep this plankton issue to ourselves until we figure out if it's a problem or not.'

Tolland gave a reluctant nod.

'I'd like to go too,' Rachel said.

Norah spun like a cobra. 'The hell you will.'

'Actually,' the administrator said, as if an idea had just occurred to him, 'I think I'd feel safer if we used the standard quad tether configuration. If you go dual, and Mike slips, you'll never hold him. Four people are a lot safer than two.' He paused glancing at Corky. 'That would mean either you or Dr Ming.' Ekstrom glanced around the habisphere. 'Where is Dr Ming, anyway?'

'I haven't seen him in a while,' Tolland said. 'He might be catching a nap.'

Ekstrom turned to Corky. 'Dr Marlinson, I cannot require that you go out with them, and yet—'

'What the hell?' Corky said. 'Seeing as everyone is getting along so well.'

'No!' Norah exclaimed. 'Four people will slow us down. Mike and I are going alone.'

'You are *not* going alone.' The administrator's tone was final.

'There's a reason tethers are built as quads, and we're going to do this as safely as possible. The last thing I need is an accident a couple hours before the biggest press conference in NASA's history.'

CHAPTER **43**

Gabrielle Ashe felt a precarious uncertainty as she sat in the heavy air of Marjorie Tench's office. *What could this woman possibly want with me?* Behind the room's sole desk, Tench leaned back in her chair, her hard features seeming to radiate pleasure with Gabrielle's discomfort.

'Does the smoke bother you?' Tench asked, tapping a fresh cigarette from her pack.

'No,' Gabrielle lied.

Tench was already lighting up anyway. 'You and your candidate have taken quite an interest in NASA during this campaign.'

'True,' Gabrielle snapped, making no effort to hide her anger, 'thanks to some creative encouragement. I'd like an explanation.'

Tench gave an innocent pout. 'You want to know why I've been sending you e-mail fodder for your attack on NASA?'

'The information you sent me hurt your President.'

'In the short run, yes.'

The ominous tone in Tench's voice made Gabrielle uneasy. 'What's that supposed to mean?'

'Relax, Gabrielle. My e-mails didn't change things much. Senator Sexton was NASA-bashing long before I stepped in. I simply helped him clarify his message. Solidify his position.'

'Solidify his position?'

'Exactly.' Tench smiled, revealing stained teeth. 'Which, I must say, he did quite effectively this afternoon on CNN.'

Gabrielle recalled the senator's reaction to Tench's fence-buster question. *Yes, I would act to abolish NASA.* Sexton had gotten himself cornered, but he'd played out of the rough with a strong drive. It was the right move. Wasn't it? From Tench's contented look, Gabrielle sensed there was information missing.

Tench stood suddenly, her lanky frame dominating the cramped space. With the cigarette dangling from her lips, she walked over to a wall safe, removed a thick manila envelope, returned to the desk, and sat back down.

Gabrielle eyed the burgeoning envelope.

Tench smiled, cradling the envelope in her lap like a poker player holding a royal flush. Her yellowed fingertips flicked at the corner, making an annoying repetitive scratch, as if savoring the anticipation.

Gabrielle knew it was just her own guilty conscience, but her first fears were that the envelope contained some kind of proof of her sexual indiscretion with the senator. *Ridiculous*, she thought. The encounter had occurred after hours in Sexton's locked senatorial office. Not to mention, if the White House actually had any evidence, they would have gone public with it already.

They may be suspicious, Gabrielle thought, *but they don't have proof.*

Tench crushed out her cigarette. 'Ms Ashe, whether or not you are aware, you are caught in the middle of a battle that has been raging behind the scenes in Washington since 1996.'

This opening gambit was not at all what Gabrielle expected. 'I beg your pardon?'

Tench lit another cigarette. Her spindly lips curled around it, and the tip glowed red. 'What do you know about a bill called the Space Commercialization Promotions Act?'

Gabrielle had never heard of it. She shrugged, lost.

'Really?' Tench said. 'That surprises me. Considering your candidate's platform. The Space Commercialization Promotions Act was proposed back in 1996 by Senator Walker. The bill, in essence, cites the failure of NASA to do anything worthwhile since putting a man on the moon. It calls for the privatization of NASA by immediately selling off NASA assets to private aerospace companies and allowing the free-market system to explore space more efficiently, thus relieving the burden NASA now places on taxpayers.'

Gabrielle had heard NASA critics suggest privatization as a solution to NASA's woes, but she was not aware the idea had actually taken the form of an official bill.

'This commercialization bill,' Tench said, 'has been presented to Congress four times now. It is similar to bills that have successfully privatized government industries like uranium production. Congress has passed the space commercialization bill all four times it has seen it. Thankfully, the White House vetoed it on all occasions. Zachary Herney has had to veto it twice.'

'Your point?'

'My point is that this bill is one Senator Sexton will certainly support if he becomes President. I have reason to believe Sexton will have no qualms about selling off NASA assets to commercial bidders the first chance he gets. In short, your candidate would support privatization over having American tax dollars fund space explora-tion.'

'To my knowledge, the senator has never commented publicly about his stance on any Space Commercialization Promotions Act.'

'True. And yet knowing his politics, I assume you would not be surprised if he supported it.'

'Free-market systems tend to breed efficiency.'

'I'll take that as a "yes." ' Tench stared. 'Sadly, privatizing NASA is an abominable idea, and there are countless reasons why every White House administration since the bill's inception has shot it down.'

'I've heard the arguments against privatizing space,' Gabrielle said, 'and I understand your concerns.'

'Do you?' Tench leaned toward her. '*Which* arguments have you heard?'

Gabrielle shifted uneasily. 'Well, the standard academic fears mostly – the most common being that if we privatize NASA, our current pursuit of scientific space knowledge would be quickly abandoned in favor of profitable ventures.'

'True. Space science would die in a heartbeat. Instead of spending money to study our universe, private space companies would strip-mine asteroids, build tourist hotels in space, offer commercial satellite launch services. Why would private companies bother studying the origins of our universe when it would cost them billions and show no financial return?'

'They wouldn't,' Gabrielle countered. 'But certainly a National

Endowment for Space Science could be founded to fund academic missions.'

'We already have that system in place. It's called NASA.'

Gabrielle fell silent.

'The abandonment of science in favor of profits is a side issue,' Tench said. 'Hardly relevant compared to the utter chaos that would result by permitting the private sector to run free in space. We would have the wild west all over again. We would see pioneers staking claims on the moon and on asteroids and protecting those claims with force. I've heard petitions from companies who want to build neon billboards that blink advertisements in the nighttime sky. I've seen petitions from space hotels and tourist attractions whose proposed operations include ejecting their trash into the void of space and creating orbiting trash heaps. In fact, I just read a proposal yesterday from a company that wants to turn space into a mausoleum by launching the deceased into orbit. Can you imagine our telecommunications satellites colliding with dead bodies? Last week, I had a billionaire CEO in my office who was petitioning to launch a mission to a near-field asteroid, drag it closer to earth, and mine it for precious minerals. I actually had to remind this guy that dragging asteroids into near earth orbit posed potential risks of global catastrophe! Ms Ashe, I can assure you, if this bill passes, the throngs of entrepreneurs rushing into space will not be rocket scientists. They will be entrepreneurs with deep pockets and shallow minds.'

'Persuasive arguments,' Gabrielle said, 'and I'm sure the senator would weigh those issues carefully if he ever found himself in a position to vote on the bill. Might I ask what any of this has to do with me?'

Tench's gaze narrowed over her cigarette. 'A lot of people stand to make a lot of money in space, and the political lobby is mounting to remove all restrictions and open the floodgates. The veto power of the office of the President is the only remaining barrier against privatization . . . against complete anarchy in space.'

'Then I commend Zach Herney for vetoing the bill.'

'My fear is that your candidate would not be so prudent if elected.'

'Again, I assume the senator would carefully weigh all the issues if he were ever in a position to pass judgment on the bill.'

Tench did not look entirely convinced. 'Do you know how much Senator Sexton spends on media advertising?'

The question came out of left field. 'Those figures are public domain.'

'More than three million a month.'

Gabrielle shrugged. 'If you say so.' The figure was close.

'That's a lot of money to spend.'

'He's *got* a lot of money to spend.'

'Yes, he planned well. Or rather, *married* well.' Tench paused to blow smoke. 'It's sad about his wife, Katherine. Her death hit him hard.' A tragic sigh followed, clearly feigned. 'Her death was not all that long ago, was it?'

'Come to your point, or I'm leaving.'

Tench let out a lung-shaking cough and reached for the burgeoning manila folder. She pulled out a small stack of stapled papers and handed them to Gabrielle. 'Sexton's financial records.'

Gabrielle studied the documents in astonishment. The records went back several years. Although Gabrielle was not privy to the internal workings of Sexton's finances, she sensed this data was authentic – banking accounts, credit card accounts, loans, stock assets, real estate assets, debts, capital gains and losses. 'This is private data. Where did you get this?'

'My source is not your concern. But if you spend some time studying these figures, you will clearly see that Senator Sexton does not have the kind of money he is currently spending. After Katherine died, he squandered the vast majority of her legacy on bad investments, personal comforts, and buying himself what appears to be certain victory in the primaries. As of six months ago, your candidate was broke.'

Gabrielle sensed this had to be a bluff. If Sexton were broke, he sure wasn't acting it. He was buying advertising time in bigger and bigger blocks every week.

'Your candidate,' Tench continued, 'is currently outspending the President four to one. And he has no personal money.'

'We get a lot of donations.'

'Yes, some of them legal.'

Gabrielle's head shot up. 'I *beg* your pardon?'

Tench leaned across the desk, and Gabrielle could smell her nicotine breath. 'Gabrielle Ashe, I am going to ask you a question, and I suggest you think very carefully before you answer. It could affect whether you spend the next few years in jail or not. Are you aware that Senator Sexton is accepting enormous illegal campaign bribes from aerospace companies who have billions to gain from the privatization of NASA?'

Gabrielle stared. 'That's an absurd allegation!'

'Are you saying you are unaware of this activity?'

'I think I would *know* if the senator were accepting bribes of the magnitude you are suggesting.'

Tench smiled coldly. 'Gabrielle, I understand that Senator Sexton has shared *a lot* of himself with you, but I assure you there is plenty you do not know about the man.'

Gabrielle stood up. 'This meeting is over.'

'On the contrary,' Tench said, removing the remaining contents of the folder and spreading it on the desk. 'This meeting is just beginning.'

CHAPTER 44

Inside the habisphere's 'staging room,' Rachel Sexton felt like an astronaut as she slid into one of NASA's Mark IX microclimate survival suits. The black, one-piece, hooded jumpsuit resembled an inflatable scuba suit. Its two-ply, memory-foam fabric was fitted with hollow channels through which a dense gel was pumped to help the wearer regulate body temperature in both hot and cold environments.

Now, as Rachel pulled the tight-fitting hood over her head, her eyes fell on the NASA administrator. He appeared as a silent sentinel at the door, clearly displeased with the necessity for this little mission.

Norah Mangor was muttering obscenities as she got everyone outfitted. 'Here's an extra pudgy,' she said, tossing Corky his suit.

Tolland was already half into his.

Once Rachel was fully zipped up, Norah found the stopcock on Rachel's side and connected her to an infusion tube that coiled out of a silver canister resembling a large scuba tank.

'Inhale,' Norah said, opening the valve.

Rachel heard a hiss and felt gel being injected into the suit. The memory foam expanded, and the suit compressed around her, pressing down on her inner layer of clothing. The sensation reminded her of sticking her hand underwater while wearing a rubber glove. As the hood inflated around her head, it pressed in on her ears, making everything sound muffled. *I'm in a cocoon.*

'Best thing about the Mark IX,' Norah said, 'is the padding. You can fall on your ass and not feel a thing.'

Rachel believed it. She felt like she was trapped inside a mattress.

Norah handed Rachel a series of tools – an ice ax, tether snaps, and carabiners, which she affixed to the belt harnessed on Rachel's waist.

'All this?' Rachel asked, eyeing the gear. 'To go two hundred yards?'

Norah's eyes narrowed. 'You want to come or not?'

Tolland gave Rachel a reassuring nod. 'Norah's just being careful.'

Corky connected to the infusion tank and inflated his suit, looking amused. 'I feel like I'm wearing a giant condom.'

Norah gave a disgusted groan. 'Like you'd know, virgin boy.'

Tolland sat down next to Rachel. He gave her a weak smile as she donned her heavy boots and crampons. 'You sure you want to come?' His eyes had a protective concern that drew her in.

Rachel hoped her confident nod belied her growing trepidation. *Two hundred yards . . . not far at all.* 'And you thought you could find excitement only on the high seas.'

Tolland chuckled, talking as he attached his own crampons. 'I've decided I like liquid water much better than this frozen stuff.'

'I've never been a big fan of either,' Rachel said. 'I fell through the ice as a kid. Water's made me nervous ever since.'

Tolland glanced over, his eyes sympathetic. 'Sorry to hear that. When this is over, you'll have to come out and visit me on the *Goya*. I'll change your mind about water. Promise.'

The invitation surprised her. The *Goya* was Tolland's research ship – well known both from its role in *Amazing Seas* as well as its reputation as one of the strangest-looking ships on the ocean.

Although a visit to the *Goya* would be unnerving for Rachel, she knew it would be hard to pass up.

'She's anchored twelve miles off the coast of New Jersey at the moment,' Tolland said, struggling with his crampon latches.

'Sounds like an unlikely spot.'

'Not at all. The Atlantic seaboard is an incredible place. We were gearing up to shoot a new documentary when I was so rudely interrupted by the President.'

Rachel laughed. 'Shooting a documentary on what?'

'*Sphyrna mokarran* and megaplumes.'

Rachel frowned. 'Glad I asked.'

Tolland finished attaching his crampons and looked up. 'Seriously, I'll be filming out there for a couple weeks. Washington's not that far from the Jersey coast. Come out when you get back home. No reason to spend your life afraid of the water. My crew would roll out the red carpet for you.'

Norah Mangor's voice blared. 'Are we going outside, or should I get you two some candles and champagne?'

CHAPTER 45

Gabrielle Ashe had no idea what to make of the documents now spread out before her on Marjorie Tench's desk. The pile included photocopied letters, faxes, transcripts of phone conversations, and they all seemed to support the allegation that Senator Sexton was in covert dialogue with private space companies.

Tench pushed a couple of grainy black-and-white photographs toward Gabrielle. 'I assume this is news to you?'

Gabrielle looked at the photos. The first candid shot showed Senator Sexton getting out of a taxi in some kind of underground garage. *Sexton never takes taxis.* Gabrielle looked at the second shot – a telephoto of Sexton climbing into a parked white minivan. An old man appeared to be in the van waiting for him.

'Who is that?' Gabrielle said, suspicious the photos might be faked.
'A big shot from the SFF.'

Gabrielle was doubtful. 'The Space Frontier Foundation?'

The SFF was like a 'union' for private space companies. It represented aerospace contractors, entrepreneurs, venture capitalists –
any private entity that wanted to go into space. They tended to be
critical of NASA, arguing that the U.S. space program employed
unfair business practices to prevent private companies from launching
missions into space.

'The SFF,' Tench said, 'now represents over a hundred major
corporations, some very wealthy enterprises who are waiting eagerly
for the Space Commercialization Promotions Act to be ratified.'

Gabrielle considered it. For obvious reasons the SFF was a vocal
supporter of Sexton's campaign, although the senator had been
careful not to get too close to them because of their controversial
lobbying tactics. Recently the SFF had published an explosive rant
charging that NASA was in fact an 'illegal monopoly' whose ability to
operate at a loss and still stay in business represented unfair competition to private firms. According to the SFF, whenever AT&T needed
a telecomm satellite launched, several private space companies offered to do the job at a reasonable $50 million. Unfortunately, NASA
always stepped in and offered to launch AT&T's satellites for a mere
$25 million, even though it cost NASA five times that to do the job!
Operating at a loss is one way NASA keeps its grip on space, the SFF
lawyers accused. *And taxpayers pick up the tab.*

'This photo reveals,' Tench said, 'that your candidate is holding
secret meetings with an organization that represents private space
enterprises.' Tench motioned to several other documents on the
table. 'We also have internal SFF memos calling for huge sums of
money to be collected from SFF member companies – in amounts
commensurate with their net worth – and transferred to accounts
controlled by Senator Sexton. In effect, these private space agencies
are anteing up to put Sexton in office. I can only assume he has
agreed to pass the commercialization bill and privatize NASA if
elected.'

Gabrielle looked at the pile of papers, unconvinced. 'Do you expect
me to believe that the White House has evidence that its opponent is

engaged in profoundly illegal campaign finance – and yet, for some reason, you are keeping it secret?'

'What would you believe?'

Gabrielle glared. 'Frankly, considering your skills for manipulation, a more logical solution seems that you are plying me somehow with phony documents and photos produced by some enterprising White House staffer and his desktop publishing computer.'

'Possible, I admit. But not true.'

'No? Then how did you get all these internal documents from corporations? The resources required to steal all of this evidence from so many companies certainly exceeds the grasp of the White House.'

'You're right. This information arrived here as an unsolicited gift.'

Gabrielle was now lost.

'Oh yes,' Tench said, 'we get a lot of it. The President has many powerful political allies who would like to see him stay in office. Remember, your candidate is suggesting cuts all over the place – a lot of them right here in Washington. Senator Sexton certainly has no qualms about citing the FBI's bloated budget as an example of government overspending. He's taken some potshots at the IRS, too. Maybe someone at the bureau or at the service got a little annoyed.'

Gabrielle got the implication. People at the FBI and IRS would have ways of getting this kind of information. They might then send it to the White House as an unsolicited favor to help the President's election. But what Gabrielle could not make herself believe was that Senator Sexton would ever be engaged in illegal campaign funding. 'If this data is accurate,' Gabrielle challenged, 'which I strongly doubt it is, why haven't you gone public?'

'Why do you think?'

'Because it was gathered illegally.'

'How we got it makes no difference.'

'Of course it makes a difference. It's inadmissible in a hearing.'

'What hearing? We'd simply leak this to a newspaper, and they'd run it as a "credible-source" story with photos and documentation. Sexton would be guilty until proven innocent. His vocal anti-NASA stance would be virtual proof that he is taking bribes.'

Gabrielle knew it was true. 'Fine,' she challenged, 'then why haven't you leaked the information?'

'Because it's a negative. The President promised not to go negative in the campaign and he wants to stick to that promise as long as he can.'

Yeah, right! 'You're telling me the President is so upstanding that he refuses to go public with this because people might consider it a negative?'

'It's a negative for the country. It implicates dozens of private companies, many of which are made up of honest people. It besmirches the office of the U.S. Senate and is bad for the country's morale. Dishonest politicians hurt *all* politicians. Americans need to trust their leaders. This would be an ugly investigation and would most likely send a U.S. senator and numerous prominent aerospace executives to jail.'

Although Tench's logic did make sense, Gabrielle still doubted the allegations. 'What does any of this have to do with me?'

'Simply put, Ms Ashe, if we release these documents, your candidate will be indicted for illegal campaign financing, lose his Senate seat, and most likely do prison time.' Tench paused. 'Unless . . .'

Gabrielle saw a snakelike glint in the senior adviser's eyes. 'Unless *what?*'

Tench took a long drag on her cigarette. 'Unless you decide to help us avoid all that.'

A murky silence settled over the room.

Tench coughed roughly. 'Gabrielle, listen, I decided to share this unfortunate information with you for three reasons. First, to show you Zach Herney is a decent man who considers the government's well-being before his personal gain. Second, to inform you that your candidate is not as trustworthy as you might think. And third, to persuade you to accept the offer I am about to make.'

'That offer being?'

'I'd like to offer you a chance to do the right thing. The *patriotic* thing. Whether you know it or not, you're in a unique position to spare Washington all kinds of unpleasant scandal. If you can do what I am about to ask, perhaps you could even earn yourself a place on the President's team.'

A place on the President's team? Gabrielle couldn't believe what she was hearing. 'Ms Tench, whatever you have in mind, I do not appreciate being blackmailed, coerced, or talked down to. I work for the senator's campaign because I believe in his politics. And if *this* is any indication of the way Zach Herney exerts political influence, I have no interest in being associated with him! If you've got something on Senator Sexton, then I suggest you leak it to the press. Frankly, I think this whole thing's a sham.'

Tench gave a dreary sigh. 'Gabrielle, your candidate's illegal funding is a fact. I'm sorry. I know you trust him.' She lowered her voice. 'Look, here's the point. The President and I will go public with the funding issue if we must, but it will get ugly on a grand scale. This scandal involves several major U.S. corporations breaking the law. A lot of innocent people will pay the price.' She took a long drag and exhaled. 'What the President and I are hoping for here . . . is some *other* way to discredit the senator's ethics. A way that is more contained . . . one in which no innocent parties get hurt.' Tench set down her cigarette and folded her hands. 'Simply put, we would like you to publicly admit that you had an affair with the senator.'

Gabrielle's entire body went rigid. Tench sounded utterly certain of herself. *Impossible*, Gabrielle knew. There was no proof. The sex had happened only once, behind locked doors in Sexton's senatorial office. *Tench has nothing. She's fishing.* Gabrielle fought to retain her steady tone. 'You assume a lot, Ms Tench.'

'Which? That you had an affair? Or that you would abandon your candidate?'

'Both.'

Tench gave a curt smile and stood up. 'Well, let's put one of those facts to rest right now, shall we?' She walked to her wall safe again and returned with a red manila folder. It was stamped with the White House seal. She unhooked the clasp, tipped the envelope over, and dumped the contents out on the desk in front of Gabrielle.

As dozens of color photographs spilled out onto the desk, Gabrielle saw her entire career come crashing down before her.

CHAPTER 46

Outside the habisphere, the katabatic wind roaring down off the glacier was nothing like the ocean winds Tolland was accustomed to. On the ocean, wind was a function of tides and pressure fronts and came in gusting ebbs and flows. The katabatic, however, was a slave to simple physics – heavy cold air rushing down a glacial incline like a tidal wave. It was the most resolute gale force Tolland had ever experienced. Had it been coming at twenty knots, the katabatic would have been a sailor's dream, but at its current eighty knots it could quickly become a nightmare even for those on solid ground. Tolland found that if he paused and leaned backward, the stalwart squall could easily prop him up.

Making the raging river of air even more unnerving to Tolland was the slight downwind grade of the ice shelf. The ice was sloped ever so slightly toward the ocean, two miles away. Despite the sharp spikes on the Pitbull Rapido crampons attached to his boots, Tolland had the uneasy feeling that any misstep might leave him caught up in a gale and sliding down the endless icy slope. Norah Mangor's two-minute course in glacier safety now seemed danger-ously inadequate.

Piranha Ice ax, Norah had said, fastening a lightweight T-shaped tool to each of their belts as they suited up in the habisphere. *Standard blade, banana blade, semitubular blade, hammer, and adze. All you need to remember is, if anyone slips or gets caught up in a gust, grab your ax with one hand on the head and one on the shaft, ram the banana blade into the ice, and fall on it, planting your crampons.*

With those words of assurance, Norah Mangor had affixed YAK belay harnesses to each of them, they all donned goggles, and headed out into the afternoon darkness.

Now, the four figures made their way down the glacier in a straight line with ten yards of belay rope separating each of them. Norah was in the lead position, followed by Corky, then Rachel, and Tolland as anchor.

As they moved farther away from the habisphere, Tolland felt a growing uneasiness. In his inflated suit, although warm, he felt like some kind of uncoordinated space traveler trekking across a distant planet. The moon had disappeared behind thick, billowing storm clouds, plunging the ice sheet into an impenetrable blackness. The katabatic wind seemed to be getting stronger by the minute, applying a constant pressure to Tolland's back. As his eyes strained through his goggles to make out the expansive emptiness around them, he began to perceive a true danger in this place. Redundant NASA safety precautions or not, Tolland was surprised the administrator had been willing to risk four lives out here instead of two. Especially when the additional two lives were that of a senator's daughter and a famous astrophysicist. Tolland was not surprised to feel a protective concern for Rachel and Corky. As someone who had captained a ship, he was used to feeling responsible for those around him.

'Stay behind me,' Norah shouted, her voice swallowed by the wind. 'Let the sled lead the way.'

The aluminum sled on which Norah was transporting her testing gear resembled an oversized Flexible Flyer. The craft was prepacked with diagnostic gear and safety accessories she'd been using on the glacier over the past few days. All of her gear – including a battery pack, safety flares, and a powerful front-mounted spotlight – was bound under a secured, plastic tarp. Despite the heavy load, the sled glided effortlessly on long, straight runners. Even on the almost imperceptible incline, the sled moved downhill on its own accord, and Norah applied a gentle restraint, almost as if allowing the sled to lead the way.

Sensing the distance growing between the group and the habisphere, Tolland looked over his shoulder. Only fifty yards away, the pale curvature of the dome had all but disappeared in the blustery blackness.

'You at all worried about finding our way back?' Tolland yelled. 'The habisphere is almost invisi—' His words were cut short by the loud hiss of a flare igniting in Norah's hand. The sudden red-white glow illuminated the ice shelf in a ten-yard radius all around them.

Norah used her heel to dig a small impression in the surface snow, piling up a protective ridge on the upwind side of the hole. Then she rammed the flare into the indentation.

'High-tech bread crumbs,' Norah shouted.

'Bread crumbs?' Rachel asked, shielding her eyes from the sudden light.

'Hansel and Gretel,' Norah shouted. 'These flares will last an hour – plenty of time to find our way back.'

With that, Norah headed out again, leading them down the glacier – into the darkness once again.

CHAPTER **47**

Gabrielle Ashe stormed out of Marjorie Tench's office and practically knocked over a secretary in doing so. Mortified, all Gabrielle could see were the photographs – images – arms and legs intertwined. Faces filled with ecstasy.

Gabrielle had no idea how the photos had been taken, but she knew damn well they were real. They had been taken in Senator Sexton's office and seemed to have been shot from above as if by hidden camera. *God help me.* One of the photos showed Gabrielle and Sexton having sex directly on top of the senator's desk, their bodies sprawled across a scatter of official-looking documents.

Marjorie Tench caught up with Gabrielle outside the Map Room. Tench was carrying the red envelope of photos. 'I assume from your reaction that you believe these photos are authentic?' The President's senior adviser actually looked like she was having a good time. 'I'm hoping they persuade you that our other data is accurate as well. They came from the same source.'

Gabrielle felt her entire body flushing as she marched down the hall. *Where the hell is the exit?*

Tench's gangly legs had no trouble keeping up. 'Senator Sexton swore to the world that you two are platonic associates. His televised statement was actually quite convincing.' Tench motioned smugly over her shoulder. 'In fact, I have a tape in my office if you'd like to refresh your memory?'

Gabrielle needed no refresher. She remembered the press conference all too well. Sexton's denial was as adamant as it was heartfelt.

'It's unfortunate,' Tench said, sounding not at all disappointed, 'but Senator Sexton looked the American people in the eye and told a bald-faced lie. The public has a right to know. And they *will* know. I'll see to it personally. The only question now is how the public finds out. We believe it's best coming from you.'

Gabrielle was stunned. 'You really think I'm going to help lynch my own candidate?'

Tench's face hardened. 'I am trying to take the high ground here, Gabrielle. I'm giving you a chance to save everyone a lot of embarrassment by holding your head high and telling the truth. All I need is a signed statement admitting your affair.'

Gabrielle stopped short. 'What?'

'Of course. A signed statement gives us the leverage we need to deal with the senator *quietly*, sparing the country this ugly mess. My offer is simple: sign a statement for me, and these photos never need to see the light of day.'

'You want a statement?'

'Technically, I would need an affidavit, but we have a notary here in the building who could—'

'You're crazy.' Gabrielle was walking again.

Tench stayed at her side, sounding more angry now. 'Senator Sexton is going down one way or another, Gabrielle, and I'm offering you a chance to get out of this without seeing your own naked ass in the morning paper! The President is a decent man and doesn't *want* these photos publicized. If you just give me an affidavit and confess to the affair on your own terms, then all of us can retain a little dignity.'

'I'm not for sale.'

'Well, your candidate certainly is. He's a dangerous man, and he's breaking the law.'

'*He's* breaking the law? You're the ones breaking into offices and taking illegal surveillance pictures! Ever heard of Watergate?'

'We had nothing to do with gathering this dirt. These photos came from the same source as the SFF campaign-funding information. Someone's been watching you two very closely.'

Gabrielle tore past the security desk where she had gotten her security badge. She ripped off the badge and tossed it to the wide-eyed guard. Tench was still on her tail.

'You'll need to decide fast, Ms Ashe,' Tench said as they neared the exit. 'Either bring me an affidavit admitting you slept with the senator, or at eight o'clock tonight, the President will be forced to go public with everything – Sexton's financial dealings, the photos of you, the works. And believe me, when the public sees that you stood idly by and let Sexton lie about your relationship, you'll go down in flames right beside him.'

Gabrielle saw the door and headed for it.

'On my desk by eight o'clock tonight, Gabrielle. Be smart.' Tench tossed her the folder of photographs on her way out. 'Keep them, sweetie. We've got plenty more.'

CHAPTER 48

Rachel Sexton felt a growing chill inside as she moved down the ice sheet into a deepening night. Disquieting images swirled in her mind – the meteorite, the phosphorescent plankton, the implications if Norah Mangor had made a mistake with the ice cores.

A solid matrix of freshwater ice, Norah had argued, reminding them all that she had drilled cores all around the area as well as directly over the meteorite. If the glacier contained saltwater interstices filled with plankton, she would have seen them. Wouldn't she? Nonetheless, Rachel's intuition kept returning to the simplest solution.

There are plankton frozen in this glacier.

Ten minutes and four flares later, Rachel and the others were approximately 250 yards from the habisphere. Without warning, Norah stopped short. 'This is the spot,' she said, sounding like a water-witch diviner who had mystically sensed the perfect spot to drill a well.

Rachel turned and glanced up the slope behind them. The habisphere had long since disappeared into the dim, moonlit night, but the line of flares was clearly visible, the farthest one twinkling reassuringly like a faint star. The flares were in a perfectly straight line, like a carefully calculated runway. Rachel was impressed with Norah's skills.

'Another reason we let the sled go first,' Norah called out when she saw Rachel admiring the line of flares. 'The runners are straight. If we let gravity lead the sled and we don't interfere, we're guaranteed to travel in a straight line.'

'Neat trick,' Tolland yelled. 'Wish there were something like that for the open sea.'

This IS the open sea, Rachel thought, picturing the ocean beneath them. For a split second, the most distant flame caught her attention. It had disappeared, as if the light had been blotted out by a passing form. A moment later, though, the light reappeared. Rachel felt a sudden uneasiness. 'Norah,' she yelled over the wind, 'did you say there were polar bears up here?'

The glaciologist was preparing a final flare and either did not hear or was ignoring her.

'Polar bears,' Tolland yelled, 'eat seals. They only attack humans when we invade their space.'

'But this *is* polar bear country, right?' Rachel could never remember which pole had bears and which had penguins.

'Yeah,' Tolland shouted back. 'Polar bears actually give the Arctic its name. *Arktos* is Greek for bear.'

Terrific. Rachel gazed nervously into the dark.

'Antarctica has *no* polar bears,' Tolland said. 'So they call it *Anti-arktos*.'

'Thanks, Mike,' Rachel yelled. 'Enough talk of polar bears.'

He laughed. 'Right. Sorry.'

Norah pressed a final flare into the snow. As before, the four of them were engulfed in a reddish glow, looking bloated in their black weather suits. Beyond the circle of light emanating from the flare, the rest of the world became totally invisible, a circular shroud of blackness engulfing them.

As Rachel and the others looked on, Norah planted her feet and used careful overhand motions to reel the sled several yards back up the slope to where they were standing. Then, keeping the rope taut, she crouched and manually activated the sled's talon brakes – four angled spikes that dug into the ice to keep the sled stationary. That done, she stood up and brushed herself off, the rope around her waist falling slack.

'All right,' Norah shouted. 'Time to go to work.'

The glaciologist circled to the downwind end of the sled and began unfastening the butterfly eyelets holding the protective canvas over the gear. Rachel, feeling like she had been a little hard on Norah, moved to help by unfastening the rear of the flap.

'Jesus, NO!' Norah yelled, her head snapping up. 'Don't *ever* do that!'

Rachel recoiled, confused.

'Never unfasten the upwind side!' Norah said. 'You'll create a wind sock! This sled would have taken off like an umbrella in a wind tunnel!'

Rachel backed off. 'I'm sorry. I . . .'

Norah glared. 'You and space boy shouldn't be out here.'

None of us should, Rachel thought.

Amateurs, Norah seethed, cursing the administrator's insistence on sending Corky and Sexton along. *These clowns are going to get someone killed out here.* The last thing Norah wanted right now was to play baby-sitter.

'Mike,' she said, 'I need help lifting the GPR off the sled.'

Tolland helped her unpack the Ground Penetrating Radar and position it on the ice. The instrument looked like three miniature snowplow blades that had been affixed in parallel to an aluminum frame. The entire device was no more than a yard long and was connected by cables to a current attenuator and a marine battery on the sled.

'That's radar?' Corky asked, yelling over the wind.

Norah nodded in silence. Ground Penetrating Radar was far more equipped to see brine ice than PODS was. The GPR transmitter sent pulses of electromagnetic energy through the ice, and the pulses bounced differently off substances of differing crystal structure. Pure freshwater froze in a flat, shingled lattice. However, seawater froze in more of a meshed or forked lattice on account of its sodium content, causing the GPR pulses to bounce back erratically, greatly diminishing the number of reflections.

Norah powered up the machine. 'I'll be taking a kind of echo-location cross-sectional image of the ice sheet around the extraction pit,' she yelled. 'The machine's internal software will render a cross section of the glacier and then print it out. Any sea ice will register as a shadow.'

'Printout?' Tolland looked surprised. 'You can *print* out here?'

Norah pointed to a cable from the GPR leading to a device still protected under the canopy. 'No choice but to print. Computer screens use too much valuable battery power, so field glaciologists print data to heat-transfer printers. Colors aren't brilliant, but laser toner clumps below neg twenty. Learned that the hard way in Alaska.'

Norah asked everyone to stand on the downhill side of the GPR as she prepared to align the transmitter such that it would scan the area of the meteorite hole, almost three football fields away. But as Norah looked back through the night in the general direction from which they had come, she couldn't see a damn thing. 'Mike, I need to align the GPR transmitter with the meteorite site, but this flare has me blinded. I'm going back up the slope just enough to get out of the light. I'll hold my arms in line with the flares, and you adjust the alignment on the GPR.'

Tolland nodded, kneeling down beside the radar device.

Norah stamped her crampons into the ice and leaned forward against the wind as she moved up the incline toward the habisphere. The katabatic today was much stronger than she'd imagined, and she sensed a storm coming in. It didn't matter. They would be done here in a matter of minutes. *They'll see I'm right*. Norah clomped twenty yards back toward the habisphere. She reached the edge of the darkness just as the belay rope went taut.

Norah looked back up the glacier. As her eyes adjusted to the dark, the line of flares slowly came into view several degrees to her left. She shifted her position until she was perfectly lined up with them. Then she held her arms out like a compass, turning her body, indicating the exact vector. 'I'm in line with them now!' she yelled.

Tolland adjusted the GPR device and waved. 'All set!'

Norah took a final look up the incline, grateful for the illuminated pathway home. As she looked out, though, something odd occurred. For an instant, one of the nearest flares entirely disappeared from view. Before Norah could worry that it was dying out, the flare reappeared. If Norah didn't know better, she would assume something had passed between the flare and her location. Certainly nobody else was out here . . . unless of course the administrator had started to feel guilty and sent a NASA team out after them. Somehow Norah doubted it. Probably nothing, she decided. A gust of wind had momentarily killed the flame.

Norah returned to the GPR. 'All lined up?'

Tolland shrugged. 'I think so.'

Norah went over to the control device on the sled and pressed a button. A sharp buzz emanated from the GPR and then stopped. 'Okay,' she said. 'Done.'

'That's it?' Corky said.

'All the work is in setup. The actual shot takes only a second.'

Onboard the sled, the heat-transfer printer had already begun to hum and click. The printer was enclosed in a clear plastic covering and was slowly ejecting a heavy, curled paper. Norah waited until the device had completed printing, and then she reached up under the plastic and removed the printout. *They'll see*, she thought, carrying the printout over to the flare so that everyone could see it. *There won't be any saltwater*.

Everyone gathered around as Norah stood over the flare, clutching the printout tightly in her gloves. She took a deep breath and uncurled the paper to examine the data. The image on the paper made her recoil in horror.

'Oh, God!' Norah stared, unable to believe what she was looking at. As expected, the printout revealed a clear cross section of the water-filled meteorite shaft. But what Norah had never expected to see was the hazy grayish outline of a humanoid form floating halfway down the shaft. Her blood turned to ice. 'Oh God . . . there's a body in the extraction pit.'

Everyone stared in stunned silence.

The ghostlike body was floating head down in the narrow shaft. Billowing around the corpse like some sort of cape was an eerie shroudlike aura. Norah now realized what the aura was. The GPR had captured a faint trace of the victim's heavy coat, what could only be a familiar, long, dense camel hair.

'It's . . . Ming,' she said in a whisper. 'He must have slipped . . .'

Norah Mangor never imagined that seeing Ming's body in the extraction pit would be the lesser of the two shocks the printout would reveal, but as her eyes traced downward in the shaft, she saw something else.

The ice beneath the extraction shaft . . .

Norah stared. Her first thought was that something had gone wrong with the scan. Then, as she studied the image more closely, an unsettling realization began to grow, like the storm gathering around them. The paper's edges flapped wildly in the wind as she turned and looked more intently at the printout.

But . . . that's impossible!

Suddenly, the truth came crashing down. The realization felt like it was going to bury her. She forgot all about Ming.

Norah now understood. *The saltwater in the shaft!* She fell to her knees in the snow beside the flare. She could barely breathe. Still clutching the paper in her hands, she began trembling.

My God . . . it didn't even occur to me.

Then, with a sudden eruption of rage, she spun her head in the direction of the NASA habisphere. 'You bastards!' she screamed, her voice trailing off in the wind. 'You goddamned *bastards!*'

In the darkness, only fifty yards away, Delta-One held his CrypTalk device to his mouth and spoke only two words to his controller. 'They know.'

CHAPTER 49

Norah Mangor was still kneeling on the ice when the bewildered Michael Tolland pulled the Ground Penetrating Radar's printout from her trembling hands. Shaken from seeing the floating body of Ming, Tolland tried to gather his thoughts and decipher the image before him.

He saw the cross section of the meteorite shaft descending from the surface down to 200 feet into the ice. He saw Ming's body floating in the shaft. Tolland's eyes drifted lower now, and he sensed something was amiss. Directly *beneath* the extraction shaft, a dark column of sea ice extended downward to the open ocean below. The vertical pillar of saltwater ice was massive – the same diameter as the shaft.

'My God!' Rachel yelled, looking over Tolland's shoulder. 'It looks like the meteorite shaft continues all the way *through* the ice shelf into the ocean!'

Tolland stood transfixed, his brain unable to accept what he knew to be the only logical explanation. Corky looked equally alarmed.

Norah shouted, 'Someone drilled up under the shelf!' Her eyes were wild with rage. 'Someone intentionally *inserted* that rock from underneath the ice!'

Although the idealist in Tolland wanted to reject Norah's words, the scientist in him knew she could easily be right. The Milne Ice Shelf was floating over the ocean with plenty of clearance for a submersible. Because everything weighed significantly less underwater, even a small submersible not much bigger than Tolland's one-man research Triton easily could have transported the meteorite in its payload arms. The sub could have approached from the ocean, submerged beneath the ice shelf, and drilled upward into the ice. Then, it could have used an extending payload arm or inflatable balloons to push the meteorite up into the shaft. Once the meteorite was in place, the ocean water that had risen into the shaft behind the meteorite would begin to freeze. As soon as the shaft closed enough to hold the meteorite in place, the sub could retract its arm and disappear, leaving Mother Nature to seal the remainder of the tunnel and erase all traces of the deception.

'But *why?*' Rachel demanded, taking the printout from Tolland and studying it. 'Why would someone do that? Are you sure your GPR is working?'

'Of course, I'm sure! And the printout perfectly explains the presence of phosphorescent bacteria in the water!'

Tolland had to admit, Norah's logic was chillingly sound. Phosphorescent dinoflagellates would have followed instinct and swum upward into the meteorite shaft, becoming trapped just beneath the meteorite and freezing into the ice. Later, when Norah heated the meteorite, the ice directly beneath would have melted, releasing the plankton. Again, they would swim upward, this time reaching the surface inside the habisphere, where they would eventually die for lack of saltwater.

'This is crazy!' Corky yelled. 'NASA has a meteorite with extraterrestrial fossils in it. Why would they care *where* it's found? Why would they go to the trouble to bury it under an ice shelf?'

'Who the hell knows,' Norah fired back, 'but GPR printouts don't lie. We were tricked. That meteorite isn't part of the Jungersol Fall. It was inserted in the ice *recently*. Within the last year, or the plankton would be dead!' She was already packing up her GPR gear on the sled and fastening it down. 'We've got to get back and tell someone! The President is about to go public with all the wrong data! NASA tricked him!'

'Wait a minute!' Rachel yelled. 'We should at least run another scan to make sure. None of this makes sense. Who will believe it?'

'Everyone,' Norah said, preparing her sled. 'When I march into the habisphere and drill another core sample out of the bottom of the meteorite shaft and it comes up as saltwater ice, I guarantee you *everyone* will believe this!'

Norah disengaged the brakes on the equipment sled, redirected it toward the habisphere, and started back up the slope, digging her crampons into the ice and pulling the sled behind her with surprising ease. She was a woman on a mission.

'Let's go!' Norah shouted, pulling the tethered group along as she headed toward the perimeter of the illuminated circle. 'I don't know what NASA's up to here, but I sure as hell don't appreciate being used as a pawn for their—'

Norah Mangor's neck snapped back as if she'd been rammed in the forehead by some invisible force. She let out a guttural gasp of pain, wavered, and collapsed backward onto the ice. Almost instantly, Corky let out a cry and spun around as if his shoulder had been propelled backward. He fell to the ice, writhing in pain.

Rachel immediately forgot all about the printout in her hand, Ming, the meteorite, and the bizarre tunnel beneath the ice. She had just felt a small projectile graze her ear, barely missing her temple. Instinctively, she dropped to her knees, yanking Tolland down with her.

'What's going on?' Tolland screamed.

A hailstorm was all Rachel could imagine – balls of ice blowing down off the glacier – and yet from the force with which Corky and Norah had just been hit, Rachel knew the hailstones would have to be moving at hundreds of miles an hour. Eerily, the sudden barrage of marble-sized objects seemed now to focus on Rachel and Tolland, pelting all around them, sending up plumes of exploding ice. Rachel rolled onto her stomach, dug her crampon's toe spikes into the ice, and launched toward the only cover available. The sled. Tolland arrived a moment later, scrambling and hunkering down beside her.

Tolland looked out at Norah and Corky unprotected on the ice. 'Pull them in with the tether!' he yelled, grabbing the rope and trying to pull.

But the tether was wrapped around the sled.

Rachel stuffed the printout in the Velcro pocket of her Mark IX suit, and scrambled on all fours toward the sled, trying to untangle the rope from the sled runners. Tolland was right behind her.

The hailstones suddenly rained down in a barrage against the sled, as if Mother Nature had abandoned Corky and Norah and was taking direct aim at Rachel and Tolland. One of the projectiles slammed into the top of the sled tarp, partially embedding itself, and then bounced over, landing on the sleeve of Rachel's coat.

When Rachel saw it, she froze. In an instant, the bewilderment she had been feeling turned to terror. These 'hailstones' were man-made. The ball of ice on her sleeve was a flawlessly shaped spheroid the size of a large cherry. The surface was polished and smooth, marred only by a linear seam around the circumference, like an old-fashioned lead musket ball, machined in a press. The globular pellets were, without a doubt, man-made.

Ice bullets . . .

As someone with military clearance, Rachel was well acquainted with the new experimental 'IM' weaponry – Improvised Munitions – snow rifles that compacted snow into ice pellets, desert rifles that melted sand into glass projectiles, water-based firearms that shot pulses of liquid water with such force that they could break bones. Improvised Munitions weaponry had an enormous advantage over conventional weapons because IM weapons used available resources and literally manufactured munitions on the spot, providing soldiers unlimited rounds without their having to carry heavy conventional bullets. The ice balls being fired at them now, Rachel knew, were being compressed 'on demand' from snow fed into the butt of the rifle.

As was often the case in the intelligence world, the more one knew, the more frightening a scenario became. This moment was no exception. Rachel would have preferred blissful ignorance, but her knowledge of IM weaponry instantly led her to a sole chilling conclusion: they were being attacked by some kind of U.S. Special Ops force, the only forces in the country currently cleared to use these experimental IM weapons in the field.

The presence of a military covert operations unit brought with it a second, even more terrifying realization: the probability of surviving this attack was close to zero.

The morbid thought was terminated as one of the ice pellets found an opening and came screaming through the wall of gear on the sled, colliding with her stomach. Even in her padded Mark IX suit, Rachel felt like an invisible prizefighter had just gut-punched her. Stars began to dance around the periphery of her vision, and she teetered backward, grabbing gear on the sled for balance. Michael Tolland dropped Norah's tether and lunged to support Rachel, but he arrived too late. Rachel fell backward, pulling a pile of equipment with her. She and Tolland tumbled to the ice in a pile of electronic apparatus.

'They're . . . bullets . . .' she gasped, the air momentarily crushed from her lungs. 'Run!'

CHAPTER **50**

The Washington MetroRail subway now leaving Federal Triangle station could not speed away from the White House fast enough for Gabrielle Ashe. She sat rigid in a deserted corner of the train as darkened shapes tore past outside in a blur. Marjorie Tench's big red envelope lay in Gabrielle's lap, pressing down like a ten-ton weight.

I've got to talk to Sexton! she thought, the train accelerating now in the direction of Sexton's office building. *Immediately!*

Now, in the dim, shifting light of the train, Gabrielle felt like she was enduring some kind of hallucinogenic drug trip. Muted lights whipped by overhead like slow-motion discotheque strobes. The ponderous tunnel rose on all sides like a deepening canyon.

Tell me this is not happening.

She gazed down at the envelope on her lap. Unclasping the flap, she reached inside and pulled out one of the photos. The internal lights of the train flickered for a moment, the harsh glare illuminating a shocking image – Sedgewick Sexton lying naked in his office, his gratified face turned perfectly toward the camera while Gabrielle's dark form lay nude beside him.

She shivered, rammed the photo back inside, and fumbled to reclasp the envelope.

It's over.

As soon as the train exited the tunnel and climbed onto the above-ground tracks near L'Enfant Plaza, Gabrielle dug out her cellphone and called the senator's private cellular number. His voice mail answered. Puzzled, she phoned the senator's office. The secretary answered.

'It's Gabrielle. Is he in?'

The secretary sounded peeved. 'Where have you been? He was looking for you.'

'I had a meeting that ran long. I need to talk to him right away.'

'You'll have to wait till morning. He's at Westbrooke.'

Westbrooke Place Luxury Apartments was the building where Sexton kept his D.C. residence. 'He's not picking up his private line,' Gabrielle said.

'He blocked off tonight as a P.E.,' the secretary reminded. 'He left early.'

Gabrielle scowled. *Personal Event.* In all the excitement, she'd forgotten Sexton had scheduled himself a night alone at home. He was very particular about not being disturbed during his P.E. blocks. *Bang on my door only if the building is on fire*, he would say. *Other than that, it can wait until morning.* Gabrielle decided Sexton's building was definitely on fire. 'I need you to reach him for me.'

'Impossible.'

'This is serious, I really—'

'No, I mean *literally* impossible. He left his pager on my desk on his way out and told me he was not to be disturbed all night. He was adamant.' She paused. 'More so than usual.'

Shit. 'Okay, thanks.' Gabrielle hung up.

'*L'Enfant Plaza,*' a recording announced in the subway car. '*Connection all stations.*'

Closing her eyes, Gabrielle tried to clear her mind, but devastating images rushed in . . . the lurid photos of herself and the senator . . . the pile of documents alleging Sexton was taking bribes. Gabrielle could still hear Tench's raspy demands. *Do the right thing. Sign the affidavit. Admit the affair.*

As the train screeched into the station, Gabrielle forced herself to imagine what the senator would do if the photos hit the presses. The first thing to pop in her mind both shocked and shamed her.

Sexton would lie.

Was this truly her first instinct regarding her candidate?

Yes. He would lie . . . brilliantly.

If these photos hit the media without Gabrielle's having admitted the affair, the senator would simply claim the photos were a cruel forgery. This was the age of digital photo editing; anyone who had ever been on-line had seen the flawlessly retouched spoof photographs of celebrities' heads digitally melded onto other people's bodies, often those of porn stars engaged in lewd acts. Gabrielle had already witnessed the senator's ability to look into a television camera and lie convincingly about their affair; she had no doubt he could persuade the world these photos were a lame attempt to derail his career. Sexton would lash out with indignant outrage, perhaps even insinuate that the President himself had ordered the forgery.

No wonder the White House hasn't gone public. The photos, Gabrielle realized, could backfire just like the initial drudge. As vivid as the pictures seemed, they were totally inconclusive.

Gabrielle felt a sudden surge of hope.

The White House can't prove any of this is real!

Tench's powerplay on Gabrielle had been ruthless in its simplicity: admit your affair or watch Sexton go to jail. Suddenly it made perfect sense. The White House *needed* Gabrielle to admit the affair, or the photos were worthless. A sudden glimmer of confidence brightened her mood.

As the train sat idling and the doors slid open, another distant door seemed to open in Gabrielle's mind, revealing an abrupt and heartening possibility.

Maybe everything Tench told me about the bribery was a lie.

After all, what had Gabrielle really seen? Yet again, nothing conclusive – some Xeroxed bank documents, a grainy photo of Sexton in a garage. All of it potentially counterfeit. Tench cunningly could have showed Gabrielle bogus financial records in the same sitting as the genuine sex photos, hoping Gabrielle would accept the *entire* package as true. It was called 'authentication by association,' and politicians used it all the time to sell dubious concepts.

Sexton is innocent, Gabrielle told herself. The White House was desperate, and they had decided to take a wild gamble on scaring Gabrielle into going public about the affair. They needed Gabrielle to desert Sexton publicly – scandalously. *Get out while you can*, Tench had told her. *You have until eight o'clock tonight.* The ultimate pressure sales job. *All of it fits*, she thought.

Except one thing . . .

The only confusing piece of the puzzle was that Tench had been sending Gabrielle anti-NASA e-mails. This certainly suggested NASA really *did* want Sexton to solidify his anti-NASA stance so they could use it against him. Or did it? Gabrielle realized that even the e-mails had a perfectly logical explanation.

What if the e-mails were not really from Tench?

It was possible Tench caught a traitor on staff sending Gabrielle data, fired that person, and then stepped in and e-mailed the final message herself, calling Gabrielle in for a meeting. *Tench could have pretended she leaked all the NASA data on purpose – to set Gabrielle up.*

The subway hydraulics hissed now in L'Enfant Plaza, the doors preparing to close.

Gabrielle stared out at the platform, her mind racing. She had no idea if her suspicions were making any sense or if they were just wishful thinking, but whatever the hell was going on, she knew she had to talk to the senator right away – P.E. night or not.

Clutching the envelope of photographs, Gabrielle hurried off the train just as the doors hissed shut. She had a new destination.

Westbrooke Place Apartments.

CHAPTER **51**

Fight or flight.

As a biologist, Tolland knew that vast physiological changes occurred when an organism sensed danger. Adrenaline flooded the cerebral cortex, jolting the heart rate and commanding the brain to make the oldest and most intuitive of all biological decisions – whether to do battle or flee.

Tolland's instinct told him to flee, and yet reason reminded him he was still tethered to Norah Mangor. There was nowhere to flee anyway. The only cover for miles was the habisphere, and the attackers, whoever the hell they were, had positioned themselves high on the glacier and cut off that option. Behind him, the wide open sheet of ice fanned out into a two-mile-long plain that terminated in a sheer drop to a frigid sea. Flight in that direction meant death by exposure. The practical barriers to fleeing notwithstanding, Tolland knew he could not possibly leave the others. Norah and Corky were still out in the open, tethered to Rachel and Tolland.

Tolland stayed down near Rachel as the ice pellets continued to slam into the side of the toppled equipment sled. He pillaged the strewn contents, searching for a weapon, a flare gun, a radio . . . anything.

'Run!' Rachel yelled, her breathing still strained.

Then, oddly, the hailstorm of ice bullets abruptly stopped. Even in the pounding wind, the night felt suddenly calm . . . as if a storm had let up unexpectedly.

It was then, peering cautiously around the sled, that Tolland witnessed one of the most chilling sights he had ever seen.

Gliding effortlessly out of the darkened perimeter into the light, three ghostly figures emerged, coasting silently in on skis. The figures wore full white weather suits. They carried no ski poles but rather large rifles that looked like no guns Tolland had ever seen. Their skis were bizarre as well, futuristic and short, more like elongated Rollerblades than skis.

Calmly, as if knowing they had already won this battle, the figures coasted to a stop beside their closest victim – the unconscious Norah Mangor. Tolland rose shakily to his knees and peered over the sled at the attackers. The visitors stared back at him through eerie electronic goggles. They were apparently uninterested.

At least for the moment.

Delta-One felt no remorse as he stared down at the woman lying unconscious on the ice before him. He had been trained to carry out orders, not to question motives.

The woman was wearing a thick, black, thermal suit and had a welt on the side of her face. Her breathing was short and labored. One of the IM ice rifles had found its mark and knocked her unconscious.

Now it was time to finish the job.

As Delta-One knelt down beside the oblivious woman, his team-mates trained their rifles on the other targets – one on the small, unconscious man lying on the ice nearby, and one on the overturned sled where the two other victims were hiding. Although his men easily could have moved in to finish the job, the remaining three victims were unarmed and had nowhere to run. Rushing to finish them all off at once was careless. *Never disperse your focus unless absolutely necessary. Face one adversary at a time.* Exactly as they had been trained, the Delta Force would kill these people one at a time. The magic, however, was that they would leave no trace to suggest how they had died.

Crouched beside the unconscious woman, Delta-One removed his thermal gloves and scooped up a handful of snow. Packing the snow, he opened the woman's mouth and began stuffing it down her throat. He filled her entire mouth, ramming the snow as deep as he could down her windpipe. She would be dead within three minutes.

This technique, invented by the Russian mafia, was called the *byelaya smert* – white death. This victim would suffocate long before the snow in her throat melted. Once dead, however, her body would stay warm long enough to dissolve the blockage. Even if foul play were suspected, no murder weapon or evidence of violence would be apparent immediately. Eventually someone might figure it out, but it would buy them time. The ice bullets would fade into the environ-ment, buried in the snow, and the welt on this woman's head would look like she'd taken a nasty spill on the ice – not surprising in these gale force winds.

The other three people would be incapacitated and killed in much the same way. Then Delta-One would load all of them on the sled, drag them several hundred yards off course, reattach their belay lines and arrange the bodies. Hours from now, the four of them would be found frozen in the snow, apparent victims of over-exposure and hypothermia. Those who discovered them would be puzzled what they were doing off course, but nobody would be surprised that they were dead. After all, their flares had burned out, the weather was perilous, and getting lost on the Milne Ice Shelf could bring death in a hurry.

Delta-One had now finished packing snow down the woman's throat. Before turning his attention to the others, Delta-One unhooked the woman's belay harness. He could reconnect it later, but at the moment, he did not want the two people behind the sled getting ideas about pulling his victim to safety.

Michael Tolland had just witnessed a murderous act more bizarre than his darkest mind could imagine. Having cut Norah Mangor free, the three attackers were turning their attention to Corky.

I've got to do something!

Corky had come to and was moaning, trying to sit up, but one of the soldiers pushed him back down on his back, straddled him, and pinned Corky's arms to the ice by kneeling on them. Corky let out a cry of pain that was instantly swallowed up by the raging wind.

In a kind of demented terror, Tolland tore through the scattered contents of the overturned sled. *There must be something here! A weapon! Something!* All he saw was diagnostic ice gear, most of it smashed beyond recognition by the ice pellets. Beside him, Rachel groggily tried to sit up, using her ice ax to prop herself up. 'Run . . . Mike . . .'

Tolland eyed the ax that was strapped to Rachel's wrist. It could be a weapon. Sort of. Tolland wondered what his chances were attacking three armed men with a tiny ax.

Suicide.

As Rachel rolled and sat up, Tolland spied something behind her. A bulky vinyl bag. Praying against fate that it contained a flare gun or radio, he clambered past her and grabbed the bag. Inside he found a large, neatly folded sheet of Mylar fabric. Worthless. Tolland had something similar on his research ship. It was a small weather balloon, designed to carry payloads of observational weather gear not much heavier than a personal computer. Norah's balloon would be no help here, particularly without a helium tank.

With the growing sounds of Corky's struggle, Tolland felt a helpless sensation he had not felt in years. Total despair. Total loss. Like the cliché of one's life passing before one's eyes before death, Tolland's mind flashed unexpectedly through long forgotten childhood images. For an instant he was sailing in San Pedro, learning the age-old sailor's pastime of spinnaker-flying – hanging on a knotted rope, suspended over the ocean, plunging laughing into the water, rising and falling like a kid hanging on a belfry rope, his fate determined by a billowing spinnaker sail and the whim of the ocean breeze.

Tolland's eyes instantly snapped back to the Mylar balloon in his hand, realizing that his mind had not been surrendering, but rather it had been trying to remind him of a solution! *Spinnaker-flying.*

Corky was still struggling against his captor as Tolland yanked open the protective bag around the balloon. Tolland had no illusions that this plan was anything other than a long shot, but he knew remaining here was certain death for all of them. He clutched the folded mass of Mylar. The payload clip warned: CAUTION: NOT FOR USE IN WINDS OVER 10 KNOTS.

The hell with that! Gripping it hard to keep it from unfurling, Tolland clambered over to Rachel, who was propped on her side. He could see the confusion in her eyes as he nestled close, yelling, 'Hold this!'

Tolland handed Rachel the folded pad of fabric and then used his free hands to slip the balloon's payload clasp through one of the carabiners on his harness. Then, rolling on his side, he slipped the clasp through one of Rachel's carabiners as well.

Tolland and Rachel were now one.

Joined at the hip.

From between them, the loose tether trailed off across the snow to the struggling Corky . . . and ten yards farther to the empty clip beside Norah Mangor.

Norah is already gone, Tolland told himself. *Nothing you can do.*

The attackers were crouched over Corky's writhing body now, packing a handful of snow, and preparing to stuff it down Corky's throat. Tolland knew they were almost out of time.

Tolland grabbed the folded balloon from Rachel. The fabric was as light as tissue paper – and virtually indestructible. *Here goes nothing.* 'Hold on!'

'Mike?' Rachel said. 'What—'

Tolland hurled the pad of wadded Mylar into the air over their heads. The howling wind snatched it up and spread it out like a parachute in a hurricane. The sheath filled instantly, billowing open with a loud snap.

Tolland felt a wrenching yank on his harness, and he knew in an instant he had grossly underestimated the power of the katabatic wind. Within a fraction of a second, he and Rachel were half airborne, being dragged down the glacier. A moment later, Tolland felt a jerk as his tether drew taut on Corky Marlinson. Twenty yards back, his terrified friend was yanked out from under his stunned attackers, sending one of them tumbling backward. Corky let out a blood-curdling scream as he too accelerated across the ice, barely missing the overturned sled, then fishtailing inward. A second rope trailed limp beside Corky . . . the rope that had been connected to Norah Mangor.

Nothing you can do, Tolland told himself.

Like a tangled mass of human marionettes, the three bodies skimmed down the glacier. Ice pellets went sailing by, but Tolland knew the attackers had missed their chance. Behind him, the white-clad soldiers faded away, shrinking to illuminated specks in the glow of the flares.

Tolland now felt the ice ripping beneath his padded suit with relentless acceleration, and the relief at having escaped faded fast. Less than two miles directly ahead of them, the Milne Ice Shelf came to an abrupt end at a precipitous cliff – and beyond it . . . a 100-foot drop to the lethal pounding surf of the Arctic Ocean.

CHAPTER **52**

Marjorie Tench was smiling as she made her way downstairs toward the White House Communications Office, the computerized broadcast facility that disseminated press releases formulated upstairs in the Communications Bullpen. The meeting with Gabrielle Ashe had gone well. Whether or not Gabrielle was scared enough to turn over an affidavit admitting the affair was uncertain, but it sure as hell was worth a try.

Gabrielle would be smart to bail out on him, Tench thought. The poor girl had no idea just how hard Sexton was about to fall.

In a few hours, the President's meteoric press conference was going to cut Sexton down at the knees. That was in the bank. Gabrielle Ashe, if she cooperated, would be the death blow that sent Sexton crawling off in shame. In the morning, Tench could release Gabrielle's affidavit to the press along with footage of Sexton denying it.

One-two punch.

After all, politics was not just about winning the election, it was about winning decisively – having the momentum to carry out one's vision. Historically, any president who squeaked into office on a narrow margin accomplished much less; he was weakened right out of the gate, and Congress never seemed to let him forget it.

Ideally, the destruction of Senator Sexton's campaign would be comprehensive – a two-pronged attack sacking *both* his politics and his ethics. This strategy, known in Washington as the 'high-low,' was stolen from the art of military warfare. *Force the enemy to battle on two fronts*. When a candidate possessed a piece of negative information about his opponent, he often waited until he had a second piece and went public with both simultaneously. A double-edged attack was always more effective than a single shot, particularly when the dual attack incorporated separate aspects of his campaign – the first against his politics, the second against his character. Rebuttal of a *political* attack took logic, while rebuttal of a *character* attack took passion; disputing both simultaneously was an almost impossible balancing act.

Tonight, Senator Sexton would find himself scrambling to extract himself from the political nightmare of an astounding NASA triumph, and yet his plight would deepen considerably if he were forced to defend his NASA position while being called a liar by a prominent female member of his staff.

Arriving now at the doorway of the Communications Office, Tench felt alive with the thrill of the fight. Politics was war. She took a deep breath and checked her watch. 6:15 P.M. The first shot was about to be fired.

She entered.

The Communications Office was small not for lack of room, but for lack of necessity. It was one of the most efficient mass communications stations in the world and employed a staff of only five people. At the moment, all five employees stood over their banks of electronic gear looking like swimmers poised for the starting gun.

They are ready, Tench saw in their eager gazes.

It always amazed her that this tiny office, given only two hours' head start, could contact more than *one third* of the world's civilized population. With electronic connections to literally tens of thousands of global news sources – from the largest television conglomerates to the smallest home-town newspapers – the White House Communications Office could, at the touch of a few buttons, reach out and touch the world.

Fax-broadcast computers churned press releases into the in-boxes of radio, television, print, and Internet media outlets from Maine to Moscow. Bulk e-mail programs blanketed on-line news wires. Telephone autodialers phoned thousands of media content managers and played recorded voice announcements. A breaking news web page provided constant updates and preformatted content. The 'live-feed-capable' news sources – CNN, NBC, ABC, CBS, foreign syndicates – would be assaulted from all angles and promised free, live television feeds. Whatever else these networks were airing would come to a screeching halt for an emergency presidential address.

Full penetration.

Like a general inspecting her troops, Tench strode in silence over to the copy desk and picked up the printout of the 'flash release' that now sat loaded in all the transmission machines like cartridges in a shotgun.

When Tench read it, she had to laugh quietly to herself. By usual standards, the release loaded for broadcast was heavy-handed – more of an advertisement than an announcement – but the President had ordered the Communications Office to pull out all the stops. And that they had. This text was perfect – keyword-rich and content light. A deadly combination. Even the news wires that used automated 'keyword-sniffer' programs to sort their incoming mail would see multiple flags on this one:

From: White House Communications Office
Subject: Urgent Presidential Address

The *President of the United States* will be holding an *urgent* press conference tonight at 8:00 P.M. Eastern Standard Time from the White House briefing room. The topic of his announcement is currently *classified*. Live A/V feeds will be available via customary outlets.

Laying the paper back down on the desk, Marjorie Tench looked around the Communications Office and gave the staff an impressed nod. They looked eager.

Lighting a cigarette, she puffed a moment, letting the anticipation build. Finally, she grinned. 'Ladies and gentlemen. Start your engines.'

CHAPTER 53

All logical reasoning had evaporated from Rachel Sexton's mind. She held no thoughts for the meteorite, the mysterious GPR printout in her pocket, Ming, the horrific attack on the ice sheet. There was one matter at hand.

Survival.

The ice skimmed by in a blur beneath her like an endless, sleek highway. Whether her body was numb with fear or simply cocooned by her protective suit, Rachel did not know, but she felt no pain. She felt nothing.

Yet.

Lying on her side, attached to Tolland at the waist, Rachel lay face-to-face with him in an awkward embrace. Somewhere ahead of them, the balloon billowed, fat with wind, like a parachute on the back of a dragster. Corky trailed behind, swerving wildly like a tractor trailer out of control. The flare marking the spot where they had been attacked had all but disappeared in the distance.

The hissing of their nylon Mark IX suits on the ice grew higher and higher in pitch as they continued to accelerate. She had no idea how fast they were going now, but the wind was at least sixty miles an hour, and the frictionless runway beneath them seemed to be racing by faster and faster with every passing second. The impervious Mylar balloon apparently had no intentions of tearing or relinquishing its hold.

We need to release, she thought. They were racing away from one deadly force – directly toward another. *The ocean is probably less than a mile ahead now!* The thought of icy water brought back terrifying memories.

The wind gusted harder, and their speed increased. Somewhere behind them Corky let out a scream of terror. At this speed, Rachel knew they had only a few minutes before they were dragged out over the cliff into the frigid ocean.

Tolland was apparently having similar thoughts because he was now fighting with the payload clasp attached to their bodies.

'I can't unhook us!' he yelled. 'There's too much tension!'

Rachel hoped a momentary lull in the wind might give Tolland some slack, but the katabatic pulled on with relentless uniformity. Trying to help, Rachel twisted her body and rammed the toe cleat of one of her crampons into the ice, sending a rooster tail of ice shards into the air. Their velocity slowed ever so slightly.

'Now!' she yelled, lifting her foot.

For an instant the payload line on the balloon slackened slightly. Tolland yanked down, trying to take advantage of the loose line to maneuver the payload clip out of their carabiners. Not even close.

'Again!' he yelled.

This time they both twisted against one another and rammed their toe prongs into the ice, sending a double plume of ice into the air. This slowed the contraption more perceptibly.

'Now!'

On Tolland's cue, they both let up. As the balloon surged forward again, Tolland rammed his thumb into the carabiner latch and twisted the hook, trying to release the clasp. Although closer this time, he still needed more slack. The carabiners, Norah had bragged, were first-rate, Joker safety clips, specifically crafted with an extra loop in the metal so they would never release if there were any tension on them at all.

Killed by safety clips, Rachel thought, not finding the irony the least bit amusing.

'One more time!' Tolland yelled.

Mustering all her energy and hope, Rachel twisted as far as she could and rammed both of her toes into the ice. Arching her back, she tried to lift all her weight onto her toes. Tolland followed her lead until they were both angled roughly on their stomachs, the connection at their belts straining their harnesses. Tolland rammed his toes down and Rachel arched farther. The vibrations sent shock waves up her legs. She felt like her ankles were going to break.

'Hold it . . . hold it . . .' Tolland contorted himself to release the Joker clip as their speed decreased. 'Almost . . .'

Rachel's crampons snapped. The metal cleats tore off of her boots and went tumbling backward into the night, bouncing over Corky. The balloon immediately lurched forward, sending Rachel and Tolland fishtailing to one side. Tolland lost his grasp on the clip.

'Shit!'

The Mylar balloon, as if angered at having been momentarily restrained, lurched forward now, pulling even harder, dragging them down the glacier toward the sea. Rachel knew they were closing fast on the cliff, although they faced danger even before the hundred-foot drop into the Arctic Ocean. Three huge snow berms stood in their path. Even protected by the padding in the Mark IX suits, the experience of launching at high speed up and over the snow mounds filled her with terror.

Fighting in desperation with their harnesses, Rachel tried to find a way to release the balloon. It was then that she heard the rhythmic ticking on the ice – the rapid-fire staccato of lightweight metal on the sheet of bare ice. The ax.

In her fear, she had entirely forgotten the ice ax attached to the rip cord on her belt. The lightweight aluminum tool was bouncing along beside her leg. She looked up at the payload cable on the balloon. Thick, heavy-duty braided nylon. Reaching down, she fumbled for the bouncing ax. She grasped the handle and pulled it toward her, stretching the elastic rip cord. Still on her side, Rachel struggled to raise her arms over her head, placing the ax's serrated edge against the thick cord. Awkwardly, she began sawing the taut cable.

'Yes!' Tolland yelled, fumbling now for his own ax.

Sliding on her side, Rachel was stretched out, her arms above her, sawing at the taut cable. The line was strong, and the individual nylon strands were fraying slowly. Tolland gripped his own ax, twisted, raised his arms over his head, and tried to saw from underneath in the same spot. Their banana blades clicked together as they worked in tandem like lumberjacks. The rope began fraying on both sides now.

We're going to do it, Rachel thought. *This thing is going to break!*

Suddenly, the silver bubble of Mylar before them swooped upward as if it had hit an updraft. Rachel realized to her horror that it was simply following the contour of the land.

They had arrived.

The berms.

The wall of white loomed only an instant before they were on it. The blow to Rachel's side as they hit the incline drove the wind from her lungs and wrenched the ax from her hand. Like a tangled water-skier being dragged up over a jump, Rachel felt her body dragged up the face of the berm and launched. She and Tolland were suddenly catapulted in a dizzying upward snarl. The trough between the berms spread out far beneath them, but the frayed payload cable held fast, lifting their accelerated bodies upward, carrying them clear out over the first trough. For an instant, she glimpsed what lay ahead. Two more berms – a short plateau – and then the drop-off to the sea.

As if to give a voice to Rachel's own dumbstruck terror, the high-pitched scream of Corky Marlinson cut through the air. Somewhere behind them, he sailed up over the first berm. All three of them went airborne, the balloon clawing upward like a wild animal trying to break its captor's chains.

Suddenly, like a gunshot in the night, a snap echoed overhead. The frayed rope gave way, and the tattered end recoiled in Rachel's face. Instantly, they were falling. Somewhere overhead the Mylar balloon billowed out of control . . . spiraling out to sea.

Tangled in carabiners and harnesses, Rachel and Tolland tumbled back toward earth. As the white mound of the second berm rose up toward them, Rachel braced for impact. Barely clearing the top of the second berm, they crashed down the far side, the blow partially cushioned by their suits and the descending contour of the berm. As the world around her turned into a blur of arms and legs and ice, Rachel felt herself rocketing down the incline out onto the central ice trough. Instinctively she spread her arms and legs, trying to slow down before they hit the next berm. She felt them slowing, but only slightly, and it seemed only seconds before she and Tolland were sliding back up an incline. At the top, there was another instant of weightlessness as they cleared the crest. Then, filled with terror, Rachel felt them begin their dead slide down the other side and out onto the final plateau . . . the last eighty feet of the Milne Glacier.

As they skidded toward the cliff, Rachel could feel the drag of Corky on the tether, and she knew they were all slowing down. She knew it was too little too late. The end of the glacier raced toward them, and Rachel let out a helpless scream.

Then it happened.

The edge of the ice slid out from underneath them. The last thing Rachel remembered was falling.

CHAPTER 54

The Westbrooke Place Apartments are located at 2201 N Street NW and promote themselves as one of the few unquestionably correct addresses in Washington. Gabrielle hurried through the gilded revolving door into the marble lobby, where a deafening waterfall reverberated.

The doorman at the front desk looked surprised to see her. 'Ms Ashe? I didn't know you were stopping by tonight.'

'I'm running late.' Gabrielle quickly signed in. The clock overhead read 6:22 P.M.

The doorman scratched his head. 'The senator gave me a list, but you weren't—'

'They always forget the people who help them most.' She gave a harried smile and strode past him toward the elevator.

Now the doorman looked uneasy. 'I better call up.'

'Thanks,' Gabrielle said, as she boarded the elevator and headed up. *The senator's phone is off the hook.*

Riding the elevator to the ninth floor, Gabrielle exited and made her way down the elegant hallway. At the end, outside Sexton's doorway, she could see one of his bulky personal safety escorts – glorified bodyguards – sitting in the hall. He looked bored. Gabrielle was surprised to see security on duty, although apparently not as surprised as the guard was to see her. He jumped to his feet as she approached.

'I know,' Gabrielle called out, still halfway down the hall. 'It's a P.E. night. He doesn't want to be disturbed.'

The guard nodded emphatically. 'He gave me very strict orders that no visitors—'

'It's an emergency.'

The guard physically blocked the doorway. 'He's in a private meeting.'

'Really?' Gabrielle pulled the red envelope from under her arm. She flashed the White House seal in the man's face. 'I was just in the Oval Office. I need to give the senator this information. Whatever old pals he's schmoozing tonight are going to have to do without him for a few minutes. Now, let me in.'

The guard withered slightly at the sight of the White House seal on the envelope.

Don't make me open this, Gabrielle thought.

'Leave the folder,' he said. 'I'll take it in to him.'

'The hell you will. I have direct orders from the White House to hand-deliver this. If I don't talk to him immediately, we can all start looking for jobs tomorrow morning. Do you understand?'

The guard looked deeply conflicted, and Gabrielle sensed the senator had indeed been unusually adamant tonight about having no visitors. She moved in for the kill. Holding the White House envelope directly in his face, Gabrielle lowered her voice to a whisper and uttered the six words all Washington security personnel feared most.

'You do *not* understand the situation.'

Security personnel for politicians *never* understood the situation, and they hated that fact. They were hired guns, kept in the dark, never sure whether to stand firm in their orders or risk losing their jobs by mule-headedly ignoring some obvious crisis.

The guard swallowed hard, eyeing the White House envelope again. 'Okay, but I'm telling the senator you *demanded* to be let in.'

He unlocked the door, and Gabrielle pushed past him before he changed his mind. She entered the apartment and quietly closed the door behind her, relocking it.

Now inside the foyer, Gabrielle, could hear muffled voices in Sexton's den down the hall – men's voices. Tonight's P.E. was obviously not the private meeting implied by Sexton's earlier call.

As Gabrielle moved down the hall toward the den, she passed an open closet where a half dozen expensive men's coats hung inside – distinctive wool and tweed. Several briefcases sat on the floor. Apparently work stayed in the hall tonight. Gabrielle would have walked right past the cases except that one of the briefcases caught her eye. The nameplate bore a distinctive company logo. A bright red rocket.

She paused, kneeling down to read it:

SPACE AMERICA, INC.

Puzzled, she examined the other briefcases.

BEAL AEROSPACE. MICROCOSM, INC. ROTARY ROCKET COMPANY. KISTLER AEROSPACE.

Marjorie Tench's raspy voice echoed in her mind. *Are you aware that Sexton is accepting bribes from private aerospace companies?*

Gabrielle's pulse began racing as she gazed down the darkened hallway toward the archway that led into the senator's den. She knew she should speak up, announce her presence, and yet she felt herself inching quietly forward. She moved to within a few feet of the archway and stood soundlessly in the shadows . . . listening to the conversation beyond.

CHAPTER 55

While Delta-Three stayed behind to collect Norah Mangor's body and the sled, the other two soldiers accelerated down the glacier after their quarry.

On their feet they wore ElektroTread-powered skis. Modeled after the consumer Fast Trax motorized skis, the classified ElektroTreads were essentially snow skis with miniaturized tank treads affixed – like snowmobiles worn on the feet. Speed was controlled by pushing the tips of the index finger and thumb together, compressing two pressure plates inside the right-hand glove. A powerful gel battery was molded around the foot, doubling as insulation and allowing the skis to run silently. Ingeniously, the kinetic energy generated by gravity and the spinning treads as the wearer glided *down* a hill was automatically harvested to recharge the batteries for the next incline.

Keeping the wind at his back, Delta-One crouched low, skimming seaward as he surveyed the glacier before him. His night vision system was a far cry from the Patriot model used by the Marines. Delta-One was looking through a hands-free face mount with a 40 x 90 mm six-element lens, three-element Magnification Doubler, and Super Long Range IR. The world outside appeared in a translucent tint of cool blue, rather than the usual green – the color scheme especially designed for highly reflective terrains like the Arctic.

As he approached the first berm, Delta-One's goggles revealed several bright stripes of freshly disturbed snow, rising up and over the berm like a neon arrow in the night. Apparently the three escapees had either not thought to unhook their makeshift sail or had been unable to. Either way, if they had not released by the final berm, they were now somewhere out in the ocean. Delta-One knew his quarry's protective clothing would lengthen the usual life expectancy in the water, but the relentless offshore currents would drag them out to sea. Drowning would be inevitable.

Despite his confidence, Delta-One had been trained never to assume. He needed to see bodies. Crouching low, he pressed his fingers together and accelerated up the first incline.

Michael Tolland lay motionless, taking stock of his bruises. He was battered, but he sensed no broken bones. He had little doubt the gel-filled Mark IX had saved him any substantial trauma. As he opened his eyes, his thoughts were slow to focus. Everything seemed softer here . . . quieter. The wind still howled, but with less ferocity.

We went over the edge – didn't we?

Focusing, Tolland found he was lying on ice, draped across Rachel Sexton, almost at right angles, their locked carabiners twisted. He could feel her breathing beneath him, but he could not see her face. He rolled off her, his muscles barely responding.

'Rachel . . . ?' Tolland wasn't sure if his lips were making sound or not.

Tolland recalled the final seconds of their harrowing ride – the upward drag of the balloon, the payload cable snapping, their bodies plummeting down the far side of the berm, sliding up and over the final mound, skimming toward the edge – the ice running out. Tolland and Rachel had fallen, but the fall had been oddly short. Rather than the expected plunge to the sea, they had fallen only ten feet or so before hitting another slab of ice and sliding to a stop with the dead weight of Corky in tow.

Now, raising his head, Tolland looked toward the sea. Not far away, the ice ended in a sheer cliff, beyond which he could hear the sounds of the ocean. Looking back up the glacier, Tolland strained to see into the night. Twenty yards back, his eyes met a high wall of ice, which seemed to hang above them. It was then that he realized what had happened. Somehow they had slid off the main glacier onto a lower terrace of ice. This section was flat, as large as a hockey rink, and had partially collapsed – preparing to cleave off into the ocean at any moment.

Ice calving, Tolland thought, eyeing the precarious platform of ice on which he was now lying. It was a broad square slab that hung off the glacier like a colossal balcony, surrounded on three sides by precipices to the ocean. The sheet of ice was attached to the glacier only at its back, and Tolland could see the connection was anything but permanent. The boundary where the lower terrace clung to the Milne Ice Shelf was marked by a gaping pressure fissure almost four feet across. Gravity was well on its way to winning this battle.

Almost more frightening than seeing the fissure was Tolland's seeing the motionless body of Corky Marlinson crumpled on the ice. Corky lay ten yards away at the end of a taut tether attached to them.

Tolland tried to stand up, but he was still attached to Rachel. Repositioning himself, he began detaching their interlocking carabiners.

Rachel looked weak as she tried to sit up. 'We didn't . . . go over?' Her voice was bewildered.

'We fell onto a lower block of ice,' Tolland said, finally unfastening himself from her. 'I've got to help Corky.'

Painfully, Tolland attempted to stand, but his legs felt feeble. He grabbed the tether and heaved. Corky began sliding toward them across the ice. After a dozen or so pulls, Corky was lying on the ice a few feet away.

Corky Marlinson looked beaten. He'd lost his goggles, suffered a bad cut on his cheek, and his nose was bleeding. Tolland's worries that Corky might be dead were quickly allayed when Corky rolled over and looked at Tolland with an angry glare.

'Jesus,' he stammered. 'What the hell was *that* little trick?'

Tolland felt a wave of relief.

Rachel sat up now, wincing. She looked around. 'We need to . . . get off of here. This block of ice looks like it's about to fall.'

Tolland couldn't have agreed more. The only question was how.

They had no time to consider a solution. A familiar high-pitched whir became audible above them on the glacier. Tolland's gaze shot up to see two white-clad figures ski effortlessly up onto the edge and stop in unison. The two men stood there a moment, peering down at their battered prey like chess masters savoring checkmate before the final kill.

Delta-One was surprised to see the three escapees alive. He knew, however, this was a temporary condition. They had fallen onto a section of the glacier that had already begun its inevitable plunge to the sea. This quarry could be disabled and killed in the same manner as the other woman, but a far cleaner solution had just presented itself. A way in which no bodies would ever be found.

Gazing downward over the lip, Delta-One focused on the gaping crevasse that had begun to spread like a wedge between the ice shelf and the clinging block of ice. The section of ice on which the three fugitives sat was dangerously perched . . . ready to break away and fall into the ocean any day now.

Why not today . . .

Here on the ice shelf, the night was rocked every few hours by deafening booms – the sound of ice cracking off parts of the glacier and plummeting into the ocean. Who would take notice?

Feeling the familiar warm rush of adrenaline that accompanied the preparation for a kill, Delta-One reached in his supply pack and pulled out a heavy, lemon-shaped object. Standard issue for military assault teams, the object was called a flash-bang – a 'nonlethal' concussion grenade that temporarily disoriented an enemy by generating a blinding flash and deafening concussion wave. Tonight, however, Delta-One knew this flash-bang would most certainly be lethal.

He positioned himself near the edge and wondered how far the crevasse descended before tapering to a close. Twenty feet? Fifty feet? He knew it didn't matter. His plan would be effective regardless.

With calm bred from the performance of countless executions, Delta-One dialed a ten-second delay into the grenade's screw-dial, slid out the pin, and threw the grenade down into the chasm. The bomb plummeted into the darkness and disappeared.

Then Delta-One and his partner cleared back up onto the top of the berm and waited. This would be a sight to behold.

Even in her delirious state of mind, Rachel Sexton had a very good idea what the attackers had just dropped into the crevasse. Whether Michael Tolland also knew or whether he was reading the fear in her eyes was unclear, but she saw him go pale, shooting a horrified glance down at the mammoth slab of ice on which they were stranded, clearly realizing the inevitable.

Like a storm cloud lit by an internal flash of lightning, the ice beneath Rachel illuminated from within. The eerie white translucence shot out in all directions. For a hundred yards around them, the glacier flashed white. The concussion came next. Not a rumble like an earthquake, but a deafening shock wave of gut-churning force. Rachel felt the impact tearing up through the ice into her body.

Instantly, as if a wedge had been driven between the ice shelf and the block of ice supporting them, the cliff began to shear off with a sickening crack. Rachel's eyes locked with Tolland's in a freeze-frame of terror. Corky let out a scream nearby.

The bottom dropped out.

Rachel felt weightless for an instant, hovering over the multi-million-pound block of ice. Then they were riding the iceberg down – plummeting into the frigid sea.

CHAPTER 56

The deafening grating of ice against ice assaulted Rachel's ears as the massive slab slid down the face of the Milne Ice Shelf, sending towering plumes of spray into the air. As the slab splashed downward, it slowed, and Rachel's previously weightless body crashed down onto the top of the ice. Tolland and Corky landed hard nearby.

As the block's downward momentum plunged it deeper into the sea, Rachel could see the foaming surface of the ocean racing upward with a kind of taunting deceleration, like the ground beneath a bungee-jumper whose cord was a few feet too long. Rising . . . rising . . . and then it was there. Her childhood nightmare was back. *The ice . . . the water . . . the darkness*. The dread was almost primal.

The top of the slab slipped below the waterline, and the frigid Arctic Ocean poured over the edges in a torrent. As the ocean rushed in all around her, Rachel felt herself sucked under. The bare skin on her face tightened and burned as the saltwater hit. The flooring of ice disappeared beneath her, and Rachel fought her way back to the surface, buoyed by the gel in her suit. She took in a mouthful of saltwater, sputtering to the surface. She could see the others floundering nearby, all of them tangled in tethers. Just as Rachel righted herself, Tolland yelled out.

'It's coming back up!'

As his words echoed above the tumult, Rachel felt an eerie upwelling in the water beneath her. Like a massive locomotive straining to reverse direction, the slab of ice had groaned to a stop underwater and was now beginning its ascent directly beneath them. Fathoms below, a sickening low frequency rumble resonated upward through the water as the gigantic submerged sheet began scraping its way back up the face of the glacier.

The slab rose fast, accelerating as it came, swooping up from the darkness. Rachel felt herself rising. The ocean roiled all around as the ice met her body. She scrambled in vain, trying to find her balance as the ice propelled her skyward along with millions of gallons of seawater. Buoying upward, the giant sheet bobbed above the surface, heaving and teetering, looking for its center of gravity. Rachel found herself scrambling in waist-deep water across the enormous, flat expanse. As the water began pouring off the surface, the current swallowed Rachel and dragged her toward the edge. Sliding, splayed flat on her stomach, Rachel could see the edge looming fast.

Hold on! Rachel's mother's voice was calling the same way it had when Rachel was just a child floundering beneath the icy pond. *Hold on! Don't go under!*

The wrenching yank on her harness expelled what little air Rachel had left in her lungs. She jerked to a dead stop only yards from the edge. The motion spun her in space. Ten yards away, she could see Corky's limp body, still tethered to her, also jolting to a stop. They had been flowing off the sheet in opposite directions and his momentum had stopped her. As the water ran off and grew more shallow, another dark form appeared over near Corky. He was on his hands and knees, grasping Corky's tether and vomiting saltwater.

Michael Tolland.

As the last of the wake drained past her and flowed off the iceberg, Rachel lay in terrified silence, listening to the sounds of the ocean. Then, feeling the onset of deadly cold, she dragged herself onto her hands and knees. The 'berg was still bobbing back and forth, like a giant ice cube. Delirious and in pain, she crawled back toward the others.

High above on the glacier, Delta-One peered through his night-vision goggles at the water churning around the Arctic Ocean's newest tabular iceberg. Although he saw no bodies in the water, he was not surprised. The ocean was dark, and his quarry's weather suits and skullcaps were black.

As he passed his gaze across the surface of the enormous floating sheet of ice, he had a hard time keeping it in focus. It was receding quickly, already heading out to sea in the strong offshore currents. He was about to turn his gaze back to the sea when he saw something unexpected. Three specks of black on the ice. *Are those bodies?* Delta-One tried to bring them into focus.

'See something?' Delta-Two asked.

Delta-One said nothing, focusing in with his magnifier. In the pale tint of the iceberg, he was stunned to see three human forms huddled motionless on the island of ice. Whether they were alive or dead, Delta-One had no idea. It hardly mattered. If they were alive, even in weather suits, they'd be dead within the hour; they were wet, a storm was coming in, and they were drifting seaward into one of the most deadly oceans on the planet. Their bodies would never be found.

'Just shadows,' Delta-One said, turning from the cliff. 'Let's get back to base.'

CHAPTER 57

Senator Sedgewick Sexton set his snifter of Courvoisier on the mantelpiece of his Westbrooke apartment and stoked the fire for several moments, gathering his thoughts. The six men in the den with him sat in silence now . . . waiting. The small talk was over. It was time for Senator Sexton to make his pitch. They knew it. He knew it.

Politics was sales.

Establish trust. Let them know you understand their problems.

'As you may know,' Sexton said, turning toward them, 'over the past months, I have met with many men in your same position.' He smiled and sat down, joining them on their level. 'You are the only ones I have ever brought into my home. You are extraordinary men, and I am honored to meet you.'

Sexton folded his hands and let his eyes circle the room, making personal contact with each of his guests. Then he focused in on his first mark – the heavyset man in the cowboy hat.

'Space Industries of Houston,' Sexton said. 'I'm glad you came.'

The Texan grunted. 'I hate this town.'

'I don't blame you. Washington has been unfair to you.'

The Texan stared out from beneath the rim of his hat but said nothing.

'Twelve years back,' Sexton began, 'you made an offer to the U.S. government. You proposed to build them a U.S. space station for a mere five billion dollars.'

'Yeah, I did. I still have the blueprints.'

'And yet NASA convinced the government that a U.S. space station should be a *NASA* project.'

'Right. NASA started building almost a decade ago.'

'A decade. And not only is the NASA space station not yet fully operational, but the project so far has cost *twenty* times your bid. As an American taxpayer, I am sickened.'

A grumble of agreement circled the room. Sexton let his eyes move, reconnecting with the group.

'I am well aware,' the senator said, addressing everyone now, 'that several of your companies have offered to launch private space shuttles for as little as fifty million dollars per flight.'

More nods.

'And yet NASA undercuts you by charging only thirty-eight million dollars per flight . . . even though their *actual* per flight cost is over one hundred and fifty million dollars!'

'It's how they keep us out of space,' one of the men said. 'The private sector cannot possibly compete with a company that can afford to run shuttle flights at a four hundred percent loss and still stay in business.'

'Nor should you *have* to,' Sexton said.

Nods all around.

Sexton turned now to the austere entrepreneur beside him, a man whose file Sexton had read with interest. Like many of the entrepreneurs funding Sexton's campaign, this man was a former military engineer who had become disillusioned with low wages and government bureaucracy and had abandoned his military post to seek his fortune in aerospace.

'Kistler Aerospace,' Sexton said, shaking his head in despair. 'Your company has designed and manufactured a rocket that can launch payloads for as little as two thousand dollars per pound compared to NASA's costs of *ten thousand dollars* per pound.' Sexton paused for effect. 'And yet you have no clients.'

'Why *would* I have any clients?' the man replied. 'Last week NASA undercut us by charging Motorola only eight hundred and twelve dollars per pound to launch a telecomm satellite. The government launched that satellite at a nine hundred percent loss!'

Sexton nodded. Taxpayers were unwittingly subsidizing an agency that was ten times less efficient than its competition. 'It has become painfully clear,' he said, his voice darkening, 'that NASA is working very hard to stifle competition in space. They crowd out private aerospace businesses by pricing services below market value.'

'It's the Wal-Marting of space,' the Texan said.

Damn good analogy, Sexton thought. *I'll have to remember that.* Wal-Mart was notorious for moving into a new territory, selling products below market value, and driving all local competition out of business.

'I'm goddamned sick and tired,' the Texan said, 'of having to pay millions in business taxes so Uncle Sam can use that money to steal my clients!'

'I hear you,' Sexton said. 'I understand.'

'It's the lack of corporate sponsorships that's killing Rotary Rocket,' a sharply dressed man said. 'The laws against sponsorship are criminal!'

'I couldn't agree more.' Sexton had been shocked to learn that another way NASA entrenched its monopoly of space was by passing federal mandates banning advertisements on space vehicles. Instead of allowing private companies to secure funding through corporate sponsorships and advertising logos – the way, for example, professional race car drivers did – space vehicles could only display the words USA and the company name. In a country that spent $185 billion a year on advertising, not one advertising dollar ever found its way into the coffers of private space companies.

'It's robbery,' one of the men snapped. 'My company hopes to stay in business long enough to launch the country's first tourist-shuttle prototype next May. We expect enormous press coverage. The Nike Corporation just offered us seven million in sponsorship dollars to paint the Nike swoosh and "Just do it!" on the side of the shuttle. Pepsi offered us twice that for "Pepsi: The choice of a new generation." But according to federal law, if our shuttle displays advertising, we are prohibited from launching it!'

'That's right,' Senator Sexton said. 'And if elected, I will work to abolish that antisponsorship legislation. That is a promise. Space should be open for advertising the way every square inch of earth is open to advertising.'

Sexton gazed out now at his audience, his eyes locking in, his voice growing solemn. 'We all need to be aware, however, that the biggest obstacle to privatization of NASA is not laws, but rather, it is public perception. Most Americans still hold a romanticized view of the American space program. They still believe NASA is a *necessary* government agency.'

'It's those goddamned Hollywood movies!' one man said. 'How many NASA-saves-the-world-from-a-killer-asteroid movies can Hollywood make, for Christ's sake? It's propaganda!'

The plethora of NASA movies coming out of Hollywood, Sexton knew, was simply a matter of economics. Following the wildly popular movie *Top Gun* – a Tom Cruise jet pilot blockbuster that played like a two-hour advertisement for the U.S. Navy – NASA realized the true potential of Hollywood as a public relations powerhouse. NASA quietly began offering film companies *free* filming access to all of NASA's dramatic facilities – launchpads, mission control, training facilities. Producers, who were accustomed to paying enormous on-site licensing fees when they filmed anywhere else, jumped at the opportunity to save millions in budget costs by making

NASA thrillers on 'free' sets. Of course, Hollywood only got access if NASA approved the script.

'Public brainwashing,' a Hispanic grunted. 'The movies aren't half as bad as the publicity stunts. Sending a senior citizen into space? And now NASA is planning an all-female shuttle crew? All for publicity!'

Sexton sighed, his tone turning tragic. 'True, and I know I don't have to remind you what happened back in the Eighties when the Department of Education was bankrupt and cited NASA as wasting millions that could be spent on education. NASA devised a PR stunt to prove NASA was education-friendly. They sent a public school teacher into space.' Sexton paused. 'You all remember Christa McAuliffe.'

The room fell silent.

'Gentlemen,' Sexton said, stopping dramatically in front of the fire. 'I believe it is time Americans understood the truth, for the good of all of our futures. It's time Americans understand that NASA is not leading us skyward, but rather is stifling space exploration. Space is no different than any other industry, and keeping the private sector grounded verges on a criminal act. Consider the computer industry, in which we see such an explosion of progress that we can barely keep up from week to week! Why? Because the computer industry is a free-market system: it rewards efficiency and vision with *profits*. Imagine if the computer industry were government-run? We would still be in the Dark Ages. We're stagnating in space. We should put space exploration into the hands of the private sector where it belongs. Americans would be stunned by the growth, jobs, and realized dreams. I believe we should let the free-market system spur us to new heights in space. If elected, I will make it my personal mission to unlock the doors to the final frontier and let them swing wide open.'

Sexton lifted his snifter of cognac.

'My friends, you came here tonight to decide if I am someone worthy of your trust. I hope I am on the way to earning it. In the same way it takes investors to build a company, it takes investors to build a presidency. In the same way corporate stockholders expect returns, you as political investors expect returns. My message to you tonight is simple: invest in me, and I will never forget you. Ever. Our missions are one and the same.'

Sexton extended his glass toward them in a toast.

'With your help, my friends, soon I will be in the White House . . . and you will all be launching your dreams.'

Only fifteen feet away, Gabrielle Ashe stood in the shadows, rigid. From the den came the harmonious clink of crystal snifters and the crackle of the fire.

CHAPTER 58

In a panic, the young NASA technician dashed through the habisphere. *Something terrible has happened!* He found Administrator Ekstrom alone near the press area.

'Sir,' the technician gasped, running up. 'There's been an accident!'

Ekstrom turned, looking distant, as if his thoughts were already deeply troubled with other matters. 'What did you say? An accident? Where?'

'In the extraction pit. A body just floated up. Dr Wailee Ming.'

Ekstrom's face was blank. 'Dr Ming? But . . .'

'We pulled him out, but it was too late. He's dead.'

'For Christ's sake. How long has he been in there?'

'We think about an hour. It looks like he fell in, sank to the bottom, but when his body bloated, he floated up again.'

Ekstrom's reddish skin turned crimson. 'Goddamn it! Who else knows about this?'

'Nobody, sir. Only two of us. We fished him out, but we thought we better tell you before—'

'You did the right thing.' Ekstrom exhaled a weighty sigh. 'Stow Dr Ming's body immediately. Say nothing.'

The technician felt perplexed. 'But, sir, I—'

Ekstrom put a large hand on the man's shoulder. 'Listen to me carefully. This is a tragic accident, one I deeply regret. Of course I will deal with it appropriately when the time comes. Now, however, is not the time.'

'You want me to *hide* his body?'

Ekstrom's cold Nordic eyes bore down. 'Think about it. We could tell everyone, but what would that accomplish? We're about an hour off from this press conference. Announcing that we've had a fatal accident would overshadow the discovery and have a devastating effect on morale. Dr Ming made a careless mistake; I have no intention of making NASA pay for it. These civilian scientists have taken enough of the spotlight without my letting one of their slipshod errors cast a shadow over our public moment of glory. Dr Ming's accident remains a secret until after the press conference. Do you understand?'

The man nodded, pale. 'I'll stow his body.'

CHAPTER 59

Michael Tolland had been at sea enough times to know the ocean took victims without remorse or hesitation. As he lay in exhaustion on the expansive sheet of ice, he could just make out the ghostly outline of the towering Milne Ice Shelf receding in the distance. He knew the powerful Arctic current flowing off the Elizabethan Islands spiraled in an enormous loop around the polar ice cap and would eventually skirt land in northern Russia. Not that it mattered. That would be months from now.

We've got maybe thirty minutes . . . forty-five at the most.

Without the protective insulation of their gel-filled suits, Tolland knew they would be dead already. Thankfully, the Mark IXs had kept them dry – the most critical aspect of surviving cold weather. The thermal gel around their bodies had not only cushioned their fall, but it was now helping their bodies retain what little heat they had left.

Soon hypothermia would set in. It would start with a vague numbness in limbs as the blood retreated to the body's core to protect the critical internal organs. Delirious hallucinations would come next, as the pulse and respiration slowed, cheating the brain of oxygen. Then, the body would make a final effort to conserve its remaining heat by shutting down all operations except the heart and respiration. Unconsciousness would follow. In the end, heart and respiration centers in the brain would stop functioning altogether.

Tolland turned his gaze toward Rachel, wishing he could do something to save her.

The numbness spreading through Rachel Sexton's body was less painful than she would have imagined. Almost a welcome anesthetic. *Nature's morphine.* She had lost her goggles in the collapse, and she could barely open her eyes against the cold.

She could see Tolland and Corky on the ice nearby. Tolland was looking at her, eyes filled with regret. Corky was moving but obviously in pain. His right cheekbone was smashed and bloody.

Rachel's body trembled wildly as her mind searched for answers. *Who? Why?* Her thoughts were muddled by a growing heaviness inside her. Nothing was making sense. She felt like her body was slowly shutting down, lulled by an invisible force pulling her to sleep. She fought it. A fiery anger ignited within her now, and she tried to fan the flames.

They tried to kill us! She peered out at the threatening sea and sensed their attackers had succeeded. *We're already dead.* Even now, knowing she would probably not live to learn the whole truth about the deadly game being played out on the Milne Ice Shelf, Rachel suspected she already knew who to blame.

Administrator Ekstrom had the most to gain. He was the one who sent them out on the ice. He had ties to the Pentagon and Special Ops. *But what did Ekstrom have to gain by inserting the meteorite beneath the ice? What did anyone have to gain?*

Rachel flashed on Zach Herney, wondering if the President was a coconspirator or an unknowing pawn? *Herney knows nothing. He's innocent.* The President obviously had been duped by NASA. Now Herney was only about an hour away from making NASA's announcement. And he would do so armed with a video documentary containing endorsements from four civilian scientists.

Four *dead* civilian scientists.

Rachel could do nothing to stop the press conference now, but she vowed that whoever was responsible for this attack would not get away with it.

Summoning her strength, Rachel tried to sit up. Her limbs felt like granite, all her joints screaming in pain as she bent her legs and arms. Slowly, she pulled herself to her knees, steadying herself on the flat ice. Her head spun. All around her the ocean churned. Tolland lay nearby, gazing up at her with inquisitive eyes. Rachel sensed he probably thought she was kneeling in prayer. She was not, of course, although prayer probably had as good a chance of saving them as what she was about to attempt.

Rachel's right hand fumbled across her waist and found the ice ax still bungeed to her belt. Her stiff fingers gripped the handle. She inverted the ax, positioning it like an upside down T. Then, with all her energy, she drove the butt downward into the ice. *Thud.* Again. *Thud.* The blood felt like cold molasses in her veins. *Thud.* Tolland looked on in obvious confusion. Rachel drove the ax down again. *Thud.*

Tolland tried to lift himself onto his elbow. 'Ra . . . chel?'

She did not answer. She needed all her energy. *Thud. Thud.*

'I don't think . . .' Tolland said, 'this far north . . . that the SAA . . . could hear . . .'

Rachel turned, surprised. She had forgotten Tolland was an oceanographer and might have some idea what she was up to. *Right idea . . . but I'm not calling the SAA.*

She kept pounding.

The SAA stood for a Suboceanic Acoustic Array, a relic of the Cold War now used by oceanographers worldwide to listen for whales. Because underwater sounds carried for hundreds of miles, the SAA network of fifty-nine underwater microphones around the world could listen to a surprisingly large percentage of the planet's oceans. Unfortunately, this remote section of the Arctic was not part of that percentage, but Rachel knew there were others out there listening to the ocean floor – others that few on earth knew existed. She kept pounding. Her message was simple and clear.

THUD. THUD. THUD.

THUD . . . THUD . . . THUD . . .

THUD. THUD. THUD.

Rachel had no delusions that her actions would save their lives; she could already feel a frosty tightness gripping her body. She doubted she had a half hour of life left in her. Rescue was beyond the realm of possibility now. But this was not about rescue.

THUD. THUD. THUD.

THUD . . . THUD . . . THUD . . .

THUD. THUD. THUD.

'There's . . . no time . . .' Tolland said.

It's not . . . about us, she thought. *It's about the information in my pocket.* Rachel pictured the incriminating GPR printout inside the Velcro pocket of her Mark IX suit. *I need to get the GPR printout into the hands of the NRO . . . and soon.*

Even in her delirious state, Rachel was certain her message would be received. In the mid-Eighties, the NRO had replaced the SAA with an array thirty times as powerful. Total global coverage: Classic Wizard, the NRO's $12 million ear to the ocean floor. In the next few hours the Cray supercomputers at the NRO/NSA listening post in Menwith Hill, England, would flag an anomalous sequence in one of the Arctic's hydrophones, decipher the pounding as an SOS, triangulate the coordinates, and dispatch a rescue plane from Thule Air Force Base in Greenland. The plane would find three bodies on an iceberg. Frozen. Dead. One would be an NRO employee . . . and she would be carrying a strange piece of thermal paper in her pocket.

A GPR printout.

Norah Mangor's final legacy.

When the rescuers studied the printout, the mysterious insertion tunnel beneath the meteorite would be revealed. From there, Rachel had no idea what would happen, but at least the secret would not die with them here on the ice.

CHAPTER **60**

Every president's transition into the White House involves a
private tour of three heavily guarded warehouses containing priceless
collections of past White House furniture: desks, silverware, bureaus,
beds, and other items used by past presidents as far back as George
Washington. During the tour, the transitioning president is invited to
select any heirlooms he likes and use them as furnishings inside the
White House during his term. Only the bed in the Lincoln Bedroom
is a permanent White House fixture. Ironically, Lincoln never slept
in it.

The desk at which Zach Herney was currently sitting inside the Oval
Office had once belonged to his idol, Harry Truman. The desk, though
small by modern standards, served as a daily reminder to Zach Herney
that the 'buck' did indeed stop here, and that Herney was ultimately
responsible for any shortcomings of his administration. Herney
accepted the responsibility as an honor and did his best to instill in his
staff the motivations to do whatever it took to get the job done.

'Mr President?' his secretary called out, peering into the office.
'Your call just went through.'

Herney waved. 'Thank you.'

He reached for his phone. He would have preferred some privacy
for this call, but he sure as hell was not going to get any of that right
now. Two makeup specialists hovered like gnats, poking and primping
at his face and hair. Directly in front of his desk, a television crew was
setting up, and an endless swarm of advisers and PR people scurried
around the office, excitedly discussing strategy.

T minus one hour . . .

Herney pressed the illuminated button on his private phone.
'Lawrence? You there?'

'I'm here.' The NASA administrator's voice sounded consumed,
distant.

'Everything okay up there?'

'Storm's still moving in, but my people tell me the satellite link will not be affected. We're good to go. One hour and counting.'

'Excellent. Spirits high, I hope.'

'Very high. My staff's excited. In fact, we just shared some beers.'

Herney laughed. 'Glad to hear it. Look, I wanted to call and thank you before we do this thing. Tonight's going to be one hell of a night.'

The administrator paused, sounding uncharacteristically uncertain. 'That it will, sir. We've been waiting a long time for this.'

Herney hesitated. 'You sound exhausted.'

'I need some sunlight and a real bed.'

'One more hour. Smile for the cameras, enjoy the moment, and then we'll get a plane up there to bring you back to D.C.'

'Looking forward to it.' The man fell silent again.

As a skilled negotiator, Herney was trained to listen, to hear what was being said between the lines. Something in the administrator's voice sounded off somehow. 'You sure everything's okay up there?'

'Absolutely. All systems go.' The administrator seemed eager to change the subject. 'Did you see the final cut of Michael Tolland's documentary?'

'Just watched it,' Herney said. 'He did a fantastic job.'

'Yes. You made a good call bringing him in.'

'Still mad at me for involving civilians?'

'Hell, yes,' the administrator growled good-naturedly, his voice with the usual strength to it.

It made Herney feel better. *Ekstrom's fine*, Herney thought. *Just a little tired*. 'Okay, I'll see you in an hour via satellite. We'll give 'em something to talk about.'

'Right.'

'Hey, Lawrence?' Herney's voice grew low and solemn now. 'You've done a hell of thing up there. I won't ever forget it.'

Outside the habisphere, buffeted by wind, Delta-Three struggled to right and repack Norah Mangor's toppled equipment sled. Once all the equipment was back onboard, he battened down the vinyl top and draped Mangor's dead body across the top, tying her down. As he was preparing to drag the sled off course, his two partners came skimming up the glacier toward him.

'Change of plans,' Delta-One called out above the wind. 'The other three went over the edge.'

Delta-Three was not surprised. He also knew what it meant. The Delta Force's plan to stage an accident by arranging four dead bodies on the ice shelf was no longer a viable option. Leaving a lone body would pose more questions than answers. 'Sweep?' he asked.

Delta-One nodded. 'I'll recover the flares and you two get rid of the sled.'

While Delta-One carefully retraced the scientists' path, collecting every last clue that anyone had been there at all, Delta-Three and his partner moved down the glacier with the laden equipment sled. After struggling over the berms, they finally reached the precipice at the end of the Milne Ice Shelf. They gave a push, and Norah Mangor and her sled slipped silently over the edge, plummeting into the Arctic Ocean.

Clean sweep, Delta-Three thought.

As they headed back to base, he was pleased to see the wind obliterating the tracks made by their skis.

CHAPTER 61

The nuclear submarine *Charlotte* had been stationed in the Arctic Ocean for five days now. Its presence here was highly classified.

A Los Angeles-class sub, the *Charlotte* was designed to 'listen and not be heard.' Its 42 tons of turbine engines were suspended on springs to dampen any vibration they might cause. Despite its requirement for stealth, the LA-class sub had one of the largest footprints of any reconnaissance sub in the water. Stretching more than 360 feet from nose to stern, the hull, if placed on an NFL football field, would crush both goalposts and then some. Seven times the length of the

U.S. Navy's first Holland-class submarine, the *Charlotte* displaced 6,927 tons of water when fully submerged and could cruise at an astounding 35 knots.

The vessel's normal cruising depth was just below the thermocline, a natural temperature gradient that distorted sonar reflections from above and made the sub invisible to surface radar. With a crew of 158 and max dive depth of over 1,500 feet, the vessel represented the state-of-the-art submersible and was the oceanic workhorse of the United States Navy. Its evaporative electrolysis oxygenation system, two nuclear reactors, and engineered provisions gave it the ability to circumnavigate the globe twenty-one times without surfacing. Human waste from the crew, as on most cruise ships, was compressed into sixty-pound blocks and ejected into the ocean – the huge bricks of feces jokingly referred to as 'whale turds.'

The technician sitting at the oscillator screen in the sonar room was one of the best in the world. His mind was a dictionary of sounds and waveforms. He could distinguish between the sounds of several dozen Russian submarine propellers, hundreds of marine animals, and even pinpoint underwater volcanoes as far away as Japan.

At the moment, however, he was listening to a dull, repetitive echo. The sound, although easily distinguishable, was most unexpected.

'You aren't going to believe what's coming through my listening cans,' he said to his catalog assistant, handing over the headphones.

His assistant donned the headphones, an incredulous look crossing his face. 'My God. It's clear as day. What do we do?'

The sonar man was already on the phone to the captain.

When the submarine's captain arrived in the sonar room, the technician piped a live sonar feed over a small set of speakers. The captain listened, expressionless.

THUD. THUD. THUD.

THUD . . . THUD . . . THUD . . .

Slower. Slower. The pattern was becoming looser. More and more faint.

'What are the coordinates?' the captain demanded.

The technician cleared his throat. 'Actually, sir, it's coming from the surface, about three miles to our starboard.'

CHAPTER 62

In the darkened hallway outside Senator Sexton's den, Gabrielle
Ashe's legs were trembling. Not so much out of exhaustion from
standing motionless, but from disillusionment over what she was
listening to. The meeting in the next room was still going, but
Gabrielle didn't have to hear another word. The truth seemed
painfully obvious.

Senator Sexton is taking bribes from private space agencies. Marjorie
Tench had been telling the truth.

The revulsion Gabrielle felt spreading through her now was one of
betrayal. She had believed in Sexton. She'd fought for him. *How can
he do this?* Gabrielle had seen the senator lie publicly from time to
time to protect his private life, but that was politics. *This* was breaking
the law.

*He's not even elected yet, and he's already selling out the White
House!*

Gabrielle knew she could no longer support the senator. Promising
to deliver the NASA privatization bill could be done only with a
contemptuous disregard for both the law and the democratic system.
Even if the senator *believed* it would be in everyone's best interest,
to sell that decision flat out, in advance, slammed the door on the
checks and balances of government, ignoring potentially persuasive
arguments from Congress, advisers, voters, and lobbyists. Most
important, guaranteeing the privatization of NASA, Sexton had paved
the way for endless abuses of that advanced knowledge – insider
trading the most common – blatantly favoring the wealthy inside
cadre at the expense of honest public investors.

Feeling sick to her stomach, Gabrielle wondered what she should
do.

A telephone rang sharply behind her, shattering the silence of
the hallway. Startled, Gabrielle turned. The sound was coming from

the closet in the foyer – a cellphone in the pocket of one of the visitors' coats.

' 'Scuse me, friends,' a Texas drawl said in the den. 'That's me.'

Gabrielle could hear the man get up. *He's coming this way!* Wheeling, she dashed back up the carpet the way she'd come. Halfway up the hall, she cut left, ducking into the darkened kitchen just as the Texan exited the den and turned up the hall. Gabrielle froze, motionless in the shadows.

The Texan strode by without noticing.

Over the sound of her pounding heart, Gabrielle could hear him rustling in the closet. Finally, he answered the ringing phone.

'Yeah? . . . When? . . . Really? We'll switch it on. Thanks.' The man hung up and headed back toward the den, calling out as he went, 'Hey! Turn on the television. Sounds like Zach Herney's giving an urgent press conference tonight. Eight o'clock. All channels. Either we're declaring war on China, or the International Space Station just fell into the ocean.'

'Now wouldn't *that* be something to toast!' someone called out.

Everyone laughed.

Gabrielle felt the kitchen spinning around her now. *An eight P.M. press conference?* Tench, it seemed, had not been bluffing after all. She had given Gabrielle until 8:00 P.M. to give her an affidavit admitting the affair. *Distance yourself from the senator before it's too late,* Tench had told her. Gabrielle had assumed the deadline was so the White House could leak the information to tomorrow's papers, but now it seemed the White House intended to go public with the allegations themselves.

An urgent press conference? The more Gabrielle considered it, though, the stranger it seemed. *Herney is going live with this mess? Personally?*

The television came on in the den. Blaring. The news announcer's voice was bursting with excitement. 'The White House has offered no clues as to the topic of tonight's surprise presidential address, and speculation abounds. Some political analysts now think that following the President's recent absence on the campaign trail, Zach Herney may be preparing to announce he will not be running for a second term.'

A hopeful cheer arose in the den.

Absurd, Gabrielle thought. With all the dirt the White House had on Sexton right now, there was no way in hell the President was throwing in the towel tonight. *This press conference is about something else.* Gabrielle had a sinking feeling she'd already been warned what it was.

With rising urgency, she checked her watch. Less than an hour. She had a decision to make, and she knew exactly to whom she needed to talk. Clutching the envelope of photos under her arm, she quietly exited the apartment.

In the hallway, the bodyguard looked relieved. 'I heard some cheering inside. Sounds like you were a hit.'

She smiled curtly and headed for the elevator.

Outside in the street, the settling night felt unusually bitter. Flagging a cab, she climbed in and tried to reassure herself she knew exactly what she was doing.

'ABC television studios,' she told the driver. 'And hurry.'

CHAPTER **63**

As Michael Tolland lay on his side on the ice, he rested his head on an outstretched arm, which he could no longer feel. Although his eyelids felt heavy, he fought to keep them open. From this odd vantage point, Tolland took in the final images of his world – now just sea and ice – in a strange sideways tilt. It seemed a fitting end to a day in which nothing had been what it seemed.

An eerie calm had begun to settle over the floating raft of ice. Rachel and Corky had both fallen silent, and the pounding had stopped. The farther from the glacier they floated, the calmer the wind became. Tolland heard his own body getting quieter too. With the tight skullcap over his ears, he could hear his own breathing amplified in his head. It was getting slower . . . shallower. His body was no longer able to fight off the compressing sensation that accompanied his own blood racing from his extremities like a crew abandoning ship, flowing instinctively to his vital organs in a last-ditch effort to keep him conscious.

A losing battle, he knew.

Strangely, there was no pain anymore. He had passed through that stage. The sensation now was that of having been inflated. Numbness. Floating. As the first of his reflexive operations – blinking – began to shut down, Tolland's vision blurred. The aqueous humor that circulated between his cornea and lens was freezing repeatedly. Tolland gazed back toward the blur of the Milne Ice Shelf, now only a faint white form in the hazy moonlight.

He felt his soul admitting defeat. Teetering on the brink between presence and absence, he stared out at the ocean waves in the distance. The wind howled all around him.

It was then that Tolland began hallucinating. Strangely, in the final seconds before unconsciousness, he did not hallucinate rescue. He did not hallucinate warm and comforting thoughts. His final delusion was a terrifying one.

A leviathan was rising from the water beside the iceberg, breaching the surface with an ominous hiss. Like some mythical sea monster, it came – sleek, black, and lethal, with water foaming around it. Tolland forced himself to blink his eyes. His vision cleared slightly. The beast was close, bumping up against the ice like a huge shark butting a small boat. Massive, it towered before him, its skin shimmering and wet.

As the hazy image went black, all that was left were the sounds. Metal on metal. Teeth gnashing at the ice. Coming closer. Dragging bodies away.

Rachel . . .

Tolland felt himself being grabbed roughly.

And then everything went blank.

CHAPTER **64**

Gabrielle Ashe was at a full jog when she entered the third-floor production room of ABC News. Even so, she was moving slower than everyone else in the room. The intensity in production was at a fever pitch twenty-four hours a day, but at the moment the cubicle grid in front of her looked like the stock exchange on speed. Wild-eyed editors screamed to one another over the tops of their compartments, fax-waving reporters darted from cubicle to cubicle comparing notes, and frantic interns inhaled Snickers and Mountain Dew between errands.

Gabrielle had come to ABC to see Yolanda Cole.

Usually Yolanda could be found in production's high-rent district – the glass-walled private offices reserved for the decision makers who actually required some quiet to think. Tonight, however, Yolanda was out on the floor, in the thick of it. When she saw Gabrielle, she let out her usual shriek of exuberance.

'Gabs!' Yolanda was wearing a batik body-wrap and tortoiseshell glasses. As always, several pounds of garish costume jewelry were draped off her like tinsel. Yolanda waddled over, waving. 'Hug!'

Yolanda Cole had been a content editor with ABC News in Washington for sixteen years. A freckle-faced Pole, Yolanda was a squat, balding woman whom everyone affectionately called 'Mother.' Her matronly presence and good humor disguised a street-savvy ruthlessness for getting the story. Gabrielle had met Yolanda at a Women in Politics mentoring seminar she'd attended shortly after her arrival in Washington. They'd chatted about Gabrielle's background, the challenges of being a woman in D.C., and finally about Elvis Presley – a passion they were surprised to discover they shared. Yolanda had taken Gabrielle under her wing and helped her make connections. Gabrielle still stopped by every month or so to say hello.

Gabrielle gave her a big hug, Yolanda's enthusiasm already lifting her spirits.

Yolanda stepped back and looked Gabrielle over. 'You look like you aged a hundred years, girl! What happened to you?'

Gabrielle lowered her voice. 'I'm in trouble, Yolanda.'

'That's not the word on the street. Sounds like your man is on the rise.'

'Is there some place we can talk in private?'

'Bad timing, honey. The President is holding a press conference in about half an hour, and we still haven't a clue what it's all about. I've got to line up expert commentary, and I'm flying blind.'

'I know what the press conference is about.'

Yolanda lowered her glasses, looking skeptical. 'Gabrielle, our correspondent *inside* the White House is in the dark on this one. You say Sexton's campaign has advance knowledge?'

'No, I'm saying *I* have advance knowledge. Give me five minutes. I'll tell you everything.'

Yolanda glanced down at the red White House envelope in Gabrielle's hand. 'That's a White House internal. Where'd you get that?'

'In a private meeting with Marjorie Tench this afternoon.'

Yolanda stared a long moment. 'Follow me.'

Inside the privacy of Yolanda's glass-walled cubicle, Gabrielle confided in her trusted friend, confessing to a one-night affair with Sexton and the fact that Tench had photographic evidence.

Yolanda smiled broadly and shook her head laughing. Apparently she had been in Washington journalism so long that nothing shocked her. 'Oh, Gabs, I had a hunch you and Sexton had probably hooked up. Not surprising. He's got a reputation, and you're a pretty girl. Too bad about the photos. I wouldn't worry about it, though.'

Don't worry about it?

Gabrielle explained that Tench had accused Sexton of taking illegal bribes from space companies and that Gabrielle had just overheard a secret SFF meeting confirming that fact. Again Yolanda's expression conveyed little surprise or concern – until Gabrielle told her what she was thinking of doing about it.

Yolanda now looked troubled. 'Gabrielle, if you want to hand over a legal document saying you slept with a U.S. senator and stood by while he lied about it, that's your business. But I'm telling you, it's a very bad move for you. You need to think long and hard about what it could mean for you.'

'You're not listening. I don't have that kind of time!'

'I *am* listening, and sweetheart, whether or not the clock is ticking, there are certain things you just do not do. You do *not* sell out a U.S. senator in a sex scandal. It's suicide. I'm telling you, girl, if you take down a presidential candidate, you better get in your car and drive as far from D.C. as possible. You'll be a marked woman. A lot of people spend a lot of money to put candidates at the top. There's big finances and power at stake here – the kind of power people kill for.'

Gabrielle fell silent now.

'Personally,' Yolanda said, 'I think Tench was leaning on you in hopes you'd panic and do something dumb – like bail out and confess to the affair.' Yolanda pointed to the red envelope in Gabrielle's hands. 'Those shots of you and Sexton don't mean squat unless you or Sexton admit they're accurate. The White House knows if they leak those photos, Sexton will just claim they're phony and throw them back in the President's face.'

'I thought of that, but still the campaign finance bribery issue is—'

'Honey, think about it. If the White House hasn't gone public yet with bribery allegations, they probably don't intend to. The President is pretty serious about no negative campaigning. My guess is he decided to save an aerospace industry scandal and sent Tench after you with a bluff in hopes he might scare you out of hiding on the sex thing. Make you stab your candidate in the back.'

Gabrielle considered it. Yolanda was making sense, and yet something still felt odd. Gabrielle pointed through the glass at the bustling news room. 'Yolanda, you guys are gearing up for a big presidential press conference. If the President is not going public about bribery or sex, what's it all about?'

Yolanda looked stunned. 'Hold on. You think this press conference is about you and Sexton?'

'Or the bribery. Or both. Tench told me I had until eight tonight to sign a confession or else the President was going to announce—'

Yolanda's laughter shook the entire glass cubicle. 'Oh please! Wait! You're killing me!'

Gabrielle was in no mood for joking. 'What?'

'Gabs, listen,' Yolanda managed, between laughs, 'trust me on this. I've been dealing with the White House for sixteen years, and there's no way Zach Herney has called together the *global* media to tell them he suspects Senator Sexton is accepting shady campaign financing or sleeping with you. That's the kind of information you *leak*. Presidents don't gain popularity by interrupting regularly scheduled pro-gramming to bitch and moan about sex or alleged infractions of cloudy campaign finance laws.'

'Cloudy?' Gabrielle snapped. 'Flat out selling your decision on a space bill for millions in ad money is hardly a cloudy issue!'

'Are you *sure* that's what he is doing?' Yolanda's tone hardened now. 'Are you sure enough to drop your skirt on national TV? Think about it. It takes a lot of alliances to get anything done these days, and campaign finance is complex stuff. Maybe Sexton's meeting was perfectly legal.'

'He's breaking the law,' Gabrielle said. *Isn't he?*

'Or so Marjorie Tench would have you believe. Candidates accept behind-the-scenes donations all the time from big corporations. It may not be pretty, but it's not necessarily illegal. In fact, most legal issues deal not with where the money comes from but *how* the candidate chooses to spend it.'

Gabrielle hesitated, feeling uncertain now.

'Gabs, the White House played you this afternoon. They tried to turn you against your candidate, and so far you've called their bluff. If I were looking for someone to trust, I think I'd stick with Sexton before jumping ship to someone like Marjorie Tench.'

Yolanda's phone rang. She answered, nodding, uh-huh-ing, taking notes. 'Interesting,' she finally said. 'I'll be right there. Thanks.'

Yolanda hung up and turned with an arched brow. 'Gabs, sounds like you're off the hook. Just as I predicted.'

'What's going on?'

'I don't have a specific yet, but I can tell you this much – the President's press conference has nothing to do with sex scandals or campaign finance.'

Gabrielle felt a flash of hope and wanted badly to believe her. 'How do you know that?'

'Someone on the inside just leaked that the press conference is NASA-related.'

Gabrielle sat up suddenly. 'NASA?'

Yolanda winked. 'This could be your lucky night. My bet is President Herney is feeling so much pressure from Senator Sexton that he's decided the White House has no choice but to pull the plug on the International Space Station. That explains all the global media coverage.'

A press conference killing the space station? Gabrielle could not imagine.

Yolanda stood up. 'That Tench attack this afternoon? It was probably just a last-ditch effort to get a foothold over Sexton before the President had to go public with the bad news. Nothing like a sex scandal to take the attention away from another presidential flop. Anyhow, Gabs, I've got work to do. My advice to you – get yourself a cup of coffee, sit right here, turn on my television, and ride this out like the rest of us. We've got twenty minutes until show time, and I'm telling you, there is no way the President is going Dumpster-diving tonight. He's got the whole world watching. Whatever he has to say carries some serious weight.' She gave a reassuring wink. 'Now give me the envelope.'

'What?'

Yolanda held out a demanding hand. 'These pictures are getting locked in my desk until this is over. I want to be sure you don't do something idiotic.'

Reluctantly, Gabrielle handed over the envelope.

Yolanda locked the photos carefully in a desk drawer and pocketed the keys. 'You'll thank me, Gabs. I swear it.' She playfully ruffled Gabrielle's hair on her way out. 'Sit tight. I think good news is on the way.'

Gabrielle sat alone in the glass cubicle and tried to let Yolanda's upbeat attitude lift her mood. All Gabrielle could think of, though, was the self-satisfied smirk on the face of Marjorie Tench this afternoon. Gabrielle could not imagine what the President was about to tell the world, but it was definitely not going to be good news for Senator Sexton.

CHAPTER **65**

Rachel Sexton felt like she was being burned alive.

It's raining fire!

She tried to open her eyes, but all she could make out were foggy shapes and blinding lights. It was raining all around her. Scalding hot rain. Pounding down on her bare skin. She was lying on her side and could feel hot tiles beneath her body. She curled more tightly into the fetal position, trying to protect herself from the scalding liquid falling from above. She smelled chemicals. Chlorine, maybe. She tried to crawl away, but she could not. Powerful hands pressed down on her shoulders, holding her down.

Let me go! I'm burning!

Instinctively, she again fought to escape, and again she was rebuffed, the strong hands clamping down. 'Stay where you are,' a man's voice said, the accent was American. Professional. 'It will be over soon.'

What will be over? Rachel wondered. *The pain? My life?* She tried to focus her vision. The lights in this place were harsh. She sensed the room was small. Cramped. Low ceilings.

'I'm burning!' Rachel's scream was a whisper.

'You're fine,' the voice said. 'This water is lukewarm. Trust me.'

Rachel realized she was mostly undressed, wearing only her soaked underwear. No embarrassment registered; her mind was filled with too many other questions.

The memories were coming back now in a torrent. The ice shelf. The GPR. The attack. *Who? Where am I?* She tried to put the pieces together, but her mind felt torpid, like a set of clogged gears. From out of the muddled confusion came a single thought: *Michael and Corky . . . where are they?*

Rachel tried to focus her bleary vision but saw only the men standing over her. They were all dressed in the same blue jumpsuits.

She wanted to speak, but her mouth refused to formulate a single word. The burning sensation in her skin was now giving way to sudden deep waves of aching that rolled through the muscles like seismic tremors.

'Let it happen,' the man over her said. 'The blood needs to flow back into your musculature.' He spoke like a doctor. 'Try to move your limbs as much as you can.'

The pain racking Rachel's body felt as if every muscle was being beaten with a hammer. She lay there on the tile, her chest contracting, and she could barely breathe.

'Move your legs and arms,' the man insisted. 'No matter what it feels like.'

Rachel tried. Each movement felt like a knife being thrust into her joints. The jets of water grew hotter again. The scalding was back. The crushing pain went on. At the precise instant she thought she could not withstand another moment, Rachel felt someone giving her an injection. The pain seemed to subside quickly, less and less violent, releasing. The tremors slowed. She felt herself breathing again.

A new sensation was spreading through her body now, the eerie bite of pins and needles. Everywhere – stabbing – sharper and sharper. Millions of tiny needlepoint jabs, intensifying whenever she moved. She tried to hold motionless, but the water jets continued to buffet her. The man above her was holding her arms, moving them.

God that hurts! Rachel was too weak to fight. Tears of exhaustion and pain poured down her face. She shut her eyes hard, blocking out the world.

Finally, the pins and needles began to dissipate. The rain from above stopped. When Rachel opened her eyes, her vision was clearer.

It was then that she saw them.

Corky and Tolland lay nearby, quivering, half-naked and soaked. From the looks of anguish on their faces, Rachel sensed that they had just endured similar experiences. Michael Tolland's brown eyes were bloodshot and glassy. When he saw Rachel, he managed a weak smile, his blue lips trembling.

Rachel tried to sit up, to take in their bizarre surroundings. The three of them were lying in a trembling twist of half-naked limbs on the floor of a tiny shower room.

CHAPTER **66**

Strong arms lifted her.

Rachel felt the powerful strangers drying her body and wrapping her in blankets. She was being placed on a medical bed of some sort and vigorously massaged on her arms, legs, and feet. Another injection in her arm.

'Adrenaline,' someone said.

Rachel felt the drug coursing through her veins like a life force, invigorating her muscles. Although she still felt an icy hollowness tight like a drum in her gut, Rachel sensed the blood slowly returning to her limbs.

Back from the dead.

She tried to focus her vision. Tolland and Corky were lying nearby, shivering in blankets as the men massaged their bodies and gave them injections as well. Rachel had no doubt that this mysterious assemblage of men had just saved their lives. Many of them were soaking wet, apparently having jumped into the showers fully clothed to help. Who they were or how they had gotten to Rachel and the others in time was beyond her. It made no difference at the moment. *We're alive.*

'Where . . . are we?' Rachel managed, the simple act of trying to speak bringing on a crashing headache.

The man massaging her replied, 'You're on the medical deck of a Los Angeles class—'

'*On deck!*' someone called out.

Rachel sensed a sudden commotion all around her, and she tried to sit up. One of the men in blue helped, propping her up, and pulling the blankets up around her. Rachel rubbed her eyes and saw someone striding into the room.

The newcomer was a powerful African-American man. Handsome and authoritative. His uniform was khaki. 'At ease,' he declared, moving toward Rachel, stopping over her and gazing down at her with strong black eyes. 'Harold Brown,' he said, his voice deep and commanding. 'Captain of the U.S.S. *Charlotte*. And you are?'

U.S.S. Charlotte, Rachel thought. The name seemed vaguely familiar. 'Sexton . . .' she replied. 'I'm Rachel Sexton.'

The man looked puzzled. He stepped closer, studying her more carefully. 'I'll be damned. So you are.'

Rachel felt lost. *He knows me?* Rachel was certain she did not recognize the man, although as her eyes dropped from his face to the patch on his chest, she saw the familiar emblem of an eagle clutching an anchor surrounded by the words U.S. NAVY.

It now registered why she knew the name *Charlotte*.

'Welcome aboard, Ms Sexton,' the captain said. 'You've gisted a number of this ship's recon reports. I know who you are.'

'But what are you doing in these waters?' she stammered.

His face hardened somewhat. 'Frankly, Ms Sexton, I was about to ask you the same question.'

Tolland sat up slowly now, opening his mouth to speak. Rachel silenced him with a firm shake of her head. *Not here. Not now.* She had no doubt the first thing Tolland and Corky would want to talk about was the meteorite and the attack, but this was certainly not a topic to discuss in front of a Navy submarine crew. In the world of intelligence, regardless of crisis, CLEARANCE remained king; the meteorite situation remained highly classified.

'I need to speak to NRO director William Pickering,' she told the captain. 'In private, and immediately.'

The captain arched his eyebrows, apparently unaccustomed to taking orders on his own ship.

'I have classified information I need to share.'

The captain studied her a long moment. 'Let's get your body temperature back, and then I'll put you in contact with the NRO director.'

'It's urgent, sir. I—' Rachel stopped short. Her eyes had just seen a clock on the wall over the pharmaceutical closet.

19:51 HOURS.

Rachel blinked, staring. 'Is . . . is that clock *right?*'

'You're on a navy vessel, ma'am. Our clocks are accurate.'

'And is that . . *Eastern* time?'

'7:51 P.M. Eastern Standard. We're out of Norfolk.'

My God! she thought, stunned. *It's only 7:51 P.M.?* Rachel had the impression hours had passed since she passed out. It was not even past eight o'clock? *The President has not yet gone public about the meteorite! I still have time to stop him!* She immediately slid down off the bed, wrapping the blanket around her. Her legs felt shaky. 'I need to speak to the President right away.'

The captain looked confused. 'The president of what?'

'Of the United States!'

'I thought you wanted William Pickering.'

'I don't have time. I need the President.'

The captain did not move, his huge frame blocking her way. 'My understanding is that the President is about to give a very important live press conference. I doubt he's taking personal phone calls.'

Rachel stood as straight as she could on her wobbly legs and fixed her eyes on the captain. 'Sir, you do not have the clearance for me to explain the situation, but the President is about to make a terrible mistake. I have information he desperately needs to hear. Now. You need to trust me.'

The captain stared at her a long moment. Frowning, he checked the clock again. 'Nine minutes? I can't get you a secure connection to the White House in that short a time. All I could offer is a radiophone. Unsecured. And we'd have to go to antenna depth, which will take a few—'

'Do it! Now!'

CHAPTER 67

The White House telephone switchboard was located on the lower level of the East Wing. Three switchboard operators were always on duty. At the moment, only two were seated at the controls. The third operator was at a full sprint toward the Briefing Room. In her hand, she carried a cordless phone. She'd tried to patch the call through to the Oval Office, but the President was already en route to the press conference. She'd tried to call his aides on their cellulars, but before televised briefings, all cellular phones in and around the Briefing Room were turned off so as not to interrupt the proceedings.

Running a cordless phone directly to the President at a time like this seemed questionable at best, and yet when the White House's NRO liaison called claiming she had emergency information that the President must get before going live, the operator had little doubt she needed to jump. The question now was whether she would get there in time.

In a small medical office onboard the U.S.S. *Charlotte*, Rachel Sexton clutched a phone receiver to her ear and waited to talk to the President. Tolland and Corky sat nearby, still looking shaken. Corky had five stitches and a deep bruise on his cheekbone. All three of them had been helped into Thinsulate thermal underwear, heavy navy flight suits, oversized wool socks, and deck boots. With a hot cup of stale coffee in her hand, Rachel was starting to feel almost human again.

'What's the holdup?' Tolland pressed. 'It's seven fifty-six!'

Rachel could not imagine. She had successfully reached one of the White House operators, explained who she was and that this was an emergency. The operator seemed sympathetic, had placed Rachel on hold, and was now, supposedly, making it her top priority to patch Rachel through to the President.

Four minutes, Rachel thought. *Hurry up!*

Closing her eyes, Rachel tried to gather her thoughts. It had been one hell of a day. *I'm on a nuclear submarine*, she said to herself, knowing she was damned lucky to be anywhere at all. According to the submarine captain, the *Charlotte* had been on a routine patrol in the Bering Sea two days ago and had picked up anomalous underwater sounds coming from the Milne Ice Shelf – drilling, jet noise, lots of encrypted radio traffic. They had been redirected and told to lie quietly and listen. An hour or so ago, they'd heard an explosion in the ice shelf and moved in to check it out. That was when they heard Rachel's SOS call.

'Three minutes left!' Tolland sounded anxious now as he monitored the clock.

Rachel was definitely getting nervous now. What was taking so long? Why hadn't the President taken her call? If Zach Herney went public with the data as it stood—

Rachel forced the thought from her mind and shook the receiver. *Pick up!*

As the White House operator dashed toward the stage entrance of the Briefing Room, she was met with a gathering throng of staff members. Everyone here was talking excitedly, making final preparations. She could see the President twenty yards away waiting at the entrance. The makeup people were still primping.

'Coming through!' the operator said, trying to get through the crowd. 'Call for the President. Excuse me. Coming through!'

'*Live in two minutes!*' a media coordinator called out.

Clutching the phone, the operator shoved her way toward the President. 'Call for the President!' she panted. 'Coming through!'

A towering roadblock stepped into her path. Marjorie Tench. The senior adviser's long face grimaced down in disapproval. 'What's going on?'

'I have an emergency!' The operator was breathless. '. . . phone call for the President.'

Tench looked incredulous. 'Not now, you don't!'

'It's from Rachel Sexton. She says it's urgent.'

The scowl that darkened Tench's face appeared to be more one of puzzlement than anger. Tench eyed the cordless phone. 'That's a house line. That's not secure.'

'No, ma'am. But the incoming call is open anyway. She's on a radiophone. She needs to speak to the President right away.'

'*Live in ninety seconds!*'

Tench's cold eyes stared, and she held out a spiderlike hand. 'Give me the phone.'

The operator's heart was pounding now. 'Ms Sexton wants to speak to President Herney directly. She told me to postpone the press conference until she'd talked to him. I assured—'

Tench stepped toward the operator now, her voice a seething

whisper. 'Let me tell you how this works. You do not take orders from the daughter of the President's opponent, you take them from me. I can assure you, this is as close as you are getting to the President until I find out what the hell is going on.'

The operator looked toward the President, who was now surrounded by microphone technicians, stylists, and several staff members talking him through final revisions of his speech.

'*Sixty seconds!*' the television supervisor yelled.

Onboard the *Charlotte*, Rachel Sexton was pacing wildly in the tight space when she finally heard a click on the telephone line.

A raspy voice came on. 'Hello?'

'President Herney?' Rachel blurted.

'Marjorie Tench,' the voice corrected. 'I am the President's senior adviser. Whoever this is, I must warn you that prank calls against the White House are in violation of—'

For Christ's sake! 'This is not a prank! This is Rachel Sexton. I'm your NRO liaison and—'

'I am aware of who Rachel Sexton is, ma'am. And I am doubtful that you are she. You've called the White House on an unsecured line telling me to interrupt a major presidential broadcast. That is hardly proper MO for someone with—'

'Listen,' Rachel fumed, 'I briefed your whole staff a couple of hours ago on a meteorite. You sat in the front row. You watched my briefing on a television sitting on the President's desk! Any questions?'

Tench fell silent a moment. 'Ms Sexton, what is the meaning of this?'

'The meaning is that you have to stop the President! His meteorite data is all wrong! We've just learned the meteorite was inserted from *beneath* the ice shelf. I don't know by whom, and I don't know why! But things are not what they seem up here! The President is about to endorse some seriously errant data, and I strongly advise—'

'Wait one goddamned minute!' Tench lowered her voice. 'Do you realize what you are saying?'

'Yes! I suspect the NASA administrator has orchestrated some kind of large-scale fraud, and President Herney is about to get caught in the middle. You've at least got to postpone ten minutes so I can explain to him what's been going on up here. Someone tried to kill me, for God's sake!'

Tench's voice turned to ice. 'Ms Sexton, let me give you a word of warning. If you are having second thoughts about your role in helping the White House in this campaign, you should have thought of that long before you personally endorsed that meteorite data for the President.'

'What?' *Is she even listening?*

'I'm revolted by your display. Using an unsecured line is a cheap stunt. Implying the meteorite data has been faked? What kind of intelligence official uses a radiophone to call the White House and talk about classified information? Obviously you are *hoping* someone intercepts this message.'

'Norah Mangor was killed over this! Dr Ming is also dead. You've got to warn—'

'Stop right there! I don't know what you're playing at, but I will remind you – and anyone *else* who happens to be intercepting this phone call – that the White House possesses videotaped depositions from NASA's top scientists, several renowned civilian scientists, and *yourself*, Ms Sexton, all endorsing the meteorite data as accurate. Why you are suddenly changing your story, I can only imagine. Whatever the reason, consider yourself relieved of your White House post as of this instant, and if you try to taint this discovery with any more absurd allegations of foul play, I assure you the White House and NASA will sue you for defamation so fast you won't have a chance to pack a suitcase before you go to jail.'

Rachel opened her mouth to speak, but no words came.

'Zach Herney has been generous to you,' Tench snapped, 'and frankly this smacks of a cheap Sexton publicity stunt. Drop it right now, or we'll press charges. I swear it.'

The line went dead.

Rachel's mouth was still hanging open when the captain knocked on the door.

'Ms Sexton?' the captain said, peering in. 'We're picking up a faint signal from Canadian National Radio. President Zach Herney has just begun his press conference.'

CHAPTER **68**

Standing at the podium in the White House Briefing Room, Zach Herney felt the heat of the media lights and knew the world was watching. The targeted blitz performed by the White House Press Office had created a contagion of media buzz. Those who did not hear about the address via television, radio, or on-line news, invariably heard about it from neighbors, coworkers, and family. By 8:00 P.M., anyone not living in a cave was speculating about the topic of the President's address. In bars and living rooms over the globe, millions leaned toward their televisions in apprehensive wonder.

It was during moments like these – facing the world – that Zach Herney truly felt the weight of his office. Anyone who said power was not addictive had never really experienced it. As he began his address, however, Herney sensed something was amiss. He was not a man prone to stage fright, and so the tingle of apprehension now tightening in his core startled him.

It's the magnitude of the audience, he told himself. And yet he knew something else. Instinct. Something he had seen.

It had been such a little thing, and yet . . .

He told himself to forget it. It was nothing. And yet it stuck.

Tench.

Moments ago, as Herney was preparing to take the stage, he had seen Marjorie Tench in the yellow hallway, talking on a cordless phone. This was strange in itself, but it was made more so by the White House operator standing beside her, her face white with apprehension. Herney could not hear Tench's phone conversation, but he could see it was contentious. Tench was arguing with a vehemence and anger the President had seldom seen – even from Tench. He paused a moment and caught her eye, inquisitive.

Tench gave him the thumbs-up. Herney had never seen Tench give *anyone* the thumbs-up. It was the last image in Herney's mind as he was cued onto the stage.

On the blue rug in the press area inside the NASA habisphere on Ellesmere Island, Administrator Lawrence Ekstrom was seated at the center of the long symposium table, flanked by top NASA officials and scientists. On a large monitor facing them the President's opening statement was being piped in live. The remainder of the NASA crew was huddled around other monitors, teeming with excitement as their commander-in-chief launched into his press conference.

'Good evening,' Herney was saying, sounding uncharacteristically stiff. 'To my fellow countrymen, and to our friends around the world . . .'

Ekstrom gazed at the huge charred mass of rock displayed prominently in front of him. His eyes moved to a standby monitor, where he watched himself, flanked by his most austere personnel, against a backdrop of a huge American flag and NASA logo. The dramatic lighting made the setting look like some kind of neomodern painting – the twelve apostles at the last supper. Zach Herney had turned this whole thing into a political sideshow. *Herney had no choice.* Ekstrom still felt like a televangelist, packaging God for the masses.

In about five minutes the President would introduce Ekstrom and his NASA staff. Then, in a dramatic satellite linkup from the top of the world, NASA would join the President in sharing this news with the world. After a brief account of how the discovery was made, what it meant for space science, and some mutual backpatting, NASA and the President would hand duty off to celebrity scientist, Michael Tolland, whose documentary would roll for just under fifteen minutes. Afterward, with credibility and enthusiasm at its peak, Ekstrom and the President would say their goodnights, promising more information to come in the days ahead via endless NASA press conferences.

As Ekstrom sat and waited for his cue, he felt a cavernous shame settling inside him. He'd known he would feel it. He'd been expecting it.

He'd told lies . . . endorsed untruths.

Somehow, though, the lies seemed inconsequential now. Ekstrom had a bigger weight on his mind.

*   *   *

In the chaos of the ABC production room, Gabrielle Ashe stood
shoulder to shoulder with dozens of strangers, all necks craned toward
the bank of television monitors suspended from the ceiling. A hush
fell as the moment arrived. Gabrielle closed her eyes, praying that
when she opened them she would not be looking at images of her own
naked body.

The air inside Senator Sexton's den was alive with excitement. All of
his visitors were standing now, their eyes glued to the large-screen
television.

Zach Herney stood before the world, and incredibly, his greeting
had been awkward. He seemed momentarily uncertain.

He looks shaky, Sexton thought. *He never looks shaky.*

'Look at him,' somebody whispered. 'It has to be bad news.'

The space station? Sexton wondered.

Herney looked directly into the camera and took a deep breath. 'My
friends, I have puzzled for many days now over how best to make this
announcement . . .'

Three easy words, Senator Sexton willed him. *We blew it.*

Herney spoke for a moment about how unfortunate it was that
NASA had become such an issue in this election and how, that being
the case, he felt he needed to preface the timing of his impending
statement with an apology.

'I would have preferred any other moment in history to make this
announcement,' he said. 'The political charge in the air tends to make
doubters out of dreamers, and yet as your President, I have no choice
but to share with you what I have recently learned.' He smiled. 'It
seems the magic of the cosmos is something which does not work on
any human schedule . . . not even that of a president.'

Everyone in Sexton's den seemed to recoil in unison. *What?*

'Two weeks ago,' Herney said, 'NASA's new Polar Orbiting Density
Scanner passed over the Milne Ice Shelf on Ellesmere Island, a remote
landmass located above the Eightieth Parallel in the high Arctic
Ocean.'

Sexton and the others exchanged confused looks.

'This NASA satellite,' Herney continued, 'detected a large, high-density rock buried two hundred feet under the ice.' Herney smiled now for the first time, finding his stride. 'On receiving the data, NASA immediately suspected PODS had found a meteorite.'

'A meteorite?' Sexton sputtered, standing. 'This is news?'

'NASA sent a team up to the ice shelf to take core samples. It was then that NASA made . . .' He paused. 'Frankly, they made the scientific discovery of the century.'

Sexton took an incredulous step toward the television. *No* . . . His guests shifted uneasily.

'Ladies and gentlemen,' Herney announced, 'several hours ago, NASA pulled from the Arctic ice an eight-ton meteorite, which contains . . .' The President paused again, giving the whole world time to lean forward. 'A meteorite which contains *fossils* of a life-form. Dozens of them. Unequivocal proof of extraterrestrial life.'

On cue, a brilliant image illuminated on the screen behind the President – a perfectly delineated fossil of an enormous buglike creature embedded in a charred rock.

In Sexton's den, six entrepreneurs jumped up in wide-eyed horror. Sexton stood frozen in place.

'My friends,' the President said, 'the fossil behind me is one hundred and ninety million years old. It was discovered in a fragment of a meteorite called the Jungersol Fall which hit the Arctic Ocean almost three centuries ago. NASA's exciting new PODS satellite discovered this meteorite fragment buried in an ice shelf. NASA and this administration have taken enormous care over the past two weeks to confirm every aspect of this momentous discovery before making it public. In the next half hour you will be hearing from numerous NASA and civilian scientists, as well as viewing a short documentary prepared by a familiar face whom I'm sure you all will recognize. Before I go any further, though, I absolutely must welcome, live via satellite from above the Arctic Circle, the man whose leadership, vision, and hard work is solely responsible for this historic moment. It is with great honor that I present NASA administrator Lawrence Ekstrom.'

Herney turned to the screen on perfect cue.

The image of the meteorite dramatically dissolved into a regal-looking panel of NASA scientists seated at a long table, flanked by the dominant frame of Lawrence Ekstrom.

'Thank you, Mr President.' Ekstrom's air was stern and proud as he stood up and looked directly into the camera. 'It gives me great pride to share with all of you, this – NASA's finest hour.'

Ekstrom spoke passionately about NASA and the discovery. With a fanfare of patriotism and triumph, he segued flawlessly to a documentary hosted by civilian science-celebrity Michael Tolland.

As he watched, Senator Sexton fell to his knees in front of the television, his fingers clutching at his silver mane. *No! God, no!*

CHAPTER 69

Marjorie Tench was livid as she broke away from the jovial chaos outside the Briefing Room and marched back to her private corner in the West Wing. She was in no mood for celebration. The phone call from Rachel Sexton had been most unexpected.

Most disappointing.

Tench slammed her office door, stalked to her desk, and dialed the White House operator. 'William Pickering. NRO.'

Tench lit a cigarette and paced the room as she waited for the operator to track down Pickering. Normally, he might have gone home for the night, but with the White House's big windup into tonight's press conference, Tench guessed Pickering had been in his office all evening, glued to his television screen, wondering what could possibly be going on in the world about which the NRO director did not have prior knowledge.

Tench cursed herself for not trusting her instincts when the President said he wanted to send Rachel Sexton to Milne. Tench had been wary, feeling it was an unnecessary risk. But the President had been convincing, persuading Tench that the White House staff had grown cynical over the past weeks and would be suspect of the NASA discovery if the news came from in-house. As Herney had promised, Rachel Sexton's endorsement had squelched suspicions, prevented any skeptical in-house debate, and forced the White House staff to move forward with a unified front. Invaluable, Tench had to admit. And yet now Rachel Sexton had changed her tune.

The bitch called me on an unsecured line.

Rachel Sexton was obviously intent on destroying the credibility of this discovery, and Tench's only solace was knowing the President had captured Rachel's earlier briefing on videotape. *Thank God.* At least Herney had thought to obtain that small insurance. Tench was starting to fear they were going to need it.

At the moment, however, Tench was trying to stem the bleeding in other ways. Rachel Sexton was a smart woman, and if she truly intended to go head-to-head with the White House and NASA, she would need to recruit some powerful allies. Her first logical choice would be William Pickering. Tench already knew how Pickering felt about NASA. She needed to get to Pickering before Rachel did.

'Ms Tench?' the transparent voice on the line said. 'William Pickering here. To what do I owe this honor?'

Tench could hear the television in the background – NASA commentary. She could already sense in his tone that he was still reeling from the press conference. 'Do you have a minute, Director?'

'I expected you'd be busy celebrating. Quite a night for you. Looks like NASA and the President are back in the fight.'

Tench heard stark amazement in his voice, combined with a tinge of acrimony – the latter no doubt on account of the man's legendary distaste for hearing breaking news at the same time as the rest of the world.

'I apologize,' Tench said, trying to build an immediate bridge, 'that the White House and NASA were forced to keep you unapprised.'

'You are aware,' Pickering said, 'that the NRO detected NASA activity up there a couple weeks ago and ran an inquiry?'

Tench frowned. *He's pissed.* 'Yes, I know. And yet—'

'NASA told us it was nothing. They said they were running some kind of extreme environment training exercises. Testing equipment, that sort of thing.' Pickering paused. 'We bought the lie.'

'Let's not call it a *lie*,' Tench said. 'More of a necessary misdirection. Considering the magnitude of the discovery, I trust you understand NASA's need to keep this quiet.'

'From the public, perhaps.'

Pouting was not in the repertoire of men like William Pickering, and Tench sensed this was as close as he would get. 'I only have a minute,' Tench said, working to retain her dominant position, 'but I thought I should call and warn you.'

'Warn me?' Pickering waxed wry momentarily. 'Has Zach Herney decided to appoint a new, NASA-friendly NRO director?'

'Of course not. The President understands your criticisms of NASA are simply issues of security, and he is working to plug those holes. I'm actually calling about one of your employees.' She paused. 'Rachel Sexton. Have you heard from her this evening?'

'No. I sent her to the White House this morning at the President's request. You've obviously kept her busy. She has yet to check in.'

Tench was relieved to have gotten to Pickering first. She took a drag on her cigarette and spoke as calmly as possible. 'I suspect you may be getting a call from Ms Sexton sometime soon.'

'Good. I've been expecting one. I've got to tell you, when the President's press conference began, I was concerned Zach Herney might have convinced Ms Sexton to participate publicly. I'm pleased to see he resisted.'

'Zach Herney is a decent person,' Tench said, 'which is more than I can say for Rachel Sexton.'

There was a long pause on the line. 'I hope I misunderstood that.'

Tench sighed heavily. 'No, sir, I'm afraid you did not. I'd prefer not to talk specifics on the phone, but Rachel Sexton, it seems, has decided she wants to undermine the credibility of this NASA announcement. I have no idea why, but after she reviewed and endorsed NASA's data earlier this afternoon, she has suddenly pulled an about-face and is spouting some of the most improbable allegations imaginable of NASA treachery and fraud.'

Pickering sounded intense now. 'Excuse me?'

'Troubling, yes. I hate to be the one to tell you this, but Ms Sexton contacted me two minutes before the press conference and warned me to cancel the whole thing.'

'On what grounds?'

'Absurd ones, frankly. She said she'd found serious flaws in the data.'

Pickering's long silence was more wary than Tench would have liked. 'Flaws?' he finally said.

'Ridiculous, really, after two full weeks of NASA experimentation and—'

'I find it very hard to believe someone like Rachel Sexton would have told you to postpone the President's press conference unless she had a damn good reason.' Pickering sounded troubled. 'Maybe you should have listened to her.'

'Oh, please!' Tench blurted, coughing. 'You saw the press conference. The meteorite data was confirmed and reconfirmed by countless specialists. Including civilians. Doesn't it seem suspicious to you that Rachel Sexton – the daughter of the only man whom this announcement hurts – is suddenly changing her tune?'

'It seems suspicious, Ms Tench, only because I happen to know that Ms Sexton and her father are barely civil to one another. I cannot imagine why Rachel Sexton would, after years of service to the President, suddenly decide to switch camps and tell lies to support her father.'

'Ambition, perhaps? I really don't know. Maybe the opportunity to be first daughter . . .' Tench let it hang.

Pickering's tone hardened instantly. 'Thin ice, Ms Tench. Very thin.'

Tench scowled. What the hell did she expect? She was accusing a prominent member of Pickering's staff of treason against the President. The man was going to be defensive.

'Put her on,' Pickering demanded. 'I'd like to speak to Ms Sexton myself.'

'I'm afraid that's impossible,' Tench replied. 'She's not at the White House.'

'Where is she?'

'The President sent her to Milne this morning to examine the data firsthand. She has yet to return.'

Pickering sounded livid now. 'I was never informed—'

'I do not have time for hurt pride, Director. I have simply called as a courtesy. I wanted to warn you that Rachel Sexton has decided to pursue her own agenda with respect to tonight's announcement. She will be looking for allies. If she contacts you, you would be wise to know that the White House is in possession of a video taken earlier today in which she endorsed this meteorite data in its entirety in front of the President, his cabinet, and his entire staff. If now, for whatever motives she might have, Rachel Sexton attempts to besmirch the good name of Zach Herney or of NASA, then I swear to you the White House will see to it she falls hard and far.' Tench waited a moment, to be sure her meaning had settled in. 'I expect you to repay the courtesy of this call by informing me immediately if Rachel Sexton contacts you. She is attacking the President directly, and the White House intends to detain her for questioning before she does any serious damage. I will be waiting for your call, Director. That's all. Good night.'

Marjorie Tench hung up, certain that William Pickering had never been talked to like that in his life. At least now he knew she was serious.

On the top floor of the NRO, William Pickering stood at his window and stared into the Virginia night. The call from Marjorie Tench had been deeply troubling. He chewed at his lip as he tried to assemble the pieces in his mind.

'Director?' his secretary said, knocking quietly. 'You have another phone call.'

'Not now,' Pickering said absently.

'It's Rachel Sexton.'

Pickering wheeled. Tench was apparently a fortune-teller. 'Okay. Patch her through, right away.'

'Actually, sir, it's an encrypted AV stream. Do you want to take it in the conference room?'

An AV stream? 'Where is she calling from?'

The secretary told him.

Pickering stared. Bewildered, he hurried down the hall toward the conference room. This was something he had to see.

CHAPTER 70

The *Charlotte*'s 'dead room' – designed after a similar structure at Bell Laboratories – was what was formally known as an anechoic chamber. An acoustical clean room containing no parallel or reflective surfaces, it absorbed sound with 99.4 percent efficiency. Because of the acoustically conductive nature of metal and water, conversations onboard submarines were always vulnerable to interception by nearby eavesdroppers or parasitic suction mics attached to the outer hull. The dead room was, in effect, a tiny chamber inside the submarine from which absolutely no sound could escape. All conversations inside this insulated box were entirely secure.

The chamber looked like a walk-in closet whose ceiling, walls, and floor had been completely covered with foam spires jutting inward from all directions. It reminded Rachel of a cramped underwater cave where stalagmites had run wild, growing off every surface. Most unsettling, however, was the apparent lack of a floor.

The floor was a taut, meshed chicken-wire grid strung horizontally across the room like a fishing net, giving the inhabitants the feeling that they were suspended midway up the wall. The mesh was rubberized and stiff beneath the feet. As Rachel gazed down through the webbed flooring, she felt like she was crossing a string bridge suspended over a surrealistic fractalized landscape. Three feet below, a forest of foam needles pointed ominously upward.

Instantly upon entering Rachel had sensed the disorientating lifelessness to the air, as if every bit of energy had been sucked out. Her ears felt as if they'd been stuffed with cotton. Only her breath was audible inside her head. She called out, and the effect was that of speaking into a pillow. The walls absorbed every reverberation, making the only perceivable vibrations those inside her head.

Now the captain had departed, closing the padded door behind him. Rachel, Corky, and Tolland were seated in the center of the room at a small U-shaped table that stood on long metal stilts that descended through the mesh. On the table were affixed several gooseneck microphones, headphones, and a video console with a fish-eye camera on top. It looked like a mini-United Nations symposium.

As someone who worked in the U.S. intelligence community – the world's foremost manufacturers of hard laser microphones, under-water parabolic eavesdroppers, and other hypersensitive listening devices – Rachel was well aware there were few places on earth where one could have a truly secure conversation. The dead room was apparently one of those places. The mics and headphones on the table enabled a face-to-face 'conference call' in which people could speak freely, knowing the vibrations of their words could not escape the room. Their voices, upon entering the microphones, would be heavily encrypted for their long journey through the atmosphere.

'Level check.' The voice materialized suddenly inside their headphones, causing Rachel, Tolland, and Corky to jump. 'Do you read me, Ms Sexton?'

Rachel leaned into the microphone. 'Yes. Thank you.' *Whoever you are.*

'I have Director Pickering on the line for you. He's accepting AV. I am signing off now. You will have your data stream momentarily.'

Rachel heard the line go dead. There was a distant whirr of static and then a rapid series of beeps and clicks in the headphones. With startling clarity, the video screen in front of them sprang to life, and Rachel saw Director Pickering in the NRO conference room. He was alone. His head snapped up and he looked into Rachel's eyes.

She felt oddly relieved to see him.

'Ms Sexton,' he said, his expression perplexed and troubled. 'What in the world is going on?'

'The meteorite, sir,' Rachel said. 'I think we may have a serious problem.'

CHAPTER 71

Inside the *Charlotte*'s dead room, Rachel Sexton introduced Michael Tolland and Corky Marlinson to Pickering. Then she took charge and launched into a quick account of the day's incredible chain of events.

The NRO director sat motionless as he listened.

Rachel told him about the bioluminescent plankton in the extraction pit, their journey onto the ice shelf and discovery of an insertion shaft beneath the meteorite, and finally of their sudden attack by a military team she suspected was Special Ops.

William Pickering was known for his ability to listen to disturbing information without so much as flinching an eye, and yet his gaze grew more and more troubled with each progression in Rachel's story. She sensed disbelief and then rage when she talked about Norah Mangor's murder and their own near-death escape. Although Rachel wanted to voice her suspicions of the NASA administrator's involvement, she knew Pickering well enough not to point fingers without evidence. She gave Pickering the story as cold hard facts. When she was finished, Pickering did not respond for several seconds.

'Ms Sexton,' he finally said, 'all of you . . .' He moved his gaze to each of them. 'If what you're saying is true, and I cannot imagine why three of you would lie about this, you are all very lucky to be alive.'

They all nodded in silence. The President had called in four civilian scientists . . . and two of them were now dead.

Pickering heaved a disconsolate sigh, as if he had no idea what to say next. The events clearly made little sense. 'Is there any way,' Pickering asked, 'that this insertion shaft you're seeing in that GPR printout is a natural phenomenon?'

Rachel shook her head. 'It's too perfect.' She unfolded the soggy GPR printout and held it up in front of the camera. 'Flawless.'

Pickering studied the image, scowling in agreement. 'Don't let that out of your hands.'

'I called Marjorie Tench to warn her to stop the President,' Rachel said. 'But she shut me down.'

'I know. She told me.'

Rachel looked up, stunned. 'Marjorie Tench called you?' *That was fast.*

'Just now. She's very concerned. She feels you are attempting some kind of stunt to discredit the President and NASA. Perhaps to help your father.'

Rachel stood up. She waved the GPR printout and motioned to her two companions. 'We were almost killed! Does this look like some kind of stunt? And why would I—'

Pickering held up his hands. 'Easy. What Ms Tench failed to tell me was that there were three of you.'

Rachel could not recall if Tench had even given her time to mention Corky and Tolland.

'Nor did she tell me you had physical evidence,' Pickering said. 'I was skeptical of her claims before I spoke to you, and now I am convinced she is mistaken. I do not doubt your claims. The question at this point is what it all means.'

There was a long silence.

William Pickering rarely looked confused, but he shook his head, seeming lost. 'Let's assume for the moment that someone *did* insert this meteorite beneath the ice. That begs the obvious issue of *why*. If NASA has a meteorite with fossils in it, why would they, or anyone else for that matter, care where it is found?'

'It appears,' Rachel said, 'that the insertion was performed such that PODS would make the discovery, and the meteorite would appear to be a fragment from a known impact.'

'The Jungersol Fall,' Corky prompted.

'But of what *value* is the meteorite's association with a known impact?' Pickering demanded, sounding almost mad. 'Aren't these fossils an astounding discovery anywhere and anytime? No matter what meteoritic event they are associated with?'

All three nodded.

Pickering hesitated, looking displeased. 'Unless . . . of course . . .'

Rachel saw the wheels turning behind the director's eyes. He had found the simplest explanation for placing the meteorite concurrent with the Jungersol strata, but the simplest explanation was also the most troubling.

'Unless,' Pickering continued, 'the careful placement was intended to lend credibility to totally false data.' He sighed, turning to Corky. 'Dr Marlinson, what is the possibility that this meteorite is a counterfeit?'

'Counterfeit, sir?'

'Yes. A fake. Manufactured.'

'A *fake* meteorite?' Corky gave an awkward laugh. 'Utterly impossible! That meteorite was examined by countless professionals. *Myself* included. Chemical scans, spectrograph, rubidium-strontium dating. It is unlike any kind of rock ever seen on earth. The meteorite is authentic. Any astrogeologist would agree.'

Pickering seemed to consider this a long time, gently stroking his tie. 'And yet taking into account the amount NASA has to gain from this discovery right now, the apparent signs of tampering with evidence, and your being attacked . . . the first and only logical conclusion I can draw is that this meteorite is a well-executed fraud.'

'Impossible!' Corky sounded angry now. 'With all respect, sir, meteorites are not some Hollywood special effect that can be conjured up in a lab to fool a bunch of unsuspecting astrophysicists. They are chemically complex objects with unique crystalline structures and element ratios!'

'I am not challenging you, Dr Marlinson. I am simply following a logical chain of analysis. Considering someone wanted to kill you to keep you from revealing it was inserted under the ice, I'm inclined to entertain all kinds of wild scenarios here. What specifically makes you certain this rock is indeed a meteorite?'

'Specifically?' Corky's voice cracked in the headphones. 'A flawless fusion crust, the presence of chondrules, a nickel ratio unlike anything ever found on earth. If you're suggesting that someone tricked us by manufacturing this rock in a lab, then all I can say is that the lab was about one hundred and ninety million years old.' Corky dug in his pocket and pulled out a stone shaped like a CD. He held it in front of the camera. 'We chemically dated samples like this with numerous methods. Rubidium-strontium dating is *not* something you can fake!'

Pickering looked surprised. 'You have a sample?'

Corky shrugged. 'NASA had dozens of them floating around.'

'You mean to tell me,' Pickering said, looking at Rachel now, 'that NASA discovered a meteorite they think contains life, and they're letting people walk off with samples?'

'The point,' Corky said, 'is that the sample in my hands is genuine.' He held the rock close to the camera. 'You could give this to any petrologist or geologist or astronomer on earth, they would run tests, and they would tell you two things: one, it is one hundred and ninety million years old; and two, it is chemically dissimilar from the kind of rock we have here on earth.'

Pickering leaned forward, studying the fossil embedded in the rock. He seemed momentarily transfixed. Finally, he sighed. 'I am not a scientist. All I can say is that if that meteorite is genuine, which it appears it is, I would like to know why NASA didn't present it to the world at face value? Why has someone carefully placed it under the ice as if to *persuade* us of its authenticity?'

*   *   *

At that moment, inside the White House, a security officer was dialing Marjorie Tench.

The senior adviser answered on the first ring. 'Yeah?'

'Ms Tench,' the officer said, 'I have the information you requested earlier. The radiophone call that Rachel Sexton placed to you earlier this evening. We have the trace.'

'Tell me.'

'Secret Service ops says the signal originated aboard the naval submarine U.S.S. *Charlotte*.'

'What?'

'They don't have coordinates, ma'am, but they are certain of the vessel code.'

'Oh, for Christ's sake!' Tench slammed down the receiver without another word.

CHAPTER 72

The muted acoustics of the *Charlotte*'s dead room were starting to make Rachel feel mildly nauseated. On-screen, William Pickering's troubled gaze moved now to Michael Tolland. 'You're quiet, Mr Tolland.'

Tolland glanced up like a student who had been called on unexpectedly. 'Sir?'

'You just gave quite a convincing documentary on television,' Pickering said. 'What's your take on the meteorite now?'

'Well, sir,' Tolland said, his discomfort obvious, 'I have to agree with Dr Marlinson. I believe the fossils and meteorite are authentic. I'm fairly well versed in dating techniques, and the age of that stone was confirmed by multiple tests. The nickel content as well. These data cannot be forged. There exists no doubt the rock, formed one hundred and ninety million years ago, exhibits nonterrestrial nickel ratios and contains dozens of confirmed fossils whose formation is also dated at one hundred and ninety million years. I can think of no other possible explanation than that NASA has found an authentic meteorite.'

Pickering fell silent now. His expression was one of quandary, a look Rachel had never before seen on William Pickering.

'What should we do, sir?' Rachel asked. 'Obviously we need to alert the President there are problems with the data.'

Pickering frowned. 'Let's hope the President doesn't *already* know.'

Rachel felt a knot rise in her throat. Pickering's implication was clear. *President Herney could be involved.* Rachel strongly doubted it, and yet both the President and NASA had plenty to gain here.

'Unfortunately,' Pickering said, 'with the exception of this GPR printout revealing an insertion shaft, all of the scientific data points to a credible NASA discovery.' He paused, dire. 'And this issue of your being attacked . . .' He looked up at Rachel. 'You mentioned Special Ops.'

'Yes, sir.' She told him again about the Improvised Munitions and tactics.

Pickering looked more and more unhappy by the moment. Rachel sensed her boss was contemplating the number of people who might have access to a small military kill force. Certainly the President had access. Probably Marjorie Tench too, as senior adviser. Quite possibly NASA administrator Lawrence Ekstrom with his ties to the Pentagon. Unfortunately, as Rachel considered the myriad of possibilities, she realized the controlling force behind the attack could have been almost anyone with high-level political clout and the right connections.

'I could phone the President right now,' Pickering said, 'but I don't think that's wise, at least until we know who's involved. My ability to protect you becomes limited once we involve the White House. In addition, I'm not sure what I would tell him. If the meteorite is real, which you all feel it is, then your allegation of an insertion shaft and attack doesn't make sense; the President would have every right to question the validity of my claim.' He paused as if calculating the options. 'Regardless . . . whatever the truth is or who the players are, some very powerful people will take hits if this information goes public. I suggest we get you to safety right away, before we start rocking any boats.'

Get us to safety? The comment surprised Rachel. 'I think we're fairly safe on a nuclear submarine, sir.'

Pickering looked skeptical. 'Your presence on that submarine won't stay secret long. I'm pulling you out immediately. Frankly, I'll feel better when the three of you are sitting in my office.'

CHAPTER 73

Senator Sexton huddled alone on his couch feeling like a refugee. His Westbrooke Place apartment that had only an hour ago been filled with new friends and supporters now looked forsaken, scattered with the rubble of snifters and business cards, abandoned by men who had quite literally dashed out the door.

Now Sexton crouched in solitude before his television, wanting more than anything to turn it off and yet being unable to pull himself from the endless media analyses. This was Washington, and it didn't take long for the analysts to rush through their pseudoscientific and philosophical hyperbole and lock in on the ugly stuff – the politics. Like torture masters rubbing acid in Sexton's wounds, the newscasters were stating and restating the obvious.

'Hours ago, Sexton's campaign was soaring,' one analyst said. 'Now, with NASA's discovery, the senator's campaign has crashed back to earth.'

Sexton winced, reaching for the Courvoisier and taking a hit right out of the bottle. Tonight, he knew, would be the longest and loneliest night of his life. He despised Marjorie Tench for setting him up. He despised Gabrielle Ashe for mentioning NASA in the first place. He despised the President for being so goddamned lucky. And he despised the world for laughing at him.

'Obviously, this is devastating for the senator,' the analyst was saying. 'The President and NASA have claimed an incalculable triumph with this discovery. News like this would revitalize the President's campaign regardless of Sexton's position on NASA, but with Sexton's admission today that he would go so far as to abolish NASA funding outright if need be . . . well, this presidential announcement is a one-two punch from which the senator will not recover.'

I was tricked, Sexton said. *The White House fucking set me up.*

The analyst was smiling now. 'All of the credibility NASA has lost with Americans recently has just been restored in spades. There's a real feeling of national pride out there on the streets right now.'

'As there should be. They love Zach Herney, and they were losing faith. You've got to admit, the President was lying down and taking some pretty big hits recently, but he's come out of it smelling like a rose.'

Sexton thought of the CNN debate that afternoon and hung his head, thinking he might be sick to his stomach. All of the NASA inertia he had so carefully built up over the last months had not only come to a screeching halt, but it had become an anchor around his neck. He looked like a fool. He'd been brazenly played by the White House. He was already dreading all the cartoons in tomorrow's paper. His name would be the punch line to every joke in the country. Obviously, there would be no more quiet SFF campaign funding. Everything had changed. All of the men who had been in his apartment had just seen their dreams go down the toilet. The privatization of space had just struck a brick wall.

Taking another hit of cognac, the senator stood up and walked unevenly to his desk. He gazed down at the unhooked phone receiver. Knowing it was an act of masochistic self-flagellation, he slowly replaced the phone receiver in its cradle and began counting the seconds.

One . . . two . . . The phone rang. He let the machine pick up.

'Senator Sexton, Judy Oliver from CNN. I'd like to give you an opportunity to react to the NASA discovery this evening. Please call me.' She hung up.

Sexton started counting again. *One . . .* The phone started ringing. He ignored it, letting the machine get it. Another reporter.

Holding his bottle of Courvoisier, Sexton wandered toward the sliding door of his balcony. He pulled it aside and stepped out into the cool air. Leaning against the railing, he gazed out across town to the illuminated facade of the White House in the distance. The lights seemed to twinkle gleefully in the wind.

Bastards, he thought. *For centuries we've been looking for proof of*

life in the heavens. Now we find it in the same fucking year as my
election? This wasn't propitious, this was goddamned clairvoyant.
Every apartment window, for as far as Sexton could see, had a
television on. Sexton wondered where Gabrielle Ashe was tonight.
This was all her fault. She'd fed him NASA failure after NASA failure.

He raised the bottle to take another swig.

Goddamned Gabrielle . . . she's the reason I'm in this so deep.

Across town, standing amid the chaos of the ABC production room,
Gabrielle Ashe felt numb. The President's announcement had come
out of left field, leaving her suspended in a semicatatonic haze. She
stood, lock-kneed in the center of the production room floor, staring
up at one of the television monitors while pandemonium raged
around her.

The initial seconds of the announcement had brought dead silence
to the newsroom floor. It had lasted only moments before the place
erupted into a deafening carnival of scrambling reporters. These
people were professionals. They had no time for personal reflection.
There would be time for that after the work was done. At the
moment, the world wanted to know more, and ABC had to provide
it. This story had everything – science, history, political drama –
an emotional mother lode. Nobody in the media was sleeping tonight.

'Gabs?' Yolanda's voice was sympathetic. 'Let's get you back into
my office before someone realizes who you are and starts grilling you
on what this means for Sexton's campaign.'

Gabrielle felt herself guided through a haze into Yolanda's glass-
walled office. Yolanda sat her down and handed her a glass of water.
She tried to force a smile. 'Look on the bright side, Gabs. Your
candidate's campaign is fucked, but at least you're not.'

'Thanks. Terrific.'

Yolanda's tone turned serious. 'Gabrielle, I know you feel like shit.
Your candidate just got hit by a Mack truck, and if you ask me, he's
not getting up. At least not in time to turn this thing around. But at
least nobody's splashing your picture all over the television. Seriously.
This is good news. Herney won't need a sex scandal now. He's looking
far too presidential right now to talk sex.'

It seemed a small consolation to Gabrielle.

'As for Tench's allegations of Sexton's illegal campaign finance . . .'
Yolanda shook her head. 'I have my doubts. Granted, Herney is
serious about no negative campaigning. And granted, a bribery
investigation would be bad for the country. But is Herney really so
patriotic that he would forgo a chance to crush his opposition, simply
to protect national morale? My guess is Tench stretched the truth
about Sexton's finances in an effort to scare. She gambled, hoping
you'd jump ship and give the President a free sex scandal. And you've
got to admit, Gabs, *tonight* would have been a hell of a night for
Sexton's morals to come into question!'

Gabrielle nodded vaguely. A sex scandal would have been a
one-two punch from which Sexton's career never would have recovered . . . ever.

'You outlasted her, Gabs. Marjorie Tench went fishing, but you
didn't bite. You're home free. There'll be other elections.'

Gabrielle nodded vaguely, unsure what to believe anymore.

'You've got to admit,' Yolanda said, 'the White House played
Sexton brilliantly – hurling him down the NASA path, getting him to
commit, coaxing him to put all his eggs in the NASA basket.'

Totally my fault, Gabrielle thought.

'And this announcement we just watched, my God, it was genius!
The importance of the discovery entirely aside, the production
values were brilliant. Live feeds from the Arctic? A Michael Tolland
documentary? Good God, how can you compete? Zach Herney nailed
it tonight. There's a reason the guy is President.'

And will be for another four years . . .

'I've got to get back to work, Gabs,' Yolanda said. 'You sit right
there as long as you want. Get your feet under you.' Yolanda headed
out the door. 'Hon, I'll check back in a few minutes.'

Alone now, Gabrielle sipped her water, but it tasted foul. Everything did. *It's all my fault*, she thought, trying to ease her conscience
by reminding herself of all the glum NASA press conferences of the
past year – the space station setbacks, the postponement of the X-33,
all the failed Mars probes, continuous budget bailouts. Gabrielle
wondered what she could have done differently.

Nothing, she told herself. *You did everything right.*

It had simply backfired.

CHAPTER 74

The thundering navy SeaHawk chopper had been scrambled under a covert operation status out of Thule Air Force Base in northern Greenland. It stayed low, out of radar range, as it shot through the gale winds across seventy miles of open sea. Then, executing the bizarre orders they had been given, the pilots fought the wind and brought the craft to a hover above a preordained set of coordinates on the empty ocean.

'Where's the rendezvous?' the copilot yelled, confused. They had been told to bring a chopper with a rescue winch, so he anticipated a search-and-retrieve operation. 'You sure these are the right co-ordinates?' He scanned the choppy seas with a search light, but there was nothing below them except—

'Holy shit!' The pilot pulled back on the stick, jolting upward.

The black mountain of steel rose before them out of the waves without warning. A gargantuan unmarked submarine blew its ballast and rose on a cloud of bubbles.

The pilots exchanged uneasy laughs. 'Guess that's them.'

As ordered, the transaction proceeded under complete radio silence. The doublewide portal on the peak of the sail opened and a seaman flashed them signals with a strobe light. The chopper then moved over the sub and dropped a three-man rescue harness, essentially three rubberized loops on a retractable cable. Within sixty seconds, the three unknown 'danglers' were swinging beneath the chopper, ascending slowly against the downdraft of the rotors.

When the copilot hauled them aboard – two men and a woman – the pilot flashed the sub the 'all clear.' Within seconds, the enormous vessel disappeared beneath the windswept sea, leaving no trace it had ever been there.

With the passengers safely aboard, the chopper pilot faced front, dipped the nose of the chopper, and accelerated south to complete his mission. The storm was closing fast, and these three strangers were to be brought safely back to Thule AFB for further jet transport. Where they were headed, the pilot had no idea. All he knew was that his orders had been from high up, and he was transporting very precious cargo.

CHAPTER 75

When the Milne storm finally exploded, unleashing its full force on the NASA habisphere, the dome shuddered as if ready to lift off the ice and launch out to sea. The steel stabilizing cables pulled taut against their stakes, vibrating like huge guitar strings and letting out a doleful drone. The generators outside stuttered, causing the lights to flicker, threatening to plunge the huge room into total blackness.

NASA administrator Lawrence Ekstrom strode across the interior of the dome. He wished he were getting the hell out of here tonight, but that was not to be. He would remain another day, giving additional on-site press conferences in the morning and overseeing preparations to transport the meteorite back to Washington. He wanted nothing more at the moment than to get some sleep; the day's unexpected problems had taken a lot out of him.

Ekstrom's thoughts turned yet again to Wailee Ming, Rachel Sexton, Norah Mangor, Michael Tolland, and Corky Marlinson. Some of the NASA staff had begun noticing the civilians were missing.

Relax, Ekstrom told himself. *Everything is under control.*

He breathed deeply, reminding himself that everyone on the planet was excited about NASA and space right now. Extraterrestrial life hadn't been this exciting a topic since the famous 'Roswell incident' back in 1947 – the alleged crash of an alien spaceship in Roswell, New Mexico, which was now the shrine to millions of UFO-conspiracy theorists even today.

During Ekstrom's years working at the Pentagon, he had learned that the Roswell incident had been nothing more than a military accident during a classified operation called Project Mogul – the flight test of a spy balloon being designed to listen in on Russian atomic tests. A prototype, while being tested, had drifted off course and crashed in the New Mexico desert. Unfortunately, a civilian found the wreckage before the military did.

Unsuspecting rancher William Brazel had stumbled across a debris field of radical synthesized neoprene and lightweight metals unlike anything he'd ever seen, and he immediately called in the sheriff. Newspapers carried the story of the bizarre wreckage, and public interest grew fast. Fueled by the military's denial that the wreckage was theirs, reporters launched investigations, and the covert status of Project Mogul came into serious jeopardy. Just as it seemed the sensitive issue of a spy balloon was about to be revealed, something wonderful happened.

The media drew an unexpected conclusion. They decided the scraps of futuristic substance could only have come from an extra-terrestrial source – creatures more scientifically advanced than humans. The military's denial of the incident obviously had to be one thing only – a cover-up of contact with aliens! Although baffled by this new hypothesis, the air force was not about to look a gift horse in the mouth. They grabbed the alien story and ran with it; the world's suspicion that aliens were visiting New Mexico was far less a threat to national security than that of the Russians catching wind of Project Mogul.

To fuel the alien cover story, the intelligence community shrouded the Roswell incident in secrecy and began orchestrating 'security leaks' – quiet murmurings of alien contacts, recovered spaceships, and even a mysterious 'Hangar 18' at Dayton's Wright-Patterson Air Force Base where the government was keeping alien bodies on ice. The world bought the story, and Roswell fever swept the globe. From that moment on, whenever a civilian mistakenly spotted an advanced U.S. military aircraft, the intelligence community simply dusted off the old conspiracy.

That's not an aircraft, that's an alien spaceship!

Ekstrom was amazed to think this simple deception was still working today. Every time the media reported a sudden flurry of UFO sightings, Ekstrom had to laugh. Chances were some lucky civilian had caught a glimpse of one of the NRO's fifty-seven fast-moving, unmanned reconnaissance aircraft known as Global Hawks – oblong, remote-controlled aircraft that looked like nothing else in the sky.

Ekstrom found it pathetic that countless tourists still made pilgrimages to the New Mexico desert to scan the night skies with their video cameras. Occasionally one got lucky and captured 'hard evidence' of a UFO – bright lights flitting around the sky with more maneuverability and speed than any aircraft humans had ever built. What these people failed to realize, of course, was that there existed a twelve-year lag between what the government could build and what the public knew about. These UFO-gazers were simply catching a glimpse of the next generation of U.S. aircraft being developed out at Area 51 – many of which were the brainstorms of NASA engineers. Of course, intelligence officials never corrected the misconception; it was obviously preferable that the world read about another UFO sighting than to have people learn the U.S. military's true flight capabilities.

But everything has changed now, Ekstrom thought. In a few hours, the extraterrestrial myth would become a confirmed reality, forever.

'Administrator?' A NASA technician hurried across the ice behind him. 'You have an emergency secure call in the PSC.'

Ekstrom sighed, turning. *What the hell could it be now?* He headed for the communications trailer.

The technician hurried along beside him. 'The guys manning the radar in the PSC were curious, sir . . .'

'Yeah?' Ekstrom's thoughts were still far away.

'The fat-body sub stationed off the coast here? We were wondering why you didn't mention it to us.'

Ekstrom glanced up. 'I'm sorry?'

'The submarine, sir? You could have at least told the guys on radar. Additional seaboard security is understandable, but it took our radar team off guard.'

Ekstrom stopped short. '*What* submarine?'

The technician stopped now too, clearly not expecting the administrator's surprise. 'She's not part of our operation?'

'No! Where is it?'

The technician swallowed hard. 'About three miles out. We caught her on radar by chance. Only surfaced for a couple minutes. Pretty big blip. Had to be a fat-body. We figured you'd asked the navy to stand watch over this op without telling any of us.'

Ekstrom stared. 'I most certainly did not!'

Now the technician's voice wavered. 'Well, sir, then I guess I should inform you that a sub just rendezvoused with an aircraft right off the coast here. Looked like a personnel change. Actually, we were all pretty impressed anyone would attempt a wet-dry vertical in this kind of wind.'

Ekstrom felt his muscles stiffen. *What the hell is a submarine doing directly off the coast of Ellesmere Island without my knowledge?* 'Did you see what direction the aircraft flew after rendezvous?'

'Back toward Thule air base. For connecting transport to the mainland, I assume.'

Ekstrom said nothing the rest of the way to the PSC. When he entered the cramped darkness, the hoarse voice on the line had a familiar rasp.

'We've got a problem,' Tench said, coughing as she spoke. 'It's about Rachel Sexton.'

CHAPTER 76

Senator Sexton was not sure how long he had been staring into space when he heard the pounding. When he realized the throbbing in his ears was not from the alcohol but rather from someone at his apartment door, he got up from the couch, stowed the bottle of Courvoisier, and made his way to the foyer.

'Who is it?' Sexton yelled, in no mood for visitors.

His bodyguard's voice called in with the identity of Sexton's unexpected guest. Sexton sobered instantly. *That was fast.* Sexton had hoped not to have to have this conversation until morning.

Taking a deep breath and straightening his hair, Sexton opened the door. The face before him was all too familiar – tough and leathery despite the man's seventy-something years. Sexton had met with him only this morning in the white Ford Windstar minivan in a hotel parking garage. *Was it only this morning?* Sexton wondered. God, how things had changed since then.

'May I come in?' the dark-haired man asked.

Sexton stepped aside, allowing the head of the Space Frontier Foundation to pass.

'Did the meeting go well?' the man asked, as Sexton closed the door.

Did it go well? Sexton wondered if the man lived in a cocoon. 'Things were terrific until the President came on television.'

The old man nodded, looking displeased. 'Yes. An incredible victory. It will hurt our cause greatly.'

Hurt our cause? Here was an optimist. With NASA's triumph tonight, this guy would be dead and buried before the Space Frontier Foundation attained their goals of privatization.

'For years I have suspected proof was forthcoming,' the old man said. 'I did not know how or when, but sooner or later we had to know for sure.'

Sexton was stunned. 'You're not surprised?'

'The mathematics of the cosmos virtually requires other life-forms,' the man said, moving toward Sexton's den. 'I am not surprised that this discovery has been made. Intellectually, I am thrilled. Spiritually, I am in awe. Politically, I am deeply disturbed. The timing could not be worse.'

Sexton wondered why the man had come. It sure as hell wasn't to cheer him up.

'As you know,' the man said, 'SFF member companies have spent millions trying to open the frontier of space to private citizens. Recently, much of that money has gone to your campaign.'

Sexton felt suddenly defensive. 'I had no control over tonight's fiasco. The White House baited me to attack NASA!'

'Yes. The President played the game well. And yet, all may not be lost.' There was an odd glint of hope in the old man's eyes.

He's senile, Sexton decided. All was definitely lost. Every station on television right now was talking about the destruction of the Sexton campaign.

The old man showed himself into the den, sat on the couch, and fixed his tired eyes on the senator. 'Do you recall,' the man said, 'the problems NASA initially had with the anomaly software onboard the PODS satellite?'

Sexton could not imagine where this was headed. *What the hell difference does that make now? PODS found a goddamned meteorite with fossils!*

'If you remember,' the man said, 'the onboard software did not function properly at first. You made a big deal of it in the press.'

'As I should have!' Sexton said, sitting down opposite the man. 'It was another NASA failure!'

The man nodded. 'I agree. But shortly after that, NASA held a press conference announcing they had come up with a work-around – some sort of patch for the software.'

Sexton hadn't actually seen the press conference, but he'd heard it was short, flat, and hardly newsworthy – the PODS project leader giving a dull technical description of how NASA had overcome a minor glitch in PODS's anomaly-detection software and gotten everything up and running.

'I have been watching PODS with interest ever since it failed,' the man said. He produced a videocassette and walked to Sexton's television, putting the video in the VCR. 'This should interest you.'

The video began to play. It showed the NASA press room at headquarters in Washington. A well-dressed man was taking the podium and greeting the audience. The subtitle beneath the podium read:

CHRIS HARPER, Section Manager
Polar Orbiting Density Scanner Satellite (PODS)

Chris Harper was tall, refined, and spoke with the quiet dignity of a European American who still clung proudly to his roots. His accent was erudite and polished. He was addressing the press with confidence, giving them some bad news about PODS.

'Although the PODS satellite is in orbit and functioning well, we have a minor setback with the onboard computers. A minor programming error for which I take full responsibility. Specifically, the FIR filter has a faulty voxel index, which means the PODS's anomaly-detection software is not functioning properly. We're working on a fix.'

The crowd sighed, apparently accustomed to NASA letdowns.

'What does that mean for the current effectiveness of the satellite?'
someone asked.

Harper took it like a pro. Confident and matter-of-fact. 'Imagine a
perfect set of eyes without a functioning brain. Essentially the PODS
satellite is seeing twenty-twenty, but it has no idea what it's looking at.
The purpose of the PODS mission is to look for melt pockets in the
polar ice cap, but without the computer to analyze the density data
PODS receives from its scanners, PODS cannot discern where the
points of interest are. We should have the situation remedied after the
next shuttle mission can make an adjustment to the onboard computer.'

A groan of disappointment rose in the room.

The old man glanced over at Sexton. 'He presents bad news pretty
well, doesn't he?'

'He's from NASA,' Sexton grumbled. 'That's what they do.'

The VCR tape went blank for an instant and then switched to
another NASA press conference.

'This second press conference,' the old man said to Sexton, 'was
given only a few weeks ago. Quite late at night. Few people saw it.
This time Dr Harper is announcing *good* news.'

The footage launched. This time Chris Harper looked disheveled
and uneasy. 'I am pleased to announce,' Harper said, sounding
anything but pleased, 'that NASA has found a work-around for
the PODS satellite's software problem.' He fumbled through an
explanation of the work-around – something about redirecting the raw
data from PODS and sending it through computers here on earth
rather than relying on the onboard PODS computer. Everyone seemed
impressed. It all sounded quite feasible and exciting. When Harper was
done, the room gave him an enthusiastic round of applause.

'So we can expect data soon?' someone in the audience asked.

Harper nodded, sweating. 'A couple of weeks.'

More applause. Hands shot up around the room.

'That's all I have for you now,' Harper said, looking ill as he packed
up his papers. 'PODS is up and running. We'll have data soon.' He
practically ran off the stage.

Sexton scowled. He had to admit, this was odd. Why did Chris
Harper look so comfortable giving bad news and so uncomfortable
giving good news? It should have been in reverse. Sexton hadn't

actually seen this press conference when it aired, although he'd read
about the software fix. The fix, at the time, seemed an inconsequential NASA salvage; the public perception remained unimpressed –
PODS was just another NASA project that had malfunctioned and
was being awkwardly patched together with a less than ideal solution.

The old man turned off the television. 'NASA claimed Dr Harper
was not feeling well that night.' He paused. 'I happen to think Harper
was lying.'

Lying? Sexton stared, his fuzzy thoughts unable to piece together any
logical rationale for why Harper would have lied about the software.
Still, Sexton had told enough lies in his life to recognize a poor liar when
he saw one. He had to admit, Dr Harper sure looked suspicious.

'Perhaps you don't realize?' the old man said. 'This little announcement you just heard Chris Harper give is the single most
important press conference in NASA history.' He paused. 'That
convenient software fix he just described is what allowed PODS to
find the meteorite.'

Sexton puzzled. *And you think he was lying about it?* 'But, if Harper
was lying, and the PODS software isn't really working, then how the
hell did NASA find the meteorite?'

The old man smiled. 'Exactly.'

CHAPTER 77

The U.S. military's fleet of 'repo' aircraft repossessed during
drug-trade arrests consisted of over a dozen private jets, including
three reconditioned G4s used for transporting military VIPs. A half
hour ago, one of those G4s had lifted off the Thule runway, fought its
way above the storm, and was now pounding southward into the
Canadian night en route to Washington. Onboard, Rachel Sexton,
Michael Tolland, and Corky Marlinson had the eight-seat cabin to
themselves, looking like some kind of disheveled sports team in their
matching blue U.S.S. *Charlotte* jumpsuits and caps.

Despite the roar of the Grumman engines, Corky Marlinson was asleep in the rear. Tolland sat near the front, looking exhausted as he gazed out the window at the sea. Rachel was beside him, knowing she could not sleep even if she'd been sedated. Her mind churned through the mystery of the meteorite, and, most recently, the dead room conversation with Pickering. Before signing off, Pickering had given Rachel two additional pieces of disturbing information.

First, Marjorie Tench claimed to possess a video recording of Rachel's private deposition to the White House staff. Tench was now threatening to use the video as evidence if Rachel tried to go back on her confirmation of the meteorite data. The news was particularly unsettling because Rachel had specifically told Zach Herney that her remarks to the staff were for in-house use only. Apparently Zach Herney had ignored that request.

The second bit of troubling news dealt with a CNN debate her father had attended earlier in the afternoon. Apparently, Marjorie Tench had made a rare appearance and deftly baited Rachel's father into crystallizing his position against NASA. More specifically, Tench had cajoled him into crudely proclaiming his skepticism that extraterrestrial life would ever be found.

Eat his hat? That's what Pickering said her father had offered to do if NASA ever found extraterrestrial life. Rachel wondered how Tench had managed to coax out that propitious little sound bite. Clearly, the White House had been setting the stage carefully – ruthlessly lining up all the dominoes, preparing for the big Sexton collapse. The President and Marjorie Tench, like some sort of political tag team wrestling duo, had maneuvered for the kill. While the President remained dignified outside the ring, Tench had moved in, circling, cunningly lining up the senator for the presidential body slam.

The President had told Rachel he'd asked NASA to delay announcing the discovery in order to provide time to confirm the accuracy of the data. Rachel now realized there were other advantages to waiting. The extra time had given the White House time to dole out the rope with which the senator would hang himself.

Rachel felt no sympathy for her father, and yet she now realized that beneath the warm and fuzzy exterior of President Zach Herney, a shrewd shark lurked. You did not become the most powerful man in the world without a killer instinct. The question now was whether this shark was an innocent bystander – or a player.

Rachel stood, stretching her legs. As she paced the aisle of the plane, she felt frustrated that the pieces to this puzzle seemed so contradictory. Pickering, with his trademark chaste logic, had concluded the meteorite must be fake. Corky and Tolland, with scientific assurance, insisted the meteorite was authentic. Rachel only knew what she had seen – a charred, fossilized rock being pulled from the ice.

Now, as she passed beside Corky, she gazed down at the astrophysicist, battered from his ordeal on the ice. The swelling on his cheek was going down now, and the stitches looked good. He was asleep, snoring, his pudgy hands clutching the disk-shaped meteorite sample like some kind of security blanket.

Rachel reached down and gently slipped the meteorite sample away from him. She held it up, studying the fossils again. *Remove all assumptions*, she told herself, forcing herself to reorganize her thoughts. *Reestablish the chain of substantiation*. It was an old NRO trick. Rebuilding a proof from scratch was a process known as a 'null start' – something all data analysts practiced when the pieces didn't quite fit.

Reassemble the proof.

She began pacing again.

Does this stone represent proof of extraterrestrial life?

Proof, she knew, was a conclusion built on a pyramid of facts, a broad base of accepted information on which more specific assertions were made.

Remove all the base assumptions. Start again.

What do we have?

A rock.

She pondered that for a moment. *A rock. A rock with fossilized creatures.* Walking back toward the front of the plane, she took her seat beside Michael Tolland.

'Mike, let's play a game.'

Tolland turned from the window, looking distant, apparently deep in his own thoughts. 'A game?'

She handed him the meteorite sample. 'Let's pretend you're seeing this fossilized rock for the first time. I've told you nothing about where it came from or how it was found. What would you tell me it is?'

Tolland heaved a disconsolate sigh. 'Funny you should ask. I just had the strangest thought . . .'

Hundreds of miles behind Rachel and Tolland, a strange-looking aircraft stayed low as it tore south above a deserted ocean. Onboard, the Delta Force was silent. They had been pulled out of locations in a hurry, but never like this.

Their controller was furious.

Earlier, Delta-One had informed the controller that unexpected events on the ice shelf had left his team with no option but to exercise force – force that had killed four civilians, including Rachel Sexton and Michael Tolland.

The controller reacted with shock. Killing, although an authorized last resort, obviously never had been part of the controller's plan.

Later, the controller's displeasure over the killings turned to outright rage when he learned the assassinations had not gone as planned.

'Your team failed!' the controller seethed, the androgynous tone hardly masking the person's rage. 'Three of your four targets are still alive!'

Impossible! Delta-One had thought. 'But we witnessed—'

'They made contact with a submarine and are now en route to Washington.'

'What?'

The controller's tone turned lethal. 'Listen carefully. I am about to give you new orders. And this time you will not fail.'

CHAPTER 78

Senator Sexton was actually feeling a flicker of hope as he walked his unexpected visitor back out to the elevator. The head of the SFF, as it turned out, had not come to chastise Sexton, but rather to give him a pep talk and tell him the battle was not yet over.

A possible chink in NASA's armor.

The videotape of the bizarre NASA press conference had convinced Sexton that the old man was right – PODS mission director Chris Harper was lying. *But why? And if NASA never fixed the PODS software, how did NASA find the meteorite?*

As they walked to the elevator, the old man said, 'Sometimes all it takes to unravel something is a single strand. Perhaps we can find a way to eat away at NASA's victory from within. Cast a shadow of distrust. Who knows where it will lead?' The old man locked his tired eyes on Sexton. 'I am not ready to lay down and die, Senator. And I trust nor are you.'

'Of course not,' Sexton said, mustering resolve in his voice. 'We've come too far.'

'Chris Harper lied about fixing PODS,' the man said as he boarded the elevator. 'And we need to know why.'

'I will get that information as fast as I can,' Sexton replied. *I have just the person.*

'Good. Your future depends on it.'

As Sexton headed back toward his apartment, his step was a little lighter, his head a little clearer. *NASA lied about PODS.* The only question was how Sexton could prove it.

His thoughts had already turned to Gabrielle Ashe. Wherever she was at the moment, she had to be feeling like shit. Gabrielle had no doubt seen the press conference and was now standing on a ledge somewhere getting ready to jump. Her proposition of making NASA a major issue in Sexton's campaign had turned out to be the biggest mistake of Sexton's career.

She owes me, Sexton thought. *And she knows it.*

Gabrielle already had proven she had a knack for obtaining NASA secrets. *She has a contact*, Sexton thought. She'd been scoring insider information for weeks now. Gabrielle had connections she was not sharing. Connections she could pump for information on PODS. Moreover, tonight Gabrielle would be motivated. She had a debt to repay, and Sexton suspected she would do anything to regain his favor.

As Sexton arrived back at his apartment door, his bodyguard nodded. 'Evening, Senator. I trust I did the right thing by letting Gabrielle in earlier? She said it was critical she talk to you.'

Sexton paused. 'I'm sorry?'

'Ms Ashe? She had important information for you earlier tonight. That's why I let her in.'

Sexton felt his body stiffen. He looked at his apartment door. *What the hell is this guy talking about?*

The guard's expression changed to one of confusion and concern. 'Senator, are you okay? You remember, right? Gabrielle arrived during your meeting. She talked to you, right? She *must* have. She was in there quite a while.'

Sexton stared a long moment, feeling his pulse skyrocket. *This moron let Gabrielle into my apartment during a private SFF meeting?* She stuck around inside and then departed without a word? Sexton could only imagine what Gabrielle might have overheard. Swallowing his anger, he forced a smile to his guard. 'Oh, yes! I'm sorry. I'm exhausted. Had a couple of drinks, too. Ms Ashe and I did indeed speak. You did the right thing.'

The guard looked relieved.

'Did she say where she went when she left?'

The guard shook his head. 'She was in a big hurry.'

'Okay, thanks.'

Sexton entered his apartment fuming. *How complicated were my goddamn directions? No visitors!* He had to assume if Gabrielle had been inside for any length of time and then snuck out without a word, she must have heard things she was not meant to hear. *Tonight of all nights.*

Senator Sexton knew above all he could not afford to lose Gabrielle Ashe's trust; women could become vengeful and stupid when they felt deceived. Sexton needed to bring her back. Tonight more than ever, he needed her in his camp.

CHAPTER **79**

On the fourth floor of the ABC television studios, Gabrielle Ashe sat alone in Yolanda's glass-walled office and stared at the fraying carpet. She had always prided herself on good instincts and knowing whom she could trust. Now, for the first time in years, Gabrielle felt alone, uncertain which way to turn.

The sound of her cellphone lifted her gaze from the carpet. Reluctant, she picked up. 'Gabrielle Ashe.'

'Gabrielle, it's me.'

She recognized the timbre of Senator Sexton's voice immediately, although he sounded surprisingly calm considering what had just transpired.

'It's been one hell of a night over here,' he said, 'so just let me talk. I'm sure you saw the President's conference. Christ, did we play the wrong cards. I'm sick over it. You're probably blaming yourself. Don't. Who the hell would have guessed? Not your fault. Anyhow, listen up. I think there may be a way to get our feet back under us.'

Gabrielle stood up, unable to imagine what Sexton could be talking about. This is hardly the reaction she had expected.

'I had a meeting tonight,' Sexton said, 'with representatives from private space industries, and—'

'You did?' Gabrielle blurted, stunned to hear him admit it. 'I mean . . . I had no idea.'

'Yeah, nothing major. I would have asked you to sit in, but these guys are touchy about privacy. Some of them are donating money to my campaign. It's not something they like to advertise.'

Gabrielle felt totally disarmed. 'But . . . isn't that illegal?'

'Illegal? Hell no! All the donations are under the two-thousand-dollar cap. Small potatoes. These guys barely make a dent, but I listen to their gripes anyway. Call it an investment in the future. I'm quiet about it because, frankly, the appearances aren't so great. If the White House caught wind, they'd spin the hell out of it. Anyhow, look, that's not the point. I called to tell you that after tonight's meeting, I was talking to the head of the SFF . . .'

For several seconds, although Sexton was still talking, all Gabrielle could hear was the blood rushing in shame to her face. Without the slightest challenge from her, the senator had calmly admitted tonight's meeting with private space companies. *Perfectly legal.* And to think what Gabrielle had almost considered doing! Thank God Yolanda had stopped her. *I almost jumped ship to Marjorie Tench!*

'. . . and so I told the head of the SFF,' the senator was saying, 'that you might be able to get that information for us.'

Gabrielle tuned back in. 'Okay.'

'The contact from whom you've been getting all your inside NASA information these past few months? I assume you still have access?'

Marjorie Tench. Gabrielle cringed, knowing she could never tell the senator that the informant had been manipulating her all along. 'Um . . . I think so,' Gabrielle lied.

'Good. There's some information I need from you. Right away.'

As she listened, Gabrielle realized just how badly she had been underestimating Senator Sedgewick Sexton lately. Some of the man's luster had worn off since she'd first begun following his career. But tonight, it was back. In the face of what appeared to be the ultimate death blow to his campaign, Sexton was plotting a counterattack. And although it had been Gabrielle who led him down this inauspicious path, he was not punishing her. Instead, he was giving her a chance to redeem herself.

And redeem herself she would.

Whatever it took.

CHAPTER **80**

William Pickering gazed out his office window at the distant line of headlights on Leesburg Highway. He often thought about her when he stood up here alone at the top of the world.

All this power . . . and I couldn't save her.

Pickering's daughter, Diana, had died in the Red Sea while stationed aboard a small navy escort ship, training to become a navigator. Her ship had been anchored in safe harbor on a sunny afternoon when a handmade dory loaded with explosives and powered by two suicide terrorists motored slowly across the harbor and exploded on contact with the hull. Diana Pickering and thirteen other young American soldiers had been killed that day.

William Pickering had been devastated. The anguish overwhelmed him for weeks. When the terrorist attack was traced to a known cell whom the CIA had been tracking unsuccessfully for years, Pickering's sadness turned into rage. He had marched into CIA headquarters and demanded answers.

The answers he got were hard to swallow.

Apparently the CIA had been prepared to move on this cell months before and was simply waiting for the high-res satellite photos so that they could plan a pinpoint attack on the terrorists' mountain hideout in Afghanistan. Those photos were scheduled to be taken by the $1.2 billion NRO satellite code-named Vortex 2, the same satellite that had been blown up on the launchpad by its NASA launch vehicle. Because of the NASA accident, the CIA strike had been postponed, and now Diana Pickering had died.

Pickering's mind told him that NASA had not been directly responsible, but his heart found it hard to forgive. The investigation of the rocket explosion revealed that the NASA engineers responsible for the fuel injection system had been forced to use second-rate materials in an effort to stay on budget.

'For nonmanned flights,' Lawrence Ekstrom explained in a press conference, 'NASA strives for cost-effectiveness above all. In this case, the results were admittedly not optimal. We will be looking into it.'

Not optimal. Diana Pickering was dead.

Furthermore, because the spy satellite was classified, the public never learned that NASA had disintegrated a $1.2 billion NRO project, and along with it, indirectly, numerous American lives.

'Sir?' Pickering's secretary's voice came over his intercom, startling him. 'Line one. It's Marjorie Tench.'

Pickering shook himself out of his daze and looked at his telephone. *Again?* The blinking light on line one seemed to pulse with an irate urgency. Pickering frowned and took the call.

'Pickering here.'

Tench's voice was seething mad. 'What did she tell you?'

'I'm sorry?'

'Rachel Sexton contacted you. What did she tell you? She was on a submarine, for God's sake! Explain that!'

Pickering could tell immediately that denying the fact was not an option; Tench had been doing her homework. Pickering was surprised she'd found out about the *Charlotte*, but she'd apparently thrown her weight around until she got some answers. 'Ms Sexton contacted me, yes.'

'You arranged a pickup. And you didn't contact me?'

'I arranged transport. That is correct.' Two hours remained until Rachel Sexton, Michael Tolland, and Corky Marlinson were scheduled to arrive at the nearby Bollings Air Force Base.

'And yet you chose not to inform me?'

'Rachel Sexton has made some very disturbing accusations.'

'Regarding the authenticity of the meteorite . . . and some kind of attack on her life?'

'Among other things.'

'Obviously, she is lying.'

'You are aware she is with two others who corroborate her story?'

Tench paused. 'Yes. Most disturbing. The White House is very concerned by their claims.'

'The White House? Or you personally?'

Her tone turned razor sharp. 'As far as you are concerned, Director, there is no difference tonight.'

Pickering was unimpressed. He was no stranger to blustering politicians and support staff trying to establish footholds over the intel community. Few put up as strong a front as Marjorie Tench. 'Does the President know you're calling me?'

'Frankly, Director, I'm shocked that you would even entertain these lunatic ravings.'

You didn't answer my question. 'I see no logical reason for these people to lie. I have to assume they are either telling the truth, or they have made an honest mistake.'

'Mistake? Claims of attacks? Flaws in the meteorite data that NASA never saw? Please! This is an obvious political ploy.'

'If so, the motives escape me.'

Tench sighed heavily and lowered her voice. 'Director, there are forces at work here of which you might not be aware. We can speak about that at length later, but at the moment I need to know where Ms Sexton and the others are. I need to get to the bottom of this before they do any lasting damage. Where are they?'

'That is not information I am comfortable sharing. I will contact you after they arrive.'

'Wrong. I will be there to greet them when they arrive.'

You and how many Secret Service agents? Pickering wondered. 'If I inform you of their arrival time and location, will we all have a chance to chat like friends, or do you intend to have a private army take them into custody?'

'These people pose a direct threat to the President. The White House has every right to detain and question them.'

Pickering knew she was right. Under Title 18, Section 3056 of the United States Code, agents of the U.S. Secret Service can carry firearms, use deadly force, and make 'un-warranted' arrests simply on suspicion that a person has committed or is intending to commit a felony or any act of aggression against the President. The service possessed carte blanche. Regular detainees included unsavory loiterers outside the White House and school kids who sent threatening e-mail pranks.

Pickering had no doubt the service could justify dragging Rachel Sexton and the others into the basement of the White House and keeping them there indefinitely. It would be a dangerous play, but Tench clearly realized the stakes were huge. The question was what would happen next if Pickering allowed Tench to take control. He had no intention of finding out.

'I will do whatever necessary,' Tench declared, 'to protect the President from false accusations. The mere implication of foul play will cast a heavy shadow on the White House and NASA. Rachel Sexton has abused the trust the President gave her, and I have no intention of seeing the President pay the price.'

'And if I request that Ms Sexton be permitted to present her case to an official panel of inquiry?'

'Then you would be disregarding a direct presidential order and giving her a platform from which to make a goddamn political mess! I will ask you one more time, Director. Where are you flying them?'

Pickering exhaled a long breath. Whether or not he told Marjorie Tench that the plane was coming into Bollings Air Force Base, he knew she had the means to find out. The question was whether or not she would do it. He sensed from the determination in her voice that she would not rest. Marjorie Tench was scared.

'Marjorie,' Pickering said, with unmistakable clarity of tone. 'Someone is lying to me. Of this I am certain. Either it is Rachel Sexton and two civilian scientists – or it is you. I believe it is you.'

Tench exploded. 'How dare—'

'Your indignity has no resonance with me, so save it. You would be wise to know that I have absolute proof NASA and the White House broadcast untruths tonight.'

Tench fell suddenly silent.

Pickering let her reel a moment. 'I'm not looking for a political meltdown any more than you are. But there have been lies. Lies that cannot stand. If you want me to help you, you've got to start by being honest with me.'

Tench sounded tempted but wary. 'If you're so certain there were lies, why haven't you stepped forward?'

'I don't interfere in political matters.'

Tench muttered something that sounded a lot like 'bullshit.'

'Are you trying to tell me, Marjorie, that the President's announcement tonight was entirely accurate?'

There was a long silence on the line.

Pickering knew he had her. 'Listen, we both know this is a time bomb waiting to explode. But it's not too late. There are compromises we can make.'

Tench said nothing for several seconds. Finally she sighed. 'We should meet.'

Touchdown, Pickering thought.

'I have something to show you,' Tench said. 'And I believe it will shed some light on this matter.'

'I'll come to your office.'

'No,' she said hurriedly. 'It's late. Your presence here would raise concerns. I'd prefer to keep this matter between us.'

Pickering read between the lines. *The President knows nothing about this.* 'You're welcome to come here,' he said.

Tench sounded distrusting. 'Let's meet somewhere discreet.'

Pickering had expected as much.

'The FDR Memorial is convenient to the White House,' Tench said. 'It will be empty at this time of night.'

Pickering considered it. The FDR Memorial sat midway between the Jefferson and Lincoln memorials, in an extremely safe part of town. After a long beat, Pickering agreed.

'One hour,' Tench said, signing off. 'And come alone.'

Immediately upon hanging up, Marjorie Tench phoned NASA Administrator Ekstrom. Her voice was tight as she relayed the bad news.

'Pickering could be a problem.'

CHAPTER 81

Gabrielle Ashe was brimming with new hope as she stood at Yolanda Cole's desk in the ABC production room and dialed directory assistance.

The allegations Sexton had just conveyed to her, if confirmed, had shocking potential. *NASA lied about PODS?* Gabrielle had seen the press conference in question and recalled thinking it was odd, and yet she'd forgotten all about it; PODS was not a critical issue a few weeks ago. Tonight, however, PODS had become *the* issue.

Now Sexton needed inside information, and he needed it fast. He was relying on Gabrielle's 'informant' to get the information. Gabrielle had assured the senator she would do her best. The problem, of course, was that her informant was Marjorie Tench, who would be no help at all. So Gabrielle would have to get the information another way.

'Directory assistance,' the voice on the phone said.

Gabrielle told them what she needed. The operator came back with three listings for a Chris Harper in Washington. Gabrielle tried them all.

The first number was a law firm. The second had no answer. The third was now ringing.

A woman answered on the first ring. 'Harper residence.'

'Mrs Harper?' Gabrielle said as politely as possible. 'I hope I haven't woken you?'

'Heavens no! I don't think anyone's asleep tonight.' She sounded excited. Gabrielle could hear the television in the background. Meteorite coverage. 'You're calling for Chris, I assume?'

Gabrielle's pulse quickened. 'Yes, ma'am.'

'I'm afraid Chris isn't here. He raced off to work as soon as the President's address was over.' The woman chuckled to herself. 'Of course, I doubt there's any work going on. Most likely a party. The announcement came as quite a surprise to him, you know. To everyone. Our phone's been ringing all night. I bet the whole NASA crew's over there by now.'

'E Street complex?' Gabrielle asked, assuming the woman meant NASA headquarters.

'Righto. Take a party hat.'

'Thanks. I'll track him down over there.'

Gabrielle hung up. She hurried out onto the production room floor and found Yolanda, who was just finishing prepping a group of space experts who were about to give enthusiastic commentary on the meteorite.

Yolanda smiled when she saw Gabrielle coming. 'You look better,' she said. 'Starting to see the silver lining here?'

'I just talked to the senator. His meeting tonight wasn't what I thought.'

'I told you Tench was playing you. How's the senator taking the meteorite news?'

'Better than expected.'

Yolanda looked surprised. 'I figured he'd jumped in front of a bus by now.'

'He thinks there may be a snag in the NASA data.'

Yolanda let out a dubious snort. 'Did he see the same press conference I just saw? How much more confirmation and reconfirmation can anyone need?'

'I'm going over to NASA to check on something.'

Yolanda's penciled eyebrows raised in cautionary arches. 'Senator Sexton's right-hand aide is going to march into NASA headquarters? Tonight? Can you say "public stoning"?'

Gabrielle told Yolanda about Sexton's suspicion that the PODS section manager Chris Harper had lied about fixing the anomaly software.

Yolanda clearly wasn't buying it. 'We covered that press conference, Gabs, and I'll admit, Harper was not himself that night, but NASA said he was sick as a dog.'

'Senator Sexton is convinced he lied. Others are convinced too. Powerful people.'

'If the PODS anomaly-detection software wasn't fixed, how did PODS spot the meteorite?'

Sexton's point exactly, Gabrielle thought. 'I don't know. But the senator wants me to get him some answers.'

Yolanda shook her head. 'Sexton is sending you into a hornets' nest on a desperate pipe dream. Don't go. You don't owe him a thing.'

'I totally screwed up his campaign.'

'Rotten luck screwed up his campaign.'

'But if the senator is right and the PODS section manager actually lied—'

'Honey, if the PODS section manager lied to the world, what makes you think he'll tell *you* the truth?'

Gabrielle had considered that and was already formulating her plan. 'If I find a story over there, I'll call you.'

Yolanda gave a skeptical laugh. 'If you find a story over there, I'll eat my hat.'

CHAPTER **82**

Erase everything you know about this rock sample.

Michael Tolland had been struggling with his own disquieting ruminations about the meteorite, but now, with Rachel's probing questions, he was feeling an added unease over the issue. He looked down at the rock slice in his hand.

Pretend someone handed it to you with no explanation of where it was found or what it is. What would your analysis be?

Rachel's question, Tolland knew, was loaded, and yet as an analytical exercise, it proved powerful. By discarding all the data he had been given on his arrival at the habisphere, Tolland had to admit that his analysis of the fossils was profoundly biased by a singular premise – that the rock in which the fossils were found was a meteorite.

What if I had NOT been told about the meteorite? he asked himself. Although still unable to fathom any other explanation, Tolland allowed himself the leeway of hypothetically removing 'the meteorite' as a presupposition, and when he did, the results were somewhat unsettling. Now Tolland and Rachel, joined by a groggy Corky Marlinson, were discussing the ideas.

'So,' Rachel repeated, her voice intense, 'Mike, you're saying that if someone handed you this fossilized rock with *no* explanation whatsoever, you would have to conclude it was from earth.'

'Of course,' Tolland replied. 'What else could I conclude? It's a far greater leap to assert you've found extraterrestrial life than it is to assert you've found a fossil of some previously undiscovered terrestrial species. Scientists discover dozens of new species every year.'

'Two-foot-long lice?' Corky demanded, sounding incredulous. 'You would assume a bug that big is from *earth*?'

'Not *now*, maybe,' Tolland replied, 'but the species doesn't necessarily have to be currently living. It's a fossil. It's one hundred and ninety million years old. About the same age as our Jurassic. A lot of prehistoric fossils are over-sized creatures that look shocking when we discover their fossilized remains – enormous winged reptiles, dinosaurs, birds.'

'Not to be the physicist here, Mike,' Corky said, 'but there's a serious flaw in your argument. The prehistoric creatures you just named – dinosaurs, reptiles, birds – they all have internal *skeletons*, which gives them the capability to grow to large sizes despite the earth's gravity. But this fossil . . .' He took the sample and held it up. 'These guys have *exo*skeletons. They're arthropods. Bugs. You yourself said that any bug this big could only have evolved in a low-gravity environment. Otherwise its outer skeleton would have collapsed under its own weight.'

'Correct,' Tolland said. 'This species would have collapsed under its own weight if it walked around on earth.'

Corky's brow furrowed with annoyance. 'Well, Mike, unless some caveman was running an antigravity louse farm, I don't see how you could possibly conclude a two-foot-long bug is *earthly* in origin.'

Tolland smiled inwardly to think Corky was missing such a simple point. 'Actually, there is another possibility.' He focused closely on his friend. 'Corky, you're used to looking *up*. Look *down*. There's an abundant antigravity environment right here on earth. And it's been here since prehistoric times.'

Corky stared. 'What the hell are you talking about?'

Rachel also looked surprised.

Tolland pointed out the window at the moonlit sea glistening beneath the plane. 'The ocean.'

Rachel let out a low whistle. 'Of course.'

'Water is a low-gravity environment,' Tolland explained. 'Everything weighs less underwater. The ocean supports enormous fragile structures that could never exist on land – jellyfish, giant squid, ribbon eels.'

Corky acquiesced, but only slightly. 'Fine, but the prehistoric ocean never had giant bugs?'

'Sure, it did. And it still does, in fact. People eat them every day. They're a delicacy in most countries.'

'Mike, who the hell eats giant sea bugs?'

'Anyone who eats lobsters, crabs, and shrimp.'

Corky stared.

'Crustaceans are essentially giant sea bugs,' Tolland explained. 'They're a suborder of the phylum Arthropoda – lice, crabs, spiders, insects, grasshoppers, scorpions, lobsters – they're all related. They're all species with jointed appendages and external skeletons.'

Corky suddenly looked ill.

'From a classification standpoint, they look a lot like bugs,' Tolland explained. 'Horseshoe crabs resemble giant trilobites. And the claws of a lobster resemble those of a large scorpion.'

Corky turned green. 'Okay, I've eaten my last lobster roll.'

Rachel looked fascinated. 'So arthropods on land stay small because the gravity selects naturally for smallness. But in the water, their bodies are buoyed up, so they can grow very large.'

'Exactly,' Tolland said. 'An Alaskan king crab could be wrongly classified as a giant spider if we had limited fossil evidence.'

Rachel's excitement seemed to fade now to concern. 'Mike, again barring the issue of the meteorite's apparent authenticity, tell me this: do you think the fossils we saw at Milne could possibly have come from the ocean? *Earth's* ocean?'

Tolland felt the directness of her gaze and sensed the true weight of her question. 'Hypothetically, I would have to say yes. The ocean floor has sections that are one hundred and ninety million years old. The same age as the fossils. And theoretically the oceans could have sustained life-forms that looked like this.'

'Oh please!' Corky scoffed. 'I can't believe what I'm hearing here. *Barring* the issue of the meteorite's authenticity? The meteorite is irrefutable. Even if earth has ocean floor the same age as that meteorite, we sure as hell don't have ocean floor that has fusion crust, anomalous nickel content, and chondrules. You're grasping at straws.'

Tolland knew Corky was right, and yet imagining the fossils as sea creatures had robbed Tolland of some of his awe over them. They seemed somehow more familiar now.

'Mike,' Rachel said, 'why didn't any of the NASA scientists con-sider that these fossils might be ocean creatures? Even from an ocean on another planet?'

'Two reasons, really. Pelagic fossil samples – those from the ocean floor – tend to exhibit a plethora of intermingled species. Anything living in the millions of cubic feet of life above the ocean floor will eventually die and sink to the bottom. This means the ocean floor becomes a graveyard for species from every depth, pressure, and temperature environment. But the sample at Milne was clean – a single species. It looked more like something we might find in the desert. A brood of similar animals getting buried in a sandstorm, for example.'

Rachel nodded. 'And the second reason you guessed land rather than sea?'

Tolland shrugged. 'Gut instinct. Scientists have always believed space, if it were populated, would be populated by *insects*. And from what we've observed of space, there's a lot more dirt and rock out there than water.'

Rachel fell silent.

'Although . . .' Tolland added. Rachel had him thinking now. 'I'll admit there are very deep parts of the ocean floor that oceanographers call dead zones. We don't really understand them, but they are areas in which the current and food sources are such that almost nothing lives there. Just a few species of bottom-dwelling scavengers. So from that standpoint, I suppose a single-species fossil is not entirely out of the question.'

'Hello?' Corky grumbled. 'Remember the fusion crust? The mid-level nickel content? The chondrules? Why are we even talking about this?'

Tolland did not reply.

'This issue of the nickel content,' Rachel said to Corky. 'Explain this to me again. The nickel content in earth rocks is either very high or very low, but in meteorites the nickel content is within a specific midrange window?'

Corky bobbed his head. 'Precisely.'

'And so the nickel content in this sample falls precisely within the expected range of values?'

'Very close, yes.'

Rachel looked surprised. 'Hold on. *Close?* What's that supposed to mean?'

Corky looked exasperated. 'As I explained earlier, all meteorite mineralogies are different. As scientists find new meteorites, we constantly need to update our calculations as to what we consider an acceptable nickel content for meteorites.'

Rachel looked stunned as she held up the sample. 'So, *this* meteorite forced you to reevaluate what you consider acceptable nickel content in a meteorite? It fell outside the established midrange nickel window?'

'Only slightly,' Corky fired back.

'Why didn't anyone mention this?'

'It's a nonissue. Astrophysics is a dynamic science which is constantly being updated.'

'*During* an incredibly important analysis?'

'Look,' Corky said with a huff, 'I can assure you the nickel content in that sample is a helluva lot closer to other meteorites than it is to any earth rock.'

Rachel turned to Tolland. 'Did you know about this?'

Tolland gave a reluctant nod. It hadn't seemed a major issue at the time. 'I was told this meteorite exhibited slightly higher nickel content than seen in other meteorites, but the NASA specialists seemed unconcerned.'

'For good reason!' Corky interjected. 'The mineralogical proof here is *not* that the nickel content is conclusively meteoritelike, but rather that it is conclusively non-earth-like.'

Rachel shook her head. 'Sorry, but in my business that's the kind of faulty logic that gets people killed. Saying a rock is non-earth-like doesn't prove it's a meteorite. It simply proves that it's not like anything we've ever seen on earth.'

'What the hell's the difference?'

'Nothing,' Rachel said. 'If you've seen every rock on earth.'

Corky fell silent a moment. 'Okay,' he finally said, 'ignore the nickel content if it makes you nervous. We still have a flawless fusion crust and chondrules.'

'Sure,' Rachel said, sounding unimpressed. 'Two out of three ain't bad.'

CHAPTER **83**

The structure housing the NASA central headquarters was a
mammoth glass rectangle located at 300 E Street in Washington, D.C.
The building was spidered with over 200 miles of data cabling and
thousands of tons of computer processors. It was home to 1,134 civil
servants who oversee NASA's $15 billion annual budget and the daily
operations of the 12 NASA bases nationwide.

Despite the late hour, Gabrielle was not at all surprised to see the
building's foyer filling with people, an apparent convergence of
excited media crews and even more excited NASA personnel.
Gabrielle hurried inside. The entryway resembled a museum,
dominated dramatically by fullsize replicas of famous mission capsules
and satellites suspended overhead. Television crews were staking
claims on the expensive marble floor, seizing wide-eyed NASA
employees who came through the door.

Gabrielle scanned the crowd, but did not see anyone who looked
like PODS mission director Chris Harper. Half the people in the
lobby had press passes and half had NASA photo IDs around their
necks. Gabrielle had neither. She spotted a young woman with a
NASA ID and hurried over to her.

'Hi. I'm looking for Chris Harper?'

The woman eyed Gabrielle strangely, as if she recognized her from
somewhere and couldn't quite place it. 'I saw Dr Harper go through a
while ago. I think he headed upstairs. Do I know you?'

'I don't think so,' Gabrielle said, turning away. 'How do I get
upstairs?'

'Do you work for NASA?'

'No, I don't.'

'Then you can't get upstairs.'

'Oh. Is there a phone I might use to—'

'Hey,' the woman said, looking suddenly angry. 'I know who you

are. I've seen you on television with Senator Sexton. I can't believe
you would have the nerve—'

Gabrielle was already gone, disappearing into the crowd. Behind
her, she could hear the woman angrily telling others Gabrielle was
here.

*Terrific. Two seconds through the door, and I'm already on the Most
Wanted List.*

Gabrielle kept her head down as she hurried to the far side of the
lobby. A building directory was mounted on the wall. She scanned
the listings, looking for Chris Harper. Nothing. The directory showed
no names at all. It was arranged by department.

PODS? she wondered, scanning the list for anything that had to do
with the Polar Orbiting Density Scanner. She saw nothing. She was
afraid to glance over her shoulder, half expecting to see a crew of
angry NASA employees coming to stone her. All she saw on the list
that looked even remotely promising was on the fourth floor:

EARTH SCIENCE ENTERPRISE, PHASE II
Earth Observing System (EOS)

Keeping her head turned away from the crowd, Gabrielle made her
way toward an alcove that housed a bank of elevators and a water
fountain. She searched for the elevator call buttons, but saw only slits.
Damn. The elevators were security controlled – key card ID access for
employees only.

A group of young men came hurrying toward the elevators, talking
exuberantly. They wore NASA photo IDs around their necks.
Gabrielle quickly bent over the fountain, watching behind her. A
pimple-faced man inserted his ID into the slot and opened the
elevator. He was laughing, shaking his head in amazement.

'The guys in SETI must be going nuts!' he said as everyone boarded
the elevator. 'Their horn carts traced drift fields under two hundred
milliJanskys for twenty years, and the physical proof was buried in the
ice here on earth the whole time!'

The elevator doors closed, and the men disappeared.

Gabrielle stood up, wiping her mouth, wondering what to do. She
looked around for an interoffice phone. Nothing. She wondered if she

could somehow steal a key card, but something told her that was probably unwise. Whatever she did, she knew she had to do it fast. She could now see the woman she'd first spoken to out in the lobby, moving through the crowd with a NASA security officer.

A trim, bald man came around the corner, hustling toward the elevators. Gabrielle again bent over the fountain. The man did not seem to notice her. Gabrielle watched in silence as the man leaned forward and inserted his ID card into the slit. Another set of elevator doors slid open, and the man stepped on.

Screw it, Gabrielle thought, making up her mind. *Now or never.*

As the elevator slid closed, Gabrielle spun from the fountain and ran over, sticking her hand out and catching the door. The doors bounced back open, and she stepped in, her face bright with excitement. 'You ever seen it like this?' she gushed to the startled bald man. 'My God. It's crazy!'

The man gave her an odd look.

'The guys at SETI must be going nuts!' Gabrielle said. 'Their horn carts traced drift fields under two hundred milliJanskys for twenty years, and the physical proof was buried in the ice here on earth the whole time!'

The man looked surprised. 'Well . . . yes, it's quite . . .' He glanced at her neck, apparently troubled not to see an ID. 'I'm sorry, do you—'

'Fourth floor please. Came in such a hurry I barely remembered to put on my underwear!' She laughed, stealing a quick look at the guy's ID: JAMES THEISEN, *Finance Administration*.

'Do you work here?' The man looked uncomfortable. 'Miss . . . ?'

Gabrielle let her mouth fall slack. 'Jim! I'm hurt! Nothing like making a woman feel unmemorable!'

The man went pale for a moment, looking uneasy, and running an embarrassed hand across his head. 'I'm sorry. All this excitement, you know. I admit, you *do* look very familiar. What program are you working on?'

Shit. Gabrielle flashed a confident smile. 'EOS.'

The man pointed to the illuminated fourth floor button. 'Obviously. I mean specifically, which *project*?'

Gabrielle felt her pulse quicken. She could only think of one. 'PODS.'

The man looked surprised. 'Really? I thought I'd met everyone on Dr Harper's team.'

She gave an embarrassed nod. 'Chris keeps me hidden away. I'm the idiot programmer who screwed up voxel index on the anomaly software.'

Now it was the bald man whose jaw dropped. 'That was *you?*'

Gabrielle frowned. 'I haven't slept in weeks.'

'But Dr *Harper* took all the heat for that!'

'I know. Chris is that kind of guy. At least he got it straightened out. What an announcement tonight, though, isn't it? This meteorite. I'm just in shock!'

The elevator stopped on the fourth floor. Gabrielle jumped out. 'Great seeing you, Jim. Give my best to the boys in budgeting!'

'Sure,' the man stammered as the doors slid shut. 'Nice seeing you again.'

CHAPTER 84

Zach Herney, like most presidents before him, survived on four or five hours of sleep a night. Over the last few weeks, however, he had survived on far less. As the excitement of the evening's events slowly began to ebb, Herney felt the late hour settling in his limbs.

He and some of his upper level staff were in the Roosevelt Room enjoying celebratory champagne and watching the endless loop of press conference replays, Tolland documentary excerpts, and pundit recaps on network television. On-screen at the moment, an exuberant network correspondent stood in front of the White House gripping her microphone.

'Beyond the mind-numbing repercussions for mankind as a species,' she announced, 'this NASA discovery has some harsh political repercussions here in Washington. The unearthing of these meteoric fossils could not have come at a better time for the embattled President.' Her voice grew somber. 'Nor at a worse time for Senator

Sexton.' The broadcast cut to a replay of the now infamous CNN debate from earlier in the day.

'After thirty-five years,' Sexton declared, 'I think it's pretty obvious we're not going to find extraterrestrial life!'

'And if you're wrong?' Marjorie Tench replied.

Sexton rolled his eyes. 'Oh, for heaven's sake, Ms Tench, if I'm wrong I'll eat my hat.'

Everyone in the Roosevelt Room laughed. Tench's cornering of the senator could have played as cruel and heavy-handed in retrospect, and yet viewers didn't seem to notice; the haughty tone of the senator's response was so smug that Sexton appeared to be getting exactly what he deserved.

The President looked around the room for Tench. He had not seen her since before his press conference, and she was not here now. *Odd*, he thought. *This is her celebration as much as it is mine.*

The news report on television was wrapping up, outlining yet again the White House's quantum political leap forward and Senator Sexton's disastrous slide.

What a difference a day makes, the President thought. *In politics, your world can change in an instant.*

By dawn he would realize just how true those words could be.

CHAPTER **85**

Pickering could be a problem, Tench had said.

Administrator Ekstrom was too preoccupied with this new information to notice that the storm outside the habisphere was raging harder now. The howling cables had increased in pitch, and the NASA staff was nervously milling and chatting rather than going to sleep. Ekstrom's thoughts were lost in a different storm – an explosive tempest brewing back in Washington. The last few hours had brought countless problems, all of which Ekstrom was trying to deal with. And yet one problem now loomed larger than all the others combined.

Pickering could be a problem.

Ekstrom could think of no one on earth against whom he'd less rather match wits than William Pickering. Pickering had ridden Ekstrom and NASA for years now, trying to control privacy policy, lobbying for different mission priorities, and railing against NASA's escalating failure ratio.

Pickering's disgust with NASA, Ekstrom knew, went far deeper than the recent loss of his billion-dollar NRO SIGINT satellite in a NASA launchpad explosion, or the NASA security leaks, or the battle over recruiting key aerospace personnel. Pickering's grievances against NASA were an ongoing drama of disillusionment and resentment.

NASA's X-33 space plane, which was supposed to be the shuttle replacement, had run five years overdue, meaning dozens of NRO satellite maintenance and launch programs were scrapped or put on hold. Recently, Pickering's rage over the X-33 reached a fever pitch when he discovered NASA had canceled the project entirely, swallowing an estimated $900 million loss.

Ekstrom arrived at his office, pulled the curtain aside, and entered. Sitting down at his desk he put his head in his hands. He had some decisions to make. What had started as a wonderful day was becoming a nightmare unraveling around him. He tried to put himself in the mindset of William Pickering. What would the man do next? Someone as intelligent as Pickering *had* to see the importance of this NASA discovery. He had to forgive certain choices made in desperation. He had to see the irreversible damage that would be done by polluting this moment of triumph.

What would Pickering do with the information he had? Would he let it ride, or would he make NASA pay for their shortcomings?

Ekstrom scowled, having little doubt which it would be.

After all, William Pickering had deeper issues with NASA . . . an ancient personal bitterness that went far deeper than politics.

CHAPTER **86**

Rachel was quiet now, staring blankly at the cabin of the G4 as the plane headed south along the Canadian coastline of the Gulf of St Lawrence. Tolland sat nearby, talking to Corky. Despite the majority of evidence suggesting the meteorite was authentic, Corky's admission that the nickel content was 'outside the preestablished midrange values' had served to rekindle Rachel's initial suspicion. Secretly planting a meteorite beneath the ice only made sense as part of a brilliantly conceived fraud.

Nonetheless, the remaining scientific evidence pointed toward the meteorite's validity.

Rachel turned from the window, glancing down at the disk-shaped meteorite sample in her hand. The tiny chondrules shimmered. Tolland and Corky had been discussing these metallic chondrules for some time now, talking in scientific terms well over Rachel's head – equilibrated olivine levels, metastable glass matrices, and metamorphic rehomogenation. Nonetheless, the upshot was clear: Corky and Tolland were in agreement that the chondrules were *decidedly* meteoric. No fudging of that data.

Rachel rotated the disk-shaped specimen in her hand, running a finger over the rim where part of the fusion crust was visible. The charring looked relatively fresh – certainly not 300 years old – although Corky had explained that the meteorite had been hermetically sealed in ice and avoided atmospheric erosion. This seemed logical. Rachel had seen programs on television where human remains were dug from the ice after 4,000 years and the person's skin looked almost perfect.

As she studied the fusion crust, an odd thought occurred to her – an obvious piece of data had been omitted. Rachel wondered if it had simply been an oversight in all the data that was thrown at her or did someone simply forget to mention it.

She turned suddenly to Corky. 'Did anyone date the fusion crust?'

Corky glanced over, looking confused. 'What?'

'Did anyone date the burn? That is, do we know for a fact that the burn on the rock occurred at exactly the time of the Jungersol Fall?'

'Sorry,' Corky said, 'that's impossible to date. Oxidation resets all the necessary isotopic markers. Besides, radioisotope decay rates are too slow to measure anything under five hundred years.'

Rachel considered that a moment, understanding now why the burn date was not part of the data. 'So, as far as we know, this rock could have been burned in the Middle Ages or last weekend, right?'

Tolland chuckled. 'Nobody said science had all the answers.'

Rachel let her mind wander aloud. 'A fusion crust is essentially just a severe burn. Technically speaking, the burn on this rock could have happened at any time in the past half century, in any number of different ways.'

'Wrong,' Corky said. 'Burned in any number of different ways? No. Burned in *one* way. Falling through the atmosphere.'

'There's no other possibility? How about in a furnace?'

'A furnace?' Corky said. 'These samples were examined under an electron microscope. Even the cleanest furnace on earth would have left fuel residue all over the stone – nuclear, chemical, fossil fuel. Forget it. And how about the striations from streaking through the atmosphere? You wouldn't get those in a furnace.'

Rachel had forgotten about the orientation striations on the meteorite. It did indeed appear to have fallen through the air. 'How about a volcano?' she ventured. 'Ejecta thrown violently from an eruption?'

Corky shook his head. 'The burn is far too clean.'

Rachel glanced at Tolland.

The oceanographer nodded. 'Sorry, I've had some experience with volcanoes, both above and below water. Corky's right. Volcanic ejecta is penetrated by dozens of toxins – carbon dioxide, sulfur dioxide, hydrogen sulfide, hydrochloric acid – all of which would have been detected in our electronic scans. That fusion crust, whether we like it or not, is the result of a clean atmospheric friction burn.'

Rachel sighed, looking back out the window. *A clean burn.* The phrase stuck with her. She turned back to Tolland. 'What do you mean by a clean burn?'

He shrugged. 'Simply that under an electron microscope, we see no remnants of fuel elements, so we know heating was caused by kinetic energy and friction, rather than chemical or nuclear ingredients.'

'If you didn't find any foreign fuel elements, what did you find? Specifically, what was the composition of the fusion crust?'

'We found,' Corky said, 'exactly what we *expected* to find. Pure atmospheric elements. Nitrogen, oxygen, hydrogen. No petroleums. No sulfurs. No volcanic acids. Nothing peculiar. All the stuff we see when meteorites fall through the atmosphere.'

Rachel leaned back in her seat, her thoughts focusing now.

Corky leaned forward to look at her. 'Please don't tell me your new theory is that NASA took a fossilized rock up in the space shuttle and sent it hurtling toward earth hoping nobody would notice the fireball, the massive crater, or the explosion?'

Rachel had not thought of that, although it was an interesting premise. Not feasible, but interesting all the same. Her thoughts were actually closer to home. *All natural atmospheric elements. Clean burn. Striations from racing through the air.* A faint light had gone off in a distant corner of her mind. 'The ratios of the atmospheric elements you saw,' she said. 'Were they *exactly* the same ratios you see on every other meteorite with a fusion crust?'

Corky seemed to hedge slightly at the question. 'Why do you ask?'

Rachel saw him hesitate and felt her pulse quicken. 'The ratios were off, weren't they?'

'There is a scientific explanation.'

Rachel's heart was suddenly pounding. 'Did you by any chance see an unusually high content of *one* element in particular?'

Tolland and Corky exchanged startled looks. 'Yes,' Corky said, 'but—'

'Was it ionized hydrogen?'

The astrophysicist's eyes turned to saucers. 'How could you possibly know that?'

Tolland also looked utterly amazed.

Rachel stared at them both. 'Why didn't anyone mention this to me?'

'Because there's a perfectly sound scientific explanation!' Corky declared.

'I'm all ears,' Rachel said.

'There was surplus ionized hydrogen,' Corky said, 'because the meteorite passed through the atmosphere near the North Pole, where the earth's magnetic field causes an abnormally high concentration of hydrogen ions.'

Rachel frowned. 'Unfortunately, I have another explanation.'

CHAPTER 87

The fourth floor of NASA headquarters was less impressive than the lobby – long sterile corridors with office doors equally spaced along the walls. The corridor was deserted. Laminated signs pointed in all directions.

← LANDSAT 7

TERRA →

← ACRIMSAT

← JASON 1

AQUA →

PODS →

Gabrielle followed the signs for PODS. Winding her way down a series of long corridors and intersections, she came to a set of heavy steel doors. The stencil read:

POLAR ORBITING DENSITY SCANNER (PODS)
Section Manager, Chris Harper

The doors were locked, secured both by key card and a PIN pad access. Gabrielle put her ear to the cold metal door. For a moment, she thought she heard talking. Arguing. Maybe not. She wondered if she should just bang on the door until someone inside let her in. Unfortunately, her plan for dealing with Chris Harper required a bit more subtlety than banging on doors. She looked around for another entrance but saw none. A custodial alcove stood adjacent to the door, and Gabrielle stepped in, searching the dimly lit niche for a janitor's key ring or key card. Nothing. Just brooms and mops.

Returning to the door, she put her ear to the metal again. This time she definitely heard voices. Getting louder. And footsteps. The latch engaged from inside.

Gabrielle had no time to hide as the metal door burst open. She jumped to the side, plastering herself against the wall behind the door as a group of people hurried through, talking loudly. They sounded angry.

'What the hell is Harper's problem? I thought he'd be on cloud nine!'

'On a night like tonight,' another said as the group passed by, 'he wants to be alone? He should be celebrating!'

As the group moved away from Gabrielle, the heavy door started swinging closed on pneumatic hinges, revealing her location. She remained rigid as the men continued down the hall. Waiting as long as she possibly could, until the door was only inches from closing, Gabrielle lunged forward and caught the door handle with just inches to spare. She stood motionless as the men turned the corner down the hall, too engaged in their conversation to look back.

Heart pounding, Gabrielle pulled open the door and stepped into the dimly lit area beyond. She quietly closed the door.

The space was a wide open work area that reminded her of a college physics laboratory: computers, work islands, electronic gear. As her eyes became accustomed to the darkness, Gabrielle could see blueprints and sheets of calculations scattered around. The entire area was dark except for an office on the far side of the lab, where a light shone under the door. Gabrielle walked over quietly. The door was closed, but through the window she could see a man sitting at a computer. She recognized the man from the NASA press conference. The nameplate on the door read:

Chris Harper
Section Manager, PODS

Having come this far, Gabrielle suddenly felt apprehensive, wondering if she could actually pull this off. She reminded herself how certain Sexton was that Chris Harper had lied. *I would bet my campaign on it*, Sexton had said. Apparently there were others who felt the same, others who were waiting for Gabrielle to uncover the truth so they could close in on NASA, attempting to gain even a tiny foothold after tonight's devastating developments. After the way Tench and the Herney administration had played Gabrielle this afternoon, she was eager to help.

Gabrielle raised her hand to knock on the door but paused, Yolanda's voice running through her mind. *If Chris Harper lied to the world about PODS, what makes you think he'll tell YOU the truth?*

Fear, Gabrielle told herself, having almost fallen victim to it herself today. She had a plan. It involved a tactic she'd seen the senator use on occasion to scare information out of political opponents. Gabrielle had absorbed a lot under Sexton's tutelage, and not all of it attractive or ethical. But tonight she needed every advantage. If she could persuade Chris Harper to admit he had lied – for whatever reason – Gabrielle would open a small door of opportunity for the senator's campaign. Beyond that, Sexton was a man whom, if given an inch to maneuver, could wriggle his way out of almost any jam.

Gabrielle's plan for dealing with Harper was something Sexton called 'overshooting' – an interrogation technique invented by the early Roman authorities to coax confessions from criminals they suspected were lying. The method was deceptively simple:

Assert the information you want confessed.

Then allege something far worse.

The object was to give the opponent a chance to choose the lesser of two evils – in this case, the truth.

The trick was exuding confidence, something Gabrielle was not feeling at the moment. Taking a deep breath, Gabrielle ran through the script in her mind, and then knocked firmly on the office door.

'I told you I'm busy!' Harper called out, his English accent familiar. She knocked again. Louder.

'I told you I'm not interested in coming down!'

This time she banged on the door with her fist.

Chris Harper came over and yanked open the door. 'Bloody hell, do you—' He stopped short, clearly surprised to see Gabrielle.

'Dr Harper,' she said, infusing her voice with intensity.

'How did you get up here?'

Gabrielle's face was stern. 'Do you know who I am?'

'Of course. Your boss has been slamming my project for months. How did you get in?'

'Senator Sexton sent me.'

Harper's eyes scanned the lab behind Gabrielle. 'Where is your staff escort?'

'That's not your concern. The senator has influential connections.'

'In this building?' Harper looked dubious.

'You've been dishonest, Dr Harper. And I'm afraid the senator has called a special senatorial justice board to look into your lies.'

A pall crossed Harper's face. 'What are you talking about?'

'Smart people like yourself don't have the luxury of playing stupid, Dr Harper. You're in trouble, and the senator sent me up here to offer you a deal. The senator's campaign took a huge hit tonight. He's got nothing left to lose, and he's ready to take you down with him if he needs to.'

'What the devil are you talking about?'

Gabrielle took a deep breath and made her play. 'You lied in your press conference about the PODS anomaly-detection software. We know that. A lot of people know that. That's not the issue.' Before Harper could open his mouth to argue, Gabrielle steamed onward. 'The senator could blow the whistle on your lies right now, but he's not interested. He's interested in the bigger story. I think you know what I'm talking about.'

'No, I—'

'Here's the senator's offer. He'll keep his mouth shut about your software lies if you give him the name of the top NASA executive with whom you're embezzling funds.'

Chris Harper's eyes seemed to cross for a moment. 'What? I'm not embezzling!'

'I suggest you watch what you say, sir. The senatorial committee has been collecting documentation for months now. Did you really think you two would slip by undetected? Doctoring PODS paperwork and redirecting allocated NASA funds to private accounts? Lying and embezzling can put you in jail, Dr Harper.'

'I did no such thing!'

'You're saying you didn't lie about PODS?'

'No, I'm saying I bloody well didn't embezzle money!'

'So, you're saying you *did* lie about PODS.'

Harper stared, clearly at a loss for words.

'Forget about the lying,' Gabrielle said, waving it off. 'Senator Sexton is not interested in the issue of your lying in a press conference. We're used to that. You guys found a meteorite, nobody cares how you did it. The issue for him is the embezzlement. He needs to take down someone high in NASA. Just tell him who you're working with, and he'll steer the investigation clear of you entirely. You can make it easy and tell us who the other person is, or the senator will make it ugly and start talking about anomaly-detection software and phony work-arounds.'

'You're bluffing. There are no embezzled funds.'

'You're an awful liar, Dr Harper. I've seen the documentation. Your name is on all the incriminating paperwork. Over and over.'

'I swear I know nothing about any embezzlement!'

Gabrielle let out a disappointed sigh. 'Put yourself in my position, Dr Harper. I can only draw two conclusions here. Either you're lying to me, the same way you lied in that press conference. Or you're telling the truth, and someone powerful in the agency is setting you up as a fall guy for his own misdealings.'

The proposition seemed to give Harper pause.

Gabrielle checked her watch. 'The senator's deal is on the table for an hour. You can save yourself by giving him the name of the NASA exec with whom you're embezzling taxpayers' money. He doesn't care about you. He wants the big fish. Obviously the individual in question has some power here at NASA; he or she has managed to keep his or her identity off the paper trail, allowing you to be the fall guy.'

Harper shook his head. 'You're lying.'

'Would you like to tell that to a court?'

'Sure. I'll deny the whole thing.'

'Under oath?' Gabrielle grunted in disgust. 'Suppose you'll also deny you lied about fixing the PODS software?' Gabrielle's heart was pounding as she stared straight into the man's eyes. 'Think carefully about your options here, Dr Harper. American prisons can be most unpleasant.'

Harper glared back, and Gabrielle willed him to fold. For a moment she thought she saw a glimmer of surrender, but when Harper spoke, his voice was like steel.

'Ms Ashe,' he declared, anger simmering in his eyes, 'you are clutching at thin air. You and I both know there is no embezzlement going on at NASA. The only liar in this room is *you*.'

Gabrielle felt her muscles go rigid. The man's gaze was angry and sharp. She wanted to turn and run. *You tried to bluff a rocket scientist. What the hell did you expect?* She forced herself to hold her head high. 'All I know,' she said, feigning utter confidence and indifference to his position, 'is the incriminating documents I've seen – conclusive evidence that you and another are embezzling NASA funds. The senator simply asked me to come here tonight and offer you the option of giving up your partner instead of facing the inquiry alone. I will tell the senator you prefer to take your chances with a judge. You can tell the court what you told me – you're not embezzling funds and you didn't lie about the PODS software.' She gave a grim smile. 'But after that lame press conference you gave two weeks ago, somehow I doubt it.' Gabrielle spun on her heel and strode across the darkened PODS laboratory. She wondered if maybe *she'd* be seeing the inside of a prison instead of Harper.

Gabrielle held her head high as she walked off, waiting for Harper to call her back. Silence. She pushed her way through the metal doors and strode out into the hallway, hoping the elevators up here were not key-card operated like the lobby. She'd lost. Despite her best efforts, Harper wasn't biting. *Maybe he was telling the truth in his PODS press conference*, Gabrielle thought.

A crash resounded down the hall as the metal doors behind her burst open. 'Ms Ashe,' Harper's voice called out. 'I swear I know nothing about any embezzlement. I'm an honest man!'

Gabrielle felt her heart skip a beat. She forced herself to keep walking. She gave a casual shrug and called out over her shoulder, 'And yet you lied in your press conference.'

Silence. Gabrielle kept moving down the hallway.

'Hold on!' Harper yelled. He came jogging up beside her, his face pale. 'This embezzlement thing,' he said, lowering his voice. 'I think I know who set me up.'

Gabrielle stopped dead in her tracks, wondering if she had heard him correctly. She turned as slowly and casually as she could. 'You expect me to believe someone is setting you up?'

Harper sighed. 'I swear I know nothing about embezzlement. But if there's evidence against me . . .'

'Mounds of it.'

Harper sighed. 'Then it's all been planted. To discredit me if need be. And there's only one person who would have done that.'

'Who?'

Harper looked her in the eye. 'Lawrence Ekstrom hates me.'

Gabrielle was stunned. 'The *administrator* of NASA?'

Harper gave a grim nod. 'He's the one who forced me to lie in that press conference.'

CHAPTER **88**

Even with the Aurora aircraft's misted-methane propulsion system at half power, the Delta Force was hurtling through the night at three times the speed of sound – over two thousand miles an hour. The repetitive throb of the Pulse Detonation Wave Engines behind them gave the ride a hypnotic rhythm. A hundred feet below, the ocean churned wildly, whipped up by the Aurora's vacuum wake, which sucked fifty-foot rooster tails skyward in long parallel sheets behind the plane.

This is the reason the SR-71 Blackbird was retired, Delta-One thought.

The Aurora was one of those secret aircraft that nobody was supposed to know existed, but everyone did. Even the Discovery channel had covered Aurora and its testing out at Groom Lake in

Nevada. Whether the security leaks had come from the repeated 'skyquakes' heard as far away as Los Angeles, or the fortunate eyewitness sighting by a North Sea oil-rig driller, or the administrative gaffe that left a description of Aurora in a public copy of the Pentagon budget, nobody would ever know. It hardly mattered. The word was out: the U.S. military had a plane capable of Mach 6 flight, and it was no longer on the drawing board. It was in the skies overhead.

Built by Lockheed, the Aurora looked like a flattened American football. It was 110 feet long, 60 feet wide, smoothly contoured with a crystalline patina of thermal tiles much like the space shuttle. The speed was primarily the result of an exotic new propulsion system known as a Pulse Detonation Wave Engine, which burned a clean, misted, liquid hydrogen and left a tell-tale pulse contrail in the sky. For this reason, it only flew at night.

Tonight, with the luxury of enormous speed, the Delta Force was taking the long way home, out across the open ocean. Even so, they were overtaking their quarry. At this rate, the Delta Force would be arriving on the eastern seaboard in under an hour, a good two hours before its prey. There had been discussion of tracking and shooting down the plane in question, but the controller rightly feared a radar capture of the incident or the burned wreckage might bring on a massive investigation. It was best to let the plane land as scheduled, the controller had decided. Once it became clear where their quarry intended to land, the Delta Force would move in.

Now, as Aurora streaked over the desolate Labrador Sea, Delta-One's CrypTalk indicated an incoming call. He answered.

'The situation has changed,' the electronic voice informed them. 'You have another mark before Rachel Sexton and the scientists land.'

Another mark. Delta-One could feel it. Things were unraveling. The controller's ship had sprung another leak, and the controller needed them to patch it as fast as possible. *The ship would not be leaking,* Delta-One reminded himself, *if we had hit our marks successfully on the Milne Ice Shelf.* Delta-One knew damn well he was cleaning up his own mess.

'A fourth party has become involved,' the controller said.

'Who?'

The controller paused a moment – and then gave them a name.

The three men exchanged startled looks. It was a name they knew well.

No wonder the controller sounded reluctant! Delta-One thought. For an operation conceived as a 'zero-casualty' venture, the body count and target profile was climbing fast. He felt his sinews tighten as the controller prepared to inform them exactly how and where they would eliminate this new individual.

'The stakes have increased considerably,' the controller said. 'Listen closely. I will give you these instructions only once.'

CHAPTER 89

High above northern Maine, a G4 jet continued speeding toward Washington. Onboard, Michael Tolland and Corky Marlinson looked on as Rachel Sexton began to explain her theory for why there might be increased hydrogen ions in the fusion crust of the meteorite.

'NASA has a private test facility called Plum Brook Station,' Rachel explained, hardly able to believe she was going to talk about this. Sharing classified information out of protocol was not something she had ever done, but considering the circumstances, Tolland and Corky had a right to know this. 'Plum Brook is essentially a test chamber for NASA's most radical new engine systems. Two years ago I wrote a gist about a new design NASA was testing there – something called an expander cycle engine.'

Corky eyed her suspiciously. 'Expander cycle engines are still in the theoretical stage. On paper. Nobody's actually testing. That's decades away.'

Rachel shook her head. 'Sorry, Corky. NASA has prototypes. They're testing.'

'What?' Corky looked skeptical. 'ECE's run on liquid oxygen-hydrogen, which freezes in space, making the engine worthless to NASA. They said they were not even going to try to build an ECE until they overcame the freezing fuel problem.'

'They overcame it. They got rid of the oxygen and turned the fuel into a "slush-hydrogen" mixture, which is some kind of cryogenic fuel consisting of pure hydrogen in a semifrozen state. It's very powerful and very clean burning. It's also a contender for the propulsion system if NASA runs missions to Mars.'

Corky looked amazed. 'This can't be true.'

'It *better* be true,' Rachel said. 'I wrote a brief about it for the President. My boss was up in arms because NASA wanted to publicly announce slush-hydrogen as a big success, and Pickering wanted the White House to force NASA to keep slush-hydrogen classified.'

'Why?'

'Not important,' Rachel said, having no intention of sharing more secrets than she had to. The truth was that Pickering's desire to classify slush-hydrogen's success was to fight a growing national security concern few knew existed – the alarming expansion of China's space technology. The Chinese were currently developing a deadly 'for-hire' launch platform, which they intended to rent out to high bidders, most of whom would be U.S. enemies. The implications for U.S. security were devastating. Fortunately, the NRO knew China was pursuing a doomed propulsion-fuel model for their launch platform, and Pickering saw no reason to tip them off about NASA's more promising slush-hydrogen propellant.

'So,' Tolland said, looking uneasy, 'you're saying NASA has a clean-burning propulsion system that runs on pure hydrogen?'

Rachel nodded. 'I don't have figures, but the exhaust temperatures of these engines are apparently several times hotter than anything ever before developed. They're requiring NASA to develop all kinds of new nozzle materials.' She paused. 'A large rock, placed behind one of these slush-hydrogen engines, would be scalded by a hydrogen-rich blast of exhaust fire coming out at an unprecedented temperature. You'd get quite a fusion crust.'

'Come on now!' Corky said. 'Are we back to the fake meteorite scenario?'

Tolland seemed suddenly intrigued. 'Actually, that's quite an idea. The setup would be more or less like leaving a boulder on the launchpad under the space shuttle during liftoff.'

'God save me,' Corky muttered. 'I'm airborne with idiots.'

'Corky,' Tolland said. 'Hypothetically speaking, a rock placed in an exhaust field would exhibit similar burn features to one that fell through the atmosphere, wouldn't it? You'd have the same directional striations and backflow of the melting material.'

Corky grunted. 'I suppose.'

'And Rachel's clean-burning hydrogen fuel would leave no chemical residue. Only hydrogen. Increased levels of hydrogen ions in the fusion pocking.'

Corky rolled his eyes. 'Look, if one of these ECE engines actually exists, and runs on slush-hydrogen, I suppose what you're talking about is possible. But it's extremely far-fetched.'

'Why?' Tolland asked. 'The process seems fairly simple.'

Rachel nodded. 'All you need is a one-hundred-and-ninety-million-year-old fossilized rock. Blast it in a slush-hydrogen-engine exhaust fire, and bury it in the ice. Instant meteorite.'

'To a tourist, maybe,' Corky said, 'but not to a NASA scientist! You still haven't explained the chondrules!'

Rachel tried to recall Corky's explanation of how chondrules formed. 'You said chondrules are caused by rapid heating and cooling events in space, right?'

Corky sighed. 'Chondrules form when a rock, chilled in space, suddenly becomes superheated to a partial-melt stage – somewhere near 1,550 Celsius. Then the rock must cool again, extremely rapidly, hardening the liquid pockets into chondrules.'

Tolland studied his friend. 'And this process can't happen on earth?'

'Impossible,' Corky said. 'This planet does not have the temperature variance to cause that kind of rapid shift. You're talking here about nuclear heat and the absolute zero of space. Those extremes simply don't exist on earth.'

Rachel considered it. 'At least not *naturally*.'

Corky turned. 'What's that supposed to mean?'

'Why couldn't the heating and cooling event have occurred here on earth artificially?' Rachel asked. 'The rock could have been blasted by a slush-hydrogen engine and then rapidly cooled in a cryogenic freezer.'

Corky stared. 'Manufactured chondrules?'

'It's an idea.'

'A ridiculous one,' Corky replied, flashing his meteorite sample. 'Perhaps you forget? These chondrules were irrefutably dated at one hundred and ninety million years.' His tone grew patronizing. 'To the best of my knowledge, Ms Sexton, one hundred and ninety million years ago, nobody was running slush-hydrogen engines and cryogenic coolers.'

Chondrules or not, Tolland thought, *the evidence is piling up.* He had been silent now for several minutes, deeply troubled by Rachel's newest revelation about the fusion crust. Her hypothesis, though staggeringly bold, had opened all kinds of new doors and gotten Tolland thinking in new directions. *If the fusion crust is explainable . . . what other possibilities does that present?*

'You're quiet,' Rachel said, beside him.

Tolland glanced over. For an instant, in the muted lighting of the plane, he saw a softness in Rachel's eyes that reminded him of Celia. Shaking off the memories, he gave her a tired sigh. 'Oh, I was just thinking . . .'

She smiled. 'About meteorites?'

'What else?'

'Running through all the evidence, trying to figure out what's left?'

'Something like that.'

'Any thoughts?'

'Not really. I'm troubled by how much of the data has collapsed in light of discovering that insertion shaft beneath the ice.'

'Hierarchical evidence is a house of cards,' Rachel said. 'Pull out your primary assumption, and everything gets shaky. The *location* of the meteorite find was a primary assumption.'

I'll say. 'When I arrived at Milne, the administrator told me the meteorite had been found inside a pristine matrix of three-hundred-year-old ice and was more dense than any rock found anywhere in the area, which I took as logical proof that the rock had to fall from space.'

'You and the rest of us.'

'The midrange nickel content, though persuasive, is apparently not conclusive.'

'It's *close*,' Corky said nearby, apparently listening in.

'But not exact.'

Corky acquiesced with a reluctant nod.

'And,' Tolland said, 'this never before seen species of space bug, though shockingly bizarre, in reality could be nothing more than a very old, deepwater crustacean.'

Rachel nodded. 'And now the fusion crust . . .'

'I hate to say it,' Tolland said, glancing at Corky, 'but it's starting to feel like there's more negative evidence than positive.'

'Science is not about hunches,' Corky said. 'It's about evidence. The chondrules in this rock are decidedly meteoric. I agree with you both that everything we've seen is deeply disturbing, but we cannot ignore these chondrules. The evidence in favor is conclusive, while the evidence against is circumstantial.'

Rachel frowned. 'So where does that leave us?'

'Nowhere,' Corky said. 'The chondrules prove we are dealing with a meteorite. The only question is why someone stuck it under the ice.'

Tolland wanted to believe his friend's sound logic, but something just felt wrong.

'You don't look convinced, Mike,' Corky said.

Tolland gave his friend a bewildered sigh. 'I don't know. Two out of three wasn't bad, Corky. But we're down to one out of three. I just feel like we're missing something.'

CHAPTER 90

I got caught, Chris Harper thought, feeling a chill as he pictured an American prison cell. *Senator Sexton knows I lied about the PODS software.*

As the PODS section manager escorted Gabrielle Ashe back into his office and closed the door, he felt his hatred of the NASA administrator grow deeper by the instant. Tonight Harper had learned just how deep the administrator's lies truly ran. In addition to forcing

Harper to lie about having fixed PODS's software, the administrator
had apparently set up some insurance just in case Harper got cold feet
and decided not to be a team player.

Evidence of embezzlement, Harper thought. *Blackmail. Very sly.* After
all, who would believe an embezzler trying to discredit the single
greatest moment in American space history? Harper had already
witnessed to what lengths the NASA administrator would go to save
America's space agency, and now with the announcement of a
meteorite with fossils, the stakes had skyrocketed.

Harper paced for several seconds around the wide table on which
sat a scale model of the PODS satellite – a cylindrical prism with
multiple antennae and lenses behind reflective shields. Gabrielle sat
down, her dark eyes watching, waiting. The nausea in Harper's gut
reminded him of how he had felt during the infamous press conference. He'd put on a lousy show that night, and everyone had
questioned him about it. He'd had to lie again and say he was feeling
ill that night and was not himself. His colleagues and the press
shrugged off his lackluster performance and quickly forgot about it.

Now the lie had come back to haunt him.

Gabrielle Ashe's expression softened. 'Mr Harper, with the administrator as an enemy, you will need a powerful ally. Senator Sexton
could well be your only friend at this point. Let's start with the PODS
software lie. Tell me what happened.'

Harper sighed. He knew it was time to tell the truth. *I bloody well
should have told the truth in the first place!* 'The PODS launch went
smoothly,' he began. 'The satellite settled into a perfect polar orbit
just as planned.'

Gabrielle Ashe looked bored. She apparently knew all this. 'Go on.'

'Then came the trouble. When we geared up to start searching the
ice for density anomalies, the onboard anomaly-detection software
failed.'

'Uh . . . huh.'

Harper's words came faster now. 'The software was supposed to be
able to rapidly examine thousands of acres of data and find parts of
the ice that fell outside the range of normal ice density. Primarily the
software was looking for soft spots in the ice – global warming
indicators – but if it stumbled across other density incongruities, it

was programmed to flag those as well. The plan was for PODS to scan the Arctic Circle over several weeks and identify any anomalies that we could use to measure global warming.'

'But without functioning software,' Gabrielle said, 'PODS was no good. NASA would have had to examine images of every square inch of the Arctic by hand, looking for trouble spots.'

Harper nodded, reliving the nightmare of his programming gaffe. 'It would take decades. The situation was terrible. Because of a flaw in my programming, PODS was essentially worthless. With the election coming up and Senator Sexton being so critical of NASA . . .' He sighed.

'Your mistake was devastating to NASA and the President.'

'It couldn't have come at a worse time. The administrator was livid. I promised him I could fix the problem during the next shuttle mission – a simple matter of swapping out the chip that held the PODS software system. But it was too little too late. He sent me home on leave – but essentially I was fired. That was a month ago.'

'And yet you were back on television two weeks ago announcing you'd found a work-around.'

Harper slumped. 'A terrible mistake. That was the day I got a desperate call from the administrator. He told me something had come up, a possible way to redeem myself. I came into the office immediately and met with him. He asked me to hold a press conference and tell everyone I'd found a work-around for the PODS software and that we would have data in a few weeks. He said he'd explain it to me later.'

'And you agreed.'

'No, I refused! But an hour later, the administrator was back in my office – with the White House senior adviser!'

'What?' Gabrielle looked astounded by this. 'Marjorie Tench?'

An awful creature, Harper thought, nodding. 'She and the administrator sat me down and told me *my* mistake had quite literally put NASA and the President on the brink of total collapse. Ms Tench told me about the senator's plans to privatize NASA. She told me I owed it to the President and space agency to make it all right. Then she told me how.'

Gabrielle leaned forward. 'Go on.'

'Marjorie Tench informed me that the White House, by sheer good fortune, had intercepted strong geologic evidence that an enormous meteorite was buried in the Milne Ice Shelf. One of the biggest ever. A meteorite of that size would be a major find for NASA.'

Gabrielle looked stunned. 'Hold on, so you're saying someone already *knew* the meteorite was there before PODS discovered it?'

'Yes. PODS had nothing to do with the discovery. The administrator knew the meteorite existed. He simply gave me the coordinates and told me to reposition PODS over the ice shelf and *pretend* PODS made the discovery.'

'You're kidding me.'

'That was my reaction when they asked me to participate in the sham. They refused to tell me how they'd found out the meteorite was there, but Ms Tench insisted it didn't matter and that this was the ideal opportunity to salvage my PODS fiasco. If I could pretend the PODS satellite located the meteorite, then NASA could praise PODS as a much needed success and boost the President before the election.'

Gabrielle was awestruck. 'And of course you couldn't claim PODS had detected a meteorite until you'd announced that the PODS anomaly-detection software was up and running.'

Harper nodded. 'Hence the press conference lie. I was forced into it. Tench and the administrator were ruthless. They reminded me I'd let everyone down – the President had funded my PODS project, NASA had spent years on it, and now I'd ruined the whole thing with a programming blunder.'

'So you agreed to help.'

'I didn't have a choice. My career was essentially over if I didn't. And the reality was that if I hadn't muffed the software, PODS *would have* found that meteorite on its own. So, it seemed a small lie at the time. I rationalized it by telling myself that the software would be fixed in a few months when the space shuttle went up, so I would simply be announcing the fix a little early.'

Gabrielle let out a whistle. 'A tiny lie to take advantage of a meteoric opportunity.'

Harper was feeling ill just talking about it. 'So . . . I did it. Following the administrator's orders, I held a press conference announcing that

I'd found a work-around for my anomaly-detection software, I waited a few days, and then I repositioned PODS over the administrator's meteorite coordinates. Then, following the proper chain of command, I phoned the EOS director and reported that PODS had located a hard density anomaly in the Milne Ice Shelf. I gave him the coordinates and told him the anomaly appeared to be dense enough to be a meteorite. Excitedly, NASA sent a small team up to Milne to take some drill cores. That's when the operation got very hush-hush.'

'So, you had no idea the meteorite had *fossils* until tonight?'

'Nobody here did. We're all in shock. Now everyone is calling me a hero for finding proof of extraterrestrial bioforms, and I don't know what to say.'

Gabrielle was silent a long moment, studying Harper with firm black eyes. 'But if PODS didn't locate the meteorite in the ice, how did the administrator know the meteorite was there?'

'Someone else found it first.'

'Someone *else*? Who?'

Harper sighed. 'A Canadian geologist named Charles Brophy – a researcher on Ellesmere Island. Apparently he was doing geologic ice soundings on the Milne Ice Shelf when he by chance discovered the presence of what appeared to be a huge meteorite in the ice. He radioed it in, and NASA happened to intercept the transmission.'

Gabrielle stared. 'But isn't this Canadian furious that NASA is taking all the credit for the find?'

'No,' Harper said, feeling a chill. 'Conveniently, he's dead.'

CHAPTER 91

Michael Tolland closed his eyes and listened to the drone of the G4 jet engine. He had given up trying to think anymore about the meteorite until they got back to Washington. The chondrules, according to Corky, were conclusive; the rock in the Milne Ice Shelf could only be a meteorite. Rachel had hoped to have a conclusive answer for William Pickering by the time they landed, but her thought experiments had run into a dead end with the chondrules. As suspicious as the meteorite evidence was, the meteorite appeared to be authentic.

So be it.

Rachel had obviously been shaken by the trauma in the ocean. Tolland was amazed, though, by her resilience. She was focused now on the issue at hand – to find a way to debunk or authenticate the meteorite, and to assess who had tried to kill them.

For most of the trip, Rachel had been in the seat beside Tolland. He'd enjoyed talking to her, despite the trying circumstances. Several minutes ago, she'd headed back to the restroom, and now Tolland was surprised to find himself missing her beside him. He wondered how long it had been since he'd missed a woman's presence – a woman other than Celia.

'Mr Tolland?'

Tolland glanced up.

The pilot was sticking his head into the cabin. 'You asked me to tell you when we were in telephone range of your ship? I can get you that connection if you want.'

'Thanks.' Tolland made his way up the aisle.

Inside the cockpit, Tolland placed a call to his crew. He wanted to let them know he would not be back for another day or two. Of course, he had no intention of telling them what trouble he'd run into.

The phone rang several times, and Tolland was surprised to hear the ship's SHINCOM 2100 communications system pick up. The outgoing message was not the usual professional-sounding greeting but rather the rowdy voice of one of Tolland's crew, the onboard joker.

'Hiya, hiya, this is the *Goya*,' the voice announced. 'We're sorry nobody's here right now, but we've all been abducted by very large lice! Actually, we've taken temporary shore leave to celebrate Mike's huge night. Gosh, are we proud! You can leave your name and number, and maybe we'll be back tomorrow when we're sober. Ciao! Go ET!'

Tolland laughed, missing his crew already. Obviously they'd seen the press conference. He was glad they'd gone ashore; he'd abandoned them rather abruptly when the President called, and their sitting idle at sea was crazy. Although the message said everyone had gone ashore, Tolland had to assume they would not have left his ship unattended, particularly in the strong currents where it was now anchored.

Tolland pressed the numeric code to play any internal voice mail messages they'd left for him. The line beeped once. One message. The voice was the same rowdy crewmember.

'Hi, Mike, hell of a show! If you're hearing this, you're probably checking your messages from some swanky White House party and wondering where the hell we are. Sorry we abandoned ship, buddy, but this was not a dry-celebration kind of night. Don't worry, we anchored her really good and left the porch light on. We're secretly hoping she gets pirated so you'll let NBC buy you that new boat! Just kidding, man. Don't worry, Xavia agreed to stay onboard and mind the fort. She said she preferred time alone to partying with a bunch of drunken fishmongers. Can you believe that?'

Tolland chuckled, relieved to hear someone was aboard watching the ship. Xavia was responsible, definitely not the partying type. A respected marine geologist, Xavia had the reputation for speaking her mind with a caustic honesty.

'Anyhow, Mike,' the message went on, 'tonight was incredible. Kind of makes you proud to be a scientist, doesn't it? Everyone's talking about how good this looks for NASA. Screw NASA, I say! This looks even better for *us*! *Amazing Seas* ratings must have gone up a few million points tonight. You're a star, man. A real one. Congrats. Excellent job.'

There was hushed talking on the line, and the voice came back. 'Oh, yeah, and speaking of Xavia, just so you don't get too big a head, she wants to razz you about something. Here she is.'

Xavia's razor voice came on the machine. 'Mike, Xavia, you're a God, yada yada. And because I love you so much, I've agreed to baby-sit this antediluvian wreck of yours. Frankly, it will be nice to be away from these hoodlums you call scientists. Anyhow, in addition to baby-sitting the ship, the crew has asked me, in my role as onboard bitch, to do everything in my power to keep you from turning into a conceited bastard, which after tonight I realize is going to be difficult, but I had to be the first to tell you that you made a boo-boo in your documentary. Yes, you heard me. A rare Michael Tolland brain fart. Don't worry, there are only about three people on earth who will notice, and they're all anal-retentive marine geologists with no sense of humor. A lot like me. But you know what they say about us geologists – always looking for *faults*!' She laughed. 'Anyhow, it's nothing, a minuscule point about meteorite petrology. I only mention it to ruin your night. You might get a call or two about it, so I thought I'd give you the heads-up so you don't end up sounding like the moron we all know you really are.' She laughed again. 'Anyhow, I'm not much of a party animal, so I'm staying onboard. Don't bother calling me; I had to turn on the machine because the goddamned press have been calling all night. You're a real star tonight, despite your screwup. Anyhow, I'll fill you in on it when you get back. Ciao.'

The line went dead.

Michael Tolland frowned. *A mistake in my documentary?*

Rachel Sexton stood in the restroom of the G4 and looked at herself in the mirror. She looked pale, she thought, and more frail than she'd imagined. Tonight's scare had taken a lot out of her. She wondered how long it would be before she would stop shivering, or before she would go near an ocean. Removing her U.S.S. *Charlotte* cap, she let her hair down. *Better*, she thought, feeling more like herself.

Looking into her eyes, Rachel sensed a deep weariness. Beneath it, though, she saw the resolve. She knew that was her mother's gift. *Nobody tells you what you can and can't do.* Rachel wondered if her mother had seen what happened tonight. *Someone tried to kill me, Mom. Someone tried to kill all of us . . .*

Rachel's mind, as it had for several hours now, scrolled through the list of names.

Lawrence Ekstrom . . . Marjorie Tench . . . President Zach Herney. All had motives. And, more chillingly, all had means. *The President is not involved*, Rachel told herself, clinging to her hope that the President she respected so much more than her own father was an innocent bystander in this mysterious incident.

We still know nothing.

Not who . . . not if . . . not why.

Rachel had wanted to have answers for William Pickering but, so far, all she'd managed to do was raise more questions.

When Rachel left the restroom, she was surprised to see Michael Tolland was not in his seat. Corky was dozing nearby. As Rachel looked around, Mike stepped out of the cockpit as the pilot hung up a radiophone. His eyes were wide with concern.

'What is it?' Rachel asked.

Tolland's voice was heavy as he told her about the phone message.

A mistake in his presentation? Rachel thought Tolland was overreacting. 'It's probably nothing. She didn't tell you specifically what the error was?'

'Something to do with meteorite petrology.'

'Rock structure?'

'Yeah. She said the only people who would notice the mistake were a few other geologists. It sounds like whatever error I made was relating to the composition of the meteorite itself.'

Rachel drew a quick breath, understanding now. 'Chondrules?'

'I don't know, but it seems pretty coincidental.'

Rachel agreed. The chondrules were the one remaining shred of evidence that categorically supported NASA's claim that this was indeed a meteorite.

Corky came over, rubbing his eyes. 'What's going on?'

Tolland filled him in.

Corky scowled, shaking his head. 'It's not a problem with the chondrules, Mike. No way. All of your data came from NASA. And from *me*. It was flawless.'

'What other petrologic error could I have made?'

'Who the hell knows? Besides, what do marine geologists know about chondrules?'

'I have no idea, but she's damned sharp.'

'Considering the circumstances,' Rachel said, 'I think we should talk to this woman before we talk to Director Pickering.'

Tolland shrugged. 'I called her four times and got the machine. She's probably in the hydrolab and can't hear a damn thing anyway. She won't get my messages until morning at the earliest.' Tolland paused, checking his watch. 'Although . . .'

'Although what?'

Tolland eyed her intensely. 'How important do you think it is that we talk to Xavia before we talk to your boss?'

'If she has something to say about chondrules? I'd say it's critical. Mike,' Rachel said, 'at the moment, we've got all kinds of contradictory data. William Pickering is a man accustomed to having clear answers. When we meet him, I'd love to have something substantial for him to act on.'

'Then we should make a stop.'

Rachel did a double take. 'On your ship?'

'It's off the coast of New Jersey. Almost directly on our way to Washington. We can talk to Xavia, find out what she knows. Corky still has the meteorite sample, and if Xavia wants to run some geologic tests on it, the ship has a fairly well-equipped lab. I can't imagine it would take us more than an hour to get some conclusive answers.'

Rachel felt a pulse of anxiety. The thought of having to face the ocean again so soon was unnerving. *Conclusive answers*, she told herself, tempted by the possibility. *Pickering will definitely want answers.*

CHAPTER 92

Delta-One was glad to be back on solid ground.

The Aurora aircraft, despite running at only one-half power and taking a circuitous ocean route, had completed its journey in under two hours and afforded the Delta Force a healthy head start to take up position and prepare themselves for the additional kill the controller had requested.

Now, on a private military runway outside D.C., the Delta Force left the Aurora behind and boarded their new transport – a waiting OH-58D Kiowa Warrior helicopter.

Yet again, the controller has arranged for the best, Delta-One thought.

The Kiowa Warrior, originally designed as a light observation helicopter, had been 'expanded and improved' to create the military's newest breed of attack helicopter. The Kiowa boasted infrared thermal imaging capability enabling its designator/laser range finder to provide autonomous designation for laser-guided precision weapons like Air-to-Air Stinger missiles and the AGM-1148 Hellfire Missile System. A high-speed digital signal processor provided simultaneous multitarget tracking of up to six targets. Few enemies had ever seen a Kiowa up close and survived to tell the tale.

Delta-One felt a familiar rush of power as he climbed into the Kiowa pilot's seat and strapped himself in. He had trained on this craft and flown it in covert ops three times. Of course, never before had he been gunning for a prominent *American* official. The Kiowa, he had to admit, was the perfect aircraft for the job. Its Rolls-Royce Allison engine and twin semirigid blades were 'silent running,' which essentially meant targets on the ground could not hear the chopper until it was directly over them. And because the aircraft was capable of flying blind without lights and was painted flat black with no reflective tail numbers, it was essentially invisible unless the target had radar.

Silent black helicopters.

The conspiracy theorists were going nuts over these. Some claimed the invasion of silent black helicopters was proof of 'New World Order storm troopers' under the authority of the United Nations. Others claimed the choppers were silent alien probes. Still others who saw the Kiowas in tight formation at night were deceived into thinking they were looking at fixed running lights on a much larger craft – a single flying saucer that was apparently capable of vertical flight.

Wrong again. But the military loved the diversion.

During a recent covert mission, Delta-One had flown a Kiowa armed with the most secretive new U.S. military technology – an ingenious holographic weapon nicknamed S&M. Despite conjuring associations with sadomasochism, S&M stood for 'smoke and mirrors' – holographic images 'projected' into the sky over enemy territory. The Kiowa had used S&M technology to project holograms of U.S. aircraft over an enemy anti-aircraft installation. The panicked anti-aircraft gunners fired maniacally at the circling ghosts. When all of their ammunition was gone, the United States sent in the real thing.

As Delta-One and his men lifted off the runway, Delta-One could still hear the words of his controller. *You have another mark.* It seemed an egregious understatement considering their new target's identity. Delta-One reminded himself, however, that it was not his place to question. His team had been given an order, and they would carry it out in the exact method instructed – as shocking as that method was.

I hope to hell the controller is certain this is the right move.

As the Kiowa lifted off the runway, Delta-One headed southwest. He had seen the FDR Memorial twice, but tonight would be his first time from the air.

CHAPTER **9 3**

'This meteorite was originally discovered by a Canadian geologist?' Gabrielle Ashe stared in astonishment at the young programmer, Chris Harper. 'And this Canadian is now *dead*?'

Harper gave a grim nod.

'How long have you known this?' she demanded.

'A couple of weeks. After the administrator and Marjorie Tench forced me to perjure myself in the press conference, they knew I couldn't go back on my word. They told me the truth about how the meteorite was really discovered.'

PODS is not responsible for finding the meteorite! Gabrielle had no idea where all of this information would lead, but clearly it was scandalous. Bad news for Tench. Great news for the senator.

'As I mentioned,' Harper said, looking somber now, 'the true way the meteorite was discovered was through an intercepted radio transmission. Are you familiar with a program called INSPIRE? The Interactive NASA Space Physics Ionosphere Radio Experiment.'

Gabrielle had heard of it only vaguely.

'Essentially,' Harper said, 'it's a series of very low frequency radio receivers near the North Pole that listen to the sounds of the earth –

plasma wave emissions from the northern lights, broadband pulses from lightning storms, that sort of thing.'

'Okay.'

'A few weeks ago, one of INSPIRE's radio receivers picked up a stray transmission from Ellesmere Island. A Canadian geologist was calling for help at an exceptionally low frequency.' Harper paused. 'In fact, the frequency was *so* low that nobody other than NASA's VLF receivers could possibly have heard it. We assumed the Canadian was long-waving.'

'I'm sorry?'

'Broadcasting at the lowest possible frequency to get maximum distance on his transmission. He was in the middle of nowhere, remember; a standard frequency transmission probably would not have made it far enough to be heard.'

'What did his message say?'

'The transmission was short. The Canadian said he had been out doing ice soundings on the Milne Ice Shelf, had detected an ul-tradense anomaly buried in the ice, suspected it was a giant meteorite, and while taking measurements had become trapped in a storm. He gave his coordinates, asked for rescue from the storm, and signed off. The NASA listening post sent a plane from Thule to rescue him. They searched for hours and finally discovered him, miles off course, dead at the bottom of a crevasse with his sled and dogs. Apparently he tried to outrun the storm, got blinded, went off course, and fell into a crevasse.'

Gabrielle considered the information, intrigued. 'So suddenly NASA knew about a meteorite that nobody else knew about?'

'Exactly. And ironically, if my software had been working properly, the PODS satellite would have spotted that same meteorite – a week before the Canadian did.'

The coincidence gave Gabrielle pause. 'A meteorite buried for three hundred years was almost discovered *twice* in the same week?'

'I know. A little bizarre, but science can be like that. Feast or famine. The point is that the administrator felt like the meteorite *should* have been our discovery anyway – if I had done my job correctly. He told me that because the Canadian was dead, nobody would be the wiser if I simply redirected PODS to the coordinates the Canadian had transmitted in his SOS. Then I could pretend to discover the meteorite from scratch, and we could salvage some respect from an embarrassing failure.'

'And that's what you did.'

'As I said, I had no choice. I had let down the mission.' He paused. 'Tonight, though, when I heard the President's press conference and found out the meteorite I'd pretended to discover contained *fossils* . . .'

'You were stunned.'

'Bloody well floored, I'd say!'

'Do you think the administrator knew the meteorite contained fossils before he asked you to pretend PODS found it?'

'I can't imagine how. That meteorite was buried and untouched until the first NASA team got there. My best guess is that NASA had no idea what they'd really found until they got a team up there to drill cores and X-ray. They asked me to lie about PODS, thinking they'd have a moderate victory with a big meteorite. Then when they got there, they realized just how big a find it really was.'

Gabrielle's breath was shallow with excitement. 'Dr Harper, will you testify that NASA and the White House forced you to lie about the PODS software?'

'I don't know.' Harper looked frightened. 'I can't imagine what kind of damage that would do to the agency . . . to this discovery.'

'Dr Harper, you and I both know this meteorite remains a *wonderful* discovery, regardless of how it came about. The point here is that you lied to the American people. They have a right to know that PODS is not everything NASA says it is.'

'I don't know. I despise the administrator, but my *coworkers* . . . they are good people.'

'And they deserve to know they are being deceived.'

'And this evidence against me of embezzlement?'

'You can erase that from your mind,' Gabrielle said, having almost forgotten her con. 'I will tell the senator you know nothing of the embezzlement. It is simply a frame job – insurance set up by the administrator to keep you quiet about PODS.'

'Can the senator protect me?'

'Fully. You've done nothing wrong. You were simply following orders. Besides, with the information you've just given me about this Canadian geologist, I can't imagine the senator will even need to raise the issue of embezzlement at all. We can focus entirely on NASA's misinformation regarding PODS and the meteorite. Once the senator breaks the information about the Canadian, the administrator won't be able to risk trying to discredit you with lies.'

Harper still looked worried. He fell silent, somber as he pondered his options. Gabrielle gave him a moment. She'd realized earlier that there was another troubling coincidence to this story. She wasn't going to mention it, but she could see Dr Harper needed a final push.

'Do you have dogs, Dr Harper?'

He glanced up. 'I'm sorry?'

'I just thought it was odd. You told me that shortly after this Canadian geologist radioed in the meteorite coordinates, his sled dogs ran blindly into a crevasse?'

'There was a storm. They were off course.'

Gabrielle shrugged, letting her skepticism show. 'Yeah . . . okay.'

Harper clearly sensed her hesitation. 'What are you saying?'

'I don't know. There's just a lot of coincidence surrounding this discovery. A Canadian geologist transmits meteorite coordinates on a frequency that *only* NASA can hear? And then his sled dogs run blindly off a cliff?' She paused. 'You obviously understand that this geologist's death paved the way for this entire NASA triumph.'

The color drained from Harper's face. 'You think the administrator would *kill* over this meteorite.'

Big politics. Big money, Gabrielle thought. 'Let me talk to the senator and we'll be in touch. Is there a back way out of here?'

Gabrielle Ashe left a pale Chris Harper and descended a fire stairwell into a deserted alley behind NASA. She flagged down a taxi that had just dropped off more NASA celebrators.

'Westbrooke Place Luxury Apartments,' she told the driver. She was about to make Senator Sexton a much happier man.

CHAPTER **94**

Wondering what she had agreed to, Rachel stood near the entrance of the G4 cockpit, stretching a radio transceiver cable into the cabin so she could place her call out of earshot of the pilot. Corky and Tolland looked on. Although Rachel and NRO director William Pickering had planned to maintain radio silence until her arrival at Bollings Air Force Base outside of D.C., Rachel now had information she was certain Pickering would want to hear immediately. She had phoned his secure cellular, which he carried at all times.

When William Pickering came on the line, he was all business. 'Speak with care, please. I cannot guarantee this connection.'

Rachel understood. Pickering's cellular, like most NRO field phones, had an indicator that detected unsecured incoming calls. Because Rachel was on a radio-phone, one of the least secure communication modes available, Pickering's phone had warned him. This conversation would need to be vague. No names. No locations.

'My voice is my identity,' Rachel said, using the standard field greeting in this situation. She had expected the director's response would be displeasure that she had risked contacting him, but Pickering's reaction sounded positive.

'Yes, I was about to make contact with you myself. We need to redirect. I'm concerned you may have a welcoming party.'

Rachel felt a sudden trepidation. *Someone is watching us.* She could hear the danger in Pickering's tone. *Redirect.* He would be pleased to know she had called to make that exact request, albeit for entirely different reasons.

'The issue of authenticity,' Rachel said. 'We've been discussing it. We may have a way to confirm or deny categorically.'

'Excellent. There have been developments, and at least then I would have solid ground on which to proceed.'

'The proof involves our making a quick stop. One of us has access to a laboratory facility—'

'No exact locations, please. For your own safety.'

Rachel had no intention of broadcasting her plans over this line. 'Can you get us clearance to land at GAS-AC?'

Pickering was silent a moment. Rachel sensed he was trying to process the word. GAS-AC was an obscure NRO gisting shorthand for the Coast Guard's Group Air Station Atlantic City. Rachel hoped the director would know it.

'Yes,' he finally said. 'I can arrange that. Is that your final destination?'

'No. We will require further helicopter transport.'

'An aircraft will be waiting.'

'Thank you.'

'I recommend you exercise extreme caution until we know more. Speak to no one. Your suspicions have drawn deep concern among powerful parties.'

Tench, Rachel thought, wishing she had managed to make contact with the President directly.

'I am currently in my car, en route to meet the woman in question. She has requested a private meeting in a neutral location. It should reveal much.'

Pickering is driving somewhere to meet Tench? Whatever Tench was going to tell him must be important if she refused to tell him on the phone.

Pickering said, 'Do not discuss your final coordinates with anyone. And no more radio contact. Is that clear?'

'Yes, sir. We'll be at GAS-AC in an hour.'

'Transport will be arranged. When you reach your ultimate destination, you can call me via more secure channels.' He paused. 'I cannot overstate the importance of secrecy to your safety. You have made powerful enemies tonight. Take appropriate caution.' Pickering was gone.

Rachel felt tense as she closed the connection and turned to Tolland and Corky.

'Change of destination?' Tolland said, looking eager for answers.

Rachel nodded, feeling reluctant. 'The *Goya*.'

Corky sighed, glancing down at the meteorite sample in his hand. 'I still can't imagine NASA could possibly have . . .' He faded off, looking more worried with every passing minute.

We'll know soon enough, Rachel thought.

She went into the cockpit and returned the radio transceiver. Glancing out the windscreen at the rolling plateau of moonlit clouds racing beneath them, she had the unsettling feeling they were not going to like what they found onboard Tolland's ship.

CHAPTER 95

William Pickering felt an unusual solitude as he drove his sedan down the Leesburg Highway. It was almost 2:00 A.M., and the road was empty. It had been years since he'd been driving this late.

Marjorie Tench's raspy voice still grated on his mind. *Meet me at the FDR Memorial.*

Pickering tried to recall the last time he had seen Marjorie Tench face-to-face – never a pleasant experience. It had been two months ago. At the White House. Tench was seated opposite Pickering at a long oak table surrounded by members of the National Security Council, Joint Chiefs, CIA, President Herney, and the administrator of NASA.

'Gentlemen,' the head of the CIA had said, looking directly at Marjorie Tench. 'Yet again, I am before you to urge this administration to confront the ongoing security crisis of NASA.'

The declaration took no one in the room by surprise. NASA's security woes had become a tired issue in the intelligence community. Two days previously, more than three hundred high-resolution satellite photos from one of NASA's earth-observing satellites had been stolen by hackers out of a NASA database. The photos – inadvertently revealing a classified U.S. military training facility in North Africa – had turned up on the black market, where they had been purchased by hostile intelligence agencies in the Middle East.

'Despite the best of intentions,' the CIA director said with a weary voice, 'NASA continues to be a threat to national security. Simply put, our space agency is not equipped to protect the data and technologies they develop.'

'I realize,' the President replied, 'that there have been indiscretions. Damaging leaks. And it troubles me deeply.' He motioned across the table to the stern face of NASA administrator Lawrence Ekstrom. 'We are yet again looking into ways to tighten NASA's security.'

'With due respect,' the CIA director said, 'whatever security changes NASA implements will be ineffective as long as NASA operations remain outside the umbrella of the United States intelligence community.'

The statement brought an uneasy rustle from those assembled. Everyone knew where this was headed.

'As you know,' the CIA director went on, his tone sharpening, 'all U.S. government entities who deal with sensitive intelligence information are governed by strict rules of secrecy – military, CIA, NSA, NRO – all of them must abide by stringent laws regarding the concealment of the data they glean and the technologies they develop. I ask you all, yet again, why NASA – the agency currently producing the largest portion of cutting-edge aerospace, imaging, flight, software, reconnaissance, and telecomm technologies used by the military and intelligence community – exists *outside* this umbrella of secrecy.'

The President heaved a weighty sigh. The proposal was clear. *Restructure NASA to become part of the U.S. military intelligence community.* Although similar restructurings had happened with other agencies in the past, Herney refused to entertain the idea of placing NASA under the auspices of the Pentagon, the CIA, the NRO, or any other military directive. The National Security Council was starting to splinter on the issue, many siding with the intelligence community.

Lawrence Ekstrom never looked pleased at these meetings, and this was no exception. He shot an acrimonious glare toward the CIA director. 'At the risk of repeating myself, sir, the technologies NASA develops are for nonmilitary, academic applications. If your intelligence community wants to turn one of our space telescopes around and look at China, that's your choice.'

The CIA director looked like he was about to boil over.

Pickering caught his eye and stepped in. 'Larry,' he said, careful to keep an even tone, 'every year NASA kneels before Congress and begs for money. You're running operations with too little funding, and you're paying the price in failed missions. If we incorporate NASA into the intelligence community, NASA will no longer need to ask Congress for help. You would be funded by the black budget at significantly higher levels. It's a win-win. NASA will have the money it needs to run itself properly, and the intelligence community will have peace of mind that NASA technologies are protected.'

Ekstrom shook his head. 'On principle, I cannot endorse painting NASA with that brush. NASA is about space science; we have nothing to do with national security.'

The CIA director stood up, something never done when the President was seated. Nobody stopped him. He glared down at the administrator of NASA. 'Are you telling me you think science has *nothing* to do with national security? Larry, they are synonymous, for God's sake! It is only this country's scientific and technological edge that keeps us secure, and whether we like it or not, NASA is playing a bigger and bigger part in developing those technologies. Unfortunately, your agency leaks like a sieve and has proven time and again that its security is a liability!'

The room fell silent.

Now the administrator of NASA stood up and locked eyes with his attacker. 'So you suggest locking twenty thousand NASA scientists in airtight military labs and making them work for you? Do you really think NASA's newest space telescopes would have been conceived had it not been for our scientists' *personal* desire to see deeper into space? NASA makes astonishing breakthroughs for one reason only – our employees want to understand the cosmos more deeply. They are a community of dreamers who grew up staring at starry skies and asking themselves what was up there. Passion and curiosity are what drive NASA's innovation, not the promise of military superiority.'

Pickering cleared his throat, speaking softly, trying to lower the temperatures around the table. 'Larry, I'm certain the director is not talking about recruiting NASA scientists to build military satellites. Your NASA mission statement would not change. NASA would carry on business as usual, except you would have increased funding and increased security.' Pickering turned now to the President. 'Security is expensive. Everyone in this room certainly realizes that NASA's security leaks are a result of underfunding. NASA has to toot its own horn, cut corners on security measures, run joint projects with other countries so they can share the price tag. I am proposing that NASA remain the superb, scientific, nonmilitary entity it currently is, but with a bigger budget, and some discretion.'

Several members of the security council nodded in quiet agreement.

President Herney stood slowly, staring directly at William Pickering, clearly not at all amused with the way Pickering had just taken over. 'Bill, let me ask you this: NASA is hoping to go to Mars in the next decade. How will the intelligence community feel about spending a hefty portion of the black budget running a mission to Mars – a mission that has no immediate national security benefits?'

'NASA will be able to do as they please.'

'Bullshit,' Herney replied flatly.

Everyone's eyes shot up. President Herney seldom used profanity.

'If there is one thing I've learned as president,' Herney declared, 'it's that those who control the dollars control the direction. I refuse to put NASA's purse strings in the hands of those who do not share the objectives for which the agency was founded. I can only imagine how much pure science would get done with the *military* deciding which NASA missions are viable.'

Herney's eyes scanned the room. Slowly, purposefully, he returned his rigid gaze to William Pickering.

'Bill,' Herney sighed, 'your displeasure that NASA is engaged in joint projects with foreign space agencies is painfully shortsighted. At least *someone* is working constructively with the Chinese and Russians. Peace on this planet will not be forged by military strength. It will be forged by those who come together *despite* their governments' differences. If you ask me, NASA's joint missions do more to promote national security than any billion-dollar spy satellite, and with a hell of a lot better hope for the future.'

Pickering felt an anger welling deep within him. *How dare a politician talk down to me this way!* Herney's idealism played fine in a boardroom, but in the real world, it got people killed.

'Bill,' Marjorie Tench interrupted, as if sensing Pickering was about to explode, 'we know you lost a child. We know this is a personal issue for you.'

Pickering heard nothing but condescension in her tone.

'But please remember,' Tench said, 'that the White House is currently holding back a floodgate of investors who want us to open space to the private sector. If you ask me, for all its mistakes, NASA has been one hell of a friend to the intel community. You all might just want to count your blessings.'

A rumble strip on the shoulder of the highway jolted Pickering's mind back to the present. His exit was coming up. As he approached the exit for D.C., he passed a bloody deer lying dead by the side of the road. He felt an odd hesitation . . . but he kept driving.

He had a rendezvous to keep.

CHAPTER 96

The Franklin Delano Roosevelt Memorial is one of the largest memorials in the nation. With a park, waterfalls, statuary, alcoves, and basin, the memorial is divided into four outdoor galleries, one for each of FDR's terms in office.

A mile from the memorial, a lone Kiowa Warrior coasted in, high over the city, its running lights dimmed. In a town boasting as many VIPs and media crews as D.C., helicopters in the skies were as common as birds flying south. Delta-One knew that as long as he stayed well outside what was known as 'the dome' – a bubble of protected airspace around the White House – he should draw little attention. They would not be here long.

The Kiowa was at 2,100 feet when it slowed adjacent to, but not directly over, the darkened FDR Memorial. Delta-One hovered, checking his position. He looked to his left, where Delta-Two was manning the night vision telescopic viewing system. The video feed showed a greenish image of the entry drive of the memorial. The area was deserted.

Now they would wait.

This would not be a quiet kill. There were some people you simply did not kill quietly. Regardless of the method, there would be repercussions. Investigations. Inquiries. In these cases, the best cover was to make a lot of noise. Explosions, fire, and smoke made it appear you were making a statement, and the first thought would be foreign terrorism. Especially when the target was a high-profile official.

Delta-One scanned the night-vision transmission of the tree-shrouded memorial below. The parking lot and entry road were empty. *Soon*, he thought. The location of this private meeting, though in an urban area, was fortuitously desolate at this hour. Delta-One turned his eyes from the screen to his own weapons controls.

The Hellfire system would be the weapon of choice tonight. A laser-guided, anti-armor missile, the Hellfire provided fire-and-forget capability. The projectile could home in on a laser spot that was projected from ground observers, other aircraft, or the launching aircraft itself. Tonight, the missile would be guided autonomously through the laser designator in a mast-mounted sight. Once the Kiowa's designator had 'painted' the target with a laser beam, the Hellfire missile would be self-directing. Because the Hellfire could be fired either from the air or ground, its employment here tonight would not necessarily imply an aircraft's involvement. In addition, the Hellfire was a popular munition among black-market arms dealers, so terrorist activity could certainly be blamed.

'Sedan,' Delta-Two said.

Delta-One glanced at the transmission screen. A nondescript, black luxury sedan was approaching on the access road exactly on schedule. This was the typical motor pool car of large government agencies. The driver dimmed the car's headlights on entering the memorial. The car circled several times and then parked near a grove of trees. Delta-One watched the screen as his partner trained the telescopic night vision on the driver's side window. After a moment, the person's face came into view.

Delta-One drew a quick breath.

'Target confirmed,' his partner said.

Delta-One looked at the night-vision screen – with its deadly crucifix of cross-hairs – and he felt like a sniper aiming at royalty. *Target confirmed.*

Delta-Two turned to the left side avionics compartment and activated the laser designator. He aimed, and 2,000 feet below, a pinpoint of light appeared on the roof of the sedan, invisible to the occupant. 'Target painted,' he said.

Delta-One took a deep breath. He fired.

A sharp hissing sound sizzled beneath the fuselage, followed by a remarkably dim trail of light streaking toward the earth. One second later, the car in the parking lot blew apart in a blinding eruption of flames. Twisted metal flew everywhere. Burning tires rolled into the woods.

'Kill complete,' Delta-One said, already accelerating the helicopter away from the area. 'Call the controller.'

Less than two miles away, President Zach Herney was preparing for bed. The Lexan bullet-proof windows of 'the residence' were an inch thick. Herney never heard the blast.

CHAPTER 97

The Coast Guard Group Air Station Atlantic City is located in a secure section of William J. Hughes Federal Aviation Administration Technical Center at the Atlantic City International Airport. The group's area of responsibility includes the Atlantic seaboard from Asbury Park to Cape May.

Rachel Sexton jolted awake as the plane's tires screeched down on the tarmac of the lone runway nestled between two enormous cargo buildings. Surprised to find she had fallen asleep, Rachel groggily checked her watch.

2:13 A.M. She felt like she'd been asleep for days.

A warm onboard blanket was tucked carefully around her, and

Michael Tolland was also just waking up beside her. He gave her a weary smile.

Corky staggered up the aisle and frowned when he saw them. 'Shit, you guys are still here? I woke up hoping tonight had been a bad dream.'

Rachel knew exactly how he felt. *I'm headed back out to sea.*

The plane taxied to a stop, and Rachel and the others climbed out onto a barren runway. The night was overcast, but the coastal air felt heavy and warm. In comparison to Ellesmere, New Jersey felt like the tropics.

'Over here!' a voice called out.

Rachel and the others turned to see one of the Coast Guard's classic, crimson-colored HH-65 Dolphin helicopters waiting nearby. Framed by the brilliant white stripe on the chopper's tail, a fully suited pilot waved them over.

Tolland gave Rachel an impressed nod. 'Your boss certainly gets things done.'

You have no idea, she thought.

Corky slumped. 'Already? No dinner stop?'

The pilot welcomed them over and helped them aboard. Never asking their names, he spoke exclusively in pleasantries and safety precautions. Pickering had apparently made it clear to the Coast Guard that this flight was not an advertised mission. Nonetheless, despite Pickering's discretion, Rachel could see that their identities had remained a secret for only a matter of seconds; the pilot failed to hide his wide-eyed double take upon seeing television celebrity Michael Tolland.

Rachel was already feeling tense as she buckled herself in beside Tolland. The Aerospatiale engine overhead shrieked to life, and the Dolphin's sagging 39-foot rotors began to flatten out into a silver blur. The whine turned to a roar, and it lifted off the runway, climbing into the night.

The pilot turned in the cockpit and called out, 'I was informed you would tell me your destination once we were airborne.'

Tolland gave the pilot the coordinates of an offshore location about thirty miles southeast of their current position.

His ship is twelve miles off the coast, Rachel thought, feeling a shiver.

The pilot typed the coordinates into his navigation system. Then he settled in and gunned the engines. The chopper tipped forward and banked southeast.

As the dark dunes of the New Jersey coast slipped away beneath the aircraft, Rachel turned her eyes away from the blackness of the ocean spreading out beneath her. Despite the wariness of being back over the water again, she tried to take comfort in knowing she was accompanied by a man who had made the ocean a lifetime friend. Tolland was pressed close beside her in the narrow fuselage, his hips and shoulders touching hers. Neither made any attempt to shift positions.

'I know I shouldn't say this,' the pilot sputtered suddenly, as if ready to burst with excitement, 'but you're obviously Michael Tolland, and I've got to say, well, we've been watching you on TV all night! The *meteorite!* It's absolutely incredible! You must be in awe!'

Tolland nodded patiently. 'Speechless.'

'The documentary was fantastic! You know, the networks keep playing it over and over. None of tonight's duty pilots wanted this gig because everyone wanted to keep watching television, but I drew short straw. Can you believe it? Short straw! And here I am! If the boys had any idea I'd be flying the actual—'

'We appreciate the ride,' Rachel interrupted, 'and we need you to keep our presence here to yourself. Nobody's supposed to know we're here.'

'Absolutely, ma'am. My orders were very clear.' The pilot hesitated, and then his expression brightened. 'Hey, we aren't by any chance heading for the *Goya*, are we?'

Tolland gave a reluctant nod. 'We are.'

'Holy shit!' the pilot exclaimed. 'Excuse me. Sorry, but I've seen her on your show. The twin-hull, right? Strange-looking beast! I've never actually been on a SWATH design. I never dreamed *yours* would be the first!'

Rachel tuned the man out, feeling a rising uneasiness to be heading out to sea.

Tolland turned to her. 'You okay? You could have stayed onshore. I told you that.'

I should have stayed onshore, Rachel thought, knowing pride would never have let her. 'No thanks, I'm fine.'

Tolland smiled. 'I'll keep an eye on you.'

'Thanks.' Rachel was surprised how the warmth in his voice made her feel more secure.

'You've seen the *Goya* on television, right?'

She nodded. 'It's a . . . um . . . an *interesting*-looking ship.'

Tolland laughed. 'Yeah. She was an extremely progressive proto-type in her day, but the design never quite caught on.'

'Can't imagine why,' Rachel joked, picturing the ship's bizarre profile.

'Now NBC is pressuring me to use a newer ship. Something . . . I don't know, flashier, sexier. Another season or two, and they'll make me part with her.' Tolland sounded melancholy at the thought.

'You wouldn't love a brand-new ship?'

'I don't know . . . a lot of memories onboard the *Goya*.'

Rachel smiled softly. 'Well, as my mom used to say, sooner or later we've all got to let go of our past.'

Tolland's eyes held hers for a long moment. 'Yeah, I know.'

CHAPTER 98

'Shit,' the taxi driver said, looking over his shoulder at Gabrielle. 'Looks like an accident up ahead. We ain't going nowhere. Not for a while.'

Gabrielle glanced out the window and saw the spinning lights of emergency vehicles piercing the night. Several policemen stood in the road ahead, halting traffic around the Mall.

'Must be a hell of an accident,' the driver said, motioning toward some flames near the FDR Memorial.

Gabrielle frowned at the flickering glow. *Now, of all times.* She needed to get to Senator Sexton with this new information about PODS and the Canadian geologist. She wondered if NASA's lies about how they found the meteorite would be a big enough scandal to breathe life back into Sexton's campaign. *Maybe not for most politicians*, she thought, but this was Sedgewick Sexton, a man who had built his campaign on amplifying the failures of others.

Gabrielle was not always proud of the senator's ability to put negative ethical spin on opponents' political misfortunes, but it was effective. Sexton's mastery of innuendo and indignity could probably turn this one compartmentalized NASA fib into a sweeping question of character that infected the entire space agency – and by association, the President.

Outside the window, the flames at the FDR Memorial seemed to climb higher. Some nearby trees had caught fire, and the fire trucks were now hosing them down. The taxi driver turned on the car radio and began channel-surfing.

Sighing, Gabrielle closed her eyes and felt the exhaustion roll over her in waves. When she'd first come to Washington, she'd dreamed of working in politics forever, maybe someday in the White House. At the moment, however, she felt like she'd had enough politics for a lifetime – the duel with Marjorie Tench, the lewd photographs of herself and the senator, all of NASA's lies . . .

A newscaster on the radio was saying something about a car bomb and possible terrorism.

I've got to get out of this town, Gabrielle thought for the first time since coming to the nation's capital.

CHAPTER 99

The controller seldom felt weary, but today had taken its toll. Nothing had gone as anticipated – the tragic discovery of the insertion shaft in the ice, the difficulties of keeping the information a secret, and now the growing list of victims.

Nobody was supposed to die . . . except the Canadian.

It seemed ironic that the most technically difficult part of the plan had turned out to be the least problematic. The insertion, completed months ago, had come off without a hitch. Once the anomaly was in place, all that remained was to wait for the Polar Orbiting Density Scanner (PODS) satellite to launch. PODS was slated to scan enormous sections of the Arctic Circle, and sooner or later the anomaly software onboard would detect the meteorite and give NASA a major find.

But the damned software didn't work.

When the controller learned that the anomaly software had failed and had no chance of being fixed until after the election, the entire plan was in jeopardy. Without PODS, the meteorite would go undetected. The controller had to come up with some way to surreptitiously alert someone in NASA to the meteorite's existence. The solution involved orchestrating an emergency radio transmission from a Canadian geologist in the general vicinity of the insertion. The geologist, for obvious reasons, had to be killed immediately and his death made to look accidental. Throwing an innocent geologist from a helicopter had been the beginning. Now things were unraveling fast.

Wailee Ming. Norah Mangor. Both dead.

The bold kill that had just taken place at the FDR Memorial.

Soon to be added to the list were Rachel Sexton, Michael Tolland, and Dr Marlinson.

There is no other way, the controller thought, fighting the growing remorse. *Far too much is at stake.*

CHAPTER **100**

The Coast Guard Dolphin was still two miles from the *Goya's* coordinates and flying at 3,000 feet when Tolland yelled up to the pilot.

'Do you have NightSight onboard this thing?'

The pilot nodded. 'I'm a rescue unit.'

Tolland had expected as much. NightSight was Raytheon's marine thermal imaging system, capable of locating wreck survivors in the dark. The heat given off by a swimmer's head would appear as a red speck on an ocean of black.

'Switch it on,' Tolland said.

The pilot looked confused. 'Why? You missing someone?'

'No. I want everyone to see something.'

'We won't see a thing on thermal from this high up unless there's a burning oil slick.'

'Just switch it on,' Tolland said.

The pilot gave Tolland an odd look and then adjusted some dials, commanding the thermal lens beneath the chopper to survey a three-mile swatch of ocean in front of them. An LCD screen on his dashboard lit up. The image came into focus.

'Holy shit!' The helicopter lurched momentarily as the pilot re-coiled in surprise and then recovered, staring at the screen.

Rachel and Corky leaned forward, looking at the image with equal surprise. The black background of the ocean was illuminated by an enormous swirling spiral of pulsating red.

Rachel turned to Tolland with trepidation. 'It looks like a cyclone.'

'It is,' Tolland said. 'A cyclone of warm currents. About a half mile across.'

The Coast Guard pilot chuckled in amazement. 'That's a big one. We see these now and then, but I hadn't heard about this one yet.'

'Just surfaced last week,' Tolland said. 'Probably won't last more than another few days.'

'What causes it?' Rachel asked, understandably perplexed by the huge vortex of swirling water in the middle of the ocean.

'Magma dome,' the pilot said.

Rachel turned to Tolland, looking wary. 'A volcano?'

'No,' Tolland said. 'The East Coast typically doesn't have active volcanoes, but occasionally we get rogue pockets of magma that well up under the seafloor and cause hot spots. The hot spot causes a reverse temperature gradient – hot water on the bottom and cooler water on top. It results in these giant spiral currents. They're called megaplumes. They spin for a couple of weeks and then dissipate.'

The pilot looked at the pulsating spiral on his LCD screen. 'Looks like this one's still going strong.' He paused, checking the coordinates of Tolland's ship and then looked over his shoulder in surprise. 'Mr Tolland, it looks like you're parked fairly near the middle of it.'

Tolland nodded. 'Currents are a little slower near the eye. Eighteen knots. Like anchoring in a fast-moving river. Our chain's been getting a real workout this week.'

'Jesus,' the pilot said. 'Eighteen-knot current? Don't fall overboard!' He laughed.

Rachel did not laugh. 'Mike, you didn't mention this megaplume, magma dome, hot-current situation.'

He put a reassuring hand on her knee. 'It's perfectly safe, trust me.'

Rachel frowned. 'So this documentary you were making out here was about this magma dome phenomenon?'

'Megaplumes and *Sphyrna mokarran.*'

'That's right. You mentioned that earlier.'

Tolland gave a coy smile. '*Sphyrna mokarran* love warm water, and right now, every last one for a hundred miles is congregating in this milewide circle of heated ocean.'

'Neat.' Rachel gave an uneasy nod. 'And what, pray tell, are *Sphyrna mokarran?*'

'Ugliest fish in the sea.'

'Flounder?'

Tolland laughed. 'Great hammerhead shark.'

Rachel stiffened beside him. 'You've got hammerhead *sharks* around your boat?'

Tolland winked. 'Relax, they're not dangerous.'

'You wouldn't say that unless they were dangerous.'

Tolland chuckled. 'I guess you're right.' He called playfully up to the pilot. 'Hey, how long has it been since you guys saved anyone from an attack by a hammerhead?'

The pilot shrugged. 'Gosh. We haven't saved anyone from a hammerhead in decades.'

Tolland turned to Rachel. 'See. *Decades.* No worries.'

'Just last month,' the pilot added, 'we had an attack where some idiot skin diver was chumming—'

'Hold on!' Rachel said. 'You said you hadn't saved anyone in *decades!*'

'Yeah,' the pilot replied. '*Saved* anyone. Usually, we're too late. Those bastards kill in a hurry.'

CHAPTER 101

From the air, the flickering outline of the *Goya* loomed on the horizon. At half a mile, Tolland could make out the brilliant deck lights that his crewmember Xavia had wisely left glowing. When he saw the lights, he felt like a weary traveler pulling into his driveway.

'I thought you said only one person was onboard,' Rachel said, looking surprised to see all the lights.

'Don't you leave a light on when you're home alone?'

'One light. Not the entire house.'

Tolland smiled. Despite Rachel's attempts to be lighthearted, he could tell she was extremely apprehensive about being out here. He wanted to put an arm around her and reassure her, but he knew there was nothing he could say. 'The lights are on for security. Makes the ship look active.'

Corky chuckled. 'Afraid of pirates, Mike?'

'Nope. Biggest danger out here is the idiots who don't know how to read radar. Best defense against getting rammed is to make sure everyone can see you.'

Corky squinted down at the glowing vessel. '*See* you? It looks like a Carnival Cruise line on New Year's Eve. Obviously, NBC pays your electric.'

The Coast Guard chopper slowed and banked around the huge illuminated ship, and the pilot began maneuvering toward the helipad on the stern deck. Even from the air, Tolland could make out the raging current pulling at the ship's hull struts. Anchored from its bow, the *Goya* was aimed into the current, straining at its massive anchor line like a chained beast.

'She really is a beauty,' the pilot said, laughing.

Tolland knew the comment was sarcastic. The *Goya* was ugly. 'Butt-ugly' according to one television reviewer. One of only seventeen SWATH ships ever built, the *Goya*'s Small-Waterplane-Area Twin-Hull was anything but attractive.

The vessel was essentially a massive horizontal platform floating thirty feet above the ocean on four huge struts affixed to pontoons. From a distance, the ship looked like a low-slung drilling platform. Up close, it resembled a deck barge on stilts. The crew quarters, research labs, and navigation bridge were housed in a series of tiered structures on top, giving one the rough impression of a giant floating coffee table supporting a hodgepodge of multistaged buildings.

Despite its less than streamlined appearance, the *Goya*'s design enjoyed significantly less water-plane area, resulting in increased stability. The suspended platform enabled better filming, easier lab work, and fewer seasick scientists. Although NBC was pressuring Tolland to let them buy him something newer, Tolland had refused. Granted, there were better ships out there now, even more stable ones, but the *Goya* had been his home for almost a decade now – the ship on which he had fought his way back after Celia's death. Some nights he still heard her voice in the wind out on deck. If and when the ghosts ever disappeared, Tolland would consider another ship.

Not yet.

When the chopper finally set down on the *Goya*'s stern deck, Rachel Sexton felt only half relieved. The good news was that she was no longer flying over the ocean. The bad news was that she was now standing on it. She fought off the shaky sensation in her legs as she climbed onto the deck and looked around. The deck was surprisingly cramped, particularly with the helicopter on its pad. Moving her eyes toward the bow, Rachel gazed at the ungainly, stacked edifice that made up the bulk of the ship.

Tolland stood close beside her. 'I know,' he said, talking loudly over the sound of the raging current. 'It looks bigger on television.'

Rachel nodded. 'And more stable.'

'This is one of the safest ships on the sea. I promise.' Tolland put a hand on her shoulder and guided her across the deck.

The warmth of his hand did more to calm Rachel's nerves than anything he could have said. Nonetheless, as she looked toward the rear of the ship, she saw the roiling current streaming out behind them as though the ship was at full throttle. *We're sitting on a megaplume*, she thought.

Centered on the foremost section of rear deck, Rachel spied a familiar, one-man Triton submersible hanging on a giant winch. The Triton – named for the Greek god of the sea – looked nothing like its predecessor, the steel-encased Alvin. The Triton had a hemispherical acrylic dome in front, making it look more like a giant fishbowl than a sub. Rachel could think of few things more terrifying than submerging hundreds of feet into the ocean with nothing between her face and the ocean but a sheet of clear acrylic. Of course, according to Tolland, the only unpleasant part of riding in the Triton was the initial deployment – being slowly winched down through the trap door in the *Goya*'s deck, hanging like a pendulum thirty feet above the sea.

'Xavia is probably in the hydrolab,' Tolland said, moving across the deck. 'This way.'

Rachel and Corky followed Tolland across the stern deck. The Coast Guard pilot remained in his chopper with strict instructions not to use the radio.

'Have a look at this,' Tolland said, pausing at the stern railing of the ship.

Hesitantly, Rachel neared the railing. They were very high up. The water was a good thirty feet below them, and yet Rachel could still feel the heat rising off the water.

'It's about the temperature of a warm bath,' Tolland said over the sound of the current. He reached toward a switch-box on the railing. 'Watch this.' He flipped a switch.

A wide arc of light spread through the water behind the ship, illuminating it from within like a lit swimming pool. Rachel and Corky gasped in unison.

The water around the ship was filled with dozens of ghostly shadows. Hovering only feet below the illuminated surface, armies of sleek, dark forms swam in parallel against the current, their unmistakable hammer-shaped skulls wagging back and forth as if to the beat of some prehistoric rhythm.

'Christ, Mike,' Corky stammered. 'So glad you shared this with us.'

Rachel's body went rigid. She wanted to step back from the

railing, but she could not move. She was transfixed by the petrifying vista.

'Incredible, aren't they?' Tolland said. His hand was on her shoulder again, comforting. 'They'll tread water in the warm spots for weeks. These guys have the best noses in the sea – enhanced telencephalon olfactory lobes. They can smell blood up to a mile away.'

Corky looked skeptical. 'Enhanced telencephalon olfactory lobes?'

'Don't believe me?' Tolland began rooting around in an aluminum cabinet adjacent to where they were standing. After a moment, he pulled out a small, dead fish. 'Perfect.' He took a knife from the cooler and cut the limp fish in several places. It started to drip blood.

'Mike, for God's sake,' Corky said. 'That's disgusting.'

Tolland tossed the bloody fish overboard and it fell thirty feet. The instant it hit the water, six or seven sharks darted in a tumbling ferocious brawl, their rows of silvery teeth gnashed wildly at the bloody fish. In an instant, the fish was gone.

Aghast, Rachel turned and stared at Tolland, who was already holding another fish. Same kind. Same size.

'This time, no blood,' Tolland said. Without cutting the fish, he threw it in the water. The fish splashed down, but nothing happened. The hammerheads seemed not to notice. The bait carried away on the current, having drawn no interest whatsoever.

'They attack *only* on sense of smell,' Tolland said, leading them away from the railing. 'In fact, you could swim out here in total safety – provided you didn't have any open wounds.'

Corky pointed to the stitches on his cheek.

Tolland frowned. 'Right. No swimming for you.'

CHAPTER 102

Gabrielle Ashe's taxi was not moving.

Sitting at a roadblock near the FDR Memorial, Gabrielle looked out at the emergency vehicles in the distance and felt as if a surrealistic fog bank had settled over the city. Radio reports were coming in now that the exploded car might have contained a high-level government official.

Pulling out her cellphone, she dialed the senator. He was no doubt starting to wonder what was taking Gabrielle so long.

The line was busy.

Gabrielle looked at the taxi's clicking meter and frowned. Some of the other cars stuck here were pulling up onto the curbs and turning around to find alternative routes.

The driver looked over his shoulder. 'You wanna wait? Your dime.'

Gabrielle saw more official vehicles arriving now. 'No. Let's go around.'

The driver grunted in the affirmative and began maneuvering the awkward multipoint turn. As they bounced over the curbs, Gabrielle tried Sexton again.

Still busy.

Several minutes later, having made a wide loop, the taxi was traveling up C Street. Gabrielle saw the Philip A. Hart Office Building looming. She had intended to go straight to the senator's apartment, but with her office this close . . .

'Pull over,' she blurted to the driver. 'Right there. Thanks.' She pointed.

The cab stopped.

Gabrielle paid the amount on the meter and added $10. 'Can you wait ten minutes?'

The cabbie looked at the money and then at his watch. 'Not a minute longer.'

Gabrielle hurried off. *I'll be out in five.*

The deserted marble corridors of the Senate office building felt almost sepulchral at this hour. Gabrielle's muscles were tense as she hurried through the gauntlet of austere statues lining the third-floor entryway. Their stony eyes seemed to follow her like silent sentinels.

Arriving at the main door of Senator Sexton's five-room office suite, Gabrielle used her key card to enter. The secretarial lobby was dimly lit. Crossing through the foyer, she went down a hallway to her office. She entered, flicked on the fluorescent lights, and strode directly to her file cabinets.

She had an entire file on the budgeting of NASA's Earth Observing

System, including plenty of information on PODS. Sexton would certainly want all the data he could possibly get on PODS as soon as she told him about Harper.

NASA lied about PODS.

As Gabrielle fingered her way through her files, her cellphone rang. 'Senator?' she answered.

'No, Gabs. It's Yolanda.' Her friend's voice had an unusual edge to it. 'You still at NASA?'

'No. At the office.'

'Find anything at NASA?'

You have no idea. Gabrielle knew she couldn't tell Yolanda anything until she'd talked to Sexton; the senator would have very specific ideas about how best to handle the information. 'I'll tell you all about it after I talk to Sexton. Heading over to his place now.'

Yolanda paused. 'Gabs, you know this thing you were saying about Sexton's campaign finance and the SFF?'

'I told you I was wrong and—'

'I just found out two of our reporters who cover the aerospace industry have been working on a similar story.'

Gabrielle was surprised. 'Meaning?'

'I don't know. But these guys are good, and they seem pretty convinced that Sexton is taking kickbacks from the Space Frontier Foundation. I just figured I should call you. I know I told you earlier that the idea was insane. Marjorie Tench as a source seemed spotty, but these guys of ours . . . I don't know, you might want to talk to them before you see the senator.'

'If they're so convinced, why haven't they gone to press?' Gabrielle sounded more defensive than she wanted to.

'They have no solid evidence. The senator apparently is good at covering his tracks.'

Most politicians are. 'There's nothing there, Yolanda. I told you the senator admitted taking SFF donations, but the gifts are all under the cap.'

'I know that's what he *told* you, Gabs, and I'm not claiming to know what's true or false here. I just felt obliged to call because I told you not to trust Marjorie Tench, and now I find out people *other* than Tench think the senator may be on the dole. That's all.'

'Who were these reporters?' Gabrielle felt an unexpected anger simmering now.

'No names. I can set up a meeting. They're smart. They understand campaign finance law . . .' Yolanda hesitated. 'You know, these guys actually believe Sexton is hurting for cash – bankrupt even.'

In the silence of her office, Gabrielle could hear Tench's raspy accusations echoing. *After Katherine died, the senator squandered the vast majority of her legacy on bad investments, personal comforts, and buying himself what appears to be certain victory in the primaries. As of six months ago, your candidate was broke.*

'Our men would love to talk to you,' Yolanda said.

I bet they would, Gabrielle thought. 'I'll call you back.'

'You sound pissed.'

'Never at you, Yolanda. Never at you. Thanks.'

Gabrielle hung up.

Dozing on a chair in the hallway outside Senator Sexton's Westbrooke apartment, a security guard awoke with a start at the sound of his cellular phone. Bolting up in his chair, he rubbed his eyes and pulled his phone from his blazer pocket.

'Yeah?'

'Owen, this is Gabrielle.'

Sexton's guard recognized her voice. 'Oh, hi.'

'I need to talk to the senator. Would you knock on his door for me? His line is busy.'

'It's kind of late.'

'He's awake. I'm sure of it.' Gabrielle sounded anxious. 'It's an emergency.'

'*Another* one?'

'Same one. Just get him on the phone, Owen. There's something I really need to ask him.'

The guard sighed, standing up. 'Okay, okay. I'll knock.' He stretched and made his way toward Sexton's door. 'But I'm only doing it because he was glad I let you in earlier.' Reluctantly, he raised his fist to knock.

'What did you just say?' Gabrielle demanded.

The guard's fist stopped in midair. 'I said the senator was glad I let you in earlier. You were right. It was no problem at all.'

'You and the senator *talked* about that?' Gabrielle sounded surprised.

'Yeah. So what?'

'No, I just didn't think . . .'

'Actually, it was kind of weird. The senator needed a couple of seconds to even remember you'd been in there. I think the boys were tossing back a few.'

'When did you two talk, Owen?'

'Right after you left. Is something wrong?'

A momentary silence. 'No . . . no. Nothing. Look, now that I think of it, let's not bother the senator this instant. I'll keep trying his house line, and if I don't have any luck, I'll call you back and you can knock.'

The guard rolled his eyes. 'Whatever you say, Ms Ashe.'

'Thanks, Owen. Sorry to bother you.'

'No problem.' The guard hung up, flopped back in his chair, and went to sleep.

Alone in her office, Gabrielle stood motionless for several seconds before hanging up the phone. *Sexton knows I was inside his apartment . . . and he never mentioned it to me?*

Tonight's ethereal strangeness was getting murkier. Gabrielle flashed on the senator's phone call to her while she was at ABC. The senator had stunned her with his unprovoked admission that he was meeting with space companies and accepting money. His honesty had brought her back to him. Shamed her even. His confession now seemed one hell of a lot less noble.

Soft money, Sexton had said. *Perfectly legal.*

Suddenly, all the vague misgivings Gabrielle had ever felt about Senator Sexton seemed to resurface all at once.

Outside, the taxi was honking.

CHAPTER **103**

The bridge of the *Goya* was a Plexiglas cube situated two levels above the main deck. From here Rachel had a 360-degree view of the surrounding darkened sea, an unnerving vista she looked at only once before blocking it out and turning her attention to the matter at hand.

Having sent Tolland and Corky to find Xavia, Rachel prepared to contact Pickering. She'd promised the director she would call him when they arrived, and she was eager to know what he had learned in his meeting with Marjorie Tench.

The *Goya*'s SHINCOM 2100 digital communications system was a platform with which Rachel was familiar enough. She knew if she kept her call short, her communication should be secure.

Dialing Pickering's private number, she waited, clutching the SHINCOM 2100 receiver to her ear. She expected Pickering to pick up on the first ring. But the line just kept ringing.

Six rings. Seven. Eight . . .

Rachel gazed out at the darkened ocean, her inability to reach the director doing nothing to quell her uneasiness about being at sea.

Nine rings. Ten rings. *Pick up!*

She paced, waiting. What was going on? Pickering carried his phone with him at all times, and he had expressly told Rachel to call him.

After fifteen rings, she hung up.

With growing apprehension, she picked up the SHINCOM receiver and dialed again.

Four rings. Five rings.

Where is he?

Finally, the connection clicked open. Rachel felt a surge of relief, but it was short-lived. There was no one on the line. Only silence.

'Hello,' she prompted. 'Director?'

Three quick clicks.

'Hello?' Rachel said.

A burst of electronic static shattered the line, blasting in Rachel's ear. She yanked the receiver away from her head in pain. The static abruptly stopped. Now she could hear a series of rapidly oscillating tones that pulsed in half-second intervals. Rachel's confusion quickly gave way to realization. And then fear.

'Shit!'

Wheeling back to the controls on the bridge, she slammed the receiver down in its cradle, severing the connection. For several moments she stood terrified, wondering if she'd hung up in time.

Amidships, two decks below, the *Goya*'s hydrolab was an expansive work space segmented by long counters and islands packed to the gills with electronic gear – bottom profilers, current analyzers, wet sinks, fume hoods, a walk-in specimen cooler, PCs, and a stack of organizer crates for research data and the spare electronics to keep everything running.

When Tolland and Corky entered, the *Goya*'s onboard geologist, Xavia, was reclining in front of a blaring television. She didn't even turn around.

'Did you guys run out of beer money?' she called over her shoulder, apparently thinking some of her crew had returned.

'Xavia,' Tolland said. 'It's Mike.'

The geologist spun, swallowing part of a prepackaged sandwich she was eating. 'Mike?' she stammered, clearly stunned to see him. She stood up, turned down the television, and came over, still chewing. 'I thought some of the guys had come back from bar-hopping. What are you doing here?' Xavia was heavyset and dark-skinned, with a sharp voice and a surly air about her. She motioned to the television, which was broadcasting replays of Tolland's on-site meteorite documentary. 'You sure didn't hang around on the ice shelf very long, did you?'

Something came up, Tolland thought. 'Xavia, I'm sure you recognize Corky Marlinson.'

Xavia nodded. 'An honor, sir.'

Corky was eyeing the sandwich in her hand. 'That looks good.'

Xavia gave him an odd look.

'I got your message,' Tolland said to Xavia. 'You said I made a mistake in my presentation? I want to talk to you about it.'

The geologist stared at him and let out a shrill laugh. *'That's* why you're back? Oh, Mike, for God's sake, I told you, it was nothing. I was just pulling your chain. NASA obviously gave you some old data. Inconsequential. Seriously, only three or four marine geologists in the world might have noticed the oversight!'

Tolland held his breath. 'This oversight. Does it by any chance have anything to do with chondrules?'

Xavia's face went blank with shock. 'My God. One of those geologists called you already?'

Tolland slumped. *The chondrules.* He looked at Corky and then back to the marine geologist. 'Xavia, I need to know everything you can tell me about these chondrules. What was the mistake I made?'

Xavia stared at him, apparently now sensing he was dead serious. 'Mike, it's really nothing. I read a small article in a trade journal a while back. But I don't understand why you're so worried about this.'

Tolland sighed. 'Xavia, as strange as this may sound, the less you know tonight, the better. All I'm asking is for you to tell us what you know about chondrules, and then we'll need you to examine a rock sample for us.'

Xavia looked mystified and vaguely perturbed to be out of the loop. 'Fine, let me get you that article. It's in my office.' She set her sandwich down and headed for the door.

Corky called after her, 'Can I finish that?'

Xavia paused, sounding incredulous. 'You want to *finish* my sandwich?'

'Well, I just thought if you—'

'Get your *own* damn sandwich.' Xavia left.

Tolland chuckled, motioning across the lab toward a specimen cooler. 'Bottom shelf, Corky. Between the sambuca and squid sacs.'

Outside on deck, Rachel descended the steep stairway from the bridge and strode toward the chopper pad. The Coast Guard pilot was dozing but sat up when Rachel rapped on the cockpit.

'Done already?' he asked. 'That was fast.'

Rachel shook her head, on edge. 'Can you run both surface and air radar?'

'Sure. Ten-mile radius.'

'Turn it on, please.'

Looking puzzled, the pilot threw a couple of switches and the radar screen lit up. The sweep arm spun lazy circles.

'Anything?' Rachel asked.

The pilot let the arm make several complete rotations. He adjusted some controls and watched. It was all clear. 'Couple of small ships way out on the periphery, but they're heading away from us. We're clear. Miles and miles of open sea in all directions.'

Rachel Sexton sighed, although she did not feel particularly relieved. 'Do me a favor, if you see anything approaching – boats, aircraft, anything – will you let me know immediately?'

'Sure thing. Is everything okay?'

'Yeah. I'd just like to know if we're having company.'

The pilot shrugged. 'I'll watch the radar, ma'am. If anything blips, you'll be the first to know.'

Rachel's senses were tingling as she headed for the hydrolab. When she entered, Corky and Tolland were standing alone in front of a computer monitor and chewing sandwiches.

Corky called out to her with his mouth full, 'What'll it be? Fishy chicken, fishy bologna, or fishy egg salad?'

Rachel barely heard the question. 'Mike, how fast can we get this information and get off this ship?'

CHAPTER 104

Tolland paced the hydrolab, waiting with Rachel and Corky for Xavia's return. The news about the chondrules was almost as discomforting as Rachel's news about her attempted contact with Pickering.

The director didn't answer.

And someone tried to pulse-snitch the Goya's location.

'Relax,' Tolland told everyone. 'We're safe. The Coast Guard pilot is watching the radar. He can give us plenty of warning if anyone is headed our way.'

Rachel nodded in agreement, although she still looked on edge.

'Mike, what the hell is *this*?' Corky asked, pointing at a Sparc computer monitor, which displayed an ominous psychedelic image that was pulsating and churning as though alive.

'Acoustic Doppler Current Profiler,' Tolland said. 'It's a cross section of the currents and temperature gradients of the ocean underneath the ship.'

Rachel stared. 'That's what we're anchored on *top* of?'

Tolland had to admit, the image looked frightening. At the surface, the water appeared as a swirling bluish green, but tracing downward, the colors slowly shifted to a menacing red-orange as the temperatures heated up. Near the bottom, over a mile down, hovering above the ocean floor, a blood-red cyclone vortex raged.

'That's the megaplume,' Tolland said.

Corky grunted. 'Looks like an underwater tornado.'

'Same principle. Oceans are usually colder and more dense near the bottom, but here the dynamics are reversed. The deepwater is heated and lighter, so it rises toward the surface. Meanwhile, the surface water is heavier, so it races downward in a huge spiral to fill the void. You get these drainlike currents in the ocean. Enormous whirlpools.'

'What's that big bump on the seafloor?' Corky pointed at the flat expanse of ocean floor, where a large dome-shaped mound rose up like a bubble. Directly above it swirled the vortex.

'That mound is a magma dome,' Tolland said. 'It's where lava is pushing up beneath the ocean floor.'

Corky nodded. 'Like a huge zit.'

'In a manner of speaking.'

'And if it pops?'

Tolland frowned, recalling the famous 1986 megaplume event off the Juan de Fuca Ridge, where thousands of tons of 1,200 degrees Celsius magma spewed up into the ocean all at once, magnifying the plume's intensity almost instantly. Surface currents amplified as the vortex expanded rapidly upward. What happened next was something Tolland had no intention of sharing with Corky and Rachel this evening.

'Atlantic magma domes don't pop,' Tolland said. 'The cold water circulating over the mound continually cools and hardens the earth's crust, keeping the magma safely under a thick layer of rock. Eventually the lava underneath cools, and the spiral disappears. Megaplumes are generally not dangerous.'

Corky pointed toward a tattered magazine sitting near the computer. 'So you're saying *Scientific American* publishes fiction?'

Tolland saw the cover, and winced. Someone had apparently pulled it from the *Goya*'s archive of old science magazines: *Scientific American*, February 1999. The cover showed an artist's rendering of a supertanker swirling out of control in an enormous funnel of ocean. The heading read: MEGAPLUMES – GIANT KILLERS FROM THE DEEP?

Tolland laughed it off. 'Totally irrelevant. That article is talking about megaplumes in *earthquake* zones. It was a popular Bermuda Triangle hypothesis a few years back, explaining ship disappearances. Technically speaking, if there's some sort of cataclysmic geologic event on the ocean floor, which is unheard of around here, the dome could rupture, and the vortex could get big enough to . . . well, you know . . .'

'No, we *don't* know,' Corky said.

Tolland shrugged. 'Rise to the surface.'

'Terrific. So glad you had us aboard.'

Xavia entered carrying some papers. 'Admiring the megaplume?'

'Oh, yes,' Corky said sarcastically. 'Mike was just telling us how if that little mound ruptures, we all go spiraling around in a big drain.'

'Drain?' Xavia gave a cold laugh. 'More like getting flushed down the world's largest toilet.'

Outside on the deck of the *Goya*, the Coast Guard helicopter pilot vigilantly watched the EMS radar screen. As a rescue pilot he had seen his share of fear in people's eyes; Rachel Sexton had definitely been afraid when she asked him to keep an eye out for unexpected visitors to the *Goya*.

What kind of visitors is she expecting? he wondered.

From all the pilot could see, the sea and air for ten miles in all directions contained nothing that looked out of the ordinary. A fishing boat eight miles off. An occasional aircraft slicing across an edge of their radar field and then disappearing again toward some unknown destination.

The pilot sighed, gazing out now at the ocean rushing all around the ship. The sensation was a ghostly one – that of sailing full speed despite being anchored.

He returned his eyes to the radar screen and watched. Vigilant.

CHAPTER 105

Onboard the *Goya*, Tolland had now introduced Xavia and Rachel. The ship's geologist was looking increasingly baffled by the distinguished entourage standing before her in the hydrolab. In addition, Rachel's eagerness to run the tests and get off the ship as fast as possible was clearly making Xavia uneasy.

Take your time, Xavia, Tolland willed her. *We need to know everything.*

Xavia was talking now, her voice stiff. 'In your documentary, Mike, you said those little metallic inclusions in the rock could form *only* in space.'

Tolland already felt a tremor of apprehension. *Chondrules form only in space. That's what NASA told me.*

'But according to these notes,' Xavia said, holding up the pages, 'that's not entirely true.'

Corky glared. 'Of course it's true!'

Xavia scowled at Corky and waved the notes. 'Last year a young geologist named Lee Pollock out of Drew University was using a new breed of marine robot to do Pacific deepwater crust sampling in the Mariana Trench and pulled up a loose rock that contained a geologic feature he had never seen before. The feature was quite similar in appearance to chondrules. He called them "plagioclase stress inclusions" – tiny bubbles of metal that apparently had been rehomogenized during deep ocean pressurization events. Dr Pollock was amazed to find metallic bubbles in an ocean rock, and he formulated a unique theory to explain their presence.'

Corky grumbled, 'I suppose he would *have* to.'

Xavia ignored him. 'Dr Pollock asserted that the rock formed in an ultradeep oceanic environment where extreme pressure metamorphosed a pre-existing rock, permitting some of the disparate metals to fuse.'

Tolland considered it. The Mariana Trench was seven miles down, one of the last truly unexplored regions on the planet. Only a handful of robotic probes had ever ventured that deep, and most had collapsed well before they reached the bottom. The water pressure in the trench was enormous – an astounding 18,000 pounds per square inch, as opposed to a mere 24 pounds on the ocean's surface. Oceanographers still had very little understanding of the geologic forces at the deepest ocean floor. 'So, this guy Pollock thinks the Mariana Trench can make rocks with chondrulelike features?'

'It's an extremely obscure theory,' Xavia said. 'In fact, it's never even been formally published. I only happened to stumble across Pollock's personal notes on the Web by chance last month when I was doing research on fluid-rock interactions for our upcoming megaplume show. Otherwise, I never would have heard of it.'

'The theory has never been published,' Corky said, 'because it's ridiculous. You need *heat* to form chondrules. There's no way water pressure could rearrange the crystalline structure of a rock.'

'Pressure,' Xavia fired back, 'happens to be the single biggest contributor to geologic change on our planet. A little something called a *metamorphic* rock? Geology 101?'

Corky scowled.

Tolland realized Xavia had a point. Although heat did play a role in some of earth's metamorphic geology, most metamorphic rocks were formed by extreme pressure. Incredibly, rocks deep in the earth's crust were under so much pressure that they acted more like thick molasses than solid rock, becoming elastic and undergoing chemical changes as they did. Nonetheless, Dr Pollock's theory still seemed like a stretch.

'Xavia,' Tolland said. 'I've never heard of water pressure alone chemically altering a rock. You're the geologist, what's your take?'

'Well,' she said, flipping through her notes, 'it sounds like water pressure isn't the only factor.' Xavia found a passage and read Pollock's notes verbatim. ' "Oceanic crust in the Mariana Trench, already under enormous hydrostatic pressurization, can find itself further compressed by tectonic forces from the region's subduction zones." '

Of course, Tolland thought. The Mariana Trench, in addition to being crushed under seven miles of water, was a subduction zone – the compression line where the Pacific and Indian plates moved toward one another and collided. Combined pressures in the trench could be enormous, and because the area was so remote and dangerous to study, if there were chondrules down there, chances of anyone knowing about it were very slim.

Xavia kept reading. ' "Combined hydrostatic and tectonic pressures could potentially force crust into an elastic or semiliquid state, allowing lighter elements to fuse into chondrulelike structures thought to occur only in space." '

Corky rolled his eyes. 'Impossible.'

Tolland glanced at Corky. 'Is there any alternative explanation for the chondrules in the rock Dr Pollock found?'

'Easy,' Corky said. 'Pollock found an actual *meteorite*. Meteorites fall into the ocean all the time. Pollock would not have suspected it was a meteorite because the fusion crust would have eroded away from years under the water, making it look like a normal rock.' Corky turned to Xavia. 'I don't suppose Pollock had the brains to measure the *nickel* content, did he?'

'Actually, yes,' Xavia fired back, flipping through the notes again. 'Pollock writes: "I was surprised to find the nickel content of the specimen falling within a midrange value not usually associated with terrestrial rocks." '

Tolland and Rachel exchanged startled looks.

Xavia continued reading. ' "Although the quantity of nickel does not fall within the normally acceptable midrange window for meteoritic origin, it is surprisingly *close*." '

Rachel looked troubled. 'How close? Is there any way this ocean rock could be mistaken for a meteorite?'

Xavia shook her head. 'I'm not a chemical petrologist, but as I understand it, there are numerous chemical differences between the rock Pollock found and actual meteorites.'

'What are those differences?' Tolland pressed.

Xavia turned her attention to a graph in her notes. 'According to this, one difference is in the chemical structure of the chondrules themselves. It looks like the titanium/zirconium ratios differ. The titanium/zirconium ratio in the chondrules of the ocean sample showed ultradepleted zirconium.' She looked up. 'Only two parts per million.'

'Two ppm?' Corky blurted. 'Meteorites have *thousands* of times that!'

'Exactly,' Xavia replied. 'Which is why Pollock thinks his sample's chondrules are not from space.'

Tolland leaned over and whispered to Corky, 'Did NASA happen to measure the titanium/zirconium ratio in the Milne rock?'

'Of course not,' Corky sputtered. 'Nobody would ever measure that. It's like looking at a car and measuring the tires' rubber content to confirm you're looking at a car!'

Tolland heaved a sigh and looked back at Xavia. 'If we give you a rock sample with chondrules in it, can you run a test to determine whether these inclusions are meteoric chondrules or . . . one of Pollock's deep ocean compression things?'

Xavia shrugged. 'I suppose. The electron microprobe's accuracy should be close enough. What's this all about, anyway?'

Tolland turned to Corky. 'Give it to her.'

Corky reluctantly pulled the meteorite sample from his pocket and held it out for Xavia.

Xavia's brow furrowed as she took the stone disk. She eyed the fusion crust and then the fossil embedded in the rock. 'My God!' she said, her head rocketing upward. 'This isn't part of . . . ?'

'Yeah,' Tolland said. 'Unfortunately it is.'

CHAPTER 106

Alone in her office, Gabrielle Ashe stood at the window, wondering what to do next. Less than an hour ago, she had left NASA feeling full of excitement to share Chris Harper's PODS fraud with the senator.

Now, she wasn't so sure.

According to Yolanda, two independent ABC reporters suspected Sexton of taking SFF bribes. Furthermore, Gabrielle had just learned that Sexton actually *knew* she had snuck into his apartment during the SFF meeting, and yet he had said nothing to her about it.

Gabrielle sighed. Her taxi had long since departed, and although she would call another in a few minutes, she knew there was something she had to do first.

Am I really going to try this?

Gabrielle frowned, knowing she didn't have a choice. She no longer knew whom to trust.

Stepping out of her office, she made her way back into the secretarial lobby and into a wide hallway on the opposite side. At the far end she could see the massive oak doors of Sexton's office flanked by two flags – Old Glory on the right and the Delaware flag on the left. His doors, like those of most Senate offices in the building, were steel reinforced and secured by conventional keys, an electronic key pad entry, and an alarm system.

She knew if she could get inside, even if for only a few minutes, all the answers would be revealed. Moving now toward the heavily secured doors, Gabrielle had no illusions of getting *through* them. She had other plans.

Ten feet from Sexton's office, Gabrielle turned sharply to the right and entered the ladies' room. The fluorescents came on automatically, reflecting harshly off the white tile. As her eyes adjusted, Gabrielle paused, seeing herself in the mirror. As usual, her features looked softer than she'd hoped. Delicate almost. She always felt stronger than she looked.

Are you sure you are ready to do this?

Gabrielle knew Sexton was eagerly awaiting her arrival for a complete rundown on the PODS situation. Unfortunately, she also now realized that Sexton had deftly manipulated her tonight. Gabrielle Ashe did not like being managed. The senator had kept things from her tonight. The question was how much. The answers, she knew, lay inside his office – just on the other side of this restroom wall.

'Five minutes,' Gabrielle said aloud, mustering her resolve.

Moving toward the bathroom's supply closet, she reached up and ran a hand over the door frame. A key clattered to the floor. The cleaning crews at Philip A. Hart were federal employees and seemed to evaporate every time there was a strike of any sort, leaving this bathroom without toilet paper and tampons for weeks at a time. The women of Sexton's office, tired of being caught with their pants down, had taken matters into their own hands and secured a supply room key for 'emergencies.'

Tonight qualifies, she thought.

She opened the closet.

The interior was cramped, packed with cleansers, mops, and shelves of paper supplies. A month ago, Gabrielle had been searching for paper towels when she'd made an unusual discovery. Unable to reach the paper off the top shelf, she'd used the end of a broom to coax a roll to fall. In the process, she'd knocked out a ceiling tile. When she climbed up to replace the tile, she was surprised to hear Senator Sexton's voice.

Crystal clear.

From the echo, she realized the senator was talking to himself while in his office's private bathroom, which apparently was separated from this supply closet by nothing more than removable, fiberboard ceiling tiles.

Now, back in the closet tonight for far more than toilet paper, Gabrielle kicked off her shoes, climbed up the shelves, popped out the fiberboard ceiling tile, and pulled herself up. *So much for national security*, she thought, wondering how many state and federal laws she was about to break.

Lowering herself through the ceiling of Sexton's private restroom, Gabrielle placed her stockinged feet on his cold, porcelain sink and then dropped to the floor. Holding her breath, she exited into Sexton's private office.

His oriental carpets felt soft and warm.

CHAPTER **107**

Thirty miles away, a black Kiowa gunship chopper tore over the scrub pine treetops of northern Delaware. Delta-One checked the coordinates locked in the auto navigation system.

Although Rachel's shipboard transmission device and Pickering's cellphone were encrypted to protect the contents of their communication, intercepting *content* had not been the goal when the Delta Force pulse-snitched Rachel's call from sea. Intercepting the caller's *position* had been the goal. Global Positioning Systems and computerized triangulation made pinpointing transmission coordinates a significantly easier task than decrypting the actual content of the call.

Delta-One was always amused to think that most cellphone users had no idea that every time they made a call, a government listening post, if so inclined, could detect their position to within ten feet anywhere on earth – a small hitch the cellphone companies failed to advertise. Tonight, once the Delta Force had gained access to the reception frequencies of William Pickering's cellular phone, they could easily trace the coordinates of his incoming calls.

Flying now on a direct course toward their target, Delta-One closed to within twenty miles. 'Umbrella primed?' he asked, turning to Delta-Two, who was manning the radar and weapons system.

'Affirmative. Awaiting five-mile range.'

Five miles, Delta-One thought. He had to fly this bird well within his target's radar scopes to get within range to use the Kiowa's weapons systems. He had little doubt that someone onboard the *Goya* was nervously watching the skies, and because the Delta Force's current task was to eliminate the target without giving them a chance to radio for help, Delta-One now had to advance on his prey without alarming them.

At fifteen miles out, still safely out of radar range, Delta-One

abruptly turned the Kiowa 35 degrees off course to the west. He
climbed to 3,000 feet – small airplane range – and adjusted his speed
to 110 knots.

On the deck of the *Goya*, the Coast Guard helicopter's radar scope
beeped once as a new contact entered the ten-mile perimeter. The
pilot sat up, studying the screen. The contact appeared to be a small
cargo plane headed west up the coast.

Probably for Newark.

Although this plane's current trajectory would bring it within four
miles of the *Goya*, the flight path obviously was a matter of chance.
Nonetheless, being vigilant, the Coast Guard pilot watched the
blinking dot trace a slow-moving 110-knot line across the right side of
his scope. At its closest point, the plane was about four miles west. As
expected, the plane kept moving – heading away from them now.

4.1 miles. 4.2 miles.

The pilot exhaled, relaxing.

And then the strangest thing happened.

'Umbrella now engaged,' Delta-Two called out, giving the thumbs-up
from his weapons control seat on the port side of the Kiowa gunship.
'Barrage, modulated noise, and cover pulse are all activated and
locked.'

Delta-One took his cue and banked hard to the right, putting the
craft on a direct course with the *Goya*. This maneuver would be
invisible to the ship's radar.

'Sure beats bales of tinfoil!' Delta-Two called out.

Delta-One agreed. Radar jamming had been invented in WWII
when a savvy British airman began throwing bales of hay wrapped in
tinfoil out of his plane while on bombing runs. The Germans' radar
spotted so many reflective contacts they had no idea what to shoot.
The techniques had been improved on substantially since then.

The Kiowa's onboard 'umbrella' radar-jamming system was one of
the military's most deadly electronic combat weapons. By broadcasting an umbrella of background noise into the atmosphere above a
given set of surface coordinates, the Kiowa could erase the eyes, ears,
and voice of their target. Moments ago, all radar screens aboard the

Goya had most certainly gone blank. By the time the crew realized they needed to call for help, they would be unable to transmit. On a ship, all communications were radio- or microwave-based – no solid phone lines. If the Kiowa got close enough, all of the *Goya*'s communications systems would stop functioning, their carrier signals blotted out by the invisible cloud of thermal noise broadcast in front of the Kiowa like a blinding headlight.

Perfect isolation, Delta-One thought. *They have no defenses.*

Their targets had made a fortunate and cunning escape from the Milne Ice Shelf, but it would not be repeated. In choosing to leave shore, Rachel Sexton and Michael Tolland had chosen poorly. It would be the last bad decision they ever made.

Inside the White House, Zach Herney felt dazed as he sat up in bed holding the telephone receiver. 'Now? Ekstrom wants to speak to me *now*?' Herney squinted again at the bedside clock. *3:17 A.M.*

'Yes, Mr President,' the communications officer said. 'He says it's an emergency.'

CHAPTER 108

While Corky and Xavia huddled over the electron microprobe measuring the zirconium content in the chondrules, Rachel followed Tolland across the lab into an adjoining room. Here Tolland turned on another computer. Apparently the oceanographer had one more thing he wanted to check.

As the computer powered up, Tolland turned to Rachel, his mouth poised as if he wanted to say something. He paused.

'What is it?' Rachel asked, surprised how physically drawn to him she felt, even in the midst of all this chaos. She wished she could block it all out and be with him – just for a minute.

'I owe you an apology,' Tolland said, looking remorseful.

'For what?'

'On the deck? The hammerheads? I was excited. Sometimes I forget how frightening the ocean can be to a lot of people.'

Face to face with him, Rachel felt like a teenager standing on the doorstep with a new boyfriend. 'Thanks. No problem at all. Really.' Something inside her sensed Tolland wanted to kiss her.

After a beat, he turned shyly away. 'I know. You want to get to shore. We should get to work.'

'For now.' Rachel smiled softly.

'For now,' Tolland repeated, taking a seat at the computer.

Rachel exhaled, standing close behind now, savoring the privacy of the small lab. She watched Tolland navigate a series of files. 'What are we doing?'

'Checking the database for big ocean lice. I want to see if we can find any prehistoric marine fossils that resemble what we saw in the NASA meteorite.' He pulled up a search page with bold letters across the top: PROJECT DIVERSITAS.

Scrolling through the menus, Tolland explained, 'Diversitas is essentially a continuously updated index of oceanic biodata. When a marine biologist discovers a new ocean species or fossil, he can toot his horn and share his find by uploading data and photos to a central databank. Because there's so much new data discovered on a weekly basis, this is really the only way to keep research up-to-date.'

Rachel watched Tolland navigating the menus. 'So you're accessing the Web now?'

'No. Internet access is tricky at sea. We store all this data onboard on an enormous array of optical drives in the other room. Every time we're in port, we tie into Project Diversitas and update our databank with the newest finds. This way, we can access data at sea without a Web connection, and the data is never more than a month or two out of date.' Tolland chuckled as he began typing search keywords into the computer. 'You've probably heard of the controversial music file-sharing program called Napster?'

Rachel nodded.

'Diversitas is considered the marine biologist's version of Napster. We call it LOBSTER – Lonely Oceanic Biologists Sharing Totally Eccentric Research.'

Rachel laughed. Even in this tense situation, Michael Tolland exuded a wry humor that eased her fears. She was beginning to realize she'd had entirely too little laughter in her life lately.

'Our database is enormous,' Tolland said, completing the entry of his descriptive keywords. 'Over ten terabytes of descriptions and photos. There's information in here nobody has ever seen – and nobody ever will. Ocean species are simply too numerous.' He clicked the 'search' button. 'Okay, let's see if anyone has ever seen an oceanic fossil similar to our little space bug.'

After a few seconds, the screen refreshed, revealing four listings of fossilized animals. Tolland clicked on each listing, one by one and examined the photos. None looked remotely like the fossils in the Milne meteorite.

Tolland frowned. 'Let's try something else.' He removed the word 'fossil' from his search string and hit 'search.' 'We'll search all *living* species. Maybe we can find a living descendant that has some of the physiological characteristics of the Milne fossil.'

The screen refreshed.

Again Tolland frowned. The computer had returned hundreds of entries. He sat a moment, stroking his now stubble-darkened chin. 'Okay, this is too much. Let's refine the search.'

Rachel watched as he accessed a drop-down menu marked 'habitat.' The list of options looked endless: tide pool, marsh, lagoon, reef, mid oceanic ridge, sulfur vents. Tolland scrolled down the list and chose an option that read: DESTRUCTIVE MARGINS/OCEANIC TRENCHES.

Smart, Rachel realized. Tolland was limiting his search only to species that lived near the environment where these chondrulelike features were hypothesized to form.

The page refreshed. This time Tolland smiled. 'Great. Only three entries.'

Rachel squinted at the first name on the list. *Limulus poly . . . something*.

Tolland clicked the entry. A photo appeared; the creature looked like an oversized horseshoe crab without a tail.

'Nope,' Tolland said, returning to the previous page.

Rachel eyed the second item on the list. *Shrimpus Uglius From Hellus*. She was confused. 'Is that name for real?'

Tolland chuckled. 'No. It's a new species not yet classified. The guy who discovered it has a sense of humor. He's suggesting *Shrimpus Uglius* as the official taxonomical classification.' Tolland clicked open the photo, revealing an exceptionally ugly shrimplike creature with whiskers and fluorescent pink antennae.

'Aptly named,' Tolland said. 'But not our space bug.' He returned to the index. 'The final offering is . . .' He clicked on the third entry, and the page came up.

'*Bathynomous giganteus* . . .' Tolland read aloud as the text appeared. The photograph loaded. A full-color close-up.

Rachel jumped. 'My God!' The creature staring back at her gave her chills.

Tolland drew a low breath. 'Oh boy. This guy looks kind of familiar.'

Rachel nodded, speechless. *Bathynomous giganteus*. The creature resembled a giant swimming louse. It looked very similar to the fossil species in the NASA rock.

'There are some subtle differences,' Tolland said, scrolling down to some anatomical diagrams and sketches. 'But it's damn close. Especially considering it has had one hundred and ninety million years to evolve.'

Close is right, Rachel thought. *Too close*.

Tolland read the description on the screen: '"Thought to be one of the oldest species in the ocean, the rare and recently classified species *Bathynomous giganteus* is a deepwater scavenging isopod resembling a large pill bug. Up to two feet in length, this species exhibits a chitonous exoskeleton segemented into head, thorax, abdomen. It possesses paired appendages, antennae, and compound eyes like those of land-dwelling insects. This bottom-dwelling forager has no known predators and lives in barren pelagic environments previously thought to be uninhabitable."' Tolland glanced up. 'Which could explain the lack of other fossils in the sample!'

Rachel stared at the creature on-screen, excited and yet uncertain she completely understood what all of this meant.

'Imagine,' Tolland said excitedly, 'that one hundred and ninety million years ago, a brood of these *Bathynomous* creatures got buried in a deep ocean mud slide. As the mud turns into rock, the bugs get fossilized in stone. Simultaneously, the ocean floor, which is continuously moving like a slow conveyer belt toward the oceanic trenches, carries the fossils into a high-pressure zone where the rock forms chondrules!' Tolland was talking faster now. 'And if part of the fossilized, chondrulized crust broke off and ended up on the trench's accretionary wedge, which is not at all uncommon, it would be in a perfect position to be discovered!'

'But if NASA . . .' Rachel stammered. 'I mean, if this is all a lie, NASA *must* have known that sooner or later someone would find out this fossil resembles a sea creature, right? I mean *we* just found out!'

Tolland began printing the *Bathynomous* photos on a laser printer. 'I don't know. Even if someone stepped forward and pointed out the similarities between the fossils and a living sea louse, their physiologies are not identical. It almost proves NASA's case more strongly.'

Rachel suddenly understood. 'Panspermia.' *Life on earth was seeded from space.*

'Exactly. Similarities between space organisms and earth organisms make excellent scientific sense. This sea louse actually strengthens NASA's case.'

'Except if the meteorite's authenticity is in question.'

Tolland nodded. 'Once the meteorite comes into question, then everything collapses. Our sea louse turns from NASA friend to NASA linchpin.'

Rachel stood in silence as the *Bathynomous* pages rolled out of the printer. She tried to tell herself this was all an honest NASA mistake, but she knew it was not. People who made honest mistakes didn't try to kill people.

The nasal voice of Corky echoed suddenly across the lab. '*Impossible!*'

Both Tolland and Rachel turned.

'*Measure the damn ratio again! It makes no sense!*'

Xavia came hurrying in with a computer printout clutched in her hand. Her face was ashen. 'Mike, I don't know how to say this . . .' Her voice cracked. 'The titanium/zirconium ratios we're seeing in this sample?' She cleared her throat. 'It's pretty obvious that NASA made a huge mistake. Their meteorite is an ocean rock.'

Tolland and Rachel looked at each other but neither spoke a word.

They knew. Just like that, all the suspicions and doubts had swelled up like the crest of a wave, reaching the breaking point.

Tolland nodded, a sadness in his eyes. 'Yeah. Thanks, Xavia.'

'But I don't understand,' Xavia said. 'The fusion crust . . . the location in the ice—'

'We'll explain on the way to shore,' Tolland said. 'We're leaving.'

Quickly, Rachel collected all the papers and evidence they now had. The evidence was shockingly conclusive: the GPR printout showing the insertion shaft in the Milne Ice Shelf; photos of a living sea louse resembling NASA's fossil; Dr Pollock's article on ocean chondrules; and microprobe data showing ultra-depleted titanium in the meteorite.

The conclusion was undeniable. *Fraud.*

Tolland looked at the stack of papers in Rachel's hands and heaved a melancholy sigh. 'Well, I'd say William Pickering has his proof.'

Rachel nodded, again wondering why Pickering had not answered his phone.

Tolland lifted the receiver of a nearby phone, holding it out for her. 'You want to try him again from here?'

'No, let's get moving. I'll try to contact him from the chopper.' Rachel had already decided if she could not make contact with Pickering, she'd have the Coast Guard fly them directly to the NRO, only about 180 miles.

Tolland began to hang up the phone, but he paused. Looking confused, he listened to the receiver, frowning. 'Bizarre. No dial tone.'

'What do you mean?' Rachel said, wary now.

'Weird,' Tolland said. 'Direct COMSAT lines never lose carrier—'

'Mr Tolland?' The Coast Guard pilot came rushing into the lab, his face white.

'What is it?' Rachel demanded. 'Is someone coming?'

'That's the problem,' the pilot said. 'I don't know. All onboard radar and communications have just gone dead.'

Rachel stuffed the papers deep inside her shirt. 'Get in the helicopter. We're leaving. NOW!'

CHAPTER **109**

Gabrielle's heart was racing as she crossed the darkened office of Senator Sexton. The room was as expansive as it was elegant – ornate wood-paneled walls, oil paintings, Persian carpets, leather rivet chairs, and a gargantuan mahogany desk. The room was lit only by the eerie neon glow of Sexton's computer screen.

Gabrielle moved toward his desk.

Senator Sexton had embraced the 'digital office' to maniacal proportions, eschewing the overflow of file cabinets for the compact, searchable simplicity of his personal computer, into which he fed enormous amounts of information – digitized meeting notes, scanned articles, speeches, brain storms. Sexton's computer was his sacred ground, and he kept his office locked at all times to protect it. He even refused to connect to the Internet for fear of hackers infiltrating his sacred digital vault.

A year ago Gabrielle would never have believed any politician would be stupid enough to store copies of self-incriminating documents, but Washington had taught her a lot. *Information is power.* Gabrielle had been amazed to learn that a common practice among politicians who accepted questionable campaign contributions was to keep actual *proof* of those donations – letters, bank records, receipts, logs – all hidden away in a safe place. This counterblackmail tactic, euphemistically known in Washington as 'Siamese insurance,' protected candidates from donors who felt their generosity somehow authorized them to assert undue political pressure on a candidate. If a contributor got too demanding, the candidate could simply produce evidence of the illegal donation and remind the donor that *both* parties had broken the law. The evidence ensured that candidates and donors were joined at the hip forever – like Siamese twins.

Gabrielle slipped behind the senator's desk and sat down. She took a deep breath, looking at his computer. *If the senator is accepting SFF bribes, any evidence would be in here.*

Sexton's computer screensaver was an ongoing slideshow of the White House and its grounds created for him by one of his gung-ho staffers who was big into visualization and positive thinking. Around the images crawled a ticker-tape banner that read: *President of the United States Sedgewick Sexton . . . President of the United States Sedgewick Sexton . . . President of the . . .*

Gabrielle jostled the mouse, and a security dialogue box came up.

ENTER PASSWORD:

She expected this. It would not be a problem. Last week, Gabrielle had entered Sexton's office just as the senator was sitting down and logging onto his computer. She saw him type three short keystrokes in rapid succession.

'*That's* a password?' she challenged from the doorway as she walked in.

Sexton glanced up. 'What?'

'And here I thought you were concerned about security,' Gabrielle scolded good-naturedly. 'Your password's only three keys? I thought the tech guys told us all to use at least six.'

'The tech guys are teenagers. They should try remembering six random letters when they're over forty. Besides, the door has an alarm. Nobody can get in.'

Gabrielle walked toward him, smiling. 'What if someone slipped in while you're in the loo?'

'And tried every combination of passwords?' He gave a skeptical laugh. 'I'm slow in the bathroom, but not that slow.'

'Dinner at Davide says I can guess your password in ten seconds.'

Sexton looked intrigued and amused. 'You can't afford Davide, Gabrielle.'

'So you're saying you're chicken?'

Sexton appeared almost sorry for her as he accepted the challenge. 'Ten seconds?' He logged off and motioned for Gabrielle to sit down and give it a try. 'You know I only order the saltimbocca at Davide. And that ain't cheap.'

She shrugged as she sat down. 'It's *your* money.'

ENTER PASSWORD:

'Ten seconds,' Sexton reminded.

Gabrielle had to laugh. She would need only two. Even from the doorway she could see that Sexton had entered his three-key password in very rapid succession using only his index finger. *Obviously all the same key. Not wise.* She could also see that his hand had been positioned over the far left side of his keyboard – cutting the possible alphabet down to only about nine letters. Choosing the letter was simple; Sexton had always loved the triple alliteration of his title. Senator Sedgewick Sexton.

Never underestimate the ego of a politician.

She typed SSS, and the screensaver evaporated.

Sexton's jaw hit the floor.

That had been last week. Now, as Gabrielle faced his computer again, she was certain Sexton would not have taken time yet to figure out how to set up a different password. *Why would he? He trusts me implicitly.*

She typed in SSS.

INVALID PASSWORD – ACCESS DENIED

Gabrielle stared in shock.

Apparently she had overestimated her senator's level of trust.

CHAPTER 110

The attack came without warning. Low out of the southwest sky above the *Goya*, the lethal silhouette of a gunship helicopter bore down like a giant wasp. Rachel had no doubt what it was, or why it was here.

Through the darkness, a staccato burst from the nose of the chopper sent a torrent of bullets chewing across the *Goya*'s fiberglass deck, slashing a line across the stern. Rachel dove for cover too late and felt the searing slash of a bullet graze her arm. She hit the ground hard, then rolled, scrambling to get behind the bulbous transparent dome of the Triton submersible.

A thundering of rotors exploded overhead as the chopper swooped past the ship. The noise evaporated with an eerie hiss as the chopper rocketed out over the ocean and began a wide bank for a second pass.

Lying trembling on the deck, Rachel held her arm and looked back at Tolland and Corky. Apparently having lunged to cover behind a storage structure, the two men were now staggering to their feet, their eyes scanning the skies in terror. Rachel pulled herself to her knees. The entire world suddenly seemed to be moving in slow motion.

Crouched behind the transparent curvature of the Triton sub, Rachel looked in panic toward their only means of escape – the Coast Guard helicopter. Xavia was already climbing into the chopper's cabin, frantically waving for everyone to get aboard. Rachel could see the pilot lunging into the cockpit, wildly throwing switches and levers. The blades began to turn . . . ever so slowly.

Too slowly.

Hurry!

Rachel felt herself standing now, preparing to run, wondering if she could make it across the deck before the attackers made another pass. Behind her, she heard Corky and Tolland dashing toward her and the waiting helicopter. *Yes! Hurry!*

Then she saw it.

A hundred yards out, up in the sky, materializing out of empty darkness, a pencil-thin beam of red light slanted across the night, searching the *Goya*'s deck. Then, finding its mark, the beam came to a stop on the side of the waiting Coast Guard chopper.

The image took only an instant to register. In that horrific moment, Rachel felt all the action on the deck of the *Goya* blur into a collage of shapes and sounds. Tolland and Corky dashing toward her – Xavia motioning wildly in the helicopter – the stark red laser slicing across the night sky.

It was too late.

Rachel spun back toward Corky and Tolland, who were running full speed now toward the helicopter. She lunged outward into their path, arms outstretched trying to stop them. The collision felt like a train wreck as the three of them crashed to the deck in a tangle of arms and legs.

In the distance, a flash of white light appeared. Rachel watched in disbelief and horror as a perfectly straight line of exhaust fire followed the path of the laser beam directly toward the helicopter.

When the Hellfire missile slammed into the fuselage, the helicopter exploded apart like a toy. The concussion wave of heat and noise thundered across the deck as flaming shrapnel rained down. The helicopter's flaming skeleton lurched backward on its shattered tail, teetered a moment, and then fell off the back of the ship, crashing into the ocean in a hissing cloud of steam.

Rachel closed her eyes, unable to breathe. She could hear the flaming wreckage gurgling and sputtering as it sank, being dragged away from the *Goya* by the heavy currents. In the chaos, Michael Tolland's voice was yelling. Rachel felt his powerful hands trying to pull her to her feet. But she could not move.

The Coast Guard pilot and Xavia are dead.

We're next.

CHAPTER 111

The weather on the Milne Ice Shelf had settled, and the habisphere was quiet. Even so, NASA administrator Lawrence Ekstrom had not even tried to sleep. He had spent the hours alone, pacing the dome, staring into the extraction pit, running his hands over the grooves in the giant charred rock.

Finally, he'd made up his mind.

Now he sat at the videophone in the habisphere's PSC tank and looked into the weary eyes of the President of the United States. Zach Herney was wearing a bathrobe and did not look at all amused. Ekstrom knew he would be significantly less amused when he learned what Ekstrom had to tell him.

When Ekstrom finished talking, Herney had an uncomfortable look on his face – as if he thought he must still be too asleep to have understood correctly.

'Hold on,' Herney said. 'We must have a bad connection. Did you just tell me that NASA intercepted this meteorite's coordinates from an emergency radio transmission – and then *pretended* that PODS found the meteorite?'

Ekstrom was silent, alone in the dark, willing his body to awake from this nightmare.

The silence clearly did not sit well with the President. 'For Christ's sake, Larry, tell me this isn't true!'

Ekstrom's mouth went dry. 'The meteorite was found, Mr President. That is all that's relevant here.'

'I said tell me this is not *true!*'

The hush swelled to a dull roar in Ekstrom's ears. *I had to tell him,* Ekstrom told himself. *It's going to get worse before it gets better.* 'Mr President, the PODS failure was killing you in the polls, sir. When we intercepted a radio transmission that mentioned a large meteorite lodged in the ice, we saw a chance to get back in the fight.'

Herney sounded stunned. 'By faking a PODS discovery?'

'PODS was going to be up and running soon, but not soon enough for the election. The polls were slipping, and Sexton was slamming NASA, so—'

'Are you insane? You lied to me, Larry!'

'The opportunity was staring us in the face, sir. I decided to take it. We intercepted the radio transmission of the Canadian who made the meteorite discovery. He died in a storm. Nobody else knew the meteorite was there. PODS was orbiting in the area. NASA needed a victory. We had the coordinates.'

'Why are you telling me this now?'

'I thought you should know.'

'Do you know what Sexton would do with this information if he found out?'

Ekstrom preferred not to think about it.

'He'd tell the world that NASA and the White House lied to the American people! And you know what, he'd be right!'

'You did not lie, sir, I did. And I will step down if—'

'Larry, you're missing the point. I've tried to run this presidency on truth and decency! Goddamn it! Tonight was clean. Dignified. Now I find out I lied to the world?'

'Only a small lie, sir.'

'There's no such thing, Larry,' Herney said, steaming.

Ekstrom felt the tiny room closing in around him. There was so much more to tell the President, but Ekstrom could see it should wait until morning. 'I'm sorry to have woken you, sir. I just thought you should know.'

Across town, Sedgewick Sexton took another hit of cognac and paced his apartment with rising irritation.

Where the hell is Gabrielle?

CHAPTER **112**

Gabrielle Ashe sat in the darkness at Senator Sexton's desk and gave his computer a despondent scowl.

INVALID PASSWORD – ACCESS DENIED

She had tried several other passwords that seemed likely possibilities, but none had worked. After searching the office for any unlocked drawers or stray clues, Gabrielle had all but given up. She was about to leave when she spotted something odd, shimmering on Sexton's desk calendar. Someone had outlined the date of the election in a red, white, and blue glitter pen. Certainly not the senator. Gabrielle pulled the calendar closer. Emblazoned across the date was a frilly, glittering exclamation: POTUS!

Sexton's ebullient secretary had apparently glitter-painted some more positive thinking for him for election day. The acronym POTUS was the U.S. Secret Service's code name for President of the United States. On election day, if all went well, Sexton would become the new POTUS.

Preparing to leave, Gabrielle realigned the calendar on his desk and stood up. She paused suddenly, glancing back at the computer screen.

ENTER PASSWORD:

She looked again at the calendar.

POTUS.

She felt a sudden surge of hope. Something about POTUS struck Gabrielle as being a perfect Sexton password. *Simple, positive, self-referential.*

She quickly typed in the letters.

POTUS

Holding her breath, she hit 'return.' The computer beeped.

INVALID PASSWORD – ACCESS DENIED

Slumping, Gabrielle gave up. She headed back toward the bathroom door to exit the way she had come. She was halfway across the room, when her cellphone rang. She was already on edge, and the sound startled her. Stopping short, she pulled out her phone and glanced up to check the time on Sexton's prized Jourdain grandfather clock. *Almost 4:00 A.M.* At this hour, Gabrielle knew the caller could only be Sexton. He was obviously wondering where the hell she was. *Do I pick up or let it ring?* If she answered, Gabrielle would have to lie. But if she didn't, Sexton would get suspicious.

She took the call. 'Hello?'

'Gabrielle?' Sexton sounded impatient. 'What's keeping you?'

'The FDR Memorial,' Gabrielle said. 'The taxi got hemmed in, and now we're—'

'You don't sound like you're in a taxi.'

'No,' she said, her blood pumping now. 'I'm not. I decided to stop by my office and pick up some NASA documents that might be relevant to PODS. I'm having some trouble finding them.'

'Well, hurry up. I want to schedule a press conference for the morning, and we need to talk specifics.'

'I'm coming soon,' she said.

There was a pause on the line. 'You're in your office?' He sounded suddenly confused.

'Yeah. Another ten minutes and I'll be on my way over.'

Another pause. 'Okay. I'll see you soon.'

Gabrielle hung up, too preoccupied to notice the loud and distinctive triple-tick of Sexton's prized Jourdain grandfather clock only a few feet away.

CHAPTER **113**

Michael Tolland did not realize Rachel was hurt until he saw the blood on her arm as he pulled her to cover behind the Triton. He sensed from the catatonic look on her face that she was not aware of any pain. Steadying her, Tolland wheeled to find Corky. The astrophysicist scrambled across the deck to join them, his eyes blank with terror.

We've got to find cover, Tolland thought, the horror of what had just happened not yet fully registering. Instinctively, his eyes raced up the tiers of decks above them. The stairs leading up to the bridge were all in the open, and the bridge itself was a glass box – a transparent bull's-eye from the air. Going up was suicide, which left only one other direction to go.

For a fleeting instant, Tolland turned a hopeful gaze to the Triton submersible, wondering perhaps if he could get everyone underwater, away from the bullets.

Absurd. The Triton had room for one person, and the deployment winch took a good ten minutes to lower the sub through the trap door in the deck to the ocean thirty feet below. Besides, without properly charged batteries and compressors, the Triton would be dead in the water.

'Here they come!' Corky shouted, his voice shrill with fear as he pointed into the sky.

Tolland didn't even look up. He pointed to a nearby bulkhead, where an aluminum ramp descended belowdecks. Corky apparently needed no encouragement. Keeping his head low, Corky scurried toward the opening and disappeared down the incline. Tolland put a firm arm around Rachel's waist and followed. The two of them disappeared belowdecks just as the helicopter returned, spraying bullets overhead.

Tolland helped Rachel down the grated ramp to the suspended

platform at the bottom. As they arrived, Tolland could feel Rachel's body go suddenly rigid. He wheeled, fearing maybe she'd been hit by a ricocheting bullet.

When he saw her face, he knew it was something else. Tolland followed her petrified gaze downward and immediately understood.

Rachel stood motionless, her legs refusing to move. She was staring down at the bizarre world beneath her.

Because of its SWATH design, the *Goya* had no hull but rather struts like a giant catamaran. They had just descended through the deck onto a grated catwalk that hung above an open chasm, thirty feet straight down to the raging sea. The noise was deafening here, reverberating off the underside of the deck. Adding to Rachel's terror was the fact that the ship's underwater spotlights were still illuminated, casting a greenish effulgence deep into the ocean directly beneath her. She found herself gazing down at six or seven ghostly silhouettes in the water. Enormous hammerhead sharks, their long shadows swimming in place against the current – rubbery bodies flexing back and forth.

Tolland's voice was in her ear. 'Rachel, you're okay. Eyes straight ahead. I'm right behind you.' His hands were reaching around from behind, gently trying to coax her clenched fists off the banister. It was then that Rachel saw the crimson droplet of blood roll off her arm and fall through the grating. Her eyes followed the drip as it plummeted toward the sea. Although she never saw it hit the water, she knew the instant it happened because all at once the hammerheads spun in unison, thrusting with their powerful tails, crashing together in a roiling frenzy of teeth and fins.

Enhanced telencephalon olfactory lobes . . .

They smell blood a mile away.

'Eyes straight ahead,' Tolland repeated, his voice strong and reassuring. 'I'm right behind you.'

Rachel felt his hands on her hips now, urging her forward. Blocking out the void beneath her, Rachel started down the catwalk. Somewhere above she could hear the rotors of the chopper again. Corky was already well out in front of them, reeling across the catwalk in a kind of drunken panic.

Tolland called out to him. 'All the way to the far strut, Corky! Down the stairs!'

Rachel could now see where they were headed. Up ahead, a series of switchback ramps descended. At water level, a narrow, shelf-like deck extended the length of the *Goya*. Jutting off this deck were several small, suspended docks, creating a kind of miniature marina stationed beneath the ship. A large sign read:

DIVE AREA
Swimmers May Surface without Warning
– Boats Proceed with Caution –

Rachel could only assume Michael did not intend for them to do any swimming. Her trepidation intensified when Tolland stopped at a bank of wire-mesh storage lockers flanking the catwalk. He pulled open the doors to reveal hanging wetsuits, snorkels, flippers, life jackets, and spearguns. Before she could protest, he reached in and grabbed a flare gun. 'Let's go.'

They were moving again.

Up ahead, Corky had reached the switchback ramps and was already halfway down. 'I see it!' he shouted, his voice sounding almost joyous over the raging water.

See what? Rachel wondered as Corky ran along the narrow walkway. All she could see was a shark-infested ocean lapping dangerously close. Tolland urged her forward, and suddenly Rachel could see what Corky was so excited about. At the far end of the decking below, a small powerboat was moored. Corky ran toward it.

Rachel stared. *Outrun a helicopter in a motorboat?*

'It has a radio,' Tolland said. 'And if we can get far enough away from the helicopter's jamming . . .'

Rachel did not hear another word he said. She had just spied something that made her blood run cold. 'Too late,' she croaked, extending a trembling finger. *We're finished . . .*

When Tolland turned, he knew in an instant it was over.

At the far end of the ship, like a dragon peering into the opening of a cave, the black helicopter had dropped down low and was facing them. For an instant, Tolland thought it was going to fly directly at them through the center of the boat. But the helicopter began to turn at an angle, taking aim.

Tolland followed the direction of the gun barrels. *No!*

Crouched beside the powerboat untying the moorings, Corky glanced up just as the machine guns beneath the chopper erupted in a blaze of thunder. Corky lurched as if hit. Wildly, he scrambled over the gunwale and dove into the boat, sprawled himself on the floor for cover. The guns stopped. Tolland could see Corky crawling deeper into the powerboat. The lower part of his right leg was covered with blood. Crouched below the dash, Corky reached up and fumbled across the controls until his fingers found the key. The boat's 250 hp Mercury engine roared to life.

An instant later, a red laser beam appeared, emanating from the nose of the hovering chopper, targeting the powerboat with a missile.

Tolland reacted on instinct, aiming the only weapon he had.

The flare gun in his hand hissed when he pulled the trigger, and a blinding streak tore away on a horizontal trajectory beneath the ship, heading directly toward the chopper. Even so, Tolland sensed he had acted too late. As the streaking flare bore down on the helicopter's windshield, the rocket launcher beneath the chopper emitted its own flash of light. At the same exact instant that the missile launched, the aircraft veered sharply and pulled up out of sight to avoid the incoming flare.

'Look out!' Tolland yelled, yanking Rachel down onto the catwalk.

The missile sailed off course, just missing Corky, coming the length of the *Goya* and slamming into the base of the strut thirty feet beneath Rachel and Tolland.

The sound was apocalyptic. Water and flames erupted beneath them. Bits of twisted metal flew in the air and scattered the catwalk beneath them. Metal on metal ground together as the ship shifted, finding a new balance, slightly askew.

As the smoke cleared, Tolland could see that one of the *Goya's* four main struts had been severely damaged. Powerful currents tore past the pontoon, threatening to break it off. The spiral stairway descending to the lower deck looked to be hanging by a thread.

'Come on!' Tolland yelled, urging Rachel toward it. *We've got to get down!*

But they were too late. With a surrendering crack, the stairs peeled away from the damaged strut and crashed into the sea.

Over the ship, Delta-One grappled with the controls of the Kiowa helicopter and got it back under control. Momentarily blinded by the incoming flare, he had reflexively pulled up, causing the Hellfire missile to miss its mark. Cursing, he hovered now over the bow of the ship and prepared to drop back down and finish the job.

Eliminate all passengers. The controller's demands had been clear.

'Shit! Look!' Delta-Two yelled from the rear seat, pointing out the window. 'Speedboat!'

Delta-One spun and saw a bullet-riddled Crestliner speedboat skimming away from the *Goya* into the darkness.

He had a decision to make.

CHAPTER 114

Corky's bloody hands gripped the wheel of the Crestliner Phantom 2100 as it pounded out across the sea. He rammed the throttle all the way forward, trying to eke out maximum speed. It was not until this moment that he felt the searing pain. He looked down and saw his right leg spurting blood. He instantly felt dizzy.

Propping himself against the wheel, he turned and looked back at the *Goya*, willing the helicopter to follow him. With Tolland and Rachel trapped up on the catwalk, Corky had not been able to reach them. He'd been forced to make a snap decision.

Divide and conquer.

Corky knew if he could lure the chopper far enough away from the *Goya*, maybe Tolland and Rachel could radio for help. Unfortunately, as he looked over his shoulder at the illuminated ship, Corky could see the chopper still hovering there, as if undecided.

Come on, you bastards! Follow me!

But the helicopter did not follow. Instead it banked over the stern of the *Goya*, aligned itself, and dropped down, landing on the deck. *No!* Corky watched in horror, now realizing he'd left Tolland and Rachel behind to be killed.

Knowing it was now up to him to radio for help, Corky groped the dashboard and found the radio. He flicked the power switch. Nothing happened. No lights. No static. He turned the volume knob all the way up. Nothing. *Come on!* Letting go of the wheel, he knelt down for a look. His leg screamed in pain as he bent down. His eyes focused on the radio. He could not believe what he was looking at. The dashboard had been strafed by bullets, and the radio dial was shattered. Loose wires hung out the front. He stared, incredulous.

Of all the goddamned luck . . .

Weak-kneed, Corky stood back up, wondering how things could get any worse. As he looked back at the *Goya*, he got his answer. Two armed soldiers jumped out of the chopper onto the deck. Then the chopper lifted off again, turning in Corky's direction and coming after him at full speed.

Corky slumped. *Divide and conquer.* Apparently he was not the only one with that bright idea tonight.

As Delta-Three made his way across the deck and approached the grated ramp leading belowdecks, he heard a woman shouting somewhere beneath him. He turned and motioned to Delta-Two that he was going belowdecks to check it out. His partner nodded, remaining behind to cover the upper level. The two men could stay in contact via CrypTalk; the Kiowa's jamming system ingeniously left an obscure bandwidth open for their own communications.

Clutching his snub-nose machine gun, Delta-Three moved quietly toward the ramp that led belowdecks. With the vigilance of a trained killer, he began inching downward, gun leveled.

The incline provided limited visibility, and Delta-Three crouched low for a better view. He could hear the shouting more clearly now. He kept descending. Halfway down the stairs he could now make out the twisted maze of walkways attached to the underside of the *Goya*. The shouting grew louder.

Then he saw her. Midway across the traversing catwalk, Rachel Sexton was peering over a railing and calling desperately toward the water for Michael Tolland.

Did Tolland fall in? Perhaps in the blast?

If so, Delta-Three's job would be even easier than expected. He only needed to descend another couple of feet to have an open shot. Shooting fish in a barrel. His only vague concern was Rachel standing near an open equipment locker, which meant she might have a weapon – a speargun or a shark rifle – although neither would be any match for his machine gun. Confident he was in control of the situation, Delta-Three leveled his weapon and took another step down. Rachel Sexton was almost in perfect view now. He raised the gun.

One more step.

The flurry of movement came from beneath him, under the stairs. Delta-Three was more confused than frightened as he looked down and saw Michael Tolland thrusting an aluminum pole out toward his feet. Although Delta-Three had been tricked, he almost laughed at this lame attempt to trip him up.

Then he felt the tip of the stick connect with his heel.

A blast of white-hot pain shot through his body as his right foot exploded out from under him by a blistering impact. His balance gone, Delta-Three flailed, tumbling down the stairs. His machine gun clattered down the ramp and went overboard as he collapsed on the catwalk. In anguish, he curled up to grip his right foot, but it was no longer there.

Tolland was standing over his attacker immediately with his hands still clenching the smoking bang-stick – a five-foot Powerhead Shark-Control Device. The aluminum pole had been tipped with a pressure-sensitive, twelve-gauge shotgun shell and was intended for self-defense in the event of shark attack. Tolland had reloaded the bang-stick with another shell, and now held the jagged, smoldering point to his attacker's Adam's apple. The man lay on his back as if paralyzed, staring up at Tolland with an expression of astonished rage and agony.

Rachel came running up the catwalk. The plan was for her to take the man's machine gun, but unfortunately the weapon had gone over the edge of the catwalk into the ocean.

The communications device on the man's belt crackled. The voice coming out was robotic. 'Delta-Three? Come in. I heard a shot.'

The man made no move to answer.

The device crackled again. 'Delta-Three? Confirm. Do you need backup?'

Almost immediately, a new voice crackled over the line. It was also robotic but distinguishable by the sound of a helicopter noise in the background. 'This is Delta-One,' the pilot said. 'I'm in pursuit of the departing vessel. Delta-Three, confirm. Are you down? Do you need backup?'

Tolland pressed the bang-stick into the man's throat. 'Tell the helicopter to back off that speedboat. If they kill my friend, you die.'

The soldier winced in pain as he lifted his communication device to his lips. He looked directly at Tolland as he pressed the button and spoke. 'Delta-Three here. I'm fine. Destroy the departing vessel.'

CHAPTER 115

Gabrielle Ashe returned to Sexton's private bathroom, preparing to climb back out of his office. Sexton's phone call had left her feeling anxious. He had definitely hesitated when she told him she was in her office – as if he knew somehow she was lying. Either way, she'd failed to get into Sexton's computer and now was unsure of her next move.

Sexton is waiting.

As she climbed up onto the sink, getting ready to pull herself up, she heard something clatter to the tile floor. She looked down, irritated to see that she'd knocked off a pair of Sexton's cuff links that had apparently been sitting on the edge of the sink.

Leave things exactly as you found them.

Climbing back down, Gabrielle picked up the cuff links and put them back on the sink. As she began to climb back up, she paused, glancing again at the cuff links. On any other night, Gabrielle would have ignored them, but tonight their monogram caught her attention. Like most of Sexton's monogrammed items, they had two inter-twining letters. SS. Gabrielle flashed on Sexton's initial computer password – SSS. She pictured his calendar . . . POTUS . . . and the White House screensaver with its optimistic ticker tape crawling around the screen ad infinitum.

President of the United States Sedgewick Sexton . . . President of the United States Sedgewick Sexton . . . President of the . . .

Gabrielle stood a moment and wondered. *Could he be that confident?*

Knowing it would take only an instant to find out, she hurried back into Sexton's office, went to his computer, and typed in a seven-letter password.

POTUSSS

The screensaver evaporated instantly.

She stared, incredulous.

Never underestimate the ego of a politician.

CHAPTER 116

Corky Marlinson was no longer at the helm of the Crestliner Phantom as it raced into the night. He knew the boat would travel in a straight line with or without him at the wheel. *The path of least resistance . . .*

Corky was in the back of the bouncing boat, trying to assess the damage to his leg. A bullet had entered the front part of his calf, just missing his shinbone. There was no exit wound on the back of his calf, so he knew the bullet must still be lodged in his leg. Foraging around for something to stem the bleeding, he found nothing – some fins, a snorkel, and a couple of life jackets. No first-aid kit. Frantically, Corky opened a small utility chest and found some tools, rags, duct tape, oil, and other maintenance items. He looked at his bloody leg and wondered how far he had to go to be out of shark territory.

A hell of a lot farther than this.

Delta-One kept the Kiowa chopper low over the ocean as he scanned the darkness for the departing Crestliner. Assuming the fleeing boat would head for shore and attempt to put as much distance as possible between itself and the *Goya*, Delta-One had followed the Crestliner's original trajectory away from the *Goya*.

I should have overtaken him by now.

Normally, tracking the fleeing boat would be a simple matter of using radar, but with the Kiowa's jamming systems transmitting an umbrella of thermal noise for several miles, his radar was worthless. Turning off the jamming system was not an option until he got word that everyone onboard the *Goya* was dead. No emergency phone calls would be leaving the *Goya* this evening.

This meteorite secret dies. Right here. Right now.

Fortunately, Delta-One had other means of tracking. Even against this bizarre backdrop of heated ocean, pinpointing a powerboat's thermal imprint was simple. He turned on his thermal scanner. The ocean around him registered a warm 95 degrees. Fortunately, the emissions of a racing 250 hp outboard engine were hundreds of degrees hotter.

Corky Marlinson's leg and foot felt numb.

Not knowing what else to do, he had wiped down his injured calf with the rag and wrapped the wound in layer after layer of duct tape. By the time the tape was gone, his entire calf, from ankle to knee, was enveloped in a tight silver sheath. The bleeding had stopped, although his clothing and hands were still covered with blood.

Sitting on the floor of the runaway Crestliner, Corky felt confused about why the chopper hadn't found him yet. He looked out now, scanning the horizon behind him, expecting to see the distant *Goya* and incoming helicopter. Oddly, he saw neither. The lights of the *Goya* had disappeared. Certainly he hadn't come *that* far, had he?

Corky suddenly felt hopeful he might escape. Maybe they had lost him in the dark. Maybe he could get to shore!

It was then he noticed that the wake behind his boat was not straight. It seemed to curve gradually away from the back of his boat, as if he were traveling in an arc rather than a straight line. Confused by this, he turned his head to follow the wake's arc, extrapolating a giant curve across the ocean. An instant later, he saw it.

The *Goya* was directly off his port side, less than a half mile away. In horror, Corky realized his mistake too late. With no one at the wheel, the Crestliner's bow had continuously realigned itself with the direction of the powerful current – the megaplume's circular water flow. *I'm driving in a big friggin' circle!*

He had doubled back on himself.

Knowing he was still inside the shark-filled megaplume, Corky recalled Tolland's grim words. *Enhanced telencephalon olfactory lobes . . . hammerheads can smell a droplet of blood a mile away.* Corky looked at his bloody duct-taped leg and hands.

The chopper would be on him soon.

Ripping off his bloody clothing, Corky scrambled naked toward the stern. Knowing no sharks could possibly keep pace with the boat, he rinsed himself as best as he could in the powerful blast of the wake.

A single droplet of blood . . .

As Corky stood up, fully exposed to the night, he knew there was only one thing left to do. He had learned once that animals marked their territory with urine because uric acid was the most potent-smelling fluid the human body made.

More potent than blood, he hoped. Wishing he'd had a few more beers tonight, Corky heaved his injured leg up onto the gunwale and tried to urinate on the duct tape. *Come on!* He waited. *Nothing like the pressure of having to piss all over yourself with a helicopter chasing you.*

Finally it came. Corky urinated all over the duct tape, soaking it fully. He used what little was left in his bladder to soak a rag, which he then swathed across his entire body. *Very pleasant.*

In the dark sky overhead, a red laser beam appeared, slanting toward him like the shimmering blade of an enormous guillotine. The chopper appeared from an oblique angle, the pilot apparently confused that Corky had looped back toward the *Goya*.

Quickly donning a high-float life vest, Corky moved to the rear of the speeding craft. On the boat's bloodstained floor, only five feet from where Corky was standing, a glowing red dot appeared.

It was time.

Onboard the *Goya*, Michael Tolland did not see his Crestliner Phantom 2100 erupt in flames and tumble through the air in a cartwheel of fire and smoke.

But he heard the explosion.

CHAPTER **117**

The West Wing was usually quiet at this hour, but the President's unexpected emergence in his bathrobe and slippers had rustled the aides and on-site staff out of their 'day-timer beds' and on-site sleeping quarters.

'I can't find her, Mr President,' a young aide said, hurrying after him into the Oval Office. He had looked everywhere. 'Ms Tench is not answering her pager or cellphone.'

The President looked exasperated. 'Have you looked in the—'

'She left the building, sir,' another aide announced, hurrying in. 'She signed out about an hour ago. We think she may have gone to the NRO. One of the operators says she and Pickering were talking tonight.'

'*William* Pickering?' The President sounded baffled. Tench and Pickering were anything but social. 'Have you called him?'

'He's not answering either, sir. NRO switchboard can't reach him. They say Pickering's cellphone isn't even ringing. It's like he's dropped off the face of the earth.'

Herney stared at his aides for a moment and then walked to the bar and poured himself a bourbon. As he raised the glass to his lips, a Secret Serviceman hurried in.

'Mr President? I wasn't going to wake you, but you should be aware that there was a car bombing at the FDR Memorial tonight.'

'What?' Herney almost dropped his drink. 'When?'

'An hour ago.' His face was grim. 'And the FBI just identified the victim . . .'

CHAPTER **118**

Delta-Three's foot screamed in pain. He felt himself floating through a muddled consciousness. *Is this death?* He tried to move but felt paralyzed, barely able to breathe. He saw only blurred shapes. His mind reeled back, recalling the explosion of the Crestliner out at sea, seeing the rage in Michael Tolland's eyes as the oceanographer stood over him, holding the explosive pole to his throat.

Certainly Tolland killed me . . .

And yet the searing pain in Delta-Three's right foot told him he was very much alive. Slowly it came back. On hearing the explosion of the Crestliner, Tolland had let out a cry of anguished rage for his lost friend. Then, turning his ravaged eyes to Delta-Three, Tolland had arched as if preparing to ram the rod through Delta-Three's throat. But as he did, he seemed to hesitate, as if his own morality were holding him back. With brutal frustration and fury, Tolland yanked the rod away and drove his boot down on Delta-Three's tattered foot.

The last thing Delta-Three remembered was vomiting in agony as his whole world drifted into a black delirium. Now he was coming to, with no idea how long he had been unconscious. He could feel his arms tied behind his back in a knot so tight it could only have been tied by a sailor. His legs were also bound, bent behind him and tied to his wrists, leaving him in an immobilized backward arch. He tried to call out, but no sound came. His mouth was stuffed with something.

Delta-Three could not imagine what was going on. It was then he felt the cool breeze and saw the bright lights. He realized he was up on the *Goya's* main deck. He twisted to look for help and was met by a frightful sight, his own reflection – bulbous and misshapen in the reflective Plexiglas bubble of the *Goya*'s deepwater submersible. The sub hung right in front of him, and Delta-Three realized he was lying on a giant trapdoor in the deck. This was not nearly as unsettling as the most obvious question.

If I'm on deck . . . then where is Delta-Two?

Delta-Two had grown uneasy.

Despite his partner's CrypTalk transmission claiming he was fine, the single gunshot had not been that of a machine gun. Obviously, Tolland or Rachel Sexton had fired a weapon. Delta-Two moved over to peer down the ramp where his partner had descended, and he saw blood.

Weapon raised, he had descended belowdecks, where he followed the trail of blood along a catwalk to the bow of the ship. Here, the trail of blood had led him back up another ramp to the main deck. It was deserted. With growing wariness, Delta-Two had followed the long crimson smear along the sideboard deck back toward the rear of the ship, where it passed the opening to the original ramp he had descended.

What the hell is going on? The smear seemed to travel in a giant circle.

Moving cautiously, his gun trained ahead of him, Delta-Two passed the entrance to the laboratory section of the ship. The smear continued toward the stern deck. Carefully he swung wide, rounding the corner. His eye traced the trail.

Then he saw it.

Jesus Christ!

Delta-Three was lying there – bound and gagged – dumped unceremoniously directly in front of the *Goya*'s small submersible. Even from a distance, Delta-Two could see that his partner was missing a good portion of his right foot.

Wary of a trap, Delta-Two raised his gun and moved forward. Delta-Three was writhing now, trying to speak. Ironically, the way the man had been bound – with his knees sharply bent behind him – was probably saving his life; the bleeding in his foot appeared to have slowed.

As Delta-Two approached the submersible, he appreciated the rare luxury of being able to watch his own back; the entire deck of the ship was reflected in the sub's rounded cockpit dome. Delta-Two arrived at his struggling partner. He saw the warning in his eyes too late.

The flash of silver came out of nowhere.

One of the Triton's manipulator claws suddenly leaped forward and clamped down on Delta-Two's left thigh with crushing force. He tried to pull away, but the claw bore down. He screamed in pain, feeling a bone break. His eyes shot to the sub's cockpit. Peering through the reflection of the deck, Delta-Two could now see him, ensconced in the shadows of the Triton's interior.

Michael Tolland was inside the sub, at the controls.

Bad idea, Delta-Two seethed, blocking out his pain and shouldering his machine gun. He aimed up and to the left at Tolland's chest, only three feet away on the other side of the sub's Plexiglas dome. He pulled the trigger, and the gun roared. Wild with rage at having been tricked, Delta-Two held the trigger back until the last of his shells clattered to the deck and his gun clicked empty. Breathless, he dropped the weapon and glared at the shredded dome in front of him.

'Dead!' the soldier hissed, straining to pull his leg from the clamp. As he twisted, the metal clamp severed his skin, opening a large gash. 'Fuck!' He reached now for the CrypTalk on his belt. But as he raised it to his lips, a second robotic arm snapped open in front of him and lunged forward, clamping around his right arm. The CrypTalk fell to the deck.

It was then that Delta-Two saw the ghost in the window before him. A pale visage leaning sideways and peering out through an unscathed edge of glass. Stunned, Delta-Two looked at the center of the dome and realized the bullets had not even come close to penetrating the thick shell. The dome was cratered with pockmarks.

An instant later, the topside portal on the sub opened, and Michael Tolland emerged. He looked shaky but unscathed. Climbing down the aluminum gangway, Tolland stepped onto the deck and eyed his sub's destroyed dome window.

'Ten thousand pounds per square inch,' Tolland said. 'Looks like you need a bigger gun.'

*   *   *

Inside the hydrolab, Rachel knew time was running out. She had
heard the gunshots out on the deck and was praying that everything
had happened exactly as Tolland had planned. She no longer cared
who was behind the meteorite deception – the NASA administrator,
Marjorie Tench, or the President himself – none of it mattered
anymore.

They will not get away with this. Whoever it is, the truth will be told.

The wound on Rachel's arm had stopped bleeding, and the
adrenaline coursing through her body had muted the pain and
sharpened her focus. Finding a pen and paper, she scrawled a two-line
message. The words were blunt and awkward, but eloquence
was not a luxury she had time for at the moment. She added the note
to the incriminating stack of papers in her hand – the GPR printout, images of *Bathynomous giganteus*, photos and articles regarding
oceanic chondrules, an electron microscan printout. The meteorite
was a fake, and this was the proof.

Rachel inserted the entire stack into the hydrolab's fax machine.
Knowing only a few fax numbers by heart, she had limited choices,
but she had already made up her mind who would be receiving these
pages and her note. Holding her breath, she carefully typed in the
person's fax number.

She pressed 'send,' praying she had chosen the recipient wisely.

The fax machine beeped.

ERROR: NO DIAL TONE

Rachel had expected this. The *Goya*'s communications were still
being jammed. She stood waiting and watching the machine, hoping
it functioned like hers at home.

Come on!

After five seconds, the machine beeped again.

REDIALING . . .

Yes! Rachel watched the machine lock into an endless loop.

ERROR: NO DIAL TONE

REDIALING . . .

ERROR: NO DIAL TONE

REDIALING . . .

Leaving the fax machine in search of a dial tone, Rachel dashed out
of the hydrolab just as helicopter blades thundered overhead.

CHAPTER 119

One hundred and sixty miles away from the *Goya*, Gabrielle Ashe was staring at Senator Sexton's computer screen in mute astonishment. Her suspicions had been right.

But she had never imagined *how* right.

She was looking at digital scans of dozens of bank checks written to Sexton from private space companies and deposited in numbered accounts in the Cayman Islands. The smallest check Gabrielle saw was for $15,000. Several were upward of $500,000.

Small potatoes, Sexton had told her. *All the donations are under the $2,000 cap.*

Obviously Sexton had been lying all along. Gabrielle was looking at illegal campaign financing on an enormous scale. The pangs of betrayal and disillusionment settled hard now in her heart. *He lied.*

She felt stupid. She felt dirty. But most of all she felt mad.

Gabrielle sat alone in the darkness, realizing she had no idea what to do next.

CHAPTER 120

Above the *Goya*, as the Kiowa banked over the stern deck, Delta-One gazed down, his eyes fixating on an utterly unexpected vision.

Michael Tolland was standing on deck beside a small submersible. Dangling in the sub's robotic arms, as if in the clutches of a giant insect, hung Delta-Two, struggling in vain to free himself from two enormous claws.

What in the name of God!?

Equally as shocking an image, Rachel Sexton had just arrived on deck, taking up a position over a bound and bleeding man at the foot of the submersible. The man could only be Delta-Three. Rachel held one of the Delta Force's machine guns on him and stared up at the chopper as if daring them to attack.

Delta-One felt momentarily disoriented, unable to fathom how this possibly could have happened. The Delta Force's errors on the ice shelf earlier had been a rare but explainable occurrence. This, however, was unimaginable.

Delta-One's humiliation would have been excruciating enough under normal circumstances. But tonight his shame was magnified by the presence of another individual riding with him inside the chopper, a person whose presence here was highly unconventional.

The controller.

Following the Delta's kill at the FDR Memorial, the controller had ordered Delta-One to fly to a deserted public park not far from the White House. On the controller's command, Delta-One had set down on a grassy knoll among some trees just as the controller, having parked nearby, strode out of the darkness and boarded the Kiowa. They were all en route again in a matter of seconds.

Although a controller's direct involvement in mission operations was rare, Delta-One could hardly complain. The controller, distressed by the way the Delta Force had handled the kills on the Milne Ice Shelf and fearing increasing suspicions and scrutiny from a number of parties, had informed Delta-One that the final phase of the operation would be overseen in person.

Now the controller was riding shotgun, witnessing in person a failure the likes of which Delta-One had never endured.

This must end. Now.

The controller gazed down from the Kiowa at the deck of the *Goya* and wondered how this could possibly have happened. Nothing had gone properly – the suspicions about the meteorite, the failed Delta kills on the ice shelf, the necessity of the high-profile kill at the FDR.

'Controller,' Delta-One stammered, his tone one of stunned

disgrace as he looked at the situation on the deck of the *Goya*. 'I cannot imagine . . .'

Nor can I, the controller thought. Their quarry had obviously been grossly underestimated.

The controller looked down at Rachel Sexton, who stared up blankly at the chopper's reflective windshield and raised a CrypTalk device to her mouth. When her synthesized voice crackled inside the Kiowa, the controller expected her to demand that the chopper back off or extinguish the jamming system so Tolland could call for help. But the words Rachel Sexton spoke were far more chilling.

'You're too late,' she said. 'We're not the only ones who know.'

The words echoed for a moment inside the chopper. Although the claim seemed far-fetched, the faintest possibility of truth gave the controller pause. The success of the entire project required the elimination of all those who knew the truth, and as bloody as the containment had turned out to be, the controller had to be certain this was the conclusion.

Someone else knows . . .

Considering Rachel Sexton's reputation for following strict protocol of classified data, the controller found it very hard to believe that she would have decided to share this with an outside source.

Rachel was on the CrypTalk again. 'Back off and we'll spare your men. Come any closer and they die. Either way, the truth comes out. Cut your losses. Back off.'

'You're bluffing,' the controller said, knowing the voice Rachel Sexton was hearing was an androgynous robotic tone. 'You have told no one.'

'Are you ready to take that chance?' Rachel fired back. 'I couldn't get through to William Pickering earlier, so I got spooked and took out some insurance.'

The controller frowned. It was plausible.

'They're not buying it,' Rachel said, glancing at Tolland.

The soldier in the claws gave a pained smirk. 'Your gun is empty, and the chopper's going to blow you to hell. You're both going to die. Your only hope is to let us go.'

Like hell, Rachel thought, trying to assess their next move. She looked at the bound and gagged man who lay at her feet directly in front of the sub. He looked delirious from loss of blood. She crouched beside him, looking into the man's hard eyes. 'I'm going to take off your gag and hold the CrypTalk; you're going to convince the helicopter to back off. Is that clear?'

The man nodded earnestly.

Rachel pulled out the man's gag. The soldier spat a wad of bloody saliva up into Rachel's face.

'Bitch,' he hissed, coughing. 'I'm going to watch you die. They're going to kill you like a pig, and I'm going to enjoy every minute.'

Rachel wiped the hot saliva from her face as she felt Tolland's hands lifting her away, pulling her back, steadying her as he took her machine gun. She could feel in his trembling touch that something inside him had just snapped. Tolland walked to a control panel a few yards away, put his hand on a lever, and locked eyes with the man lying on the deck.

'Strike two,' Tolland said. 'And on my ship, that's all you get.'

With a resolute rage, Tolland yanked down on the lever. A huge trap door in the deck beneath the Triton fell open like the floor of a gallows. The bound soldier gave a short howl of fear and then disappeared, plummeting through the hole. He fell thirty feet to the ocean below. The splash was crimson. The sharks were on him instantly.

The controller shook with rage, looking down from the Kiowa at what was left of Delta-Three's body drifting out from under the boat on the strong current. The illuminated water was pink. Several fish fought over something that looked like an arm.

Jesus Christ.

The controller looked back at the deck. Delta-Two still hung in the Triton's claws, but now the sub was suspended over a gaping hole in the deck. His feet dangled over the void. All Tolland had to do was release the claws, and Delta-Two would be next.

'Okay,' the controller barked into the CrypTalk. 'Hold on. Just hold on!'

Rachel stood below on the deck and stared up at the Kiowa. Even from this height the controller sensed the resolve in her eyes. Rachel raised the CrypTalk to her mouth. 'You still think we're bluffing?' she

said. 'Call the main switchboard at the NRO. Ask for Jim Samiljan.
He's in P&A on the nightshift. I told him everything about the
meteorite. He will confirm.'

She's giving me a specific name? This did not bode well. Rachel
Sexton was no fool, and this was a bluff the controller could check in
a matter of seconds. Although the controller knew of no one at the
NRO named Jim Samiljan, the organization was enormous. Rachel
could quite possibly be telling the truth. Before ordering the final kill,
the controller had to confirm if this was a bluff – or not.

Delta-One looked over his shoulder. 'You want me to deactivate
the jammer so you can call and check it out?'

The controller peered down at Rachel and Tolland, both in plain
view. If either of them made a move for a cellphone or radio, the
controller knew Delta-One could always reactivate and cut them off.
The risk was minimal.

'Kill the jammer,' the controller said, pulling out a cellphone. 'I'll
confirm Rachel's lying. Then we'll find a way to get Delta-Two and
end this.'

In Fairfax, the operator at the NRO's central switchboard was getting
impatient. 'As I just told you, I see no Jim Samiljan in the Plans and
Analysis Division.'

The caller was insistent. 'Have you tried multiple spellings? Have
you tried other departments?'

The operator had already checked, but she checked again. After
several seconds, she said, 'Nowhere on staff do we have a Jim
Samiljan. Under any spelling.'

The caller sounded oddly pleased by this. 'So you are certain the
NRO employs no Jim Samil—'

A sudden flurry of activity erupted on the line. Someone yelled.
The caller cursed aloud and promptly hung up.

Onboard the Kiowa, Delta-One was screaming with rage as he
scrambled to reactivate the jamming system. He had made the
realization too late. In the huge array of lighted controls in
the cockpit, a tiny LED meter indicated that a SATCOM data signal
was being transmitted from the *Goya. But how? Nobody left the deck!*

Before Delta-One could engage the jammer, the connection from the *Goya* terminated on its own accord.

Inside the hydrolab, the fax machine beeped contentedly.

CARRIER FOUND . . . FAX SENT

CHAPTER **121**

Kill or *be killed*. Rachel had discovered a part of herself she never knew existed. Survival mode – a savage fortitude fueled by fear.

'What was in that outbound fax?' the voice on the CrypTalk demanded.

Rachel was relieved to hear confirmation that the fax had gone out as planned. 'Leave the area,' she demanded, speaking into the CrypTalk and glaring up at the hovering chopper. 'It's over. Your secret is out.' Rachel informed their attackers of all the information she had just sent. A half dozen pages of images and text. Incontrovertible evidence that the meteorite is a fake. 'Harming us will only make your situation worse.'

There was a heavy pause. 'Who did you send the fax to?'

Rachel had no intention of answering that question. She and Tolland needed to buy as much time as possible. They had positioned themselves near the opening in the deck, on a direct line with the Triton, making it impossible for the chopper to shoot without hitting the soldier dangling in the sub's claws.

'William Pickering,' the voice guessed, sounding oddly hopeful. 'You faxed Pickering.'

Wrong, Rachel thought. Pickering would have been her first choice, but she had been forced to choose someone else for fear her attackers had already eliminated Pickering – a move whose boldness would be a chilling testimony to her enemy's resolve. In a moment of desperate decision, Rachel had faxed the data to the only other fax number she knew by heart.

Her father's office.

Senator Sexton's office fax number had been painfully engraved into Rachel's memory after her mother's death when her father chose to work out many of the particulars of the estate without having to deal with Rachel in person. Rachel never imagined she would turn to her father in a time of need, but tonight the man possessed two critical qualities – all the correct political motivations to release the meteorite data without hesitation, and enough clout to call the White House and blackmail them into calling off this kill squad.

Although her father was most certainly not in the office at this hour, Rachel knew he kept his office locked like a vault. Rachel had, in effect, faxed the data into a time-lock safe. Even if the attackers knew where she had sent it, chances were slim they could get through the tight federal security at the Philip A. Hart Senate Office Building and break into a senator's office without anyone noticing.

'Wherever you sent the fax,' the voice from above said, 'you've put that person in danger.'

Rachel knew she had to speak from a position of power regardless of the fear she was feeling. She motioned to the soldier trapped in the Triton's claws. His legs dangled over the abyss, dripping blood thirty feet to the ocean. 'The only person in danger here is your agent,' she said into the CrypTalk. 'It's over. Back off. The data is gone. You've lost. Leave the area, or this man dies.'

The voice on the CrypTalk fired back, 'Ms Sexton, you do not understand the importance—'

'Understand?' Rachel exploded. 'I understand that you killed innocent people! I understand that you lied about the meteorite! And I understand that you won't get away with this! Even if you kill us all, it's over!'

There was a long pause. Finally the voice said, 'I'm coming down.'

Rachel felt her muscles tighten. *Coming down?*

'I am unarmed,' the voice said. 'Do not do anything rash. You and I need to talk face to face.'

Before Rachel could react, the chopper dropped onto the *Goya*'s deck. The passenger door on the fuselage opened and a figure stepped out. He was a plain-looking man in a black coat and tie. For an instant, Rachel's thoughts went totally blank.

She was staring at William Pickering.

* * *

William Pickering stood on the deck of the *Goya* and gazed with regret at Rachel Sexton. He had never imagined today would come to this. As he moved toward her, he could see the dangerous combination of emotions in his employee's eyes.

Shock, betrayal, confusion, rage.

All understandable, he thought. *There is so much she does not understand.*

For a moment, Pickering flashed on his daughter, Diana, wondering what emotions she had felt before she died. Both Diana and Rachel were casualties of the same war, a war Pickering had vowed to fight forever. Sometimes the casualties could be so cruel.

'Rachel,' Pickering said. 'We can still work this out. There's a lot I need to explain.'

Rachel Sexton looked aghast, nauseated almost. Tolland had the machine gun now and was aiming at Pickering's chest. He too looked bewildered.

'Stay back!' Tolland yelled.

Pickering stopped five yards away, focusing on Rachel. 'Your father is taking bribes, Rachel. Payoffs from private space companies. He plans to dismantle NASA and open space to the private sector. He had to be stopped, as a matter of national security.'

Rachel's expression was blank.

Pickering sighed. 'NASA, for all its flaws, *must* remain a government entity.' *Certainly she can understand the dangers.* Privatization would send NASA's best minds and ideas flooding into the private sector. The brain trust would dissolve. The military would lose access. Private space companies looking to raise capital would start selling NASA patents and ideas to the highest bidders worldwide!

Rachel's voice was tremulous. 'You faked the meteorite and killed innocent people . . . in the name of national security?'

'It was never supposed to happen like this,' Pickering said. 'The plan was to save an important government agency. Killing was not part of it.'

The meteorite deception, Pickering knew, like most intelligence proposals, had been the product of fear. Three years ago, in an effort to extend the NRO hydrophones into deeper water where they could not be touched by enemy saboteurs, Pickering spearheaded a program that utilized a newly developed NASA building material to secretly design an astonishingly durable submarine capable of carrying humans to the deepest regions of the ocean – including the bottom of the Mariana Trench.

Forged from a revolutionary ceramic, this two-man submarine was designed from blueprints hacked from the computer of a California engineer named Graham Hawkes, a genius sub designer whose life dream was to build an ultra-deepwater submersible he called Deep Flight II. Hawkes was having trouble finding funding to build a prototype. Pickering, on the other hand, had an unlimited budget.

Using the classified ceramic submersible, Pickering sent a covert team underwater to affix new hydrophones to the walls of the Mariana Trench, deeper than any enemy could possibly look. In the process of drilling, however, they uncovered geologic structures unlike any that scientists had ever seen. The discoveries included chondrules and fossils of several unknown species. Of course, because the NRO's ability to dive this deep was classified, none of the information could ever be shared.

It was not until recently, driven yet again by fear, that Pickering and his quiet team of NRO science advisers had decided to put their knowledge of the Mariana's unique geology to work to help save NASA. Turning a Mariana rock into a meteorite had proven to be a deceptively simple task. Using an ECE slush-hydrogen engine, the NRO team charred the rock with a convincing fusion crust. Then, using a small payload sub, they had descended beneath the Milne Ice Shelf and inserted the charred rock up into the ice from beneath. Once the insertion shaft refroze, the rock looked like it had been there for over three hundred years.

Unfortunately, as was often the case in the world of covert operations, the grandest of plans could be undone by the smallest of snags. Yesterday, the entire illusion had been shattered by a few bioluminescent plankton . . .

From the cockpit of the idling Kiowa, Delta-One watched the drama unfold before him. Rachel and Tolland appeared to be in clear control, although Delta-One almost had to laugh at the hollowness of the illusion. The machine gun in Tolland's hands was worthless; even from here Delta-One could see the cocking bar assembly had kicked back, indicating the clip was empty.

As Delta-One gazed out at his partner struggling in the Triton's claws, he knew he had to hurry. The focus on deck had turned completely to Pickering, and now Delta-One could make his move. Leaving the rotors idling, he slipped out of the rear of the fuselage and, using the chopper for cover, made his way unseen onto the starboard gangway. With his own machine gun in hand, he headed for the bow. Pickering had given him specific orders before they landed on deck, and Delta-One had no intention of failing at this simple task.

In a matter of minutes, he knew, *this will all be over.*

CHAPTER 122

Still wearing his bathrobe, Zach Herney sat at his desk in the Oval Office, his head throbbing. The newest piece of the puzzle had just been revealed.

Marjorie Tench is dead.

Herney's aides said they had information suggesting Tench had driven to the FDR Memorial for a private meeting with William Pickering. Now that Pickering was missing, the staff feared Pickering too might be dead.

The President and Pickering had endured their battles lately. Months ago Herney learned that Pickering had engaged in illegal activity on Herney's behalf in an attempt to save Herney's floundering campaign.

Employing NRO assets, Pickering had discreetly obtained enough dirt on Senator Sexton to sink his campaign – scandalous sexual photos of the senator with his aide Gabrielle Ashe, incriminating financial records proving Sexton was taking bribes from private space companies. Pickering anonymously sent all the evidence to Marjorie Tench, assuming the White House would use it wisely. But Herney, upon seeing the data, had forbidden Tench to use it. Sex scandals and bribery were cancers in Washington, and waving another one in front of the public only added to their distrust of government.

Cynicism is killing this country.

Although Herney knew he could destroy Sexton with scandal, the cost would be besmirching the dignity of the U.S. Senate, something Herney refused to do.

No more negatives. Herney would beat Senator Sexton on the issues.

Pickering, angered by the White House's refusal to use the evidence he had provided, tried to jump-start the scandal by leaking a rumor that Sexton had slept with Gabrielle Ashe. Unfortunately, Sexton declared his innocence with such convincing indignation that the President ended up having to apologize for the leak personally. In the end William Pickering had done more damage than good. Herney told Pickering that if he ever interfered in the campaign again, he would be indicted. The grand irony, of course, was that Pickering did not even like President Herney. The NRO director's attempts to help Herney's campaign were simply fears over the fate of NASA. Zach Herney was the lesser of two evils.

Now has someone killed Pickering?

Herney could not imagine.

'Mr President?' an aide said. 'As you requested, I called Lawrence Ekstrom and told him about Marjorie Tench.'

'Thank you.'

'He would like to speak to you, sir.'

Herney was still furious with Ekstrom for lying about PODS. 'Tell him I'll talk to him in the morning.'

'Mr Ekstrom wants to talk to you right away, sir.' The aide looked uneasy. 'He's very upset.'

HE'S upset? Herney could feel his temper fraying around the edges. As he stalked off to take Ekstrom's call, the President wondered what the hell else could possibly go wrong tonight.

CHAPTER **123**

Onboard the *Goya*, Rachel felt lightheaded. The mystification that had settled around her like a heavy fog was lifting now. The stark reality that came into focus left her feeling naked and disgusted. She looked at the stranger before her and could barely hear his voice.

'We needed to rebuild NASA's image,' Pickering was saying. 'Their declining popularity and funding had become dangerous on so many levels.' Pickering paused, his gray eyes locking on hers. 'Rachel, NASA was *desperate* for a triumph. Someone had to make it happen.'

Something had to be done, Pickering thought.

The meteorite had been a final act of desperation. Pickering and others had tried to save NASA by lobbying to incorporate the space agency into the intelligence community where it would enjoy increased funding and better security, but the White House continuously rebuffed the idea as an assault on pure science. *Shortsighted idealism*. With the rising popularity of Sexton's anti-NASA rhetoric, Pickering and his band of military powerbrokers knew time was running short. They decided that capturing the imagination of taxpayers and Congress was the only remaining way to salvage NASA's image and save it from the auction block. If the space agency was to survive, it would need an infusion of grandeur – something to remind the taxpayers of NASA's Apollo glory days. And if Zach Herney was going to defeat Senator Sexton, he was going to need help.

I tried to help him, Pickering told himself, recalling all the damaging evidence he had sent Marjorie Tench. Unfortunately, Herney had forbidden its use, leaving Pickering no choice but to take drastic measures.

'Rachel,' Pickering said, 'the information you just faxed off this ship is dangerous. You must understand that. If it gets out, the White House and NASA will look complicit. The backlash against the

President and NASA will be enormous. The President and NASA know nothing, Rachel. They are innocent. They believe the meteorite is authentic.'

Pickering had not even tried to bring Herney or Ekstrom into the fold because both were far too idealistic to have agreed to any deceit, regardless of its potential to save the presidency or space agency. Administrator Ekstrom's only crime had been persuading the PODS mission supervisor to lie about the anomaly software, a move Ekstrom no doubt regretted the moment he realized how scrutinized this particular meteorite would become.

Marjorie Tench, frustrated by Herney's insistence on fighting a clean campaign, conspired with Ekstrom on the PODS lie, hoping a small PODS success might help the President fend off the rising Sexton tide.

If Tench had used the photos and bribery data I gave her, none of this would have happened!

Tench's murder, though deeply regrettable, had been destined as soon as Rachel called Tench and made accusations of fraud. Pickering knew Tench would investigate ruthlessly until she got to the bottom of Rachel's motives for the outrageous claims, and this was one investigation Pickering obviously could never let happen. Ironically, Tench would serve her president best in death, her violent end helping cement a sympathy vote for the White House as well as cast vague suspicions of foul play on a desperate Sexton campaign which had been so publicly humiliated by Marjorie Tench on CNN.

Rachel stood her ground, glaring at her boss.

'Understand,' Pickering said, 'if news of this meteorite fraud gets out, you will destroy an innocent president and an innocent space agency. You will also put a very dangerous man in the Oval Office. I need to know where you faxed the data.'

As he spoke those words, a strange look came across Rachel's face. It was the pained expression of horror of someone who had just realized they may have made a grave mistake.

Having circled the bow and come back down the port side, Delta-One now stood in the hydrolab from which he had seen Rachel emerge as the chopper had flown in. A computer in the lab displayed an unsettling image – a polychromatic rendering of the pulsating, deep-water vortex that was apparently hovering over the ocean floor somewhere beneath the *Goya*.

Another reason to get the hell out of here, he thought, moving now toward his target.

The fax machine was on a counter on the far side of the wall. The tray was filled with a stack of papers, exactly as Pickering had guessed it would be. Delta-One picked up the stack. A note from Rachel was on top. Only two lines. He read it.

To the point, he thought.

As he flipped through the pages, he was both amazed and dismayed by the extent to which Tolland and Rachel had uncovered the meteorite deception. Whoever saw these printouts would have no doubt what they meant. Fortunately, Delta-One would not even need to hit 'redial' to find out where the printouts had gone. The last fax number was still displayed in the LCD window.

A Washington D.C. prefix.

He carefully copied the fax number down, grabbed all the papers, and exited the lab.

Tolland's hands felt sweaty on the machine gun as he gripped it, aiming the muzzle at William Pickering's chest. The NRO director was still pressuring Rachel to tell him where the data had been sent, and Tolland was starting to get the uneasy feeling that Pickering was simply trying to buy time. *For what?*

'The White House and NASA are *innocent*,' Pickering repeated. 'Work with me. Don't let my mistakes destroy what little credibility NASA has left. NASA will look guilty if this gets out. You and I can come to an arrangement. The country needs this meteorite. Tell me where you faxed the data before it's too late.'

'So you can kill someone else?' Rachel said. 'You make me sick.'

Tolland was amazed by Rachel's fortitude. She despised her father, but she clearly had no intention of putting the senator in any danger whatsoever. Unfortunately, Rachel's plan to fax her father for help had backfired. Even if the senator came into his office, saw the fax, and called the President with news of the meteorite fraud and told him to call off the attack, nobody at the White House would have any idea what Sexton was talking about, or even where they were.

'I will only say this one more time,' Pickering said, fixing Rachel with a menacing glare. 'This situation is too complex for you to fully understand. You've made an enormous mistake by sending that data off this ship. You've put your country at risk.'

William Pickering was indeed buying time, Tolland now realized. And the reason was striding calmly toward them up the starboard side of the boat. Tolland felt a flash of fear when he saw the soldier sauntering toward them carrying a stack of papers and a machine gun.

Tolland reacted with a decisiveness that shocked even himself. Gripping the machine gun, he wheeled, aimed at the soldier, and pulled the trigger.

The gun made an innocuous click.

'I found the fax number,' the soldier said, handing Pickering a slip of paper. 'And Mr Tolland is out of ammunition.'

CHAPTER 124

Sedgewick Sexton stormed up the hallway of the Philip A. Hart Senate building. He had no idea how Gabrielle had done it, but she had obviously gotten into his office. While they were speaking on the phone, Sexton had clearly heard the distinctive triple-click of his Jourdain clock in the background. All he could imagine was that Gabrielle's eavesdropping on the SFF meeting had undermined her trust in him and she had gone digging for evidence.

How the hell did she get into my office?

Sexton was glad he'd changed his computer password.

When he arrived at his private office, Sexton typed in his code to deactivate the alarm. Then he fumbled for his keys, unlocked the heavy doors, threw them open, and burst in, intent on catching Gabrielle in the act.

But the office was empty and dark, lit only by the glow of his computer screensaver. He turned on the lights, his eyes scanning. Everything looked in place. Dead silence except for the triple-tick of his clock.

Where the hell is she?

He heard something rustle in his private bathroom and raced over, turning on the light. The bathroom was empty. He looked behind the door. Nothing.

Puzzled, Sexton eyed himself in the mirror, wondering if he'd had too much to drink tonight. *I heard something.* Feeling disoriented and confused, he walked back into his office.

'Gabrielle?' he called out. He went down the hall to her office. She wasn't there. Her office was dark.

A toilet flushed in the ladies' room, and Sexton spun, striding now back in the direction of the restrooms. He arrived just as Gabrielle was exiting, drying her hands. She jumped when she saw him.

'My God! You scared me!' she said, looking genuinely frightened. 'What are you doing here?'

'You said you were getting NASA documents from your office,' he declared, eyeing her empty hands. 'Where are they?'

'I couldn't find them. I looked everywhere. That's what took so long.'

He stared directly into her eyes. 'Were you in my office?'

I owe my life to his fax machine, Gabrielle thought.

Only minutes ago she'd been sitting at Sexton's computer, trying to make printouts of the images of illegal checks on his computer. The files were protected somehow, and she was going to need more time to figure out how to print them. She would probably still be trying right now if Sexton's fax machine had not rung, startling her and snapping her back to reality. Gabrielle took it as her cue to get out. Without taking time to see what the incoming fax was, she logged off Sexton's computer, tidied up, and headed out the way she had come. She was just climbing out of Sexton's bathroom when she heard him coming in.

Now, with Sexton standing before her, staring down, she sensed him searching her eyes for a lie. Sedgewick Sexton could smell untruths like nobody Gabrielle had ever met. If she lied to him, Sexton would know.

'You've been drinking,' Gabrielle said, turning away. *How does he know I was in his office?*

Sexton put his hands on her shoulders and spun her back around. 'Were you in my office?'

Gabrielle felt a rising fear. Sexton had indeed been drinking. His touch was rough. 'In your office?' she demanded, forcing a confused laugh. 'How? *Why?*'

'I heard my Jourdain in the background when I called you.'

Gabrielle cringed inwardly. *His clock?* It had not even occurred to her. 'Do you know how ridiculous that sounds?'

'I spend all day in that office. I know what my clock sounds like.'

Gabrielle sensed she had to end this immediately. *The best defense is a good offense.* At least that's what Yolanda Cole always said. Placing her hands on her hips, Gabrielle went for him with all she had. She stepped toward him, getting in his face, glaring. 'Let me get this straight, Senator. It's four o'clock in the morning, you've been drinking, you heard a ticking on your phone, and that's why you're here?' She pointed her finger indignantly down the hall at his door. 'Just for the record, are you accusing me of disarming a federal alarm system, picking two sets of locks, breaking into your office, being stupid enough to answer my cellphone while in the process of committing a felony, rearming the alarm system on my way out, and then calmly using the ladies' room before I run off with nothing to show for it? Is that the story here?'

Sexton blinked, wide-eyed.

'There's a reason people shouldn't drink alone,' Gabrielle said. 'Now do you want to talk about NASA, or not?'

Sexton felt befuddled as he walked back into his office. He went straight to his wet bar and poured himself a Pepsi. He sure as hell didn't *feel* drunk. Could he really have been wrong about this? Across the room, his Jourdain ticked mockingly. Sexton drained his Pepsi and poured himself another, and one for Gabrielle.

'Drink, Gabrielle?' he asked, turning back into the room. Gabrielle had not followed him in. She was still standing in the doorway, rubbing his nose in it. 'Oh, for God's sake! Come in. Tell me what you found out at NASA.'

'I think I've had enough for tonight,' she said, sounding distant. 'Let's talk tomorrow.'

Sexton was in no mood for games. He needed this information now, and he had no intention of begging for it. He heaved a tired sigh. *Extend the bond of trust. It's all about trust.* 'I screwed up,' he said. 'I'm sorry. It's been a hell of a day. I don't know what I was thinking.'

Gabrielle remained in the doorway.

Sexton walked to his desk and set Gabrielle's Pepsi down on his blotter. He motioned to his leather chair – the position of power. 'Have a seat. Enjoy a soda. I'm going to go stick my head in the sink.' He headed for the bathroom.

Gabrielle still wasn't moving.

'I think I saw a fax in the machine,' Sexton called over his shoulder as he entered the bathroom. *Show her you trust her.* 'Have a look at it for me, will you?'

Sexton closed the door and filled the sink with cold water. He splashed it on his face and felt no clearer. This had never happened to him before – being so sure, and being so wrong. Sexton was a man who trusted his instincts, and his instincts told him Gabrielle Ashe had been in his office.

But how? It was impossible.

Sexton told himself to forget about it and focus on the matter at hand. *NASA.* He needed Gabrielle right now. This was no time to alienate her. He needed to know what she knew. *Forget your instincts. You were wrong.*

As Sexton dried his face, he threw his head back and took a deep breath. *Relax*, he told himself. *Don't get punchy.* He closed his eyes and inhaled deeply again, feeling better.

When Sexton exited the bathroom, he was relieved to see Gabrielle had acquiesced and come back into his office. *Good*, he thought. *Now we can get to business.* Gabrielle was standing at his fax machine flipping through whatever pages had come in. Sexton was confused, however, when he saw her face. It was a mask of disorientation and fear.

'What is it?' Sexton said, moving toward her.

Gabrielle teetered, as if she were about to pass out.

'What?'

'The meteorite . . .' she choked, her voice frail as her trembling hand held the stack of fax papers out to him. 'And your daughter . . . she's in danger.'

Bewildered, Sexton walked over, and took the fax pages from Gabrielle. The top sheet was a handwritten note. Sexton immediately recognized the writing. The communiqué was awkward and shocking in its simplicity.

> Meteorite is fake. Here's proof.
> NASA/White House trying to kill me. Help! – RS

The senator seldom felt totally at a loss of understanding, but as he reread Rachel's words, he had no idea what to make of them.

The meteorite is a fake? NASA and the White House are trying to kill her?

In a deepening haze, Sexton began sifting through the half dozen sheets. The first page was a computerized image whose heading read 'Ground Penetrating Radar (GPR).' The picture appeared to be an ice-sounding of some sort. Sexton saw the extraction pit they had talked about on television. His eye was drawn to what looked like the faint outline of a body floating in the shaft. Then he saw something even more shocking – the clear outline of a second shaft directly *beneath* where the meteorite had been – as if the stone had been inserted from underneath the ice.

What in the world?

Flipping to the next page, Sexton came face to face with a photograph of some sort of living ocean species called a *Bathynomous giganteus*. He stared in utter amazement. *That's the animal from the meteorite fossils!*

Flipping faster now, he saw a graphic display depicting the ionized hydrogen content in the meteorite's crust. This page had a hand-written scrawl on it: *Slush-hydrogen burn? NASA Expander Cycle Engine?*

Sexton could not believe his eyes. With the room starting to spin around him, he flipped to the final page – a photo of a rock containing metallic bubbles that looked exactly like those in the meteorite. Shockingly, the accompanying description said the rock was the product of oceanic volcanism. *A rock from the ocean?* Sexton wondered. *But NASA said chondrules form only in space!*

Sexton set the sheets down on his desk and collapsed in his chair. It had taken him only fifteen seconds to piece together everything he was looking at. The implications of the images on the papers were crystal clear. Anyone with half a brain could see what these photos proved.

The NASA meteorite is a fake!

No day in Sexton's career had been filled with such extreme highs and lows. Today had been a roller-coaster ride of hope and despair. Sexton's bafflement over how this enormous scam could possibly have been pulled off evaporated into irrelevance when he realized what the scam meant for him politically.

When I go public with this information, the presidency is mine!

In his upwelling of celebration, Senator Sedgewick Sexton had momentarily forgotten his daughter's claim that she was in trouble.

'Rachel is in danger,' Gabrielle said. 'Her note says NASA and the White House are trying to—'

Sexton's fax machine suddenly began ringing again. Gabrielle wheeled and stared at the machine. Sexton found himself staring too. He could not imagine what else Rachel could be sending him. More proof? How much more could there be? *This is plenty!*

When the fax machine answered the call, however, no pages came through. The machine, detecting no data signal, had switched to its answering machine feature.

'Hello,' Sexton's outbound message crackled. 'This is the office of Senator Sedgewick Sexton. If you are trying to send a fax, you may transmit at anytime. If not, you may leave a message at the tone.'

Before Sexton could pick up, the machine beeped.

'Senator Sexton?' The man's voice had a lucid rawness to it. 'This is William Pickering, director of the National Reconnaissance Office. You're probably not in the office at this hour, but I need to speak immediately.' He paused as if waiting for someone to pick up.

Gabrielle reached to pick up the receiver.

Sexton grabbed her hand and violently yanked it away.

Gabrielle looked stunned. 'But that's the director of—'

'Senator,' Pickering continued, sounding almost relieved that no one had picked up. 'I'm afraid I am calling with some very troubling news. I've just received word that your daughter Rachel is in extreme danger. I have a team trying to help her as we speak. I cannot talk in detail about the situation on the phone, but I was just informed she may have faxed you some data relating to the NASA meteorite. I have not seen the data, nor do I know what it is, but the people threatening your daughter have just warned me that if you or anyone goes public with the information, your daughter will die. I'm sorry to be so blunt, sir; I do it for clarity's sake. Your daughter's life is being threatened. If she has indeed faxed you something, do *not* share it with anyone. Not yet. Your daughter's life depends on it. Stay where you are. I will be there shortly.' He paused. 'With luck, Senator, all of this will be resolved by the time you wake up. If, by chance, you get this message before I arrive at your office, stay where you are and call no one. I am doing everything in my power to get your daughter back safely.'

Pickering hung up.

Gabrielle was trembling. 'Rachel is a hostage?'

Sexton sensed that even in her disillusionment with him, Gabrielle felt a pained empathy to think of a bright young woman in danger. Oddly, Sexton was having trouble mustering the same emotions. Most of him felt like a child who had just been given his most wanted Christmas present, and he refused to let anyone yank it out of his hands.

Pickering wants me to be quiet about this?

He stood a moment, trying to decide what all of this meant. In a cold, calculating side of his mind, Sexton felt the machinery beginning to turn – a political computer, playing out every scenario and evaluating each outcome. He glanced at the stack of faxes in his hands and began to sense the raw power of the images. This NASA meteorite had shattered his dream of the presidency. But it was all a lie. A construct. Now, those who did this would pay. The meteorite that his enemies had created to destroy him would now make him powerful beyond anyone's wildest imagination. His daughter had seen to that.

There is only one acceptable outcome, he knew. *Only one course of action for a true leader to take.*

Feeling hypnotized by the shining images of his own resurrection,

Sexton was drifting through a fog as he crossed the room. He went to his copy machine and turned it on, preparing to copy the papers Rachel had faxed him.

'What are you doing?' Gabrielle demanded, sounding bewildered.

'They won't kill Rachel,' Sexton declared. Even if something went wrong, Sexton knew losing his daughter to the enemy would only make him more powerful still. Either way he would win. Acceptable risk.

'Who are those copies for?' Gabrielle demanded. 'William Pickering said not to tell anyone!'

Sexton turned from the machine and looked at Gabrielle, amazed by how unattractive he suddenly found her. In that instant, Senator Sexton was an island. Untouchable. Everything he needed to accomplish his dreams was now in his hands. Nothing could stop him now. Not claims of bribery. Not rumors of sex. Nothing.

'Go home, Gabrielle. I have no more use for you.'

CHAPTER 125

It's over, Rachel thought.

She and Tolland sat side by side on the deck staring up into the barrel of the Delta soldier's machine gun. Unfortunately, Pickering now knew where Rachel had sent the fax. The office of Senator Sedgewick Sexton.

Rachel doubted her father would ever receive the phone message Pickering had just left him. Pickering could probably get to Sexton's office well before anyone else this morning. If Pickering could get in, quietly remove the fax, and delete the phone message before Sexton arrived, there would be no need to harm the senator. William Pickering was probably one of the few people in Washington who could finagle entry to a U.S. senator's office with no fanfare. Rachel was always amazed at what could be accomplished 'in the name of national security.'

Of course if that fails, Rachel thought, *Pickering could just fly by and send a Hellfire missile through the window and blow up the fax machine.* Something told her this would not be necessary.

Sitting close to Tolland now, Rachel was surprised to feel his hand gently slip into hers. His touch had a tender strength, and their fingers intertwined so naturally that Rachel felt like they'd done this for a lifetime. All she wanted right now was to lie in his arms, sheltered from the oppressive roar of the night sea spiraling around them.

Never, she realized. *It was not to be.*

Michael Tolland felt like a man who had found hope on the way to the gallows.

Life is mocking me.

For years since Celia's death, Tolland had endured nights when he'd wanted to die, hours of pain and loneliness that seemed only escapable by ending it all. And yet he had chosen life, telling himself he could make it alone. Today, for the first time, Tolland had begun to understand what his friends had been telling him all along.

Mike, you don't have to make it alone. You'll find another love.

Rachel's hand in his made this irony that much harder to swallow. Fate had cruel timing. He felt as if layers of armor were crumbling away from his heart. For an instant, on the tired decks of the *Goya*, Tolland sensed Celia's ghost looking over him as she often did. Her voice was in the rushing water . . . speaking the last words she'd spoken to him in life.

'You're a survivor,' her voice whispered. 'Promise me you'll find another love.'

'I'll never want another,' Tolland had told her.

Celia's smile was filled with wisdom. 'You'll have to learn.'

Now, on the deck of the *Goya*, Tolland realized, he was learning. A deep emotion welled suddenly in his soul. He realized it was happiness.

And with it came an overpowering will to live.

Pickering felt oddly detached as he moved toward the two prisoners. He stopped in front of Rachel, vaguely surprised that this was not harder for him.

'Sometimes,' he said, 'circumstances raise impossible decisions.'

Rachel's eyes were unyielding. 'You created these circumstances.'

'War involves casualties,' Pickering said, his voice firmer now. *Ask Diana Pickering, or any of those who die every year defending this nation.* 'You of all people should understand that, Rachel.' His eyes focused in on her. '*Iactura paucorum serva multos.*'

He could see she recognized the words – almost a cliché in national security circles. *Sacrifice the few to save the many.*

Rachel eyed him with obvious disgust. 'And now Michael and I have become part of your *few?*'

Pickering considered it. There was no other way. He turned to Delta-One. 'Release your partner and end this.'

Delta-One nodded.

Pickering took a long look at Rachel and then strode to the ship's nearby portside railing, staring out at the sea racing by. This was something he preferred not to watch.

Delta-One felt empowered as he gripped his weapon and glanced over at his partner dangling in the clamps. All that remained was to close the trapdoors beneath Delta-Two's feet, free him from the clamps, and eliminate Rachel Sexton and Michael Tolland.

Unfortunately, Delta-One had seen the complexity of the control panel near the trapdoor – a series of unmarked levers and dials that apparently controlled the trapdoor, the winch motor, and numerous other commands. He had no intention of hitting the wrong lever and risking his partner's life by mistakenly dropping the sub into the sea.

Eliminate all risk. Never rush.

He would force Tolland to perform the actual release. And to ensure he did not try anything tricky, Delta-One would take out insurance known in his business as 'biological collateral.'

Use your adversaries against one another.

Delta-One swung the gun barrel directly into Rachel's face, stopping only inches from her forehead. Rachel closed her eyes, and Delta-One could see Tolland's fists clench in a protective anger.

'Ms Sexton, stand up,' Delta-One said.

She did.

With the gun firmly on her back, Delta-One marched her over to an aluminum set of portable stairs that led up to the top of the Triton sub from behind. 'Climb up and stand on top of the sub.'

Rachel looked frightened and confused.

'Just do it,' Delta-One said.

Rachel felt like she was moving through a nightmare as she climbed up the aluminum gangway behind the Triton. She stopped at the top, having no desire to step out over the chasm onto the suspended Triton.

'Get on top of the sub,' the soldier said, returning to Tolland and pushing the gun against his head.

In front of Rachel the soldier who was in the clamps watched her, shifting in pain, obviously eager to get out. Rachel looked at Tolland, who now had a gun barrel to his head. *Get on top of the sub*. She had no choice.

Feeling like she was edging out onto a precipice overhanging a canyon, Rachel stepped onto the Triton's engine casing, a small flat section behind the rounded dome window. The entire sub hung like a massive plumb bob over the open trapdoor. Even suspended on its winch cable, the nine-ton sub barely registered her arrival, swinging only a few millimeters as she steadied herself.

'Okay, let's move,' the soldier said to Tolland. 'Go to the controls and close the trapdoor.'

At gunpoint, Tolland began moving toward the control panel with the soldier behind him. As Tolland came toward her, he was moving slowly, and Rachel could feel his eyes fixing hard on her as if trying to send her a message. He looked directly at her and then down at the open hatch on top of the Triton.

Rachel glanced down. The hatch at her feet was open, the heavy circular covering propped open. She could see down into the one-seater cockpit. *He wants me to get in?* Sensing she must be mistaken, Rachel looked at Tolland again. He was almost to the control panel. Tolland's eyes locked on her. This time he was less subtle.

His lips mouthed, 'Jump in! Now!'

Delta-One saw Rachel's motion out of the corner of his eye and wheeled on instinct, opening fire as Rachel fell through the sub's hatch just below the barrage of bullets. The open hatch covering rang out as the bullets ricocheted off the circular portal, sending up a shower of sparks, and slamming the lid closed on top of her.

Tolland, the instant he'd felt the gun leave his back, made his move. He dove to his left, away from the trapdoor, hitting the deck and rolling just as the soldier spun back toward him, gun blazing. Bullets exploded behind Tolland as he scrambled for cover behind the ship's stern anchor spool – an enormous motorized cylinder around which was wound several thousand feet of steel cable connected to the ship's anchor.

Tolland had a plan and would have to act fast. As the soldier dashed toward him, Tolland reached up and grabbed the anchor lock with both hands, yanking down. Instantly the anchor spool began feeding out lengths of cable, and the *Goya* lurched in the strong current. The sudden movement sent everything and everyone on the deck staggering sidelong. As the boat accelerated in reverse on the current, the anchor spool doled out cable faster and faster.

Come on, baby, Tolland urged.

The soldier regained his balance and came for Tolland. Waiting until the last possible moment, Tolland braced himself and rammed the lever back up, locking the anchor spool. The chain snapped taut, stopping the ship short and sending a tremulous shudder throughout the *Goya*. Everything on deck went flying. The soldier staggered to his knees near Tolland. Pickering fell back from the railing onto the deck. The Triton swung wildly on its cable.

A grating howl of failing metal tore up from beneath the ship like an earthquake as the damaged strut finally gave way. The right stern corner of the *Goya* began collapsing under its own weight. The ship faltered, tilting on a diagonal like a massive table losing one of its four legs. The noise from beneath was deafening – a wail of twisting, grating metal and pounding surf.

White-knuckled inside the Triton cockpit, Rachel held on as the nine-ton machine swayed over the trapdoor in the now steeply inclined deck. Through the base of the glass dome she could see the ocean raging below. As she looked up, her eyes scanning the deck for Tolland, she watched a bizarre drama on the deck unfold in a matter of seconds.

Only a yard away, trapped in the Triton's claws, the clamped Delta soldier was howling in pain as he bobbed like a puppet on a stick. William Pickering scrambled across Rachel's field of vision and grabbed on to a cleat on the deck. Near the anchor lever, Tolland was also hanging on, trying not to slide over the edge into the water. When Rachel saw the soldier with the machine gun stabilizing himself nearby, she called out inside the sub, 'Mike, look out!'

But Delta-One ignored Tolland entirely. The soldier was looking back toward the idling helicopter with his mouth open in horror. Rachel turned, following his gaze. The Kiowa gunship, with its huge rotors still turning, had started to slowly slide forward down the tipping deck. Its long metal skids were acting like skis on a slope. It was then that Rachel realized the huge machine was skidding directly toward the Triton.

Scrambling up the inclined deck toward the sliding aircraft, Delta-One clambered into the cockpit. He had no intention of letting their only means of escape slide off the deck. Delta-One seized the Kiowa's controls and heaved back on the stick. *Lift off!* With a deafening roar, the blades accelerated overhead, straining to lift the heavily armed gunship off the deck. *Up, goddamn it!* The chopper was sliding directly toward the Triton and Delta-Two suspended in its grasp.

With its nose tipped forward, the Kiowa's blades were also tipped, and when the chopper lurched off the deck, it sailed more forward than up, accelerating toward the Triton like a giant buzz saw. *Up!* Delta-One pulled the stick, wishing he could drop the half ton of Hellfire warheads weighing him down. The blades just missed the top of Delta-Two's head and the top of the Triton sub, but the chopper was moving too fast. It would never clear the Triton's winch cable.

As the Kiowa's 300-rpm steel blades collided with the sub's 15-ton capacity braided-steel winch cable, the night erupted with the shriek of metal on metal. The sounds conjured images of epic battle. From the chopper's armored cockpit, Delta-One watched his rotors tear into the sub's cable like a giant lawnmower running over a steel chain. A blinding spray of sparks erupted overhead, and the Kiowa's blades exploded. Delta-One felt the chopper bottom out, its struts hitting the deck hard. He tried to control the aircraft, but he had no lift. The chopper bounded twice down the inclined deck, then slid, crashing into the ship's guardrail.

For a moment, he thought the rail would hold.

Then Delta-One heard the crack. The heavily laden chopper listed over the brink, plummeting into the sea.

Inside the Triton, Rachel Sexton sat paralyzed, her body pressed back into the sub's seat. The minisub had been tossed violently as the chopper's rotor wrapped around the cable, but she had managed to hang on. Somehow the blades had missed the main body of the sub, but she knew there had to be major damage to the cable. All Rachel could think of at that point was escaping from the sub as fast as she could. The soldier trapped in the clamps stared in at her, delirious, bleeding, and burned from the shrapnel. Beyond him, Rachel saw William Pickering still holding on to a cleat on the slanting deck.

Where's Michael? She didn't see him. Her panic lasted only an instant as a new fear descended. Overhead, the Triton's shredded winch cable let out an ominous whipping noise as the braids unraveled. Then, there was a loud snap, and Rachel felt the cable give way.

Momentarily weightless, Rachel hovered above her seat inside the cockpit as the sub hurtled downward. The deck disappeared overhead, and the catwalks under the *Goya* raced by. The soldier trapped in the claws went white with fear, staring at Rachel as the sub accelerated downward.

The fall seemed endless.

When the sub crashed into the sea beneath the *Goya*, it plunged hard under the surf, ramming Rachel down hard into her seat. Her spine compressed as the illuminated ocean raced up over the dome. She felt a suffocating drag as the sub slowed to a stop underwater and then raced back toward the surface, bobbing up like a cork.

The sharks hit instantly. From her front-row seat, Rachel sat frozen in place as the spectacle unfolded only a few feet away.

Delta-Two felt the shark's oblong head crash into him with unimaginable force. A razor sharp clamp tightened on his upper arm, slicing to the bone and locking on. A flash of white-hot pain exploded as the shark torqued its powerful body and shook its head violently, tearing Delta-Two's arm off his body. Other sharks moved in. Knives stabbing at his legs. Torso. Neck. Delta-Two had no breath to scream in agony as the sharks ripped huge chunks of his body away. The last thing he saw was a crescent-shaped mouth, tilting sideways, a gorge of teeth clamping down across his face.

The world went black.

Inside the Triton, the thudding of heavy cartilaginous heads ramming into the dome finally subsided. Rachel opened her eyes. The man was gone. The water washing against the window was crimson.

Badly battered, Rachel huddled in her chair, knees pulled to her chest. She could feel the sub moving. It was drifting on the current, scraping along the length of the *Goya*'s lower dive deck. She could feel it moving in another direction as well. Down.

Outside, the distinctive gurgling of water into the ballast tanks grew louder. The ocean inched higher on the glass in front of her.

I'm sinking!

A jolt of terror shot through Rachel, and she was suddenly scrambling to her feet. Reaching overhead, she grabbed the hatch mechanism. If she could climb up on top of the sub, she still had time to jump onto the *Goya*'s dive deck. It was only a few feet away.

I've got to get out!

The hatch mechanism was clearly marked which way to turn it to open. She heaved. The hatch did not budge. She tried again. Nothing. The portal was jammed shut. Bent. As the fear rose in her blood like the sea around her, Rachel heaved one last time.

The hatch did not move.

The Triton sank a few inches deeper, bumping the *Goya* one last time before drifting out from underneath the mangled hull . . . and into the open sea.

CHAPTER **126**

'**Don't do** this,' Gabrielle begged the senator as he finished at the copy machine. 'You're risking your daughter's life!'

Sexton blocked out her voice, moving back to his desk now with ten identical stacks of photocopies. Each stack contained copies of the pages Rachel had faxed him, including her handwritten note claiming the meteorite was a fake and accusing NASA and the White House of trying to kill her.

The most shocking media kits ever assembled, Sexton thought, as he began carefully inserting each stack into its own large, white linen envelope. Each envelope bore his name, office address, and senatorial seal. There would be no doubt where this incredible information had originated. *The political scandal of the century*, Sexton thought, *and I will be the one to reveal it!*

Gabrielle was still pleading for Rachel's safety, but Sexton heard only silence. As he assembled the envelopes, he was in his own private world. *Every political career has a defining moment. This is mine.*

William Pickering's phone message had warned that if Sexton went public, Rachel's life would be in danger. Unfortunately for Rachel, Sexton also knew if he went public with proof of NASA's fraud, that single act of boldness would land him in the White House with more decisiveness and political drama than ever before witnessed in American politics.

Life is filled with difficult decisions, he thought. *And winners are those who make them.*

Gabrielle Ashe had seen this look in Sexton's eyes before. *Blind ambition.* She feared it. And with good reason, she now realized. Sexton was obviously prepared to risk his daughter in order to be the first to announce the NASA fraud.

'Don't you see you've already won?' Gabrielle demanded. 'There's no way Zach Herney and NASA will survive this scandal. No matter *who* makes it public! No matter when it comes out! Wait until you know Rachel is safe. Wait until you talk to Pickering!'

Sexton was clearly no longer listening to her. Opening his desk drawer, he pulled out a foil sheet on which were affixed dozens of nickel-sized, self-adhesive wax seals with his initials on them. Gabrielle knew he usually used these for formal invitations, but he apparently thought a crimson wax seal would give each envelope an extra touch of drama. Peeling the circular seals off the foil, Sexton pressed one onto the pleat of each envelope, sealing it like a mono-grammed epistle.

Gabrielle's heart pulsed now with a new anger. She thought of the digitized images of illegal checks in his computer. If she said anything, she knew he would just delete the evidence. 'Don't do this,' she said, 'or I'll go public about our affair.'

Sexton laughed out loud as he affixed the wax seals. 'Really? And you think they'll believe you – a power-hungry aide denied a post in my administration and looking for revenge at any cost? I denied our involvement once, and the world believed me. I'll simply deny it again.'

'The White House has photos,' Gabrielle declared.

Sexton did not even look up. 'They don't have photos. And even if they did, they're meaningless.' He affixed the final wax seal. 'I have immunity. These envelopes out-trump anything anyone could possibly throw at me.'

Gabrielle knew he was right. She felt utterly helpless as Sexton admired his handiwork. On his desk sat ten elegant, white linen envelopes, each embossed with his name and address and secured with a crimson wax seal bearing his scripted initials. They looked like royal letters. Certainly kings had been crowned on account of less potent information.

Sexton picked up the envelopes and prepared to leave. Gabrielle stepped over and blocked his way. 'You're making a mistake. This can wait.'

Sexton's eyes bore into her. 'I made you, Gabrielle, and now I've unmade you.'

'That fax from Rachel will give you the presidency. You owe her.'

'I've given her plenty.'

'What if something happens to her?'

'Then she'll cement my sympathy vote.'

Gabrielle could not believe the thought had even crossed his mind, much less his lips. Disgusted, she reached for the phone. 'I'm calling the White—'

Sexton spun and slapped her hard across the face.

Gabrielle staggered back, feeling her lip split open. She caught herself, grabbing on to the desk, staring up in astonishment at the man she had once worshipped.

Sexton gave her a long, hard look. 'If you so much as think of crossing me on this, I will make you regret it for the rest of your life.' He stood unflinching, clutching the stack of sealed envelopes under his arm. A harsh danger burned in his eyes.

When Gabrielle exited the office building into the cold night air, her lip was still bleeding. She hailed a taxi and climbed in. Then, for the first time since she had come to Washington, Gabrielle Ashe broke down and cried.

CHAPTER 127

The Triton fell . . .

Michael Tolland staggered to his feet on the inclined deck and peered over the anchor spool at the frayed winch cable where the Triton used to hang. Wheeling toward the stern, he scanned the water. The Triton was just now emerging from under the *Goya* on the current. Relieved at least to see the sub intact, Tolland eyed the hatch, wanting nothing more than to see it open up and Rachel climb out unscathed. But the hatch remained closed. Tolland wondered if maybe she had been knocked out by the violent fall.

Even from the deck, Tolland could see the Triton was riding exceptionally low in the water – far below its normal diving trim waterline. *It's sinking.* Tolland could not imagine why, but the reason at the moment was immaterial.

I have to get Rachel out. Now.

As Tolland stood to dash for the edge of the deck, a shower of machine-gun fire exploded above him, sparking off the heavy anchor spool overhead. He dropped back to his knees. *Shit!* He peered around the spool only long enough to see Pickering on the upper deck, taking aim like a sniper. The Delta soldier had dropped his machine gun while climbing into the doomed helicopter and Pickering had apparently recovered it. Now the director had scrambled to the high ground.

Trapped behind the spool, Tolland looked back toward the sinking Triton. *Come on, Rachel! Get out!* He waited for the hatch to open. Nothing.

Looking back to the deck of the *Goya*, Tolland's eyes measured the open area between his position and the stern railing. Twenty feet. A long way without any cover.

Tolland took a deep breath and made up his mind. Ripping off his shirt, he hurled it to his right onto the open deck. While Pickering blew the shirt full of holes, Tolland dashed left, down the inclined deck, banking toward the stern. With a wild leap he launched himself over the railing, off the back of the ship. Arcing high in the air, Tolland heard the bullets whizzing all around him and knew a single graze would make him a shark feast the instant he hit the water.

Rachel Sexton felt like a wild animal trapped in a cage. She had tried the hatch again and again with no luck. She could hear a tank somewhere beneath her filling with water, and she sensed the sub gaining weight. The darkness of the ocean was inching higher up the transparent dome, a black curtain rising in reverse.

Through the lower half of the glass, Rachel could see the void of the ocean beckoning like a tomb. The empty vastness beneath threatened to swallow her whole. She grabbed the hatch mechanism and tried to twist it open one more time, but it wouldn't budge. Her lungs strained now, the dank stench of excess carbon dioxide acrid in her nostrils. Through it all, one recurring thought haunted her.

I'm going to die alone underwater.

She scanned the Triton's control panels and levers for something that could help, but all the indicators were black. No power. She was locked in a dead steel crypt sinking toward the bottom of the sea.

The gurgling in the tanks seemed to be accelerating now, and the ocean rose to within a few feet of the top of the glass. In the distance, across the endless flat expanse, a band of crimson was inching across the horizon. Morning was on its way. Rachel feared it would be the last light she ever saw. Closing her eyes to block out her impending fate, Rachel felt the terrifying childhood images rushing into her mind.

Falling through the ice. Sliding underwater.

Breathless. Unable to lift herself. Sinking.

Her mother calling for her. 'Rachel! Rachel!'

A pounding on the outside of the sub jolted Rachel out of the delirium. Her eyes snapped open.

'Rachel!' The voice was muffled. A ghostly face appeared against the glass, upside down, dark hair swirling. She could barely make him out in the darkness.

'Michael!'

Tolland surfaced, exhaling in relief to see Rachel moving inside the sub. *She's alive.* Tolland swam with powerful strokes to the rear of the Triton and climbed up onto the submerged engine platform. The ocean currents felt hot and leaden around him as he positioned himself to grab the circular portal screw, staying low and hoping he was out of range of Pickering's gun.

The Triton's hull was almost entirely underwater now, and Tolland knew if he were going to open the hatch and pull Rachel out, he would have to hurry. He had a ten-inch draw that was diminishing fast. Once the hatch was submerged, opening it would send a torrent of seawater gushing into the Triton, trapping Rachel inside and sending the sub into a free fall to the bottom.

'Now or never,' he gasped as he grabbed the hatch wheel and heaved it counterclockwise. Nothing happened. He tried again, throwing all of his force into it. Again, the hatch refused to turn.

He could hear Rachel inside, on the other side of the portal. Her voice was stifled, but he sensed her terror. 'I tried!' she shouted. 'I couldn't turn it!'

The water was lapping across the portal lid now. 'Turn together!' he shouted to her. 'You're *clockwise* in there!' He knew the dial was clearly marked. 'Okay, now!'

Tolland braced himself against the ballast air tanks and strained with all his energy. He could hear Rachel below him doing the same. The dial turned a half inch and ground to a dead stop.

Now Tolland saw it. The portal lid was not set evenly in the aperture. Like the lid of a jar that had been placed on crooked and screwed down hard, it was stuck. Although the rubber seal was properly set, the hatchdogs were bent, meaning the only way that door was opening was with a welding torch.

As the top of the sub sank below the surface, Tolland was filled with a sudden, overwhelming dread. Rachel Sexton would not be escaping from the Triton.

Two thousand feet below, the crumpled fuselage of the bomb-laden Kiowa chopper was sinking fast, a prisoner of gravity and the powerful drag of the deepwater vortex. Inside the cockpit, Delta-One's lifeless body was no longer recognizable, disfigured by the crushing pressure of the deep.

As the aircraft spiraled downward, its Hellfire missiles still attached, the glowing magma dome waited on the ocean floor like a red-hot landing pad. Beneath its three-meter-thick crust, a head of boiling lava simmered at 1,000 degrees centigrade, a volcano waiting to explode.

CHAPTER 128

Tolland stood knee-deep in water on the engine box of the sinking Triton and searched his brain for some way to save Rachel.

Don't let the sub sink!

He looked back toward the *Goya*, wondering if there were any way to get a winch connected to the Triton to keep it near the surface. Impossible. It was fifty yards away now, and Pickering was standing high on the bridge like a Roman emperor with a prime seat to some bloody Coliseum spectacle.

Think! Tolland told himself. *Why is the sub sinking?*

The mechanics of sub buoyancy were painfully simple: ballast tanks pumped full of either air or water adjusted the sub's buoyancy to move it up or down in the water.

Obviously, the ballast tanks were filling up.

But they shouldn't be!

Every sub's ballast tanks were equipped with holes both topside and underneath. The lower openings, called 'flooding holes,' always remained open, while the holes on top, 'vent valves,' could be opened and closed to let air escape so water would flood in.

Maybe the Triton's vent valves were open for some reason? Tolland could not imagine why. He floundered across the submerged engine platform, his hands groping one of the Triton's ballast trim tanks. The vent valves were closed. But as he felt the valves, his fingers found something else.

Bullet holes.

Shit! The Triton had been riddled with bullets when Rachel jumped in. Tolland immediately dove down and swam beneath the sub, running his hand carefully across the Triton's more important ballast tank – the negative tank. The Brits called this tank 'the down express.' The Germans called it 'putting on lead shoes.' Either way, the meaning was clear. The negative tank, when filled, took the sub *down*.

As Tolland's hand felt the sides of the tank, he encountered dozens of bullet holes. He could feel the water rushing in. The Triton was preparing to dive, whether Tolland liked it or not.

The sub was now three feet beneath the surface. Moving to the bow, Tolland pressed his face against the glass and peered through the dome. Rachel was banging on the glass and shouting. The fear in her voice made him feel powerless. For an instant he was back in a cold hospital, watching the woman he loved die and knowing there was nothing he could do. Hovering underwater in front of the sinking sub, Tolland told himself he could not endure this again. *You're a survivor*, Celia had told him, but Tolland did not want to survive alone . . . not again.

Tolland's lungs ached for air and yet he stayed right there with her.

Every time Rachel pounded on the glass, Tolland heard air bubbles
gurgling up and the sub sank deeper. Rachel was yelling something
about water coming in around the window.

The viewing window was leaking.

A bullet hole in the window? It seemed doubtful. His lungs ready to
burst, Tolland prepared to surface. As he palmed upward across the
huge acrylic window, his fingers hit a piece of loose rubber caulking.
A peripheral seal had apparently been jarred in the fall. This was the
reason the cockpit was leaking. *More bad news.*

Clambering to the surface, Tolland sucked in three deep breaths,
trying to clear his thoughts. Water flowing into the cockpit would
only accelerate the Triton's descent. The sub was already five feet
underwater, and Tolland could barely touch it with his feet. He could
feel Rachel pounding desperately on the hull.

Tolland could think of only one thing to do. If he dove down to the
Triton's engine box and located the high-pressure air cylinder, he
could use it to blow the negative ballast tank. Although blowing
the damaged tank would be an exercise in futility, it might keep the
Triton near the surface for another minute or so before the perforated
tanks flooded again.

Then what?

With no other immediate option, Tolland prepared to dive. Pulling
in an exceptionally deep breath, he expanded his lungs well beyond
their natural state, almost to the point of pain. *More lung capacity.
More oxygen. Longer dive.* But as he felt his lungs expand, pressuring
his rib cage, a strange thought hit him.

What if he increased the pressure *inside* the sub? The viewing dome
had a damaged seal. Maybe if Tolland could increase the pressure
inside the cockpit, he could blow the entire viewing dome off the sub
and get Rachel out.

He exhaled his breath, treading water on the surface a moment,
trying to picture the feasibility. It was perfectly logical, wasn't it?
After all, a submarine was built to be strong in only *one* direction.
They had to withstand enormous pressure from the outside, but
almost none from within.

Moreover, the Triton used uniform regulator valves to decrease the
number of spare parts the *Goya* had to carry. Tolland could simply

unsnap the high-pressure cylinder's charging hose and reroute it into an emergency ventilation supply regulator on the port side of the sub! Pressurizing the cabin would cause Rachel substantial physical pain, but it might just give her a way out.

Tolland inhaled and dove.

The sub was a good eight feet down now, and the currents and darkness made orienting himself difficult. Once he found the pressurized tank, Tolland quickly rerouted the hose and prepared to pump air into the cockpit. As he gripped the stopcock, the reflective yellow paint on the side of the tank reminded him just how dangerous this maneuver was: CAUTION: COMPRESSED AIR – 3,000 PSI.

Three thousand pounds per square inch, Tolland thought. The hope was that the Triton's viewing dome would pop off the sub before the pressure in the cabin crushed Rachel's lungs. Tolland was essentially sticking a high-powered fire hose into a water balloon and praying the balloon would break in a hurry.

He grabbed the stopcock and made up his mind. Suspended there on the back of the sinking Triton, Tolland turned the stopcock, opening the valve. The hose went rigid immediately, and Tolland could hear the air flooding the cockpit with enormous force.

Inside the Triton, Rachel felt a sudden searing pain slice into her head. She opened her mouth to scream, but the air forced itself into her lungs with such painful pressure that she thought her chest would explode. Her eyes felt like they were being rammed backward into her skull. A deafening rumble tore through her eardrums, pushing her toward unconsciousness. Instinctively, she clenched her eyes tight and pressed her hands over her ears. The pain was increasing now.

Rachel heard a pounding directly in front of her. She forced her eyes open just long enough to see the watery silhouette of Michael Tolland in the darkness. His face was against the glass. He was motioning for her to do something.

But what?

She could barely see him in the darkness. Her vision was blurred, her eyeballs distorted from the pressure. Even so, she could tell the sub had sunk beyond the last flickering fingers of the *Goya*'s underwater lights. Around her was only an endless inky abyss.

*   *   *

Tolland spread himself against the window of the Triton and kept banging. His chest burned for air, and he knew he would have to return to the surface in a matter of seconds.

Push on the glass! he willed her. He could hear pressurized air escaping around the glass, bubbling up. Somewhere, the seal was loose. Tolland's hands groped for an edge, something to get his fingers under. Nothing.

As his oxygen ran out, tunnel vision closed in, and he banged on the glass one last time. He could not even see her anymore. It was too dark. With the last of the air in his lungs, he yelled out underwater.

'*Rachel . . . push . . . on . . . the . . . glass!*'

His words came out as a bubbling, muted garble.

CHAPTER 129

Inside the Triton, Rachel's head felt like it was being compressed in some kind of medieval torture vise. Half-standing, stooped beside the cockpit chair, she could feel death closing in around her. Directly in front of her, the hemispherical viewing dome was empty. Dark. The banging had stopped.

Tolland was gone. He had left her.

The hiss of pressurized air blasting in overhead reminded her of the deafening katabatic wind on Milne. The floor of the sub had a foot of water on it now. *Let me out!* Thousands of thoughts and memories began streaming through her mind like flashes of violet light.

In the darkness, the sub began to list, and Rachel staggered, losing her balance. Stumbling over the seat, she fell forward, colliding hard with the inside of the hemispherical dome. A sharp pain erupted in her shoulder. She landed in a heap against the window, and as she did, she felt an unexpected sensation – a sudden decrease in the pressure inside the sub. The tightened drum of Rachel's ears loosened perceptibly, and she actually heard a gurgle of air escape the sub.

It took her an instant to realize what had just happened. When she'd fallen against the dome, her weight had somehow forced the bulbous sheet outward enough for some of the internal pressure to be released around a seal. Obviously, the dome glass was loose! Rachel suddenly realized what Tolland had been trying to do by increasing the pressure inside.

He's trying to blow out the window!

Overhead, the Triton's pressure cylinder continued to pump. Even as she lay there, she felt the pressure increasing again. This time she almost welcomed it, although she felt the suffocating grip pushing her dangerously close to unconsciousness. Scrambling to her feet, Rachel pressed outward with all her force on the inside of the glass.

This time, there was no gurgle. The glass barely moved.

She threw her weight against the window again. Nothing. Her shoulder wound ached, and she looked down at it. The blood was dry. She prepared to try again, but she did not have time. Without warning, the crippled sub began to tip – backward. As its heavy engine box overcame the flooded trim tanks, the Triton rolled onto its back, sinking rear-first now.

Rachel fell onto her back against the cockpit's rear wall. Half submerged in sloshing water, she stared straight up at the leaking dome, hovering over her like a giant skylight.

Outside was only night . . . and thousands of tons of ocean pressing down.

Rachel willed herself to get up, but her body felt dead and heavy. Again her mind reeled backward in time to the icy grip of a frozen river.

'Fight, Rachel!' her mother was shouting, reaching down to pull her out of the water. 'Grab on!'

Rachel closed her eyes. *I'm sinking.* Her skates felt like lead weights, dragging her down. She could see her mother lying spread-eagle on the ice to disperse her own weight, reaching out.

'*Kick*, Rachel! Kick with your feet!'

Rachel kicked as best as she could. Her body rose slightly in the icy hole. A spark of hope. Her mother grabbed on.

'Yes!' her mother shouted. 'Help me lift you! Kick with your feet!'

With her mother pulling from above, Rachel used the last of her energy to kick with her skates. It was just enough, and her mother dragged Rachel up to safety. She dragged the soaking Rachel all the way to the snowy bank before collapsing in tears.

Now, inside the growing humidity and heat of the sub, Rachel opened her eyes to the blackness around her. She heard her mother whispering from the grave, her voice clear even here in the sinking Triton.

Kick with your feet.

Rachel looked up at the dome overhead. Mustering the last of her courage, Rachel clambered up onto the cockpit chair, which was oriented almost horizontally now, like a dental chair. Lying on her back, Rachel bent her knees, pulled her legs back as far as she could, aimed her feet upward, and exploded forward. With a wild scream of desperation and force, she drove her feet into the center of the acrylic dome. Spikes of pain shot into her shins, sending her brain reeling. Her ears thundered suddenly, and she felt the pressure equalize with a violent rush. The seal on the left side of the dome gave way, and the huge lens partially dislodged, swinging open like a barn door.

A torrent of water crashed into the sub and drove Rachel back into her chair. The ocean thundered in around her, swirling up under her back, lifting her now off the chair, tossing her upside down like a sock in a washing machine. Rachel groped blindly for something to hold on to, but she was spinning wildly. As the cockpit filled, she could feel the sub begin a rapid free fall to the bottom. Her body rammed upward in the cockpit, and she felt herself pinned. A rush of bubbles erupted around her, twisting her, dragging her to the left and upward. A flap of hard acrylic smashed into her hip.

All at once she was free.

Twisting and tumbling into the endless warmth and watery blackness, Rachel felt her lungs already aching for air. *Get to the surface!* She looked for light but saw nothing. Her world looked the same in all directions. Blackness. No gravity. No sense of up or down.

In that terrifying instant, Rachel realized she had no idea which way to swim.

*   *   *

Thousands of feet beneath her, the sinking Kiowa chopper crumpled beneath the relentlessly increasing pressure. The fifteen high-explosive, antitank AGM-114 Hellfire missiles still aboard strained against the compression, their copper liner cones and spring-detonation heads inching perilously inward.

A hundred feet above the ocean floor, the powerful shaft of the megaplume grabbed the remains of the chopper and sucked it downward, hurling it against the red-hot crust of the magma dome. Like a box of matches igniting in series, the Hellfire missiles exploded, tearing a gaping hole through the top of the magma dome.

Having surfaced for air, and then dove again in desperation, Michael Tolland was suspended fifteen feet underwater scanning the blackness when the Hellfire missiles exploded. The white flash billowed upward, illuminating an astonishing image – a freeze-frame he would remember forever.

Rachel Sexton hung ten feet below him like a tangled marionette in the water. Beneath her, the Triton sub fell away fast, its dome hanging loose. The sharks in the area scattered for the open sea, clearly sensing the danger this area was about to unleash.

Tolland's exhilaration at seeing Rachel out of the sub was instantly vanquished by the realization of what was about to follow. Memorizing her position as the light disappeared, Tolland dove hard, clawing his way toward her.

Thousands of feet down, the shattered crust of the magma dome exploded apart, and the underwater volcano erupted, spewing 1,200-degree-Celsius magma up into the sea. The scorching lava vaporized all the water it touched, sending a massive pillar of steam rocketing toward the surface up the central axis of the megaplume. Driven by the same kinematic properties of fluid dynamics that powered tornadoes, the steam's vertical transfer of energy was counterbalanced by an anticyclonic vorticity spiral that circled the shaft, carrying energy in the opposite direction.

Spiraling around this column of rising gas, the ocean currents started intensifying, twisting downward. The fleeing steam created an enormous vacuum that sucked millions of gallons of seawater downward into contact with the magma. As the new water hit bottom, it too turned into steam and needed a way to escape, joining the growing column of exhaust steam and shooting upward, pulling more water in beneath it. As more water rushed in to take its place, the vortex intensified. The hydrothermal plume elongated, and the towering whirlpool grew stronger with every passing second, its upper rim moving steadily toward the surface.

An oceanic black hole had just been born.

Rachel felt like a child in a womb. Hot, wet darkness all engulfing her. Her thoughts were muddled in the inky warmth. *Breathe.* She fought the reflex. The flash of light she had seen could only have come from the surface, and yet it seemed so far away. *An illusion. Get to the surface.* Weakly, Rachel began swimming in the direction where she had seen the light. She saw more light now . . . an eerie red glow in the distance. *Daylight?* She swam harder.

A hand caught her by the ankle.

Rachel half-screamed underwater, almost exhaling the last of her air.

The hand pulled her backward, twisting her, pointing her back in the opposite direction. Rachel felt a familiar hand grasp hers. Michael Tolland was there, pulling her along with him the other way.

Rachel's mind said he was taking her down. Her heart said he knew what he was doing.

Kick with your feet, her mother's voice whispered.

Rachel kicked as hard as she could.

CHAPTER 130

Even as Tolland and Rachel broke the surface, he knew it was over. *The magma dome erupted.* As soon as the top of the vortex reached the surface, the giant underwater tornado would begin pulling everything down. Strangely, the world above the surface was not the quiet dawn he had left only moments ago. The noise was deafening. Wind slashed at him as if some kind of storm had hit while he was underwater.

Tolland felt delirious from lack of oxygen. He tried to support Rachel in the water, but she was being pulled from his arms. *The current!* Tolland tried to hold on, but the invisible force pulled harder, threatening to tear her from him. Suddenly, his grip slipped, and Rachel's body slid through his arms – but *upward*.

Bewildered, Tolland watched Rachel's body rise out of the water.

Overhead, the Coast Guard Osprey tilt-rotor airplane hovered and winched Rachel in. Twenty minutes ago, the Coast Guard had gotten a report of an explosion out at sea. Having lost track of the Dolphin helicopter that was supposed to be in the area, they feared an accident. They typed the chopper's last known coordinates into their navigation system and hoped for the best.

About a half mile from the illuminated *Goya*, they saw a field of burning wreckage drifting on the current. It looked like a speedboat. Nearby, a man was in the water, waving his arms wildly. They winched him in. He was stark naked – all except for one leg, which was covered with duct tape.

Exhausted, Tolland looked up at the underbelly of the thundering tilt-rotor airplane. Deafening gusts pounded down off its horizontal propellers. As Rachel rose on a cable, numerous sets of hands pulled her into the fuselage. As Tolland watched her dragged to safety, his eyes spotted a familiar man crouched half naked in the doorway.

Corky? Tolland's heart soared. *You're alive!*

Immediately, the harness fell from the sky again. It landed ten feet away. Tolland wanted to swim for it, but he could already feel the sucking sensation of the plume. The relentless grip of the sea wrapped around him, refusing to let go.

The current pulled him under. He fought toward the surface, but the exhaustion was overwhelming. *You're a survivor*, someone was saying. He kicked his legs, clawing toward the surface. When he broke through into the pounding wind, the harness was still out of reach. The current strained to drag him under. Looking up into the torrent of swirling wind and noise, Tolland saw Rachel. She was staring down, her eyes willing him up toward her.

It took Tolland four powerful strokes to reach the harness. With his last ounce of strength, he slid his arm and head up into the loop and collapsed.

All at once the ocean was falling away beneath him.

Tolland looked down just as the gaping vortex opened. The megaplume had finally reached the surface.

William Pickering stood on the bridge of the *Goya* and watched in dumbstruck awe as the spectacle unfolded all around him. Off the starboard of the *Goya*'s stern, a huge basinlike depression was forming on the surface of the sea. The whirlpool was hundreds of yards across and expanding fast. The ocean spiraled into it, racing with an eerie smoothness over the lip. All around him now, a guttural moan reverberated out of the depths. Pickering's mind was blank as he watched the hole expanding toward him like the gaping mouth of some epic god hungry for sacrifice.

I'm dreaming, Pickering thought.

Suddenly, with an explosive hiss that shattered the windows of the *Goya*'s bridge, a towering plume of steam erupted skyward out of the vortex. A colossal geyser climbed overhead, thundering, its apex disappearing into the darkened sky.

Instantly, the funnel walls steepened, the perimeter expanding faster now, chewing across the ocean toward him. The stern of the *Goya* swung hard toward the expanding cavity. Pickering lost his balance and fell to his knees. Like a child before God, he gazed downward into the growing abyss.

His final thoughts were for his daughter, Diana. He prayed she had not known fear like this when she died.

The concussion wave from the escaping steam hurled the Osprey sideways. Tolland and Rachel held each other as the pilots recovered, banking low over the doomed *Goya*. Looking out, they could see William Pickering – the Quaker – kneeling in his black coat and tie at the upper railing of the doomed ship.

As the stern fishtailed out over the brink of the massive twister, the anchor cable finally snapped. With its bow proudly in the air, the *Goya* slipped backward over the watery ledge, sucked down the steep spiraling wall of water. Her lights were still glowing as she disappeared beneath the sea.

CHAPTER **131**

The Washington morning was clear and crisp.

A breeze sent eddies of leaves skittering around the base of the Washington Monument. The world's largest obelisk usually awoke to its own peaceful image in the reflecting pool, but today the morning brought with it a chaos of jostling reporters, all crowding around the monument's base in anticipation.

Senator Sedgewick Sexton felt larger than Washington itself as he stepped from his limousine and strode like a lion toward the press area awaiting him at the base of the monument. He had invited the nation's ten largest media networks here and promised them the scandal of the decade.

Nothing brings out the vultures like the smell of death, Sexton thought.

In his hand, Sexton clutched the stack of white linen envelopes, each elegantly wax-embossed with his monogrammed seal. If information was power, then Sexton was carrying a nuclear warhead.

He felt intoxicated as he approached the podium, pleased to see his improvised stage included two 'fame-frames' – large, free-standing partitions that flanked his podium like navy-blue curtains – an old Ronald Reagan trick to ensure he stood out against any backdrop.

Sexton entered stage right, striding out from behind the partition like an actor out of the wings. The reporters quickly took their seats in the several rows of folding chairs facing his podium. To the east, the sun was just breaking over the Capitol dome, shooting rays of pink and gold down on Sexton like rays from heaven.

A perfect day to become the most powerful man in the world.

'Good morning, ladies and gentlemen,' Sexton said, laying the envelopes on the lectern before him. 'I will make this as short and painless as possible. The information I am about to share with you is, frankly, quite disturbing. These envelopes contain proof of a deceit at the highest levels of government. I am ashamed to say that the President called me half an hour ago and begged me – yes, *begged* me – not to go public with this evidence.' He shook his head with dismay. 'And yet, I am a man who believes in the truth. No matter how painful.'

Sexton paused, holding up the envelopes, tempting the seated crowd. The reporters' eyes followed the envelopes back and forth, a pack of dogs salivating over some unknown delicacy.

The President had called Sexton a half hour ago and explained everything. Herney had talked to Rachel, who was safely aboard a plane somewhere. Incredibly, it seemed the White House and NASA were innocent bystanders in this fiasco, a plot masterminded by William Pickering.

Not that it matters, Sexton thought. *Zach Herney is still going down hard.*

Sexton wished he could be a fly on the wall of the White House right now to see the President's face when he realized Sexton was going public. Sexton had agreed to meet Herney at the White House right now to discuss how best to tell the nation the truth about the meteorite. Herney was probably standing in front of a television at this very moment in dumbfounded shock, realizing that there was nothing the White House could do to stop the hand of fate.

'My friends,' Sexton said, letting his eyes connect with the crowd. 'I have weighed this heavily. I have considered honoring the President's desire to keep this data secret, but I must do what is in my heart.' Sexton sighed, hanging his head like a man trapped by history. 'The truth is the truth. I will not presume to color your interpretation of these facts in any way. I will simply give you the data at face value.'

In the distance, Sexton heard the beating of huge helicopter rotors. For a moment, he wondered if maybe the President were flying over from the White House in a panic, hoping to halt the press conference. *That would be the icing on the cake*, Sexton thought mirthfully. *How guilty would Herney appear THEN?*

'I do not take pleasure in doing this,' Sexton continued, sensing his timing was perfect. 'But I feel it is my duty to let the American people know they have been lied to.'

The aircraft thundered in, touching down on the esplanade to their right. When Sexton glanced over, he was surprised to see it was not the presidential helicopter after all, but rather a large Osprey tilt-rotor airplane.

The fuselage read: UNITED STATES COAST GUARD.

Baffled, Sexton watched as the cabin door opened and a woman emerged. She wore an orange Coast Guard parka and looked disheveled, like she'd been through a war. She strode toward the press area. For a moment, Sexton didn't recognize her. Then it hit him.

Rachel? He gaped in shock. *What the hell is SHE doing here?*

A murmur of confusion went through the crowd.

Pasting a broad smile on his face, Sexton turned back to the press and raised an apologetic finger. 'If you could give me just one minute? I'm terribly sorry.' He heaved a weary, good-natured sigh. 'Family first.'

A few of the reporters laughed.

With his daughter bearing down fast from his right, Sexton had no doubt this father-daughter reunion would best be held in private. Unfortunately, privacy was scarce at the moment. Sexton's eyes darted to the large partition on his right.

Still smiling calmly, Sexton waved to his daughter and stepped away from the microphone. Moving toward her at an angle, he maneuvered such that Rachel had to pass behind the partition to get to him. Sexton met her halfway, hidden from the eyes and ears of the press.

'Honey?' he said, smiling and opening his arms as Rachel came toward him. 'What a surprise!'

Rachel walked up and slapped his face.

Alone with her father now, ensconced behind the partition, Rachel glared with loathing. She had slapped him hard, but he barely flinched. With chilling control, his phony smile melted away, mutating into an admonishing glower.

His voice turned to a demonic whisper. 'You should not be here.'

Rachel saw wrath in his eyes and for the first time in her life felt unafraid. 'I turned to you for help, and you sold me out! I was almost killed!'

'You're obviously fine.' His tone was almost disappointed.

'NASA is *innocent!*' she said. 'The President told you that! What are you doing here?' Rachel's short flight to Washington aboard the Coast Guard Osprey had been punctuated by a flurry of phone calls between herself, the White House, her father, and even a distraught Gabrielle Ashe. 'You promised Zach Herney you were going to the White House!'

'I am.' He smirked. 'On election day.'

Rachel felt sickened to think this man was her father. 'What you're about to do is madness.'

'Oh?' Sexton chuckled. He turned and motioned behind him to the podium, which was visible at the end of the partition. On the podium, a stack of white envelopes sat waiting. 'Those envelopes contain information *you* sent me, Rachel. *You.* The President's blood is on your hands.'

'I faxed you that information when I needed your help! When I thought the President and NASA were guilty!'

'Considering the evidence, NASA certainly appears guilty.'

'But they are not! They deserve a chance to admit their own mistakes. You've already won this election. Zach Herney is finished! You *know* that. Let the man retain some dignity.'

Sexton groaned. 'So naïve. It's not about winning the election, Rachel, it's about *power*. It's about decisive victory, acts of greatness, crushing opposition, and controlling the forces in Washington so you can get something done.'

'At what cost?'

'Don't be so self-righteous. I'm simply presenting the evidence. The people can draw their own conclusions as to who is guilty.'

'You know how this will look.'

He shrugged. 'Maybe NASA's time has come.'

Senator Sexton sensed the press was getting restless beyond the partition, and he had no intention of standing here all morning and being lectured by his daughter. His moment of glory was waiting.

'We're through here,' he said. 'I have a press conference to give.'

'I'm asking you as your daughter,' Rachel pleaded. 'Don't do this. Think about what you're about to do. There's a better way.'

'Not for me.'

A howl of feedback echoed out of the PA system behind him, and Sexton wheeled to see a late-arriving female reporter, huddled over his podium, attempting to attach a network microphone to one of the gooseneck clips.

Why can't these idiots arrive on time? Sexton fumed.

In her haste, the reporter knocked Sexton's stack of envelopes to the ground.

Goddamn it! Sexton marched over, cursing his daughter for distracting him. When he arrived, the woman was on her hands and knees, collecting the envelopes off the ground. Sexton couldn't see her face, but she was obviously 'network' – wearing a full-length cashmere coat, matching scarf, and low-slung mohair beret with an ABC press pass clipped to it.

Stupid bitch, Sexton thought. 'I'll take those,' he snapped, holding out his hand for the envelopes.

The woman scraped up the last of the envelopes and handed them up to Sexton without looking up. 'Sorry . . .' she muttered, obviously embarrassed. Hunkering low in shame, she scurried off into the crowd.

Sexton quickly counted the envelopes. *Ten. Good.* Nobody was going to steal his thunder today. Regrouping, he adjusted the microphones and gave a joking smile to the crowd. 'I guess I'd better hand these out before someone gets hurt!'

The crowd laughed, looking eager.

Sexton sensed his daughter nearby, standing just offstage behind the partition.

'Don't do this,' Rachel said to him. 'You'll regret it.'

Sexton ignored her.

'I'm asking you to trust me,' Rachel said, her voice growing louder. 'It's a mistake.'

Sexton picked up his envelopes, straightening the edges.

'Dad,' Rachel said, intense and pleading now. 'This is your last chance to do what's right.'

Do what's right? Sexton covered the microphone and turned as if clearing his throat. He glanced discreetly over at his daughter. 'You're just like your mother – idealistic and small. Women simply do not understand the true nature of power.'

Sedgewick Sexton had already forgotten his daughter by the time he turned back toward the jostling media. Head held high, he walked around the podium and handed the stack of envelopes into the hands of the waiting press. He watched the envelopes disseminate rapidly through the crowd. He could hear the seals being broken, the envelopes being torn apart like Christmas presents.

A sudden hush came over the crowd.

In the silence, Sexton could hear the defining moment of his career. *The meteorite is a fraud. And I am the man who revealed it.*

Sexton knew it would take the press a moment to understand the true implications of what they were looking at: GPR images of an insertion shaft in the ice; a living ocean species almost identical to the NASA fossils; evidence of chondrules that formed on earth. It all led to one shocking conclusion.

'Sir?' one reporter stammered, sounding stunned as he looked in his envelope. 'Is this for real?'

Sexton gave a somber sigh. 'Yes, I'm afraid it's very real indeed.'

Murmurs of confusion now spread through the crowd.

'I'll give everyone a moment to look through these pages,' Sexton said, 'and then I'll take questions and attempt to shed some light on what you're looking at.'

'Senator?' another reporter asked, sounding utterly bewildered. 'Are these images authentic? . . . Unretouched?'

'One hundred percent,' Sexton said, speaking more firmly now. 'I would not present the evidence to you otherwise.'

The confusion in the crowd seemed to deepen, and Sexton thought he even heard some laughter – not at all the reaction he had expected. He was starting to fear he had overestimated the media's ability to connect the obvious dots.

'Um, Senator?' someone said, sounding oddly amused. 'For the record, you stand behind the authenticity of these images?'

Sexton was getting frustrated. 'My friends, I will say this one last time, the evidence in your hands is one-hundred-percent accurate. And if anyone can prove otherwise, I'll eat my hat!'

Sexton waited for the laugh, but it never came.

Dead silence. Blank stares.

The reporter who had just spoken walked toward Sexton, shuffling through his photocopies as he came forward. 'You're right, Senator.

This is scandalous data.' The reporter paused, scratching his head. 'So I guess we're puzzled as to why you've decided to share it with us like this, especially after denying it so vehemently earlier.'

Sexton had no idea what the man was talking about. The reporter handed him the photocopies. Sexton looked at the pages – and for a moment, his mind went totally blank.

No words came.

He was staring at unfamiliar photographs. Black-and-white images. Two people. Naked. Arms and legs intertwined. For an instant, Sexton had no idea what he was looking at. Then it registered. A cannonball to the gut.

In horror, Sexton's head snapped up to the crowd. They were laughing now. Half of them were already phoning in the story to their news desks.

Sexton felt a tap on his shoulder.

In a daze, he wheeled.

Rachel was standing there. 'We tried to stop you,' she said. 'We gave you every chance.' A woman stood beside her.

Sexton was trembling as his eyes moved to the woman at Rachel's side. She was the reporter in the cashmere coat and mohair beret – the woman who had knocked over his envelopes. Sexton saw her face, and his blood turned to ice.

Gabrielle's dark eyes seemed to bore right through him as she reached down and opened her coat to reveal a stack of white envelopes tucked neatly beneath her arm.

CHAPTER 132

The Oval Office was dark, lit only by the soft glow of the brass lamp on President Herney's desk. Gabrielle Ashe held her chin high as she stood before the President. Outside the window behind him, dusk was gathering on the west lawn.

'I hear you're leaving us,' Herney said, sounding disappointed.

Gabrielle nodded. Although the President had graciously offered her indefinite sanctuary inside the White House away from the press, Gabrielle preferred not to ride out this particular storm by hiding out in the eye. She wanted to be as far away as possible. At least for a while.

Herney gazed across his desk at her, looking impressed. 'The choice you made this morning, Gabrielle . . .' He paused, as if at a loss for words. His eyes were simple and clear – nothing compared to the deep, enigmatic pools that had once drawn Gabrielle to Sedgewick Sexton. And yet, even in the backdrop of this powerful place, Gabrielle saw true kindness in his gaze, an honor and dignity she would not soon forget.

'I did it for me, too,' Gabrielle finally said.

Herney nodded. 'I owe you my thanks all the same.' He stood, motioning for her to follow him into the hall. 'I was actually hoping you'd stick around long enough that I could offer you a post on my budgeting staff.'

Gabrielle gave him a dubious look. 'Stop spending and start mending?'

He chuckled. 'Something like that.'

'I think we both know, sir, that I'm more of a liability to you at the moment than an asset.'

Herney shrugged. 'Give it a few months. It will all blow over. Plenty of great men and women have endured similar situations and gone on to greatness.' He winked. 'A few of them were even U.S. presidents.'

Gabrielle knew he was right. Unemployed for only hours, Gabrielle had already turned down two other job offers today – one from Yolanda Cole at ABC, and the other from St Martin's Press, who had offered her an obscene advance if she would publish a tell-all biography. *No thanks.*

As Gabrielle and the President moved down the hallway, Gabrielle thought of the pictures of herself that were now being splashed across televisions.

The damage to the country could have been worse, she told herself. *Much worse.*

Gabrielle, after going to ABC to retrieve the photos and borrow Yolanda Cole's press pass, had snuck back to Sexton's office to assemble the duplicate envelopes. While inside, she had also printed copies of the donation checks in Sexton's computer. After the confrontation at the Washington Monument, Gabrielle had handed copies of the checks to the dumbstruck Senator Sexton and made her demands. *Give the President a chance to announce his meteorite mistake, or the rest of this data goes public too.* Senator Sexton took one look at the stack of financial evidence, locked himself in his limousine, and drove off. He had not been heard from since.

Now, as the President and Gabrielle arrived at the backstage door of the Briefing Room, Gabrielle could hear the waiting throngs beyond. For the second time in twenty-four hours, the world was assembled to hear a special presidential broadcast.

'What are you going to tell them?' Gabrielle asked.

Herney sighed, his expression remarkably calm. 'Over the years, I've learned one thing over and over . . .' He put a hand on her shoulder and smiled. 'There's just no substitute for the truth.'

Gabrielle was filled with an unexpected pride as she watched him stride toward the stage. Zach Herney was on his way to admit the biggest mistake of his life, and oddly, he had never looked more presidential.

CHAPTER 133

When Rachel awoke, the room was dark.

A clock glowed 10:14 P.M. The bed was not her own. For several moments, she lay motionless, wondering where she was. Slowly, it all started coming back . . . the megaplume . . . this morning at the Washington Monument . . . the President's invitation to stay at the White House.

I'm at the White House, Rachel realized. *I slept here all day.*

The Coast Guard chopper, at the President's command, had transported an exhausted Michael Tolland, Corky Marlinson, and Rachel Sexton from the Washington Monument to the White House, where they had been fed a sumptuous breakfast, been seen to by doctors, and been offered any of the building's fourteen bedrooms in which to recuperate.

All of them had accepted.

Rachel could not believe she had slept this long. Turning on the television, she was stunned to see that President Herney had already completed his press conference. Rachel and the others had offered to stand beside him when he announced the meteorite disappointment to the world. *We all made the mistake together.* But Herney had insisted on shouldering the burden alone.

'Sadly,' one political analyst on TV was saying, 'it seems NASA has discovered no signs of life from space after all. This marks the second time this decade that NASA has incorrectly classified a meteorite as showing signs of extraterrestrial life. This time, however, a number of highly respected civilians were also among those fooled.'

'Normally,' a second analyst chimed in, 'I would have to say that a deception of the magnitude the President described this evening would be devastating for his career . . . and yet, considering the developments this morning at the Washington Monument, I would have to say Zach Herney's chances of taking the presidency look better than ever.'

The first analyst nodded. 'So, no life in space, but no life in Senator Sexton's campaign either. And now, as new information surfaces suggesting deep financial troubles plaguing the senator—'

A knock on the door drew Rachel's attention.

Michael, she hoped, quickly turning off the television. She hadn't seen him since breakfast. On their arrival at the White House, Rachel had wanted nothing more than to fall asleep in his arms. Although she could tell Michael felt the same, Corky had intervened, parking himself on Tolland's bed and exuberantly telling and retelling his story about urinating on himself and saving the day. Finally, utterly exhausted, Rachel and Tolland had given up, heading for separate bedrooms to sleep.

Now, walking toward the door, Rachel checked herself in the mirror, amused to see how ridiculously she was dressed. All she had found to wear to bed was an old Penn State football jersey in the dresser. It draped down to her knees like a nightshirt.

The knocking continued.

Rachel opened the door, disappointed to see a female U.S. Secret Service agent. She was fit and cute, wearing a blue blazer. 'Ms Sexton, the gentleman in the Lincoln Bedroom heard your television. He asked me to tell you that as long as you're already awake . . .' She paused, arching her eyebrows, clearly no stranger to night games on the upper floors of the White House.

Rachel blushed, her skin tingling. '*Thanks.*'

The agent led Rachel down the impeccably appointed hallway to a plain-looking doorway nearby.

'The Lincoln Bedroom,' the agent said. 'And as I am always supposed to say outside this door, "Sleep well, and beware of ghosts." '

Rachel nodded. The legends of ghosts in the Lincoln Bedroom were as old as the White House itself. It was said that Winston Churchill had seen Lincoln's ghost here, as had countless others, including Eleanor Roosevelt, Amy Carter, actor Richard Dreyfus, and decades of maids and butlers. President Reagan's dog was said to bark outside this door for hours at a time.

The thoughts of historical spirits suddenly made Rachel realize what a sacred place this room was. She felt suddenly embarrassed, standing there in her long football jersey, bare-legged, like some college coed sneaking into a boy's room. 'Is this kosher?' she whispered to the agent. 'I mean this *is* the Lincoln Bedroom.'

The agent winked. 'Our policy on this floor is "Don't ask, don't tell." '

Rachel smiled. 'Thanks.' She reached for the doorknob, already feeling the anticipation of what lay beyond.

'Rachel!' the nasal voice carried down the hallway like a buzz saw.

Rachel and the agent turned. Corky Marlinson was hobbling toward them on crutches, his leg now professionally bandaged. 'I couldn't sleep either!'

Rachel slumped, sensing her romantic tryst about to disintegrate.

Corky's eyes inspected the cute Secret Service agent. He flashed her a broad smile. 'I love women in uniform.'

The agent pulled aside her blazer to reveal a lethal-looking side-arm.

Corky backed off. 'Point taken.' He turned to Rachel. 'Is Mike awake, too? You going in?' Corky looked eager to join the party.

Rachel groaned. 'Actually, Corky . . .'

'Dr Marlinson,' the Secret Service agent intervened, pulling a note from her blazer. 'According to this note, which was given to me by Mr Tolland, I have explicit orders to escort you down to the kitchen, have our chef make you anything you want, and ask you to explain to me in vivid detail how you saved yourself from certain death by . . .' the agent hesitated, grimacing as she read the note again, '. . . by urinating on yourself?'

Apparently, the agent had said the magic words. Corky dropped his crutches on the spot and put an arm around the woman's shoulders for support, and said, 'To the kitchen, love!'

As the indisposed agent helped Corky hobble off down the hall, Rachel had no doubt Corky Marlinson was in heaven. 'The urine is the key,' she heard him saying, 'because those damned telencephalon olfactory lobes can smell everything!'

The Lincoln Bedroom was dark when Rachel entered. She was surprised to see the bed empty and untouched. Michael Tolland was nowhere to be seen.

An antique oil lamp burned near the bed, and in the soft radiance, she could barely make out the Brussels carpet . . . the famous carved rosewood bed . . . the portrait of Lincoln's wife, Mary Todd . . . even the desk where Lincoln signed the Emancipation Proclamation.

As Rachel closed the door behind her, she felt a clammy draft on her bare legs. *Where is he?* Across the room, a window was open, the white organza curtains billowing. She walked over to close the window, and an eerie whisper murmured from the closet.

'Maaaarrrrrrrry . . .'

Rachel wheeled.

'Maaaaaarrrrrrrry?' the voice whispered again. 'Is that you? . . . Mary Todd Liiiiiincoln?'

Rachel quickly closed the window and turned back toward the closet. Her heart was racing, although she knew it was foolish. 'Mike, I know that's you.'

'Noooooo . . .' the voice continued. 'I am not Mike . . . I am . . . Aaaaabe.'

Rachel put her hands on her hips. 'Oh, really? *Honest* Abe?'

A muffled laugh. 'Moderately honest Abe . . . yes.'

Rachel was laughing now too.

'Be afraaaaaaid,' the voice from the closet moaned. 'Be veeeeeery afraid.'

'I'm not afraid.'

'Please be afraid . . .' the voice moaned. 'In the human species, the emotions of fear and sexual arousal are closely linked.'

Rachel burst out laughing. 'Is this your idea of a turn-on?'

'Forgiiiive me . . .' the voice moaned. 'It's been yeeeeeeears since I've been with a woman.'

'Evidently,' Rachel said, yanking the door open.

Michael Tolland stood before her with his roguish, lopsided grin. He looked irresistible wearing a pair of navy blue satin pajamas. Rachel did a double take when she saw the presidential seal emblazoned on his chest.

'Presidential pajamas?'

He shrugged. 'They were in the drawer.'

'And all I had was this football jersey?'

'You should have chosen the Lincoln Bedroom.'

'You should have offered!'

'I heard the mattress was bad. Antique horsehair.' Tolland winked, motioning to a gift-wrapped package on a marble-topped table. 'This'll make it up to you.'

Rachel was touched. 'For me?'

'I had one of the presidential aides go out and find this for you. Just arrived. Don't shake it.'

She carefully opened the package, extracting the heavy contents. Inside was a large crystal bowl in which were swimming two ugly orange goldfish. Rachel stared in confused disappointment. 'You're joking, right?'

'*Helostoma temmincki*,' Tolland said proudly.

'You bought me *fish*?'

'Rare Chinese kissing fish. Very romantic.'

'Fish are not romantic, Mike.'

'Tell that to *these* guys. They'll kiss for hours.'

'Is this supposed to be another turn-on?'

'I'm rusty on the romance. Can you grade me on effort?'

'For future reference, Mike, fish are definitely *not* a turn-on. Try flowers.'

Tolland pulled a bouquet of white lilies from behind his back. 'I tried for red roses,' he said, 'but I almost got shot sneaking into the Rose Garden.'

As Tolland pulled Rachel's body against his and inhaled the soft fragrance of her hair, he felt years of quiet isolation dissolving inside him. He kissed her deeply, feeling her body rise against him. The white lilies fell to their feet, and barriers Tolland had never known he'd built were suddenly melting away.

The ghosts are gone.

He felt Rachel inching him toward the bed now, her whisper soft in his ear. 'You don't *really* think fish are romantic, do you?'

'I do,' he said, kissing her again. 'You should see the jellyfish mating ritual. Incredibly erotic.'

Rachel maneuvered him onto his back on the horsehair mattress, easing her slender body down on top of his.

'And seahorses . . .' Tolland said, breathless as he savored her touch through the thin satin of his pajamas. 'Seahorses perform . . . an unbelievably sensual dance of love.'

'Enough fish talk,' she whispered, unbuttoning his pajamas. 'What can you tell me about the mating rituals of advanced primates?'

Tolland sighed. 'I'm afraid I don't really do primates.'

Rachel shed her football jersey. 'Well, nature boy, I suggest you learn fast.'

EPILOGUE

The NASA transport jet banked high over the Atlantic.

Onboard, Administrator Lawrence Ekstrom took a last look at the huge charred rock in the cargo hold. *Back to the sea*, he thought. *Where they found you.*

On Ekstrom's command, the pilot opened the cargo doors and released the rock. They watched as the mammoth stone plummeted downward behind the plane, arcing across the sunlit ocean sky and disappearing beneath the waves in a pillar of silver spray.

The giant stone sank fast.

Underwater, at 300 feet, barely enough light remained to reveal its tumbling silhouette. Passing 500 feet, the rock plunged into total darkness.

Racing down.

Deeper.

It fell for almost twelve minutes.

Then, like a meteorite striking the dark side of the moon, the rock crashed into a vast plain of mud on the ocean floor, kicking up a cloud of silt. As the dust settled, one of the ocean's thousands of unknown species swam over to inspect the odd newcomer.

Unimpressed, the creature moved on.

1-V-116-44-11-89-44-46-L-51-130-19-118-L-32-
118-116-130-28-116-32-44-133-U-130